Make time for friends. Make time for

DEBBIE MACOMBER

Dear Friends,

Welcome to Cedar Cove, Washington. I hope you enjoy meeting my new friends. And I hope that once you do, you'll feel as comfortable with Olivia, Grace, Charlotte, Cecilia, Jack, Ian, Seth and all the others as you would your own next-door neighbours. You see, they're mine. Well… not exactly. Cedar Cove is based on my own home town of Port Orchard, Washington, but the characters and their stories are figments of my imagination. However, anyone who's walked the streets of Port Orchard will recognise buildings and events I've described. The library, the new city hall, even the seagull-calling contest, are part and parcel of life in Port Orchard.

So please sit back and enjoy a bit of romance, a bit of mystery with a little wisdom thrown in. Sit back and acquaint yourself with a whole community of new friends. I know they're all anxious to introduce themselves to you!

Debbie Macomber

PS I love to hear from readers. You can reach me at PO Box 1458, Port Orchard, WA 98366, USA or through my website at www.debbiemacomber.com.

DEBBIE MACOMBER

16 Lighthouse Road

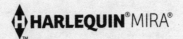

This edition published in Great Britain 2016
by Harlequin MIRA, an imprint of Harlequin (UK) Limited,
Eton House, 18-24 Paradise Road,
Richmond, Surrey, TW9 1SR

© 2001 Debbie Macomber

ISBN 978-0-7783-0480-7

Harlequin (UK) Limited's policy is to use papers that are natural, renewable and recyclable products and made from wood grown in sustainable forests. The logging and manufacturing processes conform to the legal environmental regulations of the country of origin.

Printed and bound by CPI Group (UK) Ltd, Croydon, CR0 4YY

MIX
Paper from
responsible sources
FSC
www.fsc.org   FSC® C007454

In memory of
Rita Adler
26th December, 1950 – 12th December, 2000
We miss you.

One

Cecilia Randall had heard of people who, if granted one wish, would choose to live their lives over again. Not her. She'd be perfectly content to blot just one twelve-month period from her twenty-two years.

The *past* twelve months.

Last January, shortly after New Year's, she'd met Ian Jacob Randall, a Navy man, a submariner. She'd fallen in love with him and done something completely irresponsible—she'd gotten pregnant. Then she'd complicated the whole situation by marrying him.

That was mistake number three and from there, her errors in judgment had escalated. She hadn't been stupid so much as naïve and in love and—worst of all—romantic. The Navy, and life, had cured her of that fast enough.

Their baby girl had been born premature while Ian was at sea, and it became immediately apparent that she had a defective heart. By the time Ian returned home, Allison Marie had already been laid to rest. It was Cecilia who'd stood alone in the unrelenting rain of the Pacific Northwest while her baby's tiny casket was lowered into the cold, muddy earth. She'd been forced to make life-and-death decisions without the counsel of family or the comfort of her husband.

Her mother lived on the East Coast and, because of a snowstorm, had been unable to fly into Washington State. Her father was as supportive as he knew how to be—which was damn little. His idea of "being there for her" consisted of giving Cecilia a sympathy card and writing a few lines about how sorry he was for her loss. Cecilia had spent countless days and nights by their daughter's empty crib, alternately weeping and in shock. Other Navy wives had tried to console her, but Cecilia wasn't comfortable with strangers. She'd rejected their help and their friendship. And because she'd been in Cedar Cove for such a short time, she hadn't made any close friends in the community, either. As a result, she'd borne her grief alone.

When Ian did return, he'd blamed Navy procedures for his delay. He'd tried to explain, but by then Cecilia was tired of it all. Only one reality had any meaning: her daughter was dead. Her husband didn't know and couldn't possibly understand what she'd endured in his absence. Since he was on a nuclear submarine, all transmissions during his tour of duty were limited to fifty-word "family grams." Nothing could have been done, anyway; the submarine was below the polar ice cap at the time. She did write to tell him about Allison's birth and then her death. She'd written out her grief in these brief messages, not caring that they'd be closely scrutinized by Navy personnel. But Ian's commanding officer had seen fit to postpone relaying the information until the completion of the ten-week tour. *I didn't know,* Ian had repeatedly insisted. Surely she couldn't hold him responsible. But she did. Unfair though it might be, Cecilia couldn't forgive him.

Now all she wanted was out. Out of her marriage, out of this emotional morass of guilt and regret, just *out*. The simplest form of escape was to divorce Ian.

Sitting in the hallway near the courtroom, she felt more determined than ever to terminate her marriage. With one swift strike of a judge's gavel, she could put an end to the nightmare of the past year. Eventually she would forget she'd ever met Ian Randall.

Allan Harris, Cecilia's attorney, entered the foyer outside the Kitsap County courtroom. She watched as he glanced around until he saw her. He raised his hand in a brief greeting, then walked over to where she sat on the hard wooden bench and claimed the empty space beside her.

"Tell me again what's going to happen," she said, needing the assurance that her life would return to at least an approximation of what it had been a year ago.

Allan set his briefcase on his lap. "We wait until the docket is announced. The judge will ask if we're ready, I'll announce that we are, and we'll be given a number."

Cecilia nodded, feeling numb.

"We can be assigned any number between one and fifty," her attorney continued. "Then we wait our turn."

Cecilia nodded again, hoping she wouldn't be stuck in the courthouse all day. Bad enough that she had to be here; even worse that Ian's presence was also required. She hadn't seen him yet. Maybe he was meeting somewhere with his own attorney, discussing strategies—not that she expected him to contest the divorce.

"There won't be a problem, will there?" Her palms were damp and cold sweat had broken out across her forehead. She wanted this to be over so she could get on with her life. She believed that couldn't happen until the divorce was filed. Only then would the pain start to go away.

"I can't see that there'll be any hang-ups, especially since you've agreed to divide all the debts." He frowned slightly. "Despite that prenuptial agreement you signed."

A flu-like feeling attacked Cecilia's stomach, and she clutched her purse tightly against her. *Soon,* she reminded herself, soon she could walk out these doors into a new life.

"It's a rather…unusual agreement," Allan murmured.

In retrospect, the prenuptial agreement had been another in the list of mistakes she'd made in the past year, but according to her attorney one that could easily be rectified. Back when she'd signed it, their agreement had made perfect sense. In an effort to prove their sincerity, they'd come up with the idea that the spouse who wanted the divorce should pay not only the legal costs but all debts incurred during the marriage. It could be seen as either punitive or deterrent; in either case, it hadn't worked. And now it was just one more nuisance to be dealt with.

Cecilia blamed herself for insisting on something in writing. She'd wanted to be absolutely sure that Ian wasn't marrying her out of any sense of obligation.

Yes, the pregnancy was unplanned, but she would've been perfectly content to raise her child by herself. She preferred that to being trapped in an unhappy marriage—or trapping Ian in a relationship he didn't want. Ian, however, had been adamant. He'd sworn that he loved her, loved their unborn child and wanted to marry her.

As a ten-year-old, Cecilia's entire world had been torn apart when her parents divorced. She refused to do that to her own child. In her mind, marriage was forever, so she'd wanted them to be certain before making a lifetime commitment. How naïve, she thought now. How sentimental. How *romantic*.

Ian had said he wanted their marriage to be forever, too, but like so much else this past year, that had been an illusion. Cecilia had *needed* to believe him, believe in the power of love, believe it would protect her from this kind of heartache.

In the end, blinded by the prospect of a husband who seemed totally committed to her and by the hope of a happy-ever-after kind of life, Cecilia had acquiesced to the marriage—with one stipulation. The agreement.

Their marriage was supposed to last as long as they both lived, so they'd devised an agreement that would help them stay true to their vows. Or so they'd thought…. Before the ceremony, they'd written the prenuptial contract themselves and had it notarized. She'd forgotten all about it until she'd made an appointment with Allan Harris and he'd asked if she'd signed any agreement prior to the wedding. It certainly wasn't the standard sort of document; nevertheless Allan felt they needed to have the court rescind it.

Her marriage shouldn't have ended like this, but after their baby died, everything had gone wrong. Whatever love had existed between them had been eroded by their loss. Babies weren't supposed to die— even babies born premature. Any sense of rightness, of justice, had disappeared from Cecilia's world. The marriage that was meant to sustain her had become yet another source of guilt and grief. Experience had taught her she was *alone,* and her legal status might as well reflect that.

She couldn't think about it anymore and purposely turned her thoughts elsewhere.

Attorneys milled about the crowded area, conferring with their clients, and she looked around, expecting to find Ian, bracing herself for the inevitable confrontation. She hadn't seen or talked to him in more than four months, although their attorneys were in regular contact. She wondered if all these other people were here for equally sad reasons. They must be. Why else did anyone go to court? Broken vows, fractured agreements...

"We have Judge Lockhart," Allan said, breaking into her observations.

"Is that good?"

"She's fair."

That was all Cecilia asked. "This is just a formality, right?"

"Right." Allan gave her a comforting smile.

She checked at her watch. The docket was scheduled to be announced at nine and it was five minutes before. Ian still wasn't here.

"What if Ian doesn't show up?" she asked.

"Then we'll ask for a continuance."

"Oh." Not another delay, she silently pleaded.

"He'll be here," Allan said reassuringly. "Brad told me Ian's just as keen to get this over with as you are."

The knot in her stomach tightened. This was the easy part, she told herself, dismissing her nervousness. She'd already been through the hard part—the pain and grief, the disappointment of a marriage that hadn't worked. The hearing was merely a formality; Allan had said so. Once the prenuptial agreement was rescinded, the no-contest divorce was as good as done and this nightmare would be behind her.

Then Ian appeared.

Cecilia felt his presence before she actually saw him. Felt his gaze as he came up the stairwell and into the foyer. She turned and their eyes briefly met before they each, hurriedly, looked away.

Almost simultaneous with his arrival, the courtroom doors opened. Everyone stood and began to file inside with an eagerness that defied explanation. Allan walked beside Cecilia through the mahogany doors. Ian and his attorney entered after them and sat on the opposite side of the courtroom.

The bailiff immediately started reading off names as though taking attendance. With each name or set of names, a response was made and a number assigned. It happened so quickly that Cecilia almost missed hearing her own.

"Randall."

Both Allan Harris and Brad Dumas called out.

Cecilia didn't hear the number they were given. When Allan sat down beside her, he wrote thirty on a yellow legal pad.

"Thirty?" she whispered, astonished to realize that twenty-nine other cases would have to be heard before hers.

He nodded. "Don't worry, it'll go fast. We'll probably be out of here before eleven. Depends on what else is being decided."

"Do I have to stay here?"

"Not in the courtroom. You can wait outside if you prefer."

She did. The room felt claustrophobic, unbearably so. She stood and hurried into the nearly empty hall, practically stumbling out of the courtroom in her rush to escape.

Two steps into the foyer, she stopped—barely avoiding a collision with Ian.

They both froze, staring at each other. Cecilia didn't know what to say; Ian apparently had the same problem. He looked good dressed in his Navy blues, reminding her of the first time they'd met. He was tall and fit and possessed the most mesmerizing blue eyes she'd ever seen. Cecilia thought that if Allison Marie had lived, she would have had her daddy's eyes.

"It's almost over," Ian said, his voice low and devoid of emotion.

"Yes," she returned. After a moment's silence, she added, "I didn't follow you out here." She wanted him to know that.

"I figured as much."

"It felt like the walls were closing in on me."

He didn't comment and sank onto one of the wooden benches that lined the hallway outside the courtrooms. He slouched forward, elbows braced against his knees. She sat at the other end of the bench, perched uncomfortably on the very edge. Other people left the crowded courtroom and either disappeared or found a secluded corner to confer with their lawyers. Their whispered voices echoed off the granite walls.

"I know you don't believe me, but I'm sorry it's come to this," Ian said.

"I am, too." Then, in case he assumed she might be seeking a reconciliation, she told him, "But it's necessary."

"I couldn't agree with you more." He sat upright, his back ramrod-straight as he folded his arms across his chest. He didn't look at her again.

This was awkward—both of them sitting here like this. But if he could pretend she wasn't there, she could do the same thing. Surreptitiously, she slid farther back on the bench. This was going to be a long wait.

"Well, hello there," Charlotte Jefferson said as she peeked inside the small private room at Cedar Cove Convalescent Center. "I understand you're a new arrival."

The elderly, white-haired gentleman slouched forward in his wheelchair, staring at her with clouded brown eyes. Despite the ravages of illness and age—he was in his nineties, she'd learned—she could see he'd once been a handsome man. The classic bone structure was unmistakable.

"You don't need to worry about answering," she told him. "I know you're a stroke patient. I just wanted to introduce myself. I'm Charlotte Jefferson. I stopped by to see if there's anything I can do for you."

He raised his gaze to hers and slowly, as though with great effort, shook his head.

"You don't have to tell me your name. I read it outside the door. You're Thomas Harding." She paused. "Janet Lester—the social worker here—mentioned you a few days ago. I've always been fond of the name Thomas," she chattered on. "I imagine your friends call you Tom."

A weak smile told her she was right.

"That's what I thought." Charlotte didn't mean to be pushy, but she knew how lonely it must feel to come to a strange town and not know a single, solitary soul. "One of my dearest friends was here for years, and I came to visit with her every Thursday. It got to be such a habit that after Barbara went to be with the Lord, I just continued. Last week, Janet told me you'd just arrived. So I decided to come over today and introduce myself."

He tried to move his right hand, without success.

"Is there something I can get you?" she asked, wanting to be helpful.

He shook his head again, then with a shaky index finger pointed at the chair across from him.

"Ah, I understand. You're asking me to sit down."

He managed a grin, lopsided though it was.

"Well, don't mind if I do. These dogs are barking." She sat in the chair he'd indicated and removed her right pump in order to rub some feeling back into her toes.

Tom watched her, his eyes keen with interest.

"I suppose you'd like to know a little something about Cedar Cove. Well, I don't blame you, poor man. Thank goodness you got transferred here. Janet said you'd requested Cedar Cove in the first place, but got sent to that facility in Seattle instead. I heard about what happened *there*. All I can say is it's a crying shame." According to Janet, Tom's previous facility had been closed down for a number of serious violations. The patients, most of whom were wards of the state, were assigned to a variety of care units across Washington.

"I'm so glad you're here in Cedar Cove—it's a delightful little town, Tom," she said, purposely using his name. She wanted him to feel *acknowledged*. He'd spent time in a substandard facility where he'd been treated without dignity or compassion. In fact, Janet had told her the staff there had been particularly neglectful. Charlotte was shocked to hear that; she found it incomprehensible. Imagine being cruel to a vulnerable person like Tom! Imagine ignoring him, leaving him to lie in a dirty bed, never talking to him…. "I see you've got a view of the marina from here," she said with as much enthusiasm as she could muster. "We're proud of our waterfront. During the summer there's a wonderful little festival, and of course the Farmer's Market fills the parking lot next to the library on Saturdays. Every so often, fishing boats dock at the pier and sell their wares. I swear to you, Tom, there's nothing better than Hood Canal shrimp bought fresh off the boat."

She hesitated, but Tom seemed to be listening, so she went on.

"Okay, let's see what I can tell you about Cedar Cove," she said, hardly knowing where to start. "This is a small town. Last census, I believe we totaled not quite five thousand. My husband, Clyde, and I both came from the Yakima area, in the eastern part of the state and we moved here after World War II. Back then, Cedar Cove had the only stoplight in the entire county. That was fifty years ago now." Fifty years. How could all that time have slipped away?

"Cedar Cove has changed in some ways, but it's stayed the same in others," she said. "A lot of people around here are employed by the Bremerton ship-yard, just like they were in the forties. And naturally the Navy has a real impact on the town's economy."

Tom must have guessed as much, with the Bremerton Naval shipyard on the other side of the cove. Huge aircraft carriers lined the waterfront; so did rows of diesel-powered submarines. The nuclear ones were stationed at the submarine base out in Bangor. On overcast days, the gray flotilla blended with the slate colors of the sky.

Tom jerkily placed his right hand over his heart.

"You served in the military?" she asked.

The older man's nod was barely perceptible.

"God bless you," Charlotte said. "There's all that talk about us being the greatest generation, living through the depression and the war, and you know what? They're right. Young people these days don't know what it means to sacrifice. They've had it far too easy, but then, that's just my opinion."

Tom's eyes widened, and Charlotte could tell he agreed with her.

Not wanting to get sidetracked, she paused, gnawing on her lower lip. "Now, what else can I tell you?" she murmured. "Well, for one thing, we're big on sports in Cedar Cove. Friday nights in the fall, half the town shows up for the high-school football games. This time of year, it's basketball. Two years ago, the softball team took the state championship. My oldest grandson—" She hesitated and looked away, sorry she'd followed this train of thought. "Jordan showed real promise as a baseball player, but he drowned fifteen years ago." She wasn't sure what had prompted her to mention Jordan and wished that she hadn't. A familiar sadness lodged in her heart. "I don't think I'll ever get over his death."

Tom, feeble as he was, leaned toward her, as though to rest his hand on hers.

It was a touching gesture. "I'm sorry," she whispered. "I didn't mean to talk about this. My daughter lives in Cedar Cove," she continued, forcing a cheerful note into her voice. "She's a judge—Judge Olivia Lockhart—and I'm proud as can be of her. When she was a little girl, Olivia was a skinny little thing. She grew up tall, though. Very striking. She's in her early fifties now, and she still turns heads. It's the way she carries herself. Just looking at her, people know she's someone important. That's my daughter, the judge, but to me she'll always be my little brown-eyed girl. I get a lot of joy out of sitting in her courtroom while she's presiding." She shook her head. "Here I am talking about myself instead of Cedar Cove." If she'd had questions to answer, Charlotte would've found this easier; unfortunately, it wasn't possible for Tom to ask.

"We're only a ferry ride away from Seattle, but we're a rural community. I live in the town proper, but plenty of folks have chickens and horses. Of course, that's outside the city limits."

Tom nodded in her direction.

"You're asking about me?"

His answering smile told her she'd guessed right.

Charlotte smiled, a bit flustered. She lifted her hand to her head and smoothed the soft wavy hair. At seventy-two, her hair was completely white. It suited her, if she did say so herself. Her face was relatively unlined; she'd always been proud of her complexion—a woman was allowed a little vanity, wasn't she?

"I'm a widow," she began. "Clyde's been gone nearly twenty years. He died much too young—cancer." She lowered her eyes. "He worked at the Naval shipyard. We had two children, William and Olivia. You know, the judge. William works in the energy business and travels all over the world, and Olivia married and settled down right here in Cedar Cove. Her children graduated from the same high school she did. The school hangs a picture of each year's graduating class on the wall and it's quite interesting to look back on all those young smiling faces and see what's become of them." Charlotte grew thoughtful. "Justine's picture is there. She was Jordan's twin and oh, I do worry about her. She's twenty-eight now and dating an older man neither her mother nor I trust." Charlotte stopped herself from saying more. "James is Olivia's youngest, and he's currently in the Navy. It was a shock to all of us when he enlisted. William and his wife decided against children, and I sometimes wonder if they regret that now. I think Will might, but not Georgia." Although both her children were in their fifties, Charlotte still worried about them.

Tom's eyes drifted shut, then swiftly opened.

"You're tired," Charlotte said, realizing she was discussing her concerns about her daughter and grandchildren more than she was giving Tom an overview of Cedar Cove.

He shook his head slightly, as if he didn't want her to leave.

Charlotte stood and placed her hand on his shoulder. "I'll be back soon, Tom. You should get some sleep. Besides, it's time I headed for the courthouse. Olivia's on the bench this morning and I'm finishing a baby blanket." Deciding she should explain, she added, "I do my best knitting in court. *The Chronicle* did an article about me a couple of years ago with a photo! There I was, sitting in court with my needles and my yarn. Which reminds me, if you'd like I'll bring in the local paper and read it to you. Until just this week, we only had the Wednesday edition, but the paper was recently sold and a new editor hired. He's expanded to two papers a week. Isn't that nice?"

Tom smiled.

"This is a lovely little town," Charlotte told him, leaning forward to pat his hand. "You're going to like it here so well."

She started out the door and saw that her new friend didn't have a lap robe. The ladies at the Senior Center would soon fix that. These halls got downright chilly, especially during Cedar Cove's damp winters. How sad that this man didn't have anyone who cared enough about his welfare to see that he had a basic comfort like that.

"I'll be back soon," she told him again.

Tom nodded and gave her a rakish little grin. Oh, yes, he'd been a charmer in his day.

As she walked out the main door, Janet stopped her. "Did you introduce yourself to Tom Harding?"

"I did. What a dear man."

"I knew you'd think so. You're exactly what he needs."

"He doesn't have any family?"

"There's no next of kin listed in his file. It's about five years since his stroke, and apparently he's never had visitors." She paused, frowning. "But then, I don't know how much we can trust the record-keeping at Senior Haven."

"How long was he there?"

Janet shrugged. "I don't recall exactly. At least five years. After he was released from chronic care."

"Oh, the poor man. He's—"

"In need of a friend," Janet finished for her.

"Well, he found one," Charlotte said. She'd always been a talker. Clyde used to say she could make friends with a brick wall. He meant it as a compliment and she'd taken it that way.

On second thought, she wouldn't ask the women at the Senior Center to knit Tom a lap robe; she'd do it herself, just as soon as she finished the baby blanket. By her next visit, she'd have something to give him, something to keep him warm—the lap robe…and her friendship.

Judge Olivia Lockhart had a difficult time with divorce cases, which were her least favorite duty in family court. She'd served on the bench for two years and figured she'd seen it all. Then there were cases like this one.

Ian and Cecilia Randall were asking to rescind their handwritten notarized prenuptial agreement. As soon as that was out of the way, they would file for the dissolution of their marriage. The attorneys stood before her with their clients at their sides.

Olivia glanced at the paperwork, noting that it had been dated and signed less than a year ago. How a marriage could go so wrong so quickly was beyond her. She looked up and studied the couple. So young, they were, both of them staring down at their feet. Ian Randall seemed to be a responsible young man, probably away from his home and family for the first time, serving in the military. The wife was a fragile waif, impossibly thin with dark, soulful eyes. Her straight brown hair framed her heart-shaped face; the ends straggled to her shoulders. She repeatedly looped a strand around her ear, probably out of nerves.

"I must say this is original," Olivia murmured, rereading the few lines of the text. It was straightforward enough if unusual. According to the agreement, the spouse who filed for divorce would assume all debts.

Apparently they'd had a change of heart in that, as well as in the matter of their marriage. Olivia glanced over the brief list of accumulated debts and saw that they'd been evenly split between the couple. If the marriage had lasted longer, of course, the debts would have been more punishing—a mortgage, presumably, car payments and so on. Which would have provided the discontented spouse with an incentive of sorts to stay in the marriage, Olivia supposed. In any event, the current debts amounted to seven thousand dollars. Ian Randall assumed all credit card bills and Cecilia Randall had agreed to pay the utility bills, which included a three-hundred-dollar phone bill and oddly enough, a two-hundred-dollar charge to a florist shop. The largest of the debts, she noticed, was burial costs, which they had agreed to share equally.

"Both parties have reached an agreement in regard to all debts accumulated during the time of their marriage," Allan Harris stated.

Clearly there was more to this situation than met the eye. "Was there a death in the family?" she asked, directing the question to the attorney who'd spoken.

Allan nodded. "A child."

Olivia's stomach spasmed. "I see."

"Our daughter was born premature, and she had a defective heart," Cecilia Randall said in a barely audible voice. "Her name was Allison."

"Allison Marie Randall," the sailor husband added.

Olivia watched as husband and wife exchanged glances. Cecilia looked away but not fast enough for Olivia to miss the pain, the anger, the heartache. Perhaps she recognized it because she'd experienced it herself, right along with the disintegration of her own marriage.

The two parties continued to await her decision. Since everything was in order and both were in agreement, there was little to hold up the procedure. This hearing was simply a formality so they could proceed to the dissolution of their marriage.

"Seven thousand dollars is quite a lot of debt to accumulate in just a few months," she said, prolonging their wait.

"I agree, Your Honor," Brad Dumas inserted quickly, "but there were extenuating circumstances."

Olivia caught sight of her mother in the viewing chamber. She often sat in the front row, almost always occupied with her needles and yarn. But Charlotte wasn't knitting now. Her fingers clenched the needles that rested in her lap, as though she, too, understood the significance of what was happening.

Olivia hesitated, which was completely unlike her. She was known for being swift and decisive. What this couple needed was a gentle, loving hand to guide them through the grieving process. Ending their marriage wouldn't solve the problems; personal experience had taught Olivia that. If the Randalls insisted on going through with their divorce, Olivia would be helping them pave a one-way road to pain and guilt. However, she had no legal reason not to rescind the agreement.

"I'm going to take a ten-minute recess…to review this agreement," she announced. Then, before the members of either party could reveal their shock, she got up and headed toward her chambers. She heard the rustle of the courtroom as everyone stood, followed by a flurry of hushed whispers.

Sitting at her desk, Olivia leaned her head against the high-back leather chair and closed her eyes. It was inevitable that she'd see the comparisons between herself and Cecilia Randall. Fifteen years ago, Olivia had lost her oldest son. All those years had come and gone, but the pain of Jordan's death had never faded, and it never would. In the twelve months after the drowning accident, her entire world had crumbled. First she'd lost her son and then her husband. Over the years, small problems had crept into her marriage—nothing big, nothing overwhelming or unusual, just the typical stress experienced by any couple with dual careers and three demanding children. But after Jordan's death, that stress had multiplied tenfold, had become insurmountable. Before Olivia could fully appreciate what they were doing, they'd separated. Not long afterward, Olivia and Stan found themselves standing in front of a judge, and the divorce was declared final.

Three months later, Stan had shocked her and everyone else by remarrying. Apparently he'd been confiding his problems to this other woman for some time, keeping the relationship a secret from Olivia.

A knock sounded at her door and before Olivia could answer, her mother let herself in.

Olivia straightened. She should've known her mother would take this opportunity to speak with her. "Hello, Mom."

"I'm not disturbing you, am I?"

Olivia shook her head. Her mother knew the door was always open as far as she was concerned.

"Oh, good." Charlotte immediately got to the point—*her* point. "What a shame it is, that young couple wanting out of their marriage when they've barely had a chance to get to know each other."

Olivia was thinking the same thing, although she couldn't and wouldn't admit it.

"It seems to me that neither of them is very keen on this divorce. I could be wrong, but—"

"Mother, you know I can't discuss my cases."

"Yes, yes, I know, but sometimes I just can't help myself." Charlotte started to back out the door, then apparently changed her mind. "I don't know if I ever told you this, but your father and I didn't get along the first year, either."

This was news to Olivia.

"Clyde was a stubborn man, and as you might have noticed I have a strong will of my own."

That was an understatement if ever there was one.

"Our first year, all we did was argue," Charlotte said. "And then, before I knew it, I was pregnant with your brother and well…well, we worked everything out. We had a lot of good years together, your father and I." Her hands tightened around her purse and her knitting bag. "He was the love of my life." As if she'd said more than she'd intended, Charlotte moved out of the room and gently closed the door behind her.

Grinning, Olivia got to her feet. Leave it to her mother to say exactly what she needed to hear. Her decision made, Olivia returned to the courtroom. Once she was seated, the Randalls and their attorneys approached the bench. Cecilia Randall stepped forward with her big, soulful eyes staring blankly into space. Ian Randall's expression was hard and unflinching, as though he was preparing himself for the inevitable.

"I cannot discount the possibility," Olivia began, "that these parties entered into this agreement in contemplation of the very issue—this matter of divorce—that is set before this court. They obviously placed great value on their marriage and that value served as consideration for such a contract. Their intent was clearly to avoid the outcome they now seem to be pursuing—an easy divorce. Therefore, I am not setting aside the prenuptial agreement. The issue will need to be resolved at trial. In the meantime, I strongly urge these parties to seek out counseling or apply to the Dispute Resolution Center to discuss their differences."

Both spouses and their lawyers leaned closer, as if they couldn't possibly have heard correctly.

Allan Harris and Brad Dumas immediately started

shuffling through their notes. The sight was almost comical as the two attorneys hurried to reread the prenuptial agreement.

"Excuse me, Your Honor." Brad Dumas reacted first, raising his hand.

"Both parties are in agreement," Allan Harris argued. "Mr. Randall has agreed to set aside the prenuptial and has willingly taken on responsibility for a share of the debts."

"What did she say?" Cecilia Randall asked, looking to Allan Harris.

"To clarify, Your Honor," Brad Dumas requested, his expression puzzled.

"The agreement stands as written," Olivia stated.

"You're not setting aside the agreement?" Allan Harris spoke slowly. He sounded confused.

"No, Counselors, I am not, for the reasons I've just indicated."

Allan Harris and Brad Dumas stared at her.

"Is there a problem, gentlemen?"

"Ah…"

She waved them aside. "See the clerk and set a trial date."

"Does this mean we can't go through with the divorce?" Cecilia asked her attorney.

"I want the divorce as much as you do," Ian Randall insisted.

Olivia slammed her gavel. "Order in the court," she told them. If the couple chose to argue, they could do so on their own time.

Moving as though they were in shock, Allan Harris and Brad Dumas picked up their papers and briefcases.

"Is there any other option?" Cecilia Randall asked Allan Harris as they walked toward the doors.

"We might be able to appeal, but…"

"But that'll drive up the costs even more," Ian protested, close behind with his own attorney. Apparently Brad was still too dumbfounded to speak.

"I don't understand what's happening," Cecilia muttered once she'd reached the courtroom doors. "Can't we *do* something?"

"The judge said we have to take this to trial?" Ian Randall sounded incredulous. "Just how expensive is that going to be?"

"Very," Allan Harris answered quickly, as if he'd take delight in running up his client's husband's tab.

"But that's not what I want," Cecilia wailed.

"Then I suggest you do what the judge recommended and seek counseling or contact the Dispute Resolution Center."

"I'm not airing my problems to a group of strangers." With that Ian Randall slammed his way out of the court. Brad Dumas followed his client, but not before tossing Olivia a disgruntled look.

Allan Harris stood there shaking his head, his expression incredulous.

The bailiff read off the next number and still Allan remained.

Cecilia Randall turned away, but not fast enough to disguise the fact that her eyes had filled with tears. Olivia felt her heart break just a little—and yet she was convinced she'd done the right thing.

"How did this happen?" Cecilia asked.

"I don't understand it," Olivia heard Allan Harris mumble. "This is crazy."

Cecilia Randall shook her head. "You're right," she murmured, shrugging into her coat. "None of this should have happened, but it just did."

Two

Olivia groaned when the telephone rang for the fifth time Saturday morning. No doubt this call, like all the others, was the result of Jack Griffin's newspaper piece published that morning. The newly appointed editor of *The Cedar Cove Chronicle* had for some reason decided to write an article about her. He'd run the headline Divorce Denied across the editorial page. Olivia sighed; all this unwanted attention was disrupting her weekend, and she resented it.

"Hello," she said, making sure her voice conveyed her irritation. If this caller felt compelled to discuss her judgment, then she wasn't in the mood to talk. She'd brought each of the four previous conversations to a swift end.

"Hello, Mother."

Justine, that was a relief! Olivia had been waiting to hear from her daughter all week. "How are you?" It used to be that they spoke on a regular basis, but no longer. Justine was dating a man Olivia considered disreputable, which created ongoing tension between mother and daughter. Consequently Justine avoided her. Warren Saget was a forty-eight-year-old land developer—twenty years her senior—who had put together more than one shady deal. The age difference didn't bother Olivia as much as the man himself.

"Did you know your name was in the paper this morning?" Justine asked.

As though anyone would let Olivia miss seeing it. Starting the first of the year, *The Cedar Cove Chronicle* had gone to two editions a week and this was the very first Saturday edition. Maybe Griffin should've stuck to one paper a week, Olivia thought grimly, since he obviously couldn't scrape up enough real news. His entire column had been about the day he'd spent sitting in her courtroom, listening to the judgments she'd made. Although he didn't mention the Randalls by name, he said her ruling in that instance had come from the heart rather than from any law book and he applauded her decision, calling her gutsy and unconventional. Olivia wasn't opposed to receiving praise, but she'd prefer not to have attention drawn to that particular case. While he'd mentioned her in a vaguely flattering light, he certainly hadn't been as kind to others in her profession. He appeared to have a bias against attorneys and judges, and wasn't afraid to share his opinions on the subject.

It was just Olivia's luck that Jack Griffin had chosen *her* courtroom that day. Just her *bad* luck, she amended.

"What happened?" Justine asked. "I mean, it's obvious Jack Griffin doesn't have much respect for the law, but he seems to like you."

Olivia could hear the amusement in her daughter's

voice. "I don't even know the man," she said dismissively.

"That's interesting. I thought you'd been holding out on me."

"Holding out?"

"As in you'd found yourself a man."

"Oh, please," Olivia moaned.

"Well, he seems to have made himself your champion. Especially over that 'divorce denied' thing."

Olivia had known she was taking a risk when she'd made her ruling on the Randall case. Her personal feelings had no role on the bench, but she was absolutely certain those two young people would be making a terrible mistake if they went through with the divorce. She'd merely put up a roadblock, hoping it would be enough to force them into dealing with their problems instead of running from them.

"Jack wrote that you weren't afraid of making a controversial decision."

"I've already read his column," Olivia said in an effort to keep her daughter from repeating any more of it.

"So you know all about it?"

Olivia sighed. "Unfortunately, yes." Then, hoping to change the subject, she asked, "Are you free for lunch this afternoon? It's been weeks since we had a chance to visit." Justine had come for Christmas, but she'd left as soon as the gifts were opened and dinner had been served. Olivia had no idea where she'd spent New Year's. Then again, she did know—and wished she didn't. Her daughter had spent the night with Warren Saget. "Your grandma and I are getting together. We'd love it if you could join us."

"Sorry, Mom, Warren and I already have plans."

"Oh." She should have guessed. Warren kept a tight rein on Justine. She rarely had any free time these days. That distressed and annoyed Olivia, but whenever she mentioned it, or even hinted as much, her daughter became defensive.

"We'll get together soon," Justine promised. "Gotta go now."

Olivia was about to suggest they set a day and a time right then, but before she had the opportunity, the line went dead.

Grumbling to herself, she finished writing out her grocery list, then reached for her jacket and purse. The January weather was gray and bleak. It was raining lightly—more of a fine mist, really—as she locked the front door and hurried down the porch steps to her car. Olivia loved her home, which looked out over the water on Lighthouse Road. The lighthouse itself was three miles away, situated on a jut of land that led into the protected waters of the cove. Unfortunately it couldn't be seen from her property.

She had a number of stops to make—the grocery, the dry cleaner, the library. She hoped to get everything done by noon, when she was meeting her mother for lunch. She wished again that Justine could have joined them.

She picked up her dry cleaning and returned her books to the library, then swung over to the local Safeway, where she always did her weekly shopping. Thankfully, she was early enough to avoid the usual Saturday morning crush. She began with the produce aisle, where she stood debating whether a head of lettuce was worth this outrageous price.

"Judge Lockhart. Didn't expect to run into you here."

Olivia turned to confront the very man who'd managed to upset her morning. She recognized his face from that day in her courtroom—the man who'd sat right in front, notebook and pen in hand. "Well, well, if it isn't Mr. Jack Griffin."

"I don't believe we've had the pleasure of a formal introduction."

"Trust me, Mr. Griffin, after this morning's paper, I know who you are." He was around her age, Olivia guessed, in his early fifties, and about her height. Dark hair, starting to gray. Clean-shaven, with pleasant regular features, he didn't strike her as outstandingly handsome but he had what she could only describe as an *appealing* quality. He smiled readily and his gaze was clear and direct. He seemed a bit disheveled in a loose raincoat, and she noticed that his shirt was casual, the top two buttons unfastened.

"Do I detect a note of censure?" he asked, his smile flirting with her.

Olivia wasn't sure how to answer. She was annoyed with him, but letting him know that would serve no useful purpose. "I suppose you were just doing your job," she muttered, tossing a green pepper into her cart. Rubies cost less per pound, but she had a fondness for green peppers and felt she deserved a treat. Especially after this morning. Green peppers were a whole lot better for her than butter-pecan ice cream.

She started to push her cart away, but Jack stopped her.

"They've got a coffee shop next door. Let's talk."

Olivia shook her head. "I don't think so."

Jack followed her as she sorted through the fresh green beans. "It might've been my imagination, but you didn't want to see that couple go through with the divorce, did you?"

"I don't discuss my cases outside the courtroom," she informed him stiffly.

"Naturally," he said in a reasonable tone as he continued walking at her side. "It was personal, wasn't it?"

Losing her patience, Olivia turned and glared at him. As though she'd admit such a thing to a *reporter!* He'd make the whole episode sound like a breach of professional ethics. She'd done nothing wrong, dammit. She'd acted with the best of intentions, and she'd remained steadfastly within the law.

"You lost a son, didn't you?" he pressed.

"Are you gathering information on me for your next article, Mr. Griffin?" she asked coldly.

"No—and it's Jack." He held up both hands, which was supposed to reassure her, Olivia supposed. It didn't.

"I nearly lost my own son," he said.

"Do you always pester people who prefer to go about their own business, or am I special?"

"You're special," he answered without a pause. "I knew it the minute you made your judgment in the Randall case. You were right, you know. Everyone in that courtroom could see they had no business getting divorced. What you did took guts."

"As I explained earlier, I cannot discuss my cases."

"But you could have a cup of coffee with me, couldn't you?" He didn't plead, didn't prod, but there was a good-natured quality about him that was beginning to work on her. He had a sense of humor, even a certain roguishness. She gave up. It probably wouldn't hurt to talk.

"All right," she agreed. She glanced down at her cart, calculating how long it would take her to finish.

"Thirty minutes," he suggested, grinning triumphantly. "I'll meet you there."

That settled, he walked away. Olivia couldn't help it, she was curious about this man and his comment about almost losing his own son. Perhaps they had more in common than she'd realized.

Twenty-five minutes later, her groceries in the trunk of her car, Olivia entered Java and Juice, the coffeehouse next to the Safeway. Sure enough, Jack was waiting for her, hands cupped around a steaming latte. He sat at a round table by the window and stood when she approached. It was a small thing, coming to his feet like that, a show of good manners and respect. But that one gentlemanly gesture told her as much about him as everything else he'd said and done.

She sat in the chair across from him and he waved to the waitress, who appeared promptly. Olivia ordered a regular coffee; a minute later, a thick ceramic mug was set before her.

Jack waited until the high-school girl had left before he spoke. "I just wanted you to know I meant what I said—I admire what you did last week. It couldn't have been easy." Olivia was about to remind him yet again that she couldn't discuss her court cases when he stopped her, shaking his head. "I know, I know. But in my opinion you made a bold move and I couldn't let that go unnoticed."

Olivia would have preferred he not publish his opinions for the entire town to discuss. However, there was nothing she could say or do that would change what had already seen the light of the printed page.

"How long have you been in Cedar Cove?" she asked instead.

"Three months," he answered. "Are you purposely turning the attention away from yourself?"

Olivia grinned. "I sure am," she told him. "So—you have a son?"

"Eric. He's twenty-six and lives in Seattle. When he was ten, he was diagnosed with a rare form of bone cancer. He wasn't expected to live…." His face darkened at the memory.

"But he did," Olivia said.

Jack nodded. "He's alive and healthy, and for that I'm deeply grateful." Then he went on to say that Eric worked for Microsoft and was doing very well.

Olivia's gaze went automatically to his ring finger. Jack had mentioned his son, but not his wife.

He'd obviously noticed her quick look. "Eric survived the cancer," he said, "but unfortunately my marriage didn't."

So he understood on a personal level what had occurred in her own life. "I'm sorry."

He shrugged carelessly. "That was a long time ago. Life goes on and so do I. You're divorced yourself?" Although he asked the question, she was fairly certain he already knew the answer.

"Fifteen years now."

The conversation flowed smoothly after that, and before she knew it, she had to leave to meet her mother for lunch. Reaching for her purse, Olivia stood and extended her hand to Jack.

"I enjoyed getting to know you."

He rose to his feet, taking her hand in his. "You, too, Olivia." He briefly squeezed her fingers, as if to say they'd formed a bond with one another. When they'd first met today—and definitely before that—she'd been irritated with him, but Jack had managed to thwart her displeasure. By the time she walked out the door, Olivia felt she'd made a friend. She was well aware that Jack Griffin was no ordinary man, though; she wouldn't make the mistake of underestimating him.

Ian Randall sat in his car outside his wife's apartment building, dreading what was certain to be another confrontation. The judge had made it plain that the prenuptial agreement wasn't going to be rescinded. Now what? They had a few options, none of which suited him or, apparently, his wife.

Cecilia was the one who wanted the divorce. She'd been the first to hire an attorney. Hell, she'd rammed this whole stupid idea down his throat. She wanted out. Okay, fine. If she preferred not to be with him, he was hardly going to fight for the privilege of remaining her husband. But now they were faced with a stumbling block in their attempt to end the marriage, such as it was. All because they'd written that agreement, intended to safeguard their wedding vows. Some decision had to be made.

There was no point in waiting any longer. He climbed out of his car and slowly entered the building, approaching the first-floor apartment they'd once shared.

Ian was irritated that he had to ring the doorbell to what had recently been his own home. After their separation, he'd had to move on base. Fortunately, his friend Andrew Lackey had allowed Ian to store a few things at his house. He leaned hard against the buzzer now, fighting down his resentment. Releasing the button, he retreated a step and squared his shoulders. He steeled his emotions the way he'd been taught in basic training, unwilling to reveal any of his thoughts or feelings to Cecilia.

His wife opened the door, frowning when she saw who it was.

"I thought we should come to a decision," he announced in resolute tones. No matter how many times he told himself he shouldn't feel anything for her, he did. He couldn't be in the same room with her and forget what it was like when they'd made love or when he'd first felt their baby move inside her. Nor could he forget how it had felt to stand over his daughter's grave, never having had the opportunity to hold Allison or tell her he loved her.

Cecilia held open the door. "Okay."

The hesitation in her voice was unmistakable.

Ian followed her into the compact living room and sat on the edge of the sofa. They'd picked it up second-hand at a garage sale shortly after their wedding. Ian had refused to let Cecilia help him move it, since she was already three months pregnant. His stubbornness had resulted in a wrenched back. This old sofa came with a lot of bad memories, just like his short-lived marriage.

Cecilia sat across from him, her hands folded, her face unrevealing.

"I have to tell you the judge's decision was kind of a shock," he said, opening the discussion.

"My attorney said we could appeal it."

"Oh, sure," Ian muttered, his anger flaring. "And rack up another five or six hundred dollars' worth of legal fees. I don't have that kind of money to burn and neither do you."

"You don't know the state of my finances," Cecilia snapped.

This was the way every discussion started with them. At first they were courteous, almost too polite, but within minutes they were arguing and everything exploded in his face. They seemed to reach that level of irrational anger so quickly these days, or at least since Allison Marie's birth—and death. Ian sighed, feeling a sense of hopelessness. With the way things were between them now, it was hard to believe they'd ever slept together.

Ian diverted his thoughts from their once healthy and energetic love life. In bed they'd found little to disagree about, but that was before...

"We could always do as my attorney suggested."

"And what's that?" Ian had no intention of taking Allan Harris's advice. The other man represented his wife's interests, not his.

"Allan recommended we do what the judge said and take our disagreement to the Dispute Resolution Center."

Ian remembered Judge Lockhart making some comment about that, and he remembered his own reaction at the time. "What exactly is that supposed to do?" he asked, trying to sound reasonable and conciliatory.

"Well, I can't say for certain, but I think we'd each present our sides to an impartial third party."

"What will that cost?"

"Does *everything* boil down to money with you?" Cecilia demanded.

"As a matter of fact, yes." This divorce had already set him back plenty. He wasn't the one who'd wanted it in the first place, he told himself stubbornly. Sure, after Allison died, they'd had a few arguments but he'd never expected it to lead to this.

Cecilia had never understood what it'd been like for him, although he'd tried to explain countless times. He hadn't received her "family gram" until the end of the tour. His commanding officer had withheld the information about the premature birth and death of his daughter, since there was no possibility of a humanitarian airlift or any way of contacting Cecilia. When he finally reached the base, he hadn't had a chance to absorb the reality of their loss.

His wife gave him a disgusted look. "Do *you* have any suggestions, then?" she asked in a superior tone of voice that set his teeth on edge. She knew he hated it when she spoke to him as though he was still in grade school.

"As a matter of fact, I do," he said, and got to his feet.

"Fine. I can't wait to hear it." Cecilia crossed her arms in that huffy way of hers.

"I say we simply go on with our lives."

Cecilia frowned. "What's that supposed to mean?"

"Do you plan to remarry?"

"I—I don't know. Maybe someday."

As far as he was concerned, Ian was through with

it. Never again would he subject himself to a woman's volatile emotions or fickle whims. "Not me. I've had it with marriage, with you, with the entire mess."

"Let me see if I understand what you're saying." Cecilia stood, too, and started pacing the small living room, passing directly in front of him. He caught a whiff of her perfume, and it was all he could do not to close his eyes and savor the scent. He hated that she still had the power to make him weak, to leave him wanting her....

"You can figure it out, I'm sure," he said, purposely being sarcastic because he was angry now. He couldn't be near Cecilia and not feel a rush of resentment. Not just at her but at himself for harboring emotions that wouldn't go away.

She ignored his attitude. "Are you suggesting we not divorce?"

"Sort of." He didn't want her to assume he was seeking a reconciliation. That wouldn't work; he already knew it. In the months after Allison's death, they'd both tried to make the best of a painful situation, without success.

"Sort of?" she echoed, then waved her hand at him. "Tell me more. This whole concept of yours intrigues me."

He'd just bet it did. "We could *pretend* we're divorced."

"Pretend?" Cecilia didn't bother to hide her anger. "That is the stupidest idea I've ever heard. Pretend," she repeated, shaking her head. "You think we can ignore all our problems and *pretend* they don't exist."

He glared at her, not trusting himself to speak.

Okay, maybe she was right. He didn't want to deal with this divorce.

"You're always looking for the easy way out," she said scornfully.

He might be a lot of things, but irresponsible wasn't one of them. The Navy trusted him with a multi-million-dollar nuclear submarine—didn't that prove how dependable he was? Dammit, he'd been brought up to meet his obligations, to stand by his word.

"If I was trying to escape my responsibilities, I'd never have married you." Ian knew the minute he uttered the words that he'd said the wrong thing.

Cecilia flew across the room. "I never wanted you to marry me because of Allison! We would've been fine…." She faltered and abruptly looked away. "I didn't need you…."

"The hell you didn't. You still do." If for no other reason than the health benefits the Navy provided, his wife and daughter had needed him.

"You would never have married me if it wasn't for the pregnancy."

"Not true."

She swept the hair away from her face. "I can't believe I was so stupid."

"You!" he burst out. Apparently Cecilia thought she was the only one with regrets. He had his own, and every one of them included her.

"Allison and I were…" She hesitated, suddenly inarticulate. "We…"

"Allison was my daughter, too, and I'll be damned if I'll allow you to tell me what my feelings are. Don't go putting words in my mouth, or discount the way I felt about her. Just because I couldn't be here when she was born doesn't mean I didn't care. For the love of God, I was under the polar icecap when you went into labor. You weren't even due until—"

"Now you're blaming me." She thrust her hand over her mouth as if to hold back emotion.

It didn't do any good to talk. He'd tried, damn it to hell, he'd tried, but it never got him anywhere. He just couldn't find any middle ground with her.

Rather than prolong the agony, he stormed out of the apartment. The door banged in his wake, and he wasn't sure if he'd closed it or Cecilia had slammed it after him.

He left the building, fury propelling his steps, and got into his car. Feeling the way he did just then, Ian realized he shouldn't be driving, but he wasn't about to sit outside this apartment. Not when Cecilia might think he sat there pining for her.

He revved the engine and threw the transmission into drive. The tires squealed as he sped off, burning rubber. He hadn't gone more than a quarter mile when he saw the red-and-blue lights of a police car flashing behind him.

A cop. Damn it all. He eased to a stop at the curb and rolled down his window. By the time the officer reached his vehicle, Ian had removed his military driver's license from his wallet.

"'Morning, sir," he said, wondering how good an actor he was.

"In a bit of a hurry back there, weren't you?" the policeman asked. He was middle-aged, his posture rigid, his hair worn in a crewcut. Everything about him screamed ex-military, which meant he just might be inclined to cut Ian a little slack.

"Hurry?" Ian repeated and forced himself to relax. "Not really."

"You were doing forty in a twenty-mile-an-hour zone." He glanced at the license and started writing out a ticket, apparently unimpressed by Ian's military status.

From the looks of it, Ian wasn't going to get the opportunity to talk his way out of this one. He quickly calculated what the ticket would cost him, plus the rate hike in his insurance.

Thanks, Cecilia, he thought bitterly. The price of marriage just kept going up.

Grace Sherman and Olivia Lockhart had been best friends nearly their entire lives. They'd met in seventh grade, which was when students from both South Ridge Elementary and Mariner's Glen entered Colchester Junior High. Grace had served as Olivia's maid-of-honor when she'd married Stanley Lockhart soon after her college graduation and was godmother to her youngest son, James.

The summer following their high-school graduation, Grace had married Daniel Sherman and they quickly had two daughters. When Kelly, her youngest, turned six, Grace had gone back to school and earned her Bachelor of Library Science degree. Then she'd started working for the Cedar Cove Library, and within ten years had been promoted to head librarian.

Even while Olivia was attending a prestigious women's college in Oregon and Grace was an at-home mother with two small children, they'd remained close. They still were. Because their lives were busy, they'd created routines to sustain their friendship. Lunch together once a month. And every Wednesday night at seven, they met for an aerobics class at the local YMCA.

Grace waited in the well-lit parking lot for her friend. She hadn't felt good when she left the house. The sensation was all-encompassing. Physically, she was tired, her weight was up and she didn't have her period to blame anymore. For years, she'd managed to keep within ten pounds of what she'd weighed in high school, but during the past five, she'd gained an extra fifteen pounds. It had happened despite all her efforts. Somehow the weight had crept on. She was dissatisfied with other aspects of her appearance, too. Her salt-and-pepper hair was badly in need of a cut. On second thought, perhaps she'd live dangerously and let it grow. She was in the mood for a change—although she wasn't convinced it would make much difference.

Emotionally, she wasn't feeling any better. After thirty-five years of marriage, she knew her husband as well as she did herself. Something was troubling Dan, but when she'd gently asked him about it, he'd bristled and they'd had an argument. He'd hurt her feelings and Grace had rushed away without resolving the issue.

For most of their marriage, Dan had been employed as a logger. When hard times fell on the industry, he'd taken a job with a local tree-trimming service. The work wasn't as steady as either of them would have liked, but with her income and some inventive budgeting, they managed. There wasn't any extra for small extravagances, but those had never mattered to Grace. She had her husband, her children, her friends and a decent roof over her head.

She watched Olivia's dark-blue sedan pull into the parking lot and saw her climb out, gym bag in hand.

Grace slid out of her vehicle. "So, how does it feel to be a celebrity?"

"Not you, too?" Olivia complained as they walked toward the building. She held open the door for Grace. "I've had nothing but grief over that stupid article."

Grace smiled as color instantly flooded her friend's cheeks.

"I let him have a piece of my mind," Olivia muttered, as they marched past a group of youngsters headed for the swimming pool. Once inside the locker room, they placed their bags on the bench, stripped out of their sweats and changed their shoes.

One foot braced on the side of the bench, Grace tied her running shoe. "You met Griffin? When?"

"Saturday."

Grace raised both eyebrows. She found it interesting that Olivia was skimping on the details. "Where?"

"In town."

"Hey, what's up?"

"Up? Not one thing," her friend said. "I just happened to run into Jack at the Safeway and we...chatted a bit."

"Why do I have the feeling you're not telling me something?"

Olivia slipped the sweatband around her forehead. "There's nothing to tell, trust me."

"Trust you?" Grace echoed, following her out of the locker room and into the aerobics area of the gym.

Children and adults milled about, and Grace and Olivia had to stop several times to allow others to pass by. "Have you ever noticed that the only time people ask you to trust them is when they probably *shouldn't* be trusted?"

Olivia paused, then started a few warm-up exercises on her own. "I hadn't, but you're right." She propped her leg on the ballet bar and bent her forehead to her knee.

Grace leaned against the bar, envying her friend's suppleness. Her own body was far less flexible. "Did you know people have been talking about the article all week?"

"Great."

Disregarding her sarcasm, Grace continued, her voice deceptively mild. "Actually a lot of the talk has to do with Jack Griffin."

Olivia raised her head. "Anything interesting?"

Grace shrugged and adjusted the waistband of her spandex shorts. "Oh, a few things."

"Such as?"

Grace was determined not to make this easy. Olivia had never, to her recollection, shown this much interest in any man since her divorce. Grace had felt for some time that her friend should "get back into circulation," as people called it. Appropriate comment for a librarian, she always thought. "You really want to know?"

The question seemed to require a great deal of thought. "No—forget it." Then in the next breath, Olivia changed her mind. "All right, I'm curious. What have you heard?"

"He moved to Cedar Cove three months ago."

"Old news," Olivia muttered. "If that's all you have…"

"From the Spokane area."

This appeared to be something Olivia didn't know. "Newspaper background, obviously?"

"Yes, from a paper with ten times the circulation of *The Chronicle*." Grace wasn't a gossip by nature, but she'd been wondering about Jack Griffin since she'd read his first Saturday column. She'd liked what he'd had to say, and it was apparent he approved of Olivia. She'd met him briefly at a Chamber of Commerce meeting shortly after he'd come to Cedar Cove but hadn't formed an impression one way or the other.

"Why does a man give up working for a prestigious newspaper and move across the state to a town the size of Cedar Cove?" she asked Olivia.

Her friend shrugged. "Your guess is as good as mine. Perhaps he wanted to be closer to his son."

"He has a son?" No one Grace had spoken to knew that.

"Eric. He lives in Seattle."

That was interesting. But before she could comment further, their instructor, Shannon Devlin, entered the room, clapping her hands to gather her students around her.

"Trust me. There's more to this career change than meets the eye."

"Trust *you!*"

"Yeah, trust me," Grace joked.

Olivia grinned and placed her hands on her hips as she rotated her waist, making deep bends as Shannon led the class in warm-ups. "You've been hanging around the mystery section of the library too long," she whispered as they took their places in front of the floor-to-ceiling mirror.

Shannon was twenty, if that. A pretty girl with pliant limbs and a body devoid of fat. Grace's own figure had once been that slim and perfect, she reminded herself—before two children and the onset of menopause.

The music, impossibly loud, gave her a surge of energy. She had a love/hate relationship with this class. If not for Olivia, she would have dropped out a dozen times. Unfortunately she needed the benefits of all this huffing, puffing and stretching. Despite the muscle pain, she didn't mind the mat exercises, the sit-ups and such, but she hated Shannon's little dance routines. *Step back, slide left, cross right…* Olivia never seemed to have a problem with the complicated patterns; Grace, on the other hand, had trouble living up to her name.

After fifty minutes of sweating and grumbling under her breath, plus cool-down exercises, they were finished. None too soon, as far as Grace was concerned. Not until they'd showered and changed back into their sweats did Olivia mention Jack again. The fact that she wanted to continue the conversation surprised Grace.

"Did you learn anything else about Jack Griffin?"

Grace had to think. It always seemed to take a while for her brain cells to stop bouncing around after her aerobics class. "You know more about him than I do," she finally said.

Olivia reached for her gym bag. "I doubt that."

"You're interested in him, aren't you?"

Olivia laughed off the suggestion. "Oh, hardly. I've got enough worries without adding a relationship to the mix."

"Worries?" Sure, her friend had worries, but then everyone did.

"Mom's getting on in years and Justine—I just can't seem to talk to her anymore, and I haven't heard from James in two weeks."

"I thought he was out at sea."

"He is, but he can still e-mail me."

"Okay, okay, we all have kid problems, and our parents are a concern, but that doesn't mean we have to stop living."

"You think I've stopped living?" Olivia asked. "Because I don't have a man in my life?"

Grace knew the question had offended her. First Dan and now her best friend, and Grace hadn't meant to upset either of them.

"I didn't mean it like that," she assured her. "I just think you should leave your options open when it comes to Jack."

"Why?"

"Because." And that was all the answer she was willing to give, but Grace had a very strong feeling that the new editor of *The Cedar Cove Chronicle* was going to bring something new and exciting to Olivia's life.

Three

Cecilia was working as a hostess at The Captain's Galley the night she'd met Ian Randall, and she continued to work there five evenings a week. Her father, Bobby Merrick, was one of the bartenders and had gotten her the job.

Soon after graduating from high school, Cecilia had moved to Cedar Cove at her father's urging. After a long estrangement, he'd contacted her with promises of making up for lost time. He'd seemed genuine, and because she'd felt cheated out of a father during her childhood, she'd readily agreed. Following her parents' divorce when she was ten, Cecilia hardly ever saw her father and she welcomed this unexpected opportunity. Refusing to heed her mother's warnings, she'd packed up her entire life and moved across the country, from New Hampshire to this small waterfront community in Washington. Within three months she knew she'd made a mistake. Her dreams of a college education were simply that. Dreams. Bobby's idea of setting her up for the future was talking to his boss and getting her a job at the same restaurant where he worked. Being a hostess and cocktail waitress wasn't how Cecilia wanted to spend the next few decades, but it was all too easy to imagine. Without intending it, she'd let her entire life get sidetracked.

Now she was about to be divorced, up to her ears in debt and utterly miserable. Her illusions about her father and men in general had been shattered. Bobby wanted to be her friend, but as badly as Cecilia needed a friend, she needed a father more.

One day, she vowed, she'd find a way to attend college but first she had to figure out how to pay for it. With the legal fees and what it'd cost to bury her daughter, she suspected she'd be at least thirty before she could afford to get an education. Bobby couldn't help her out financially; he'd made that completely clear.

In an effort to supplement her income, she was putting in extra hours on weekends, serving drinks in the bar once the dining room closed at ten. Often she wasn't home until two-thirty in the morning.

When she showed up for work late Friday afternoon, she knew she was in for a hectic shift. The aircraft carrier, *The Carl Vinson,* was in town, which meant a crew of 2,500 sailors. The Captain's Galley served the best seafood in the area and the bar was a popular meeting place.

It was here that Ian had come for a drink one night last January. He'd had his eye on her, and she'd been watching him just as avidly. Then he— She gave herself a mental shake. Cecilia didn't want to think about her husband, and tried to push him from her mind. It didn't work.

She hadn't seen or heard from him since he'd charged out of her apartment a week earlier. They hadn't made any decisions about what to do next. That was typical of him, she thought angrily. He left every decision to her. If they were going ahead with this divorce, then their best option was the Dispute Resolution Center. Not that *their* dispute could ever be resolved... She sighed in resignation. Obviously, she'd have to make the appointment. Ian's so-called suggestion that they pretend to be divorced was ridiculous. Absolutely ridiculous!

The bar was already hopping when the restaurant closed. Cecilia collected her tray and joined Beverly and Carla, the two other cocktail waitresses. The lounge was thick with cigarette smoke and the smell of beer hung in the air, trapped by the smoke. The music came from a jukebox and was earsplitting loud. Cecilia had to struggle to hear her customers' orders.

One man who drank alone seemed to speak softly in an effort to force her to lean closer. He was older, at least forty, and he sent out all the signals—he was interested in her. He gave her the creeps and Cecilia did her best to ignore him. The way his eyes followed her about the room made her skin crawl.

By closing time only a few patrons lingered; unfortunately her admirer was one of them. Cecilia's feet hurt and her eyes smarted from the smoke. She was eager to collect her tips and head home. Just when she thought she was finished for the night, Ian and Andrew Lackey, another sailor, walked into the bar.

Cecilia tensed, especially when she noticed Ian's demeanor. It was obvious The Captain's Galley hadn't been his first stop. Her husband didn't hold his liquor well, never had, and generally avoided anything stronger than beer.

Her attention was on Ian when she should have been keeping closer tabs on the loner whose gaze had been glued to her for the last four hours.

"You wanna bite to eat?" The husky male voice spoke from behind her.

Cecilia whirled around.

"I'm Bart, and you're Cecilia, right?"

"Right." She watched Ian and his friend stroll up to the bar. Her husband seemed to be pretending she wasn't there. But then, that was his preferred approach to anything awkward or inconvenient, wasn't it? "Actually it's been a long night," she answered, her gaze flicking back to Bart. "Another time." *In your dreams,* she added silently.

"You've gotta be hungry."

"Ah…"

Ian finally glanced in her direction, and his eyes narrowed when he saw her talking to the other man.

"Hey, it's no big deal. Breakfast, conversation." Bart continued the pressure. "You look like you could use a friend and I can be a very good…friend."

Cecilia was more concerned about Ian than ditching Bart. "I don't think so."

"Tomorrow then, just you and me."

"I…" Her gaze flew from Bart to Ian, who was scowling heavily. She was afraid he'd cause a scene, which she wanted to avoid, for everyone's sake.

Ian leaned toward his friend and whispered, but Andrew adamantly shook his head. Cecilia could see that Ian was looking for trouble and his friend was trying to dissuade him.

"Perhaps another night," Cecilia said quickly, putting Bart off. That seemed the best way of getting rid of him before Ian did something stupid.

Her husband stepped away from the bar. "Is he bothering you?" he demanded, his words half-slurred.

"Butt out," Bart snarled, angry at the interruption. He seemed to think he was making progress with Cecilia. He wasn't, but Ian didn't know that and apparently neither did he.

Andrew tried to stop him, but Ian shook off his hand and advanced a menacing step. He wasn't about to back down, even if Bart outweighed him by fifty pounds. "In case you didn't know it, you're trying to pick up my wife."

Bart glanced at Cecilia as if to gauge the truth. She didn't dare meet his look.

"We're divorced, remember?" she taunted, reminding her husband that it'd been his idea to *pretend* they were no longer married.

"The hell we are."

"You're the one who said we should just get on with our lives."

"I...I..." Ian sputtered, searching for a satisfactory reply.

"Why should you care if I date another man?"

"Because until a judge says otherwise, you're legally my wife!"

"Are you married or not?" Bart muttered.

"Married!" Ian shouted.

"Separated," Cecilia said.

Bart reached for his jacket. "In that case, let's go."

"The hell she will." Ian started toward Bart, but Andrew stepped between them.

"Anytime, buddy," Bart growled.

"Right now sounds good to me," Ian said, raising his clenched fists.

"Get out," Cecilia cried. "Both of you! I have no intention of going anywhere with either one of you." She ran toward the back room where her father had conveniently disappeared, supposedly checking inventory.

"What's happening out there?" Bobby Merrick asked as if he wasn't aware of the situation he'd left her to deal with on her own. Ian and Bobby had never gotten along, and Bobby avoided any confrontation between them by making himself scarce.

Cecilia shook her head. "Nothing."

"Everything okay?"

"Ian's here, looking for a fight. That's all."

Her father stared back, frowning. "I don't want any trouble here. Tell him to take it outside."

"Yeah." Cecilia sighed wearily. "I did. And now I'm leaving."

"Get rid of Ian first."

"Not to worry, I'm sure he's left."

She retrieved her coat and purse, got her share of the tips and walked toward the front door, hoping she wouldn't stumble upon her husband slugging it out with the loner. To Cecilia's surprise, Ian hadn't left, after all. They stared at each other from opposite sides of the room.

Beverly was the only other person in the bar, preparing the night's cash for deposit; she muttered "good night," still intent on her task.

"We're closed," Cecilia told Ian.

He paid no attention. "Were you actually going to leave with that sleazebag?"

The contempt in his voice rankled. "That's none of your business."

He looked at her for a long moment, then turned and stalked out the door.

Cecilia resisted the urge to hurry after him. Ian was in no condition to drive. She hesitated, arguing with herself. He wouldn't appreciate her concern, and it might give him the wrong impression. Just a few minutes earlier she'd demanded he stay out of her life. The least she could do was follow her own advice and stay out of his.

The door opened and she glanced up expectantly, thinking it might be Ian. Instead, it was his friend. Andrew seemed awkward and unsure. She barely knew the other sailor, who'd recently been transferred to Bremerton.

"Yes?" she asked stiffly.

"I thought you should know Ian's going to sea. He's been transferred to the *George Washington*"

That didn't make sense to her. The *George Washington* was an aircraft carrier. Ian was a submariner, a nuclear electronic technician. "He'll be away six weeks?" she asked numbly, not understanding the transfer.

"More like six months."

Six months? "Oh."

"That's why he came by tonight. He wanted you to know."

Cecilia wasn't sure what to say.

"He didn't mean to cause any trouble."

Cecilia swallowed hard. "He didn't...not really."

Andrew peered over his shoulder as if he'd heard someone call his name. "I've got to go. I just wanted to tell you I'm real sorry about your little girl."

"Th-thank you," she managed to say. But he was already gone. She waited a few moments and decided her peace of mind was worth more than her pride. She had to be sure Ian wasn't driving. Hurrying outside, she stood on the sidewalk, searching for her husband's car. He was nowhere to be seen.

A sense of loss filled her, an emptiness. Ian was going to sea for six months and she hated the thought of it. She didn't *want* to feel anything for him, but she did. At any rate, she told herself wryly, he had his wish—with Ian at sea, she couldn't proceed with the divorce.

Tired and discouraged, Cecilia strolled toward her own ramshackle car, shoulders hunched against the cold. She could smell the ocean tonight, and a low-lying fog was rolling in from the cove. A car drove slowly past. Looking up, Cecilia saw that it was Ian's. Thankfully, Andrew was behind the wheel. As she watched, her husband's gaze connected with hers.

Cecilia was shocked by the longing she saw in him. It was all she could do to keep herself from calling out. She yearned to wish Ian a safe voyage and see him off without this animosity between them.

But it was too late. Much too late.

Charlotte Jefferson wore her finest dress—Navy dotted Swiss, with long sleeves and a full skirt—on her next visit to Tom Harding at the Cedar Cove Convalescent Center. She'd worked feverishly knitting the lap robe for him, and it showed excellent workmanship, even if she said so herself.

Tom was sitting in his wheelchair when she breezed into the room. "I told you I'd be back," she said, smiling warmly, the newspaper tucked under one arm. Her new friend looked well. There was color in his cheeks and his eyes were clear and bright.

Tom nodded, obviously pleased to see her. His right hand pointed shakily to the empty chair.

"Thank you," she said, sinking gratefully onto the seat. "I don't usually dress up in my best except on Sundays, but I just came from the funeral of a friend of my husband's."

Tom stared at her blankly.

"We were friends with the Iversons for years," she said. "He was a good man. Died of lung cancer. Used to smoke like a chimney." She shook her head sadly, then crossed her legs and removed her left shoe. "I was on my feet most of the afternoon," she explained. "I'm not as young as I used to be, and Lloyd Iverson's death really shook me." Sighing, she looked over at him. "How was your week?"

Tom shrugged.

"Are they treating you well?"

He nodded as if to say he had no complaints.

"How about the food?"

Another shrug.

"Speaking of food," she said, brightening. "I got the most fabulous recipe for broccoli lasagna at the wake. I just love it when I find a good recipe. Last month we buried Marion Parsons, and a lady from her church brought the most incredible noodle salad made with—and this is the kicker—whipped cream. Spaghetti noodles with a marshmallow and cream dressing. It was out of this world." It suddenly occurred to her that Tom might not be interested in hearing about the recipe exchange that went on at wakes.

"I'm glad to hear you like it here in Cedar Cove."
He nodded again.

"I think I'll make up a batch of that broccoli lasagna and take half of it over to my daughter. She lives alone now, and I just don't think she eats enough vegetables. It doesn't matter that she's fifty-two, she's still my little girl and I worry about her."

Tom smiled faintly.

"Would you like me to bring you a piece, too?"

Grinning, Tom shook his head.

"You don't like broccoli, is that it? You and George Bush. Not George W. I don't know if he likes broccoli or not."

Once more Tom shook his head.

"Broccoli's good for the bowels. Now, that's something we both need to think about, especially at our age." She laughed outright, wondering how Olivia would react if she could hear her now.

Shuffling his right foot, Tom laboriously rolled the wheelchair over to his nightstand.

"You want me to get something for you?" she asked.

His white head bobbed.

"It's inside the drawer here?" she asked.

His brown eyes were intense, and he indicated that she'd guessed right.

Charlotte eased open the drawer and found a pen, pad and a small coin purse that closed with a zipper. Years earlier, Clyde had carried a similar one. Thinking Tom might want her to write something down, she took out the pen and paper.

He frowned and shook his head.

She reached for the coin purse, instead, and glanced at him again.

Tom smiled and nodded.

"Do you want me to open it?" She realized that he must and carefully unzipped the small leather pouch. Inside was a folded yellow sheet of paper, which she removed. She set aside the coin holder and realized there was something enclosed in the paper. A key.

"What's this?" she asked, openly curious now.

Tom sat back; he seemed to be waiting for her to discover the answer on her own.

Charlotte unfolded the single sheet of paper and saw that it was a receipt for a storage unit right here in Cedar Cove. How he'd arranged that, she couldn't guess. She'd have to ask Janet Lester.

Uncertain what she was supposed to do with the key, Charlotte looked questioningly at Tom. "Everything seems to be in order," she assured him, returning the key and the receipt to the pouch. She was about to place it in the drawer when he stopped her, leaning forward and clasping her forearm with his right hand.

His eyes pleaded with her.

"You don't want me to put it back here?" she asked.

He shook his head, breathing hard from his exertion.

"What would you like me to do with it?"

He looked directly at her purse, which rested on the floor next to her large knitting bag.

"Take it with me?"

He nodded.

"Wouldn't you rather I gave it to someone in the office?" Surely that would be more appropriate than for Charlotte to keep it.

He shook his head, his expression adamant.

"All right, but I feel I should tell Janet about this."

He shrugged.

"Don't worry, your key's in good hands. I'll make sure nothing happens to it." She slipped the pouch inside her purse, then reached for her knitting bag. "I made you a lap robe. You need something to keep your legs warm. There's a chill in the air these January mornings, isn't there?" She settled the robe over his legs and stepped back to admire it.

Tom smiled, and made a shaky gesture to show his appreciation.

"You're most welcome," she said.

Tom's eyes closed briefly and she understood that he was tired. It was time to go. "I'll be back next Thursday," she said, gathering her bags.

He gave a slight nod.

"Don't you fret about a single thing. Oh, and I'll bring you a slice of that lasagna."

He grinned and shook his head.

"All right, I'll spare you." Tom was probably on a special diet, anyway. "I promise to take good care of this key for you."

He sighed and patted the lap robe.

"The pleasure was all mine. Goodbye until next week."

She left his room more quietly than she'd entered it, and immediately sought out the social worker. She didn't want to take the key without letting someone know.

Janet was in her office, talking on the phone. When she saw Charlotte, she motioned her in and ended the conversation a minute later.

"Hello, Charlotte, what can I do for you?"

She explained about Tom Harding and the key.

Janet rolled her chair over to the filing cabinet and opened the top drawer. Extracting a file, she laid it on her desk. While she read through the file, Charlotte took a second look at the receipt for the storage unit. She saw that it was a renewal, which had been paid by the state—paid in full for the entire year. Apparently Tom had run out of funds for his care and become a ward of the state. What assets he owned were being stored in the unit and would be sold at the time of his death.

Janet continued to scan the file. "Unfortunately the information I have here is the bare minimum. Tom suffered a stroke five years ago, but there's nothing about any family—and next to nothing about his background."

"He seemed to want me to keep the key," Charlotte said, unsure what she should do.

"Then I think you should. I know you have it, and so does Tom."

"All right, I will." That settled, Charlotte stood. "He's a lovely man."

"Yes, he is, but just a little mysterious."

Charlotte had to agree and she admitted to being intrigued.

Grace Sherman grabbed a carton of milk and placed it in her grocery cart, then headed for the checkout stand. As she wheeled toward the front of the store, she decided to take a short detour and look over the paperback display. Books were her passion—books of all kinds, from classic fiction to mysteries and romances, from bestseller titles to biographies and history and…almost everything. That was why she'd gone into library work. She loved to read and often read late into the night. Her daughters shared her delight in books, although Dan had never been much of a reader.

As Grace reached the front of the store, she noticed that the lineups were long. She chose one, then got the current copy of *People* magazine and flipped through that while she waited. The truth came to her as she approached the cashier—she dreaded going home.

The realization left her breathless. They were low on milk, but it certainly hadn't been necessary to make a special trip. She could easily have waited a day or two. Since she was here anyway, she'd thrown several packets of pasta into her cart, plus toilet paper and a couple of yogurts…as though to justify being to the supermarket at all. In fact, she'd been delaying the inevitable.

Dan had been in such a bleak mood lately. There seemed to be problems at work, but that was only a guess because her husband refused to talk to her about anything beyond the mundane. Any other inquiries were met with one-word replies. Television was vastly more interesting than sharing any part of himself with her.

Grace wanted to discover what was wrong, but he snapped at her whenever she tried. Every night it was the same. Walking into the house after work was like standing in an electrical storm; she never knew when lightning might strike. Because Dan was uncommunicative and morose, she chatted endlessly about this thing and that, in an effort to lighten his mood—and to forestall his outbursts of anger. They always came without warning.

Dan listened to her remarks, nodded at the appropriate times, even smiled now and again. But he contributed nothing to the conversation. The quieter he was, the harder she tried to draw him out, to no avail. Practically every evening he settled in front of the television and didn't move until it was time for bed.

This was no marriage. They might as well be college roommates for all the love and affection they exchanged.

Their marriage had never fulfilled Grace's expectations. She'd been eighteen and pregnant with Maryellen when she married Dan. He'd enlisted in the Army and almost immediately been shipped to Vietnam. The two years he'd been away were hell, for him and for her. When he returned, Dan was a different person from the young man who'd left. He'd become bitter and cynical, prone to rages; he'd also experimented with drugs and when she refused to allow them in the house they'd briefly separated.

For Maryellen's sake, they'd managed to patch things up long enough for Grace to get pregnant a second time. Later, because of their daughters, Dan and Grace had tried hard to make their marriage work.

The war still haunted him and for years Dan used to be awakened by nightmares. He never spoke of his experiences. Those, along with everything else, were hidden away inside his head. Throughout their marriage, Grace had continually hoped things would improve. Once the girls were in school, once she finished her own studies and got the job at the library, once the girls graduated from high school—surely then everything would be better. Year after year of hoping, of looking for signs...

It wasn't all bad. There'd been good times, too. When the girls started grade school, Grace had entered Olympic College and later commuted into Seattle to attend the University of Washington. Dan had been wonderfully supportive, working two jobs and helping with all their daughters' assorted activities.

Maryellen and Kelly had both been difficult teenagers, but they'd turned into responsible young women. Dan deeply loved his daughters. Grace never questioned his devotion to them, but she seriously doubted he was still in love with her.

These last few years had been hard on his pride. His career was over, and his job with the tree service wasn't nearly as satisfying as logging had been. Her salary now paid a larger share of the expenses, and she suspected that bothered him—not that he'd actually said so. But then, they didn't talk about money, mainly because she avoided any subject that might distress him.

Although she was half an hour later than usual, Dan didn't comment when she walked into the kitchen, carrying her groceries.

"I'm home," she announced unnecessarily as she set the sack on the countertop.

Dan had already positioned himself in front of the television, watching the local news. His boots were off and his sock-covered feet rested on the footstool that matched his old overstuffed chair.

"I thought we'd have taco salad for dinner. How does that sound?"

"Great," he answered without enthusiasm.

"How was your day?"

"All right." His eyes didn't waver from the television screen.

"Are you going to ask about mine?" she asked, growing irritated. The least he could do was show some interest in her and their life together, even if it was just a token effort.

"How was your day?" he muttered, his voice impassive.

"Terrible."

No response.

"Aren't you going to ask why?"

"You can tell me if you want."

The man she'd lived with for thirty-five years couldn't have cared less. Grace couldn't stand it any longer. Each attempt to draw him out was met with denial and accusation. If she was unhappy, it was her fault, not his—that was his argument the last time she'd tried to talk to him.

Walking into the living room, Grace reached for the remote control and muted the sound. Sitting down on the footstool, she faced her husband.

"What?" he demanded, annoyed that she'd disrupted his news program.

Grace stared at him. "Do you love me?"

Dan laughed as though she'd made a joke. "Love you? We've been married for thirty-five years."

"That doesn't answer my question."

"What do you want me to say? Of course I love you. I can't believe you have to ask."

"Is there someone else?"

He sat back and looked hard at her, then shook his head. "That's a ridiculous question."

"Is there?" she repeated.

"No. When's dinner going to be ready?"

Grace had another question first. "Do you remember the last time we made love?"

"Are you keeping track?"

She wasn't fooled. Answering a question with one of his own was a familiar trick of his. "No, but I can't remember. Can you?"

"I hate it when you do this." He shoved the footstool forcefully away and got up, burying his hands in his pants pockets. "If we're going to have an argument, let's make it over something worthwhile. I didn't realize you were so insecure that you need to be told I still love you."

"What I need is some affirmation that you want to be in this marriage."

"I had no idea you were so paranoid." He walked to the other side of the room.

"I'm not!"

"You suggested I'm having an affair."

She didn't believe it, and in fact, there was no real evidence, but she'd felt it might shock him enough to get his attention.

"What do you want from me?" he asked irritably.

"Some sign of *life,*" she cried.

He glared at her. "Did it ever occur to you that I might be tired?"

"Too tired to talk?"

"I've never been a conversationalist. You knew that when you married me. I'm not going to change at this stage of my life. I don't know what's bothering you, Grace, but get over it."

"That's not fair! I'm trying to get you to take some responsibility for what's happening to us."

"You're the one who's so unhappy."

"Because I want more from our marriage than this." She motioned with her arms in a futile effort to explain.

He frowned. "I'm giving you everything I have to give."

So was she. Dear God, so was she.

"If it isn't enough, I don't know what to tell you."

Her throat thickened with heartache. This was all there was, all there would ever be, and it *wasn't* enough.

The phone rang and they both jerked their attention toward the kitchen wall. Tears rolled down her cheeks and she brushed them aside as she hurried into the other room.

"Let the machine get it," Dan said.

"Why, so we can talk some more?"

"No," he responded gruffly.

"That's what I thought." She reached for the receiver and cleared her throat before she spoke. "Hello," she said, forcing herself to sound calm.

"Mom? Oh, Mom, you'll never guess what?" Kelly cried. "I just got the news. We're pregnant!" The joy in her youngest daughter's voice was as pure and sweet as anything Grace had ever known.

"Pregnant? You're sure?" Grace felt her tears start again, but these were tears of an altogether different kind. After ten years of marriage, Kelly and Paul were desperate for a child. They'd undergone countless tests and procedures, and Grace had about given up hope that her daughter would ever conceive. She longed for grandchildren and it hadn't seemed likely. Not with Kelly's fertility problems and Maryellen divorced. This was incredible news. Fabulous news.

Dan walked into the kitchen. "It's Kelly," she said excitedly, putting her hand over the receiver. "She's pregnant."

Her husband's eyes lit up and he smiled. It was the first real smile she'd seen from him in months. "Damn, that's great."

"Oh, sweetheart, your father and I are thrilled."

"Let me talk to Daddy."

Grace handed him the receiver. Kelly had always been especially close to her father, and they chatted for several minutes.

Dan replaced the receiver and went over to the stove where she'd put the hamburger on to fry for their meal. He slid his arms around her waist from behind and hugged her.

"I love you," he whispered.

"I know. I love you, too."

"Everything's going to be all right."

"I know." And it would. Grace had faith. Hope. And now she had a reason to continue, a reason to look to the future. Her marriage wasn't everything she wanted, but maybe it was enough. She'd *make* it enough. She'd shared thirty-five years with Dan. There had been good times and some not so good.

A grandchild gave her hope for the future.

Four

"I'll drive this evening," Olivia told her mother. The previous time she'd gotten into a car with Charlotte driving, Olivia had sworn it would be the last. Her mother out on the roads was a frightening thing to contemplate. She suspected Charlotte was the type of driver who never had an accident, but caused them.

"Well, it's my turn, although I have to admit I don't like driving at night."

Olivia removed her black robe and hung it in the small closet inside her chambers. Court was over for the week and her hot Friday-night date was with her mother. In fact, she ate more meals out with Charlotte than anyone. "I don't mind driving," Olivia told her.

"All right, if you insist."

Olivia did insist. The previous driving adventure with her mother had ended up being a narrow escape. Apparently Charlotte had lost the ability to turn her neck in order to look behind her. She adjusted the rearview mirrors left and right and honked before barreling willy-nilly out of her parking space. She'd also confessed that her eyes weren't what they used to be. It was a quandary. Olivia didn't want to limit her mother's independence, but she couldn't help worrying.

"It'll be a girls' night out," Charlotte said, sounding excited at the prospect. "But I have to be home by eleven. Harry worries if I'm not there."

Her mother doted on her cat. "Not a problem. The play starts at eight, so it should be over long before eleven."

"Shall we have dinner first?" Charlotte suggested.

"Sure, why not?" Olivia was in the mood to live it up. Her best friend was about to become a grandmother. Her seventy-two-year-old mother had a beau of sorts. Charlotte talked incessantly about her friend Tom at the convalescent center. The only person without something significant happening in her life seemed to be Olivia. She was ready for a change, ready for a risk. She'd hoped to hear from Jack Griffin, but he hadn't phoned nor had he shown up in court again. He obviously wasn't interested. Well, she could deal with that.

They arrived at the Playhouse shortly after seven-thirty. Plays were staged upstairs at the Community Theater, located on Harbor Street, which was the main road through the center of what was commonly referred to as downtown. The old theater still ran movies, but generally second-run features that had appeared earlier at the six-plex on the hill. The Playhouse was above the movie theater in small but cozy quarters. Every time Olivia attended a local production, she was astonished at the talent in a town as small as Cedar Cove.

Without assigned seating, Charlotte chose the very front row. No sooner had they settled in than Jack Griffin approached.

"Is this seat taken?" he asked, looking at the empty space next to Olivia.

"Jack!" She'd blurted his name before she had a chance to restrain her delight.

"Jack Griffin? Is *this* Jack Griffin?" Charlotte was immediately on her feet. Before Olivia could even guess what her mother intended, she'd wrapped both arms around Jack and given him one of her enthusiastic hugs.

He met Olivia's gaze over Charlotte's shoulder. She noted his surprise and amusement at such a vigorous greeting.

"I've been wanting to meet you," Charlotte said, sitting down again—one seat over—and patting the empty space beside her. "That was such a *wonderful* column you wrote about Olivia. I made sure all my friends read it."

Jack arched his brows—as though to suggest her mother might have been impressed but that hadn't been the case with Olivia.

"I was so pleased with what you had to say about my daughter. She *is* a gutsy judge and an innovative thinker, too," Charlotte continued.

Olivia was mortified, but she knew better than to say anything, so she smiled blandly and felt the heat radiate from her cheeks.

Charlotte had arranged it so Jack was now sitting between the two of them. Olivia hadn't been quick enough to realize what was happening in order to avoid it. She was interested in spending time with

Jack, but she'd prefer to do so without her mother present.

Soon, Jack and her mother were deeply engrossed in conversation. At one point Jack let out a hoot of laughter and abruptly turned to look at Olivia, still smiling.

Olivia could only wonder what was so funny; she was fairly sure it had to do with her. What could her mother have told him? No doubt it was something embarrassing from her teen years.

"Your mother's hilarious," Jack said a moment later, leaning toward her.

That was true enough. Olivia merely nodded, and Jack soon turned back to Charlotte for entertainment. Meanwhile, Olivia studied the program. *To Kill a Mockingbird* was an ambitious project for so small a troupe, but those who'd seen it had raved about the performances. She assumed Jack had come to write a review.

Olivia happened to be looking idly around the theater when Justine strolled in. She wore black pants with a cropped cashmere sweater in a soft green, her long dark hair hanging loose to the middle of her back. Her arm was entwined with Warren Saget's and she gazed up at the older man with wide, adoring eyes. Olivia immediately felt her hackles rise. She didn't like Warren, never had, and hated the fact that her daughter was dating him.

Warren had moved to Cedar Cove twenty years ago. He'd bought up large parcels of land and built row upon row of tract houses. The homes had been constructed of the cheapest possible materials and had quickly developed a host of problems. First, the roofs leaked and then the siding developed mold.

Basements flooded, walls shifted, ceilings cracked. Lawsuit followed lawsuit.

Olivia didn't recall how it was all settled—her own life was undergoing a series of traumas at the time—but somehow Warren and his company had survived.

It wasn't only his business practices that distressed Olivia. Everyone knew that Warren had cheated on his wife—correction, *wives*. He'd flaunted his affairs until both women had filed for divorce and left town. The most recent Mrs. Saget had left five or so years ago, leaving Warren free to go through young women like a kid through a candy store. It hurt Olivia to see her own daughter fall victim to such an unscrupulous man.

Warren apparently liked his women young. The younger the better. A woman like Justine—tall, classy and beautiful—enhanced his image. She looked good on his arm, and Warren knew it.

Olivia wondered whose idea it was to see the play. *To Kill a Mockingbird* wasn't the sort of entertainment she suspected a man like Warren would choose. *The Best Little Whorehouse in Texas* seemed more his kind of show.

Apparently Justine hadn't noticed Olivia. Or if she had, she'd chosen to ignore the fact that her mother and grandmother were seated in the front of the theater. Justine and Warren sat in the last row, where the shadows were darkest and they couldn't easily be seen.

This relationship had worried Olivia from the start and not solely because of Warren's age and reputation. Over the years, Olivia had observed a pattern. Justine preferred older men and there'd been several, all quite similar to each other in situation and personality. Warren had lasted the longest. Olivia cringed every time she thought of her daughter marrying the likes of Warren Saget. But at twenty-eight, Justine had revealed no desire to marry. Olivia prayed Warren wouldn't be the one to change her mind.

Her heart told Olivia that her daughter's dating habits were linked to that fateful August day in 1986. Justine refused to risk the pain that real closeness could bring. She'd been with her twin brother when he died, and the love she felt for him had turned into agony. Caught up in her own grief, Olivia had failed to recognize the devastating effect his death had had on her daughter.

Olivia suspected that, deep down, Justine blamed herself. She'd been at the lake with Jordan and a whole slew of friends, not paying any attention to her twin. He'd been diving off a floating dock, joking and splashing, all of them laughing at their own antics. It'd been a hot lazy afternoon, and the world had seemed a beautiful place. Then within a matter of seconds all their lives were changed. Their capacity for innocent, uncomplicated pleasure was gone forever. Jordan, clowning around with his buddies, dove into the lake and didn't surface. By the time his friends figured out it wasn't a joke, it'd been too late. Jordan had broken his neck and drowned.

Justine had swum out to the dock and sat with Jordan's lifeless body until the paramedics arrived, but there was no hope. The poor girl hadn't slept a full night for weeks afterward. She'd been lost and confused, believing she should've been able to do *something*.

Olivia had her own share of regrets. If she'd been more focused on Justine's grief, gotten her into counseling, spent time helping her deal with the tragedy...

But it'd been all Olivia could manage to make it from one day to the next. For the sake of her husband and her two other children, she'd tried to be strong. Each day had been filled with busywork so she wouldn't have time to think. Pretending had failed miserably. Her marriage had collapsed, and her beautiful daughter had never recovered from the tragedy.

"I've been meaning to phone you," Jack said, breaking into Olivia's thoughts.

That was encouraging news. Olivia had been brought up to believe that girls shouldn't phone boys— a bit of social conditioning she'd never shaken off. She'd dated since the divorce, but not much. Friends had attempted to matchmake, without notable success.

Jack appeared to be waiting for a response from her, some indication that she would have welcomed his call.

"I wish you had." There, she'd said it, and it was true. She liked Jack Griffin and had thoroughly enjoyed their impromptu meeting and the talk that followed.

Jack stared at her as though he wasn't sure he should believe her. He seemed about to say something when Bob Beldon stepped onto the middle of the compact stage. Bob and his wife, Peggy, ran Thyme and Tide, a local bed-and-breakfast. Bob was actively involved in the theater group.

Once he had everyone's attention, Bob made several safety announcements regarding the fire codes and pointed out the exits. When he'd finished, he introduced the play and the actors. Before he left the stage, he looked at Jack Griffin and Olivia—and then Bob did the oddest thing. He winked at Jack.

"What was that about?" Olivia asked him.

"Bob's a friend."

"You knew him before moving to Cedar Cove?"

He nodded absently as he watched the actors take their places on stage. "It was Bob's way of encouraging me," he muttered.

"To do what?" Olivia pressed.

Jack squared his shoulders. "To ask you to dinner." He glanced in her direction. "Are you game?"

Are you game? was certainly an inventive invitation.

"Did you ask her yet?" Charlotte bent forward in order to get a better look at them both.

"I just did," Jack answered.

"Ask her what?" Someone Olivia didn't recognize called out from two rows back.

Mortified, Olivia slid down in her chair and hunched her shoulders.

Jack slid down, too. "Will you?"

She nodded. Well, why not? She'd already admitted that she was anxious to hear from Jack. Now he'd taken the next step. A dinner date.

She intended to have a very good time.

Cecilia woke Saturday morning feeling more than a little depressed. She hadn't heard from Ian. She'd deluded herself, thinking he'd call. He might already be out to sea; she wasn't sure whether the *George Washington* had left port, but then how would she know? She got her information from rumor and an occasional issue of *The Chronicle*. Nor had Ian mentioned being transferred from the submarine to the aircraft carrier. Apparently there was a lot he hadn't told her.

Cecilia wished now that she'd made friends with other Navy wives. She'd tried early on, but had felt like an intruder. The women had already formed cliques and she was an outsider. Between her job and the pregnancy, she didn't have the time or emotional reserves to socialize with them. She had declined the few invitations she'd received.

When Allison was born, no one had come to the hospital and after her daughter's death, Cecilia had rejected all attempts—by the other wives, by Ian's family in Georgia, by nurses and a Navy chaplain—to help her cope with the loss. As far as she was concerned, it was too little, too late. Her father hated anything to do with death and dying and avoided her entirely. Other than giving her the sympathy card, all he'd done was pat her on the back, mumbling a clichéd condolence or two.

And Ian…wasn't there.

It did no good to brood about Ian, the pending divorce and past hurts, so Cecilia showered and changed into a clean pair of jeans and a worn, comfortable sweatshirt. As always, Saturday was reserved for errands, but today she lacked the energy for it. Once she got to the grocery, her sole purchase was a big bouquet of flowers.

The cemetery was on the outskirts of town. A dense fog had rolled in; it was impossible to see across the street, let alone to the other side of the cove and the naval shipyard. Cecilia had purposely chosen this burial site because it overlooked the naval base. Maybe that didn't make sense, but she'd wanted their daughter to be close to her father, and this was the only way Cecilia knew to make that happen.

The lawn was spongy and damp, and her feet sank into the earth as she walked toward the grave. She squatted down and brushed a few dead leaves away from the small, flat headstone. The vase was too narrow to hold all the flowers, so she sorted through and removed the prettiest ones and arranged those inside. When she'd finished, she divided the remaining flowers among the other graves in the row.

Standing, she found Ian several feet back, watching her.

Neither spoke. He wore his thick Navy coat, with his white sailor's cap. His hands were buried in his coat pockets, arms pressed against his sides.

"I saw you leave the grocery store," he murmured.

"You followed me here?" She didn't like the idea of that.

He nodded. "It isn't a habit, if that's what you're thinking. I just happened to see you and wanted to talk."

Cecilia thrust her own hands into her pockets, waiting, unsure what to say.

"I wondered if this was where you were heading," Ian continued, "and I was right." He paused, shrugging. "I thought we could talk."

She stiffened. "What's there to talk about?" The last time she'd seen him, he'd been drinking and argumentative.

Ian sighed, glancing past her, past the row of graves. "I want to apologize for showing up at the restaurant the other night."

"Andrew told me you're leaving on the *George Washington.*"

"Yeah." He didn't elaborate, or explain the transfer.

"When did you get assigned to the carrier?"

"You'd know the answer to that if you hadn't been in such a hurry to file for divorce," he said with unconcealed bitterness.

"We couldn't–can't–even talk without snarling at each other." Then and now. It hurt so badly to be standing on one side of their daughter's grave while he stood on the other.

"Does it matter?" he asked. "I'm in the Navy–that hasn't changed."

She shook her head. The reasons were unimportant; he didn't owe her an explanation. Defensiveness had become an automatic response, a means of keeping people at a distance. Especially him...

"Damn," he said impatiently. "Why is it so hard to talk to you?"

Didn't he already know? What else could she say?

"Like I said, I'm sorry about the other night. It won't happen again." He turned away, his movement abrupt.

"You're leaving soon?" she called after him, not wanting him to walk off just yet.

He turned back to face her and nodded.

"I'd like to know about the transfer."

He stared down at their daughter's grave. "I requested it. If I'd been assigned to the carrier when Allison was born, I could've been airlifted home. To be with you.... It's a moot point now, but I didn't want to risk anything like that ever again."

She hadn't known such a transfer was possible.

"I'll be away for six months," he told her.

It sounded longer than a lifetime. Her reaction must have shown on her face.

"I can't help that," he said.

"I know," she whispered.

"I suppose you're worried about your divorce."

He always referred to it like that, emphasizing whose decision it had been. "The delay doesn't matter," she said. "I don't have any money for attorney's fees, anyway."

"I thought you wanted to take it to the Dispute Resolution Center?"

"I did, but with you at sea, it'd be a waste of time, wouldn't it?" She could talk to an impartial third party, but without Ian available, they wouldn't be able to resolve anything.

"We're still legally married then—right?"

Cecilia guessed this was his way of telling her he regretted last week's suggestion about pretending they were divorced.

"Yes," she said. "You don't need to worry that I'll be dating anyone else."

He frowned.

Perhaps she'd read him wrong. "That's what you were saying, wasn't it?" She couldn't help recalling his reaction to the man in the bar.

He looked at her blankly. "No, but I'm glad to hear it. No man likes to think of his wife with someone else, regardless of the situation."

Now Cecilia was confused. "Exactly what are you saying? Do you want us to be married? Or do you just want me to remember that I'm still legally bound to you?"

"I want you to keep in mind that we're stuck together—legally *and* financially—until we can sort this mess out, all right?"

Cecilia nodded, crossing her arms. She had a feeling she wasn't going to like his reasoning.

"The last time I was away…" He paused and glanced toward Allison's gravestone. "You ran up the credit cards. While we're still married, I'm legally responsible for those bills, so I'd appreciate it if you used some discretion."

It would have hurt less if he'd punched her.

"You mean you're worried about me spending money while you're at sea?" She couldn't believe he'd say such a thing. "Every penny I spent, every single penny that went on those charge cards, was so I could bury Allison." Cecilia started to shake, first with anger, then with outrage. How dared he? How dared he! If she'd needed a reminder of why she could no longer stay in this marriage, he'd certainly given it to her.

"I didn't mean that the way it sounded," he said.

"It won't happen again," she said in a deadened voice, consciously echoing his earlier words.

Ian shook his head. "I don't even know why I mentioned that. I'm sorry."

She ignored him. Her lack of response should be answer enough.

"You do this every time," he said, sounding exasperated. "I try to talk to you, get things into the open and you clam up on me like I'm not even here."

Her arms remained buried deep in her pockets, her head down. "Every penny I charged was so I could bury our daughter," she repeated dully. "And the three-hundred-dollar phone bill… I know it upset you, but—"

Suddenly she could no longer control her voice— or her emotions.

"But that was for me!" she cried, shouting the words at him, hurling them in her anger and pain. "So there wouldn't be *two* funerals that day instead of one. I'm sorry, Ian, for being so weak, but I'm not like you. I needed my mother…I needed to talk to someone. My dad couldn't deal with it and you weren't here. My mother…" Unwilling to have him witness her tears, she whirled around and started searching frantically through her purse.

"Cecilia?"

She found what she was looking for and tore open the small plastic holder. "Here," she choked, taking out the VISA card and throwing it at him. The card landed on the wet green grass. "Take it! I don't want it…."

He hesitated before picking it up. "You might need it for emergencies."

As though the death of their daughter hadn't been one.

She shook her head vehemently. She'd rot in hell before she'd use any credit card with his name on it again. She'd get one with her own name. Her maiden name.

Ian examined the card, and ran his thumb over the raised letters that spelled out *Cecilia Randall*.

"I didn't come here to get your credit card."

"Well, you have it now," she returned flippantly, refusing to look at him.

Ian said nothing. A long moment passed. "I'm sorry, Cecilia," he finally whispered.

"What for this time?"

There was another pause. "I'm going away for six months," he murmured. "I wish we'd been able to settle this divorce business before I left, but…"

They'd been over this too many times already.

"I'd like to leave without bad feelings between us. I know you'd rather not be married to me anymore, but we can't do anything about that right now."

"And your point is?" she asked, deliberately sarcastic.

"Dammit, Cecilia, would you listen to us? Is this what you *want?* Is this how you want things to be? I don't. I followed you here because I thought…I hoped there'd be a chance for us to end this on a friendly note."

"Divorces aren't friendly."

"You're right, but does that give you any pleasure?"

It didn't. She knew why he'd come. Ian would leave for sea in a few days, and when he left he wanted to go without a huge knot in his gut over her.

"Goodbye, Ian," she said softly. "Have a good tour."

He frowned, as though he wasn't sure he should trust her. "Do you mean it?"

She nodded. "I don't want to fight, I never did. Go with a clear conscience. When you get back, we'll settle all the legal stuff."

"Thank you." His relief was evident and his eyes softened as he turned away. Cecilia watched him disappear into the fog, watched until she could no longer see his dark shape.

She closed her eyes. She pictured how their parting might have been if Allison had lived. She'd be standing on the pier with all the other Navy wives and Ian would kiss her goodbye, kiss Allison and then her again, one last time. Then he'd run toward the aircraft carrier and she'd hold the baby in her arms, raise Allison's tiny arm so she could send her daddy off with a wave. Instead, they bade each other farewell standing over their daughter's grave.

Justine had avoided her mother all weekend, and with good reason. The minute they were together, Olivia would start to criticize Warren. Not openly, but she'd insinuate things. For instance, she'd mention some piece of gossip she'd supposedly heard about one of his ex-wives. Or she'd refer to problems with one or other of the homes his company constructed.

In Justine's opinion, the fact that she was seeing Warren was none of her mother's business. Okay, he was a few years older. And she'd concede that his reputation wasn't the greatest. But there were things about Warren that her mother and most other people didn't know and never would. Warren trusted her and his confidence meant a great deal to her.

The second reason Justine had been avoiding her mother had to do with her brother James. A year earlier, without warning, he'd joined the Navy and as a result, was away from home for the first time. He missed his family, and their mother fretted about him. Now her younger brother had made another life-altering decision and had left it to Justine to announce to their family.

"Tell her for me," he'd pleaded, and because she loved him she'd foolishly agreed.

Now a confrontation was inevitable. Monday

morning, she'd half decided to call her grandmother and let Charlotte deliver the news. She went as far as picking up the phone and actually dialing the number. At the first ring, she'd replaced the receiver, berating herself as a coward.

All afternoon, she'd had difficulty concentrating on loan applications and staff meetings—she was the manager of the Cedar Cove branch of First National Bank and had plenty of responsibilities to occupy her. Justine sighed; she knew she had to tell her mother in person and as soon as possible.

After work, she drove straight from the bank to the family home at 16 Lighthouse Road. She'd lived here until she left for college ten years ago; she'd returned for short periods in the intervening years. It was *home* in a way no other place had ever been. Every time she took the curve in the road and came upon it, Justine experienced a sensation that had been impossible to reproduce anywhere she'd lived since.

She parked out front. Her mother must have been looking out the window when she drove up, because she opened the door as Justine climbed the steps to the porch.

"Sweetheart," Olivia said, holding out her arms for a hug. "This is a pleasant surprise."

Justine forced a smile.

"You're just in time for dinner."

Justine could never figure out why her mother insisted on feeding her. It was the same with her grandmother. A maternal need to nurture, she supposed. Not that she needed nurturing anymore. Well, not *that* kind. "Great," she said, without enthusiasm. Her stomach was in knots already.

Olivia took a good look at her. "Something on your mind?"

Radar. Justine swore her mother had radar.

"Why don't you make a pot of tea?" she suggested.

Her mother froze. "You're pregnant, aren't you? Dear God, don't tell me you're going to marry Warren!"

"Mother, just make the tea and no, I'm not pregnant."

"Thank God." Her relief couldn't have been more evident. Did she even realize how insulting her reaction was?

Olivia moved into the kitchen and Justine followed.

"That was rude of me, honey. Forgive me," her mother said, putting the kettle on the burner. She sighed. "You know the way I feel about Warren."

Justine didn't need to be reminded.

"But you seem to enjoy his company and that's all that matters."

Justine didn't respond to her mother's halfhearted apology. What was the point? Yes, she liked Warren, but she wasn't blind to his faults, either. The most appealing thing about him was his age. Justine liked older men. They were settled, confident and, for the most part, secure. She didn't intend on having children herself and was looking for a mature relationship. She found most men her own age childish and irresponsible.

Olivia poured the tea and carried two cups to the dining-room table. "All right," she said when they'd both sat down. "If you're not pregnant, then what's wrong?"

Justine ignored the question and doctored her tea. "I heard from James last week."

Her mother stared at her blankly. "What does James have to do with this?"

"He sounded good."

"Good?"

"Happy," she elaborated.

"Does he have a new girlfriend?"

She couldn't believe her mother hadn't made the connection. "Not…exactly."

"He's seeing the same girl as before? Selina? I can't recall her surname at the moment."

"Solis."

"Hmm. Every time James mentions her, they're fighting over one thing or another."

"They're getting along just fine at the moment," Justine said, struggling not to laugh outright. Her mother appeared to be completely dense.

"I'm glad to hear it."

"Are you, Mother?" Justine pressed.

"Of course I am." Olivia hesitated. "Are you trying to tell me that James and Selina are engaged?"

"No, I'm here to tell you they're married."

"*Married?*" Olivia came out of her chair and just as quickly sat down again. "*Married?* Without letting me know? Without a word until the deed is done?"

"James was afraid of how you'd react."

"He should be a lot more afraid of what I'm going to say now," Olivia muttered grimly. "Why would he *think* such a thing? What about Selina's family? Was it as much of a shock to them?"

"Apparently not."

"How do you mean?"

"Selina's father insisted they be married by a priest."

"James isn't Catholic."

"He's converting." Justine could see from the bewilderment in her mother's eyes that she found it difficult to take in the news. The son she'd raised Protestant had converted to Catholicism overnight.

"He must love her very much," Olivia responded thoughtfully.

"I'm sure he does."

"So in other words, my son and this young woman I've never met were married in a Catholic ceremony without telling anyone from our family?"

"Yes," Justine concurred.

"Why?"

Justine held her breath for an instant. "James wanted you and Dad there, but he was afraid you might disapprove."

"For the love of heaven, why? Because Selina's Hispanic? James knows us better than that."

Justine shrugged. She disagreed with what her brother had done, but it was too late to worry about that.

"When will I meet her?"

"Mom, there's more."

Olivia set the cup back into the saucer.

"Selina's pregnant, isn't she?"

Finally, Mom. It took you long enough. "I talked to Selina myself," Justine said cheerfully. "She sounds delightful. James is crazy about her and I'm sure she's going to make him a good wife."

Her mother didn't look nearly as certain. "How far along?"

This was the hard part. "She's due in four months."

"Four months," her mother echoed. "I'm going to be a grandmother in four months?"

"It seems that way."

Her mother didn't say anything for several moments, then her eyes glistened and Justine could tell she was struggling not to cry.

"Mom, does being a grandmother bother you so much?"

Olivia shook her head and dabbed at her eyes with the napkin. "Oh, no… I just wish my son had the courage to tell me himself."

Justine hugged her close. "He's waiting to hear from you now. Do you want me to dial the phone for you?"

Her mother nodded. "Please."

Five

Cecilia arrived for work at four, an hour earlier than she was scheduled to start. The bar at The Captain's Galley was already getting crowded. She slipped onto a padded stool, hoping for an opportunity to speak to her father.

"How you doin', kiddo?" Bobby Merrick asked from the other side of the counter. "Can I get you something to drink?"

Cecilia hated it when he treated her like a customer. "Okay, how about a cup of coffee?"

"You sure you don't want anything stronger?"

"Positive." In some respects, her father had never grown up, still dressing and acting like he had as a young man. He had shoulder-length graying hair, and his wardrobe consisted of wildly printed shirts that he wore with jeans. While that didn't bother Cecilia, there were times she wanted and needed him to be a father. This afternoon was one of those times.

He brought her a mug of stale black coffee, waited

on someone else, then drifted back to visit with her. "Heard from your mother lately?" he asked.

After her parents' divorce, Bobby—which he insisted Cecilia call him—had left New Jersey and moved first to New Mexico, then Arizona and had gradually drifted north to Washington State.

"She phoned this weekend."

"She's well?" To the best of her knowledge, her parents hadn't spoken to or seen each other in years, until last May, when her mother flew out for Cecilia's wedding. Now all of a sudden Bobby was asking about her.

"Mom's doing fine."

"I'm glad to hear it," he said, leaning against the bar. "She's one hell of a woman."

That being the case, Cecilia wondered why he'd abandoned them both, but she didn't want to bring up any unpleasantness. She understood her father. He couldn't tolerate conflict of any kind. He wanted people to love each other and get along, as he'd frequently explained to Cecilia. He couldn't function if anyone was upset with him; he even disliked being around other people's arguments. When a situation became too intense for him, he simply moved on.

He'd asked about her mother, but he hadn't sought her out, hadn't called or written her in years. That made sense. He didn't want to hear about difficulties or disappointments—especially if he'd caused them. When Allison Marie died, he'd stayed away, emotionally and physically. He was incapable of giving Cecilia the support she'd needed so badly; he didn't have it in him. It'd taken her time to reach this conclusion. She could be angry with him, perhaps should have been, but it wouldn't have done any good.

Bobby was Bobby, and she either had to accept him or do without a father, lame as he was in that role.

"I was out at Olympic College this afternoon."

"You were?"

"Yeah, I signed up for an algebra class and for English." It was the 101-level, basic stuff, but she had to start somewhere. For the first time in a very long while, she was looking toward the future instead of dwelling on the past.

"Algebra?"

"I was always good with numbers." Math was something she enjoyed and she'd done well at it in high school. She liked the sense of order mathematics offered her. Everything fell neatly into place, and problems all had solutions. Perhaps that was what appealed to her most.

"How are you going to use algebra?"

Cecilia didn't know that yet, but this was more a refresher course than anything that would lead to a career. "It's important that I know how to solve for x," she said, just for fun. "That's how I can unlock the secrets of the universe. Like Einstein, you know. It all starts with x."

Bobby's eyes widened. "Really?"

It was a joke, and he'd taken her seriously. "Sure. Well, sort of." Clearly he wouldn't have been any help with high-school math if he'd been around. "What do you think about me taking these classes?" she asked, seeking his encouragement.

His returning look was blank. "Hey, that's cool."

Cool?

She'd done it again. Once more she'd set herself up for disappointment. She should've known Bobby's response would be inadequate at best.

He waited on a customer, and Cecilia slipped off the stool, ready to start her shift at the restaurant.

"We'll talk later," Bobby called after her.

She nodded. This was about as deep as any conversation went with him. The man just didn't get it, and nothing she said or did was going to change that.

Before long, the restaurant started to fill up. Escorting customers to their tables, answering the phone and manning the cash register kept her busy. She preferred it that way. It was when she had time on her hands that her thoughts automatically drifted to Ian. The *George Washington* had pulled out of Cedar Cove two days earlier. She'd watched it on the evening news, which had shown the massive aircraft carrier gliding through the protected waters of the cove.

Cecilia had sat intently in front of the television. She couldn't have stayed away even if she'd wanted to. Ian was gone. Deployed for six months. She wondered if he'd write. She could go to the library and e-mail him herself, but she wasn't convinced she should. And yet, that was exactly what she longed to do.

Dammit, everything was so complicated! She didn't understand her own feelings, and certainly not his. All these contradictory emotions—anger and yearning and regret. Well, she had six months to think about the divorce and how she should proceed. Ian had time to think, too. His leaving was good for them both, she told herself. Still, she had to admit she hated the idea of not seeing or talking to him for half a year.

Ever since the news broadcast, Cecilia had thought about what she should've said the day they met at the cemetery. She was sorry she'd been so quick to take offense and realized Ian hadn't been trying to upset her when he asked about the credit card. He'd been clumsy. It occurred to her later that he was no more skilled at expressing his real feelings than she was. She wished she'd hugged him before they parted. It would have felt good to have his arms around her again.

Cecilia was getting ready to leave for the night when her father came looking for her.

"Did you hear about Ian?" he asked.

"Hear what?"

"He might be back."

"Ian?"

"You said he was on the *George Washington,* didn't you?"

Cecilia frowned in confusion. "You mean the carrier's returning to Bremerton?"

"That's the way it sounds. I heard two sailors talking, and they said there's something wrong with the navigational gear."

Cecilia knew she shouldn't be pleased, shouldn't listen to gossip, either. She'd heard rumors such as this before, and they hadn't been true.

"You can ask them yourself," Bobby said with a shrug.

"I think I will." She entered the bar, which by this time was thick with cigarette smoke. Two sailors sat at the counter, nursing mugs of beer.

Cecilia walked over to them. Both men turned to her, smiling in welcome.

"Bobby here just told me you have some information about the *George Washington,*" she said.

The heavier of the two nodded. "Join us?"

"No, thanks, I'm on my way home. Can you tell me what you know?"

The two shared a look of disappointment. "I got a buddy on the *George Washington*," the first one said, "and he e-mailed me that they're having some technical problems."

"Then it's coming back?" Eagerness crept into her voice.

"Maybe. He thinks so, but—"

"For how long?"

"He isn't sure it's returning to port. Won't know for a day or two. Why do you ask?"

"My husband's on board," she said quickly.

Both men looked at her left hand, where she continued to wear the plain gold ring.

"You'll probably hear from him soon," the first sailor said.

"But don't get your hopes up," the second added.

Even though Cecilia knew he was right, she couldn't help feeling hopeful. Ian might be back—but only God and the Navy knew for how long.

The phone rang just as Olivia was putting the finishing touches on her makeup for her dinner date with Jack Griffin. She glanced at her watch; she still had fifteen minutes before he was due to pick her up.

"Hello," she said cheerfully, half expecting it to be her mother. Charlotte had fallen completely under Jack's spell and had been singing his praises ever since they'd met last Friday night.

"It's Stan."

Her ex-husband always did have a no-nonsense way about him. He got directly to the point. "You've heard from James?"

Olivia had spoken to her son and his wife the afternoon Justine had delivered their news. It had been an emotional conversation, filled with congratulations and with tears, on her part and Selina's. She'd called again after her head had cleared, asking all the questions she'd forgotten the first time. "I spoke to him twice last week," she responded.

"Then you know."

"That he's married and about to be a father? Yes."

"What's all this about James converting to Catholicism?"

"You'll have to ask him yourself." She paused, wondering why he'd brought up that particular aspect of their son's news. "You're not upset about it, are you?" Olivia would be astonished if he was. Stan had never been too concerned with religion; he didn't object when she attended worship services or brought the children, but it wasn't something that interested him. Sunday mornings were for golf games, in his view.

"I couldn't care less," he said. "I'm just surprised."

"That's what I thought," she murmured. "He sounds happy, don't you think? When did you speak to him?"

Stan hesitated. "Just a few minutes ago. He seemed to be in a rush so I figured I'd get the story from you."

Her ex-husband apparently believed she knew more than she did. "I'm not sure what to tell you. Our son is married and we're both about to become grandparents for the first time."

Stan chuckled, sounding slightly chagrined. "I was beginning to doubt that was ever going to happen."

The tension left her and she smiled. The circumstances weren't what she would have preferred, but she was absolutely delighted at the prospect of a grandchild.

"I suppose you're going to spoil that baby rotten."

"I certainly plan to," she said. But Stan was the indulgent one, and they both knew it.

"I wish James had been a bit more forthcoming with the details," he muttered.

Olivia concurred. "I've decided to fly down once the baby's born and meet Selina and her family and welcome her to ours."

"Good idea. I cut a five-hundred-dollar check as a wedding gift."

Stan had always been excessively generous and she said so. "I sent flowers," she added ruefully. "I'll bring a real wedding gift when I visit."

"He's the first one of the kids to marry—and he's expecting a baby. It was the least I could do."

The doorbell chimed and Olivia was surprised to realize they'd been talking for fifteen minutes. "That's my dinner date," she said.

"You're dating?" There was no jealousy in the question, just curiosity.

Olivia laughed softly. "Don't sound so shocked."

"I'm not. Who's the lucky fellow?"

"Jack Griffin. He's new in town."

"Don't keep him waiting, then."

"Goodbye, Stan. It was good to talk to you."

"You, too, Olivia, and listen…"

"Yes?" she said, eager to get off the phone.

"Have a good time. You deserve a decent man in your life."

"Thank you," she whispered, and replaced the receiver. She glanced down at the phone, overwhelmed by an unexpected rush of regret. They'd had a good marriage once…. The divorce had been final years ago, but she'd never stopped loving Stan. They'd had their problems—every marriage did—only she'd believed that the bond between them was strong enough to survive a crisis. Unfortunately she'd been wrong. Still, she'd always feel connected to him; they shared children and a history, and nothing could change that.

She hurried to answer the door. Jack stood there, looking the same way he did every time she saw him. He wore a raincoat, black slacks and a blue shirt with the top two buttons left unfastened. She was beginning to wonder if he owned more than one set of clothes.

"Ah," he said, his eyes sweeping over her. "You look fabulous. Wow."

Assuming something formal, Olivia had gone to a lot of trouble. The navy-blue wool dress was new; the straight skirt was a flattering mid-calf length, and the bodice, decorated with a row of gold buttons, was formfitting. She purposely wore heels and dark hosiery, contrasting the outfit with the pearls her father had bought in Japan fifty years ago.

"Am I overdressed?" She asked the obvious. They hadn't discussed where they'd be dining.

"No," he said. "I'm underdressed."

"Don't be ridiculous. Where are we going for dinner?" She should have asked much sooner.

Looking embarassed, he told her, "I was thinking about the Taco Shack."

The restaurant, on the highway outside town, was a roadhouse of sorts, where patrons ordered at the counter and served themselves. The food was some of the best in the area; it was also fast and cheap. The salsa was freshly made every day and known all over the county.

"I'll change," Olivia offered quickly, and left the room before Jack could protest. So much for a hot date. She'd been thinking they'd linger over wine and candlelight, and he'd envisioned tacos and margaritas. Fortunately she was a flexible person.

When she returned, Olivia had changed into blue-green plaid wool slacks and a matching green turtleneck sweater. "That's better," she said, hoping to put him at ease.

"You don't mind?"

"I love the Taco Shack," she assured him, and it was the truth. She should've known better than to expect fine French dining. Jack was a taco kind of guy.

He looked vastly relieved as he led the way to his vehicle. She could tell he'd made an effort to clean off the front seat of his car; he'd tossed everything in the back, which was littered with wadded-up bags from fast-food establishments, old newspapers, books and a variety of other junk she didn't get a chance to see.

Jack seemed oblivious to it all. By nature, Olivia was neat and orderly. One look at his Ford Taurus told her Jack Griffin was her exact opposite.

Olivia had to fumble with her seat belt before she managed to secure it. It was obvious he didn't often have anyone riding with him.

"Have you ever had the stir-fried jalapeños at the Shack?" he asked as they headed out of town.

"You can stir-fry them?" Olivia asked, thinking that sounded more like Chinese cooking than Mexican.

"Sure. Just until the skins start to blister. Then they squeeze lime juice over top, sprinkle on seasoned salt— and serve them with plenty of water."

"You eat whole jalapeños?"

"You don't?"

Olivia enjoyed a bit of spice now and then, but she wasn't interested in experiencing pain as part of her meal. "Food isn't supposed to *hurt*."

Jack laughed. "You have a sense of humor. I knew there was a reason I liked you."

Olivia liked him, too.

He pulled into the gravel parking lot outside the Taco Shack and hurried around to help her out. Not until he slammed the car door did she notice that it was dented and didn't close properly.

Ever the gentleman, he held the door to the roadhouse for her. They walked up to the counter, and stood in line; the place was deservedly popular. Olivia studied the menu, hand-printed on a large board suspended from the ceiling. She ordered the combination plate, which included a cheese enchilada and a bean burrito, and iced tea. Jack ordered something she'd never heard of, plus a side of the stir-fried jalapeños. That suggested he wasn't planning to kiss her—definitely a disappointment.

She found them a seat by the window, vacated by another couple barely a minute before. When she climbed over the bench of the red-painted picnic table, Olivia was grateful she'd changed out of her dress. She hadn't been here in ages and had forgotten just how rustic it was. The window was decorated with what resembled red Christmas lights, but on closer examination, she saw they were shiny plastic peppers. She found that an amusing detail.

Jack brought napkins and plastic forks to the table and a large container of fresh salsa. When their order was ready, he collected both plates, then went back for their drinks. The food smelled delicious and she closed her eyes and breathed in the scent of Jack's peppers and the mixture of salsa and coriander.

They talked comfortably about a variety of topics: town politics, the paper, the play they'd both seen. She felt as though she'd known him for years. She wouldn't have said he was her type, but she was beginning to believe she didn't have one. Stan was an engineer, and like her, a highly organized person.

"Did I mention my son recently got married?" she said casually.

"No." Jack grinned widely. "That's great!"

"He's about to make me a grandmother."

He gave her an engaging grin. "You're the most beautiful grandmother I've ever seen."

Her ego thanked him. "Both the marriage and the pregnancy came as a surprise, but I don't mind." Well, she did...a little. "James sounded happy and although I haven't met his wife, she seems very nice." Olivia had her fears, but she wouldn't second-guess her son and his decisions. This was his life, not hers.

"Stan and I were on the phone, discussing the prospect of becoming grandparents when you arrived. That's why it took me so long to answer the door."

"You must have a good relationship with your ex."

"I wish we'd gotten along this well while we were married," she joked. "Now his second wife's getting the benefit of all my training."

"Stan's remarried?"

Olivia nodded.

Jack studied his dinner for a moment, then said,

"Because of the treatments Eric underwent for the cancer, he'll never father children."

Which meant there was no possibility of Jack's ever being a grandfather, Olivia realized. "I'm sorry."

"No need to be." It seemed he wanted to change the subject. "Do you speak to Stan often?" he asked.

"Only in matters having to do with the children," she told him. "They're both adults now, so there isn't much reason for phone calls and so forth. I suppose we'll be in touch a little more often once James's baby is born. What about you and your ex?"

Jack tore his paper napkin in half, then looked horrified by what he'd done. "I haven't spoken to Vicki in years. Unfortunately, our divorce was bitter."

"I'm sorry," she said again because she could see that talking about his ex-wife distressed him.

"What's the matter with couples these days?" he asked. "Doesn't anyone stay together anymore?"

"The Beldons have been married since shortly after high school," Olivia said, leading into the subject of how he knew Bob.

"Ah yes, Bob and Peggy."

"I went to high school with both of them," Olivia explained.

"They were boyfriend and girlfriend back then?" Jack asked.

"From tenth grade on." Those two had been together practically as long as she could remember.

"Bob was in Vietnam," Jack said.

"Is that how you know him?" Olivia asked.

Jack shook his head. "I met him later. About ten years ago."

Olivia waited, wondering if he'd tell her how they'd come to meet. He didn't.

"Bob's the one who suggested I apply for the job here in Cedar Cove. I was looking for a slower pace and decided to take him up on his offer to visit the bed-and-breakfast. I immediately fell in love with the area."

"And so you uprooted your whole life."

She met his gaze and they shared a smile.

"I'm glad I did," he said, offering her a jalapeño.

She shook her head vigorously. "I'm glad you made the move, too."

Very glad!

In the wee hours of Sunday morning, Cecilia poured herself a soothing glass of milk and sat at the small table in her tiny kitchen. She rested her bare legs on the second chair and leaned back, closing her eyes.

After a night on her feet, her toes throbbed. It'd been much worse when she was pregnant. She remembered how badly her ankles had swollen nearly every night. From the first, the pregnancy had been hard on her. She hoped subsequent pregnancies wouldn't be as difficult, then realized there wouldn't be any more. Never again did she plan to risk that kind of emotional pain.

She sipped the milk, hoping it would help her sleep. The *George Washington* had pulled back into the naval shipyard earlier in the day, just as predicted, leaving Cecilia to wonder if she'd hear from Ian.

Probably not. She was mentally reviewing the reasons they should stay away from each other when the phone rang.

Startled by the unexpectedness of it, Cecilia grabbed the receiver.

"Hello."

Silence.

Great, a prank call. If she could afford caller ID, she would've phoned right back and given the pervert a piece of her mind.

"Hi."

Ian.

She was too breathless to respond.

"I tried calling you earlier, but you weren't home," he said.

"I was at work."

"I know. I thought of stopping by The Captain's Galley, but I promised you I wouldn't."

She supposed he was letting her know he'd kept his word. "I just got home a little while ago."

"That's what I figured. I didn't wake you or anything, did I?"

"No."

"How are you?" he asked.

Cecilia could hear background traffic and supposed he was calling from a pay phone. "I'm okay." Nothing had changed in the week since she'd seen him.

"You heard the *George Washington* had to turn back, didn't you?"

"Yeah." She didn't mention that news had drifted into town on Wednesday—four days ago.

"I don't know how long we're going to be in port, but probably not long." He paused, then added, "I'd like to see you. Would you be willing to meet?"

Cecilia squeezed her eyes shut. She wasn't thinking clearly enough to answer him. Her heart leapt at the offer, but her head told her it would be a big mistake.

"I was at the college this week," she told him, avoiding his question for the moment.

"Olympic College?"

"I signed up for two classes."

"Cecilia, that's great!" At least Ian was willing to encourage her, even if her father wasn't. "What else is new?"

"I've been working in the bar on weekends, to help pay off the credit card bills." And all the attorney-related expenses, too. "I got paid on Friday and since I'm current with everything, I thought I'd put the extra money in the bank."

"Good idea."

"That's what I thought, until I went window shopping." It'd been almost a year since she'd gotten anything new—a few maternity outfits she'd recently given to charity. Last week, the temptation to spend her extra cash had been overwhelming. The spring clothes looked so appealing. There were new books she wanted. Cosmetics. A gorgeous pair of shoes. She sighed. "Everything started calling my name."

"So you decided if you were going to spend it, you'd make sure it was on something productive."

Ian did know her. "Yes."

"Good for you. When are your classes?"

"Early mornings, three days a week." She was lucky to get in, since school had already started. The early classes meant she wasn't going to have a lot of time for sleeping in. That was all right, though. The months after she'd buried Allison, all she'd done was sleep. She'd welcomed the oblivion it offered, the release from pain.

"Are you driving to school?"

Cecilia laughed. "Of course I am."

"You don't have the most reliable car."

Her 1993 Ford Tempo had almost a hundred-and-fifty-thousand miles on it. "I'll be fine," she said, knowing she sounded defensive. "If I run into problems, I can always take the bus." It wouldn't be a short trip nor would it be convenient, but it was manageable.

Ian paused, as if silently debating with himself. "You didn't answer my question."

"You want to see me?"

"Yes."

"Why?"

"Do I need a reason? You're my wife."

"We're separated."

"Don't remind me," he muttered.

Cecilia's hand tightened around the receiver. "We didn't speak for months. Remember? Why is it so important that we see each other now?"

"I have something I want to ask you," he said.

"Ask me now."

"No." He was adamant about that. "I'd rather do it in person."

"When?" She knew all these questions of hers were nothing more than a delaying tactic.

"Soon. Listen, Cecilia, I don't know how long I'll have before I'm deployed. I've got a proposition for you." When she didn't reply, he said, "Okay, okay, you're right, we *are* separated, but you're the one who wanted that."

By the time he'd moved out of the apartment, Ian

had been in full agreement. Now he'd decided to heap all the blame for the separation on *her* shoulders.

"Fine, you don't want to see me," he said shortly.

Cecilia sighed. "It isn't that." The truth of it was she *did* want to see him. More than anything.

"Then set the day and time."

Cecilia closed her eyes and pressed her fingertips to her brow as she tried to think.

"Do you want my attorney to contact your attorney?" he asked.

"No!" she flared, angry he'd even suggest such a thing.

"Then tell me when I should come over."

"You want to come here?" That put a whole new slant on the invitation.

"Fine, we can go somewhere else," he said. "Anytime, anyplace. You just tell me. I'm not asking again, Cecilia." His voice held an edge that hadn't been there earlier.

"All right," she whispered. "How about next week? Someplace in Bremerton? You choose."

His relief was palpable, even over the phone. "That wasn't so hard, was it?"

But it was, damn hard, and Ian knew it.

"When are you free to meet?" she asked, barely able to get the words out.

"I'll let you know. All right? It depends on what's happening with the *George Washington,* but it'll be soon."

This wasn't exactly *anytime* or *anyplace,* but then he was in the Navy, and the military ruled his life—and consequently hers.

Six

Thursday afternoon was the monthly potluck at the Jackson Senior Center, named after longtime Washington State senator Henry M. Jackson. Charlotte looked forward to these get-togethers with her dearest friends. It was a time to visit, catch up on each other's lives, share a fabulous lunch and listen to a speaker. Generally it was someone from the community. A local politician had spoken in January—a real windbag, as far as Charlotte was concerned. In December, the police chief had discussed safety tips for seniors, and his talk was one of the best received in months. He'd been both interesting and informative.

It just so happened that the speaker for the first week in February was Jack Griffin. Charlotte wouldn't have missed it for the world. She arrived early, secured a table for her knitting friends and made sure the spot next to her was saved for Jack.

"Yoo-hoo, Laura," Charlotte called, waving her hand so her friend could see where she was sitting. The ladies in the knitting group always ate together at these functions. As the unofficial head of the group, Charlotte was expected to arrive early and claim the table—not that she minded.

Laura nodded in her direction and carried her dish of deviled eggs to the buffet table. Her friend made the most incredible deviled eggs. She didn't fill them with the standard yolk-and-mayonnaise mixture. Instead, Laura stuffed hard-boiled egg whites with a crabmeat-and-shrimp salad. Every month, her platter was among the first to empty.

Charlotte had brought the broccoli lasagna recipe she'd picked up at Lloyd Iverson's wake. She'd experimented with it and added her own personal touch— mushrooms to the crumbled bacon, and cheddar cheese as well as mozzarella. She hadn't been sure what to bring, seeing that she'd collected several excellent recipes lately. That was what happened when she attended three funerals in as many weeks. The dessert recipe she'd gotten last Monday, made with lemon pudding and cream cheese, was worth sitting through the two-hour wake, even if she hadn't been all that fond of Kathleen O'Hara's husband.

Laura joined her, and Evelyn and Helen followed. As soon as they were seated, they reached for their dessert plates, headed for the buffet table and took their pick. Everyone did. Charlotte disapproved of the practice, but choosing your dessert early was the only way to guarantee you'd get one.

"There's Jack now," Charlotte said, hurrying down the narrow aisle between the tables.

"Jack!" she called out. It was important after all the bragging she'd done that her friends know the newspaperman considered her his personal friend. She made a show of hugging him and was gratified when he returned the gesture.

Mary Berger, president of the Senior Center, joined them and held out her hand. "I'm so pleased you could be with us today, Mr. Griffin," she said formally, frowning at Charlotte.

"The pleasure's all mine." His gaze met Charlotte's over the top of Mary's head and he winked.

Charlotte couldn't help it; she blushed. Oh, that young man could melt a heart or two. Her own included. Now if only Olivia would wake up and realize what a catch he was. She did hope this was the man for her daughter. Charlotte had liked Jack the instant they met, and it wasn't often she felt such complete rapport with a man. It seemed to be happening more and more these days. First Tom Harding and then Jack Griffin, both newcomers to the community.

"I saved you a place at my table," Charlotte told Jack, eager for her friends to meet him.

"I've arranged a seat for Jack at the head table," Mary countered, glaring at Charlotte.

"But Jack and I are *friends,*" Charlotte said, certain that he'd prefer her company to the stuffed shirts who ran the Senior Center.

"Why don't we leave it up to Jack?" Mary offered and stepped back, crossing her arms. Her expression was confident, as if to suggest there was no contest.

Jack was smiling. "Well, it's been a long time since I've had two lovely women fighting over me."

Mary cast Charlotte a saccharine-sweet smile, and it was all Charlotte could do not to throw up.

"Why don't I sit with Charlotte and her friends for

the buffet," Jack suggested, "and join Mary and her friends for dessert?"

"An excellent suggestion," Charlotte said, firmly taking his arm. Without giving anyone an opportunity to sidetrack him, she led Jack to the table where her friends were waiting.

Evelyn and Helen were dying to talk to Jack, Charlotte knew. They both had article ideas they wanted to discuss with him. Her friends felt that the community had long ignored the contribution of its senior citizens. With Jack as editor, Charlotte believed this was about to change.

Just as she knew he would, Jack won over her friends with little more than a smile. Since she'd talked his ear off the night of the community play, Charlotte was willing to share him now. The ladies gathered around him like deer at a salt lick, each one spouting her opinion of the local newspaper.

Evelyn and Helen spoke nonstop, outlining their ideas and making suggestions.

"Ladies, you're right."

Charlotte's friends beamed at the praise.

"What *The Cedar Cove Chronicle* needs is a page specifically for seniors. Interviews, health news…"

"Recipes," Charlotte inserted.

Jack pointed his index finger in her direction. "Recipes," he agreed.

"I sometimes feel the young people don't understand or appreciate the history of this town," Laura added. "Did you know Cedar Cove has had three different names in the last hundred years?"

"Three?" Charlotte only knew of two.

"I'm more interested in why the name changed,"

Jack said. "Laura, you seem to know. Write me an article for the next edition and I'll print it."

"But will people read it?" Laura asked, sounding doubtful.

"They'll read it," Jack said. "I'll make sure of that."

Charlotte chuckled, guessing at his strategy. Jack would come up with a misleading headline guaranteed to generate interest.

"I like your ideas," he told the women. "Now, which one of you is willing to head up the senior page?"

Laura, Evelyn, Helen and Bess, who was the quietest member of the knitting group, all looked to Charlotte.

"Everyone knows if you want to get something done, you should ask Charlotte," Bess said, blushing profusely. "She's got more energy than the rest of us combined."

Jack grinned as if to say he'd find it a distinct pleasure to work with her. "All right," Charlotte muttered, thinking she needed her head examined for taking on another project. "I'll do it, but I've got to have help."

"We'll all help," Laura promised.

"Bring your ideas to me," Jack said, "and we'll work on them together."

Those few words were all the incentive Charlotte required. She wanted to encourage Jack's relationship with her daughter and she could think of no better opportunity to provide him with information about Olivia. Her daughter needed a little assistance. This wasn't so different from the way things had been when Olivia was a shy teenager and Charlotte had spoken to Betty Nelson about having her son ask

Olivia to the Junior Prom. Olivia never knew that the date had been arranged between the two mothers, and what her daughter didn't know hadn't hurt her.

Delighted with this turn of events, Charlotte enjoyed her lunch. All too soon, Jack had to move to the head table. The second he was out of earshot, Charlotte leaned toward her friends. "Isn't he a sweetheart?"

Everyone agreed. The knitting group loved him. It hadn't gone unnoticed that he'd chosen to eat at their table, either. Charlotte's stock had gone up considerably.

"He's dating my daughter, you know," she announced. It was difficult not to gloat.

"Jack's dating Olivia?" Laura's eyes widened.

"Yes, and as far as I'm concerned, they're perfect together." Charlotte had high hopes for this relationship. Very high hopes, indeed.

"He's a good man," Bess whispered. "But a bit rough around the edges, don't you think?"

"How do you mean?" Charlotte instantly took Jack's side. He might not be the smoothest dresser in town, but he was honest, open-minded and he valued their opinions. This was the first time anyone from the newspaper had taken their suggestions seriously.

"I don't know." Bess shrugged, and reached for her knitting. "Don't misunderstand me, I like Mr. Griffin, but I believe there's more to him than meets the eye."

"Do you want me to check him out on the Internet?" Evelyn asked, lowering her voice to a husky whisper.

"That's ridiculous," Charlotte muttered. The former schoolteacher had taken a computer class, and ever since, she'd been downright obnoxious, forever expounding on what she could find out about a person's background. Evelyn fancied herself a private investigator, Charlotte thought sourly.

Before anything more could be said, Mary Berger introduced Jack, and he stepped to the podium, looking completely at ease.

Charlotte found Jack's talk fascinating. He started by recounting his first visit to Cedar Cove and his impressions of the town. Bob Beldon had mentioned that *The Cedar Cove Chronicle* was planning to hire a new editor. It was Jack's luck to arrive the weekend of the Annual Seagull Calling Contest, he said, and his retelling of the day had the entire room in hysterics.

His talk was one of the most entertaining they'd ever had. Those thirty minutes passed quickly.

The seniors gave him a standing ovation.

"Did you notice," Bess said, whispering in Charlotte's ear when they stood to applaud him, "he didn't tell us a single detail about his own background?"

"Yes, he did," Charlotte argued, then realized her friend was right. Well, she didn't care. Where he'd lived and worked before moving to Cedar Cove wasn't important. She'd always been a good judge of character, and her instincts told her she could trust Jack Griffin. Besides, Olivia had said Jack was from the Spokane area.

Later, however, Charlotte decided she was curious. Bess and Laura were right; one could never be too careful. Besides, her daughter was involved now, and that meant she had an obligation to dig up whatever she could.

On the pretext of finding out more about the Seniors' Page in *The Cedar Cove Chronicle,* Charlotte stopped at *The Chronicle* headquarters next to the Laundromat on Seaview Drive. She hadn't been inside the newspaper office in years.

The building was new, and it saddened her to see a neat row of desks with computer screens. She longed for the days when the scent of ink hung in the air and reporters yelled into phones and kept bottles of booze in their bottom drawers. Like in those 1940s movies. Or maybe she was thinking of Lou Grant. They didn't make newsmen like that anymore. Jack Griffin, however, passed muster.

Jack came out of his office to greet her personally. "Did you enjoy the talk yesterday?"

"Very much," she assured him. "But I was disappointed not to learn more about you."

"Me?" He laughed lightly. "What's interesting about me?"

"Your newspaper history," she elaborated.

He rattled off a number of newspapers he'd worked for over the years. The towns and positions sounded impressive. When he'd finished, he waited as if he expected her to respond.

"Well," Charlotte said, and sighed. "That does sound grand."

"And boring. Which is why I gave a talk I hoped would be more entertaining. I'm sorry to hear you were disappointed."

"Oh, not me," she was quick to tell him. It was her suspicious friends—who didn't know Jack the way she did.

Ian asked Cecilia to meet him at the Thai restaurant in Bremerton, where he'd taken her on their first official date. He'd chosen this place on purpose and hoped his wife would remember that night with the same fondness he did.

Cecilia had agreed, although dining out on a Thursday night meant she had to find someone to cover for her at The Captain's Galley. He was sorry about that, but he didn't have any choice; he'd had three straight days of duty. The *George Washington* probably wouldn't be in dock much longer and this might well be his only opportunity to spend time with her.

He was at the table waiting when Cecilia arrived. He watched her come toward him and was struck anew by her loveliness. She looked better—healthier— than she had in months. After Allison's death, she'd lost weight. More than she could afford to lose, but it wasn't just that; it seemed as though his wife had given up caring about herself. She hadn't bothered with her hair, or her makeup or any of the other things she used to do when they were first married. Their sex life had gone to hell, along with everything else. He'd tried to help her, but everything he suggested had backfired. He'd asked his mother to call, to talk to her, but Cecilia had taken offense at that. Perhaps if they'd met face-to-face... But his home was in Georgia. His mother had offered to fly to Washington—an offer Cecilia had rejected. Ian had tried to arrange an appointment with a Navy psychologist; she'd refused to go. He'd had conversations with her mother but Cecilia had accused him of interfering. He didn't want to seem critical of Sandra Merrick, but he sensed that her sympathy wasn't entirely a positive thing. As far as he could tell, Sandra wasn't encouraging her to recover, to move on. And because Cecilia didn't know his family, she'd been uninterested in their attempts to help. His own efforts to reach her emotionally had failed. He'd been in pain, too, dammit! Cecilia was angry with him and irrational though her anger was, he understood. But he *couldn't* have been with her when Allison died. It was that simple.

"You're frowning," she said as she stepped up to the table.

She was probably right. He couldn't think about the events of last year and not feel depressed.

He stood and pulled out her chair. Ian remembered how she'd told him, after their first date, that those small old-fashioned courtesies impressed her. He had his father to thank for that. Denny Randall had been a stickler for etiquette and taught all four of his sons well.

"I'm glad you came."

Cecilia smiled as she reached for her linen napkin and set it on her lap before reading the menu. They always ordered the same dish, the Phad Thai, but it didn't hurt to look.

Ian suspected she was already regretting that she'd agreed to see him. He hoped that once he explained why he'd asked her here, she'd change her mind. It was hard to remember he wasn't supposed to love her anymore, because he did. He'd never stopped.

The waitress arrived and they ordered. Ian was mildly surprised when she asked for something different. He didn't hear the name. Perhaps this was her way of letting him know she was willing to try new things, to change. He wasn't sure if he was simply

looking for signs, reading her behaviour too closely—
and if it *was* a sign, was it a good one?

As soon as the waitress left, Ian decided to launch
into his proposition.

"I'm really glad you signed up for those college
classes," he said. "How's it going?"

"Good. Although I feel like I'm a thousand years
older than everyone else."

Actually Cecilia had left high school only four
years ago. He was two years older than she was.

"Your car's not giving you problems, is it?"

"No." She sounded almost defiant.

"That's good." He wanted her to know how
strongly he approved of her going back to school.
They'd had a number of arguments over her working at the restaurant; Cecilia thought it was because
he was jealous of her being around other men. Maybe
that was a small part of his reaction, but there was
more. He felt Cecilia was wasting her abilities, her potential. She was smart, a whole lot smarter than she
gave herself credit for.

She glanced at him, and Ian had to resist an impulse to reach across the table and put his hand over
hers. Sometimes he ached just wanting to touch her.
It'd been months since he'd held her in his arms or
kissed her. After Allison, it seemed that whatever
she'd felt for him physically had died, too.

"My car's only two years old," he said.

She didn't respond, as if she thought he was bragging or something.

"I know you're wondering why I asked to meet
you, and it has to do with my car." He had her attention, he noticed; that was a start. "I want you to drive

it while I'm away." He could see from her reaction that she was going to argue with him. "It's more dependable, especially in the mornings," he added quickly, hoping she'd see the wisdom of accepting his offer.

Cecilia shook her head. "I appreciate it, but—"

"Actually you'd be doing me a favor." Ian could tell she didn't believe him. "I mean it."

"But…"

"It's not good to have an engine sit idle for six months," he said in authoritative tones. "A lot of guys lend out their cars while they're deployed for that very reason." Ian didn't know if this was true or not, but it made sense.

"I…I don't know."

Their meals arrived, and Ian studied Cecilia's dish. Chicken breast on cooked spinach, he thought, with peanut sauce ladled over top. He hadn't known she liked spinach. That was a pretty minor thing but it made him realize there was still a great deal they didn't know about each other.

"What do you think?" he asked. "About the car…"

"We're getting a divorce, Ian."

He didn't welcome the reminder. "That doesn't have anything to do with it."

"But…"

"The choice is yours, but like I said, I'll be lending it out and if you want to use it, fine. If not, I'll leave it with a friend." He probably wouldn't, but he wanted her to think so.

"You don't have to do this."

"I'd worry about you less." That wasn't the smartest thing to admit. However, it was the truth. If she was driving twenty-plus miles every morning in the heavy shipyard traffic, he'd prefer to know she was in a more reliable vehicle than the dilapidated car she currently drove.

She smiled then, and it was as if everything in the world had righted itself. "This is really thoughtful of you."

Damn, it was hard not to touch her. He shrugged off her words. "It's more for me and my car than anything."

Her smile dimmed.

"And like I said, you'd be doing me a favor."

They ate their dinner and lingered over tea. After an hour and a half, the restaurant was getting full, and their waitress was sending some obvious signals their way. But Ian didn't want the evening to end.

"How about a movie?" he suggested, hoping she'd agree but afraid she wouldn't.

To his surprise, she smiled and nodded.

Ian felt a surge of happiness...and optimism. He didn't care what they saw, as long as he could sit at her side and pretend the last eight months had never happened.

He let Cecilia choose the movie, and while he bought the tickets, she picked up a bag of buttered popcorn. They sat in the back row of the theater. Because it was a Thursday night, the place was practically deserted. Only one other couple showed up before the previews, and they sat near the front.

Ian placed his arm along the back of Cecilia's seat.

"We went to dinner at the Thai restaurant and then a movie on our first date, too," she said casually.

As though Ian had forgotten. "Did we?"

"Yes." Cecilia scooped up a handful of popcorn.

"Did I kiss you?"

She looked at him and blinked hard. "You mean you don't remember?"

He squeezed her shoulder. "I remember everything about that date," he whispered. And every subsequent one. For the first month after they'd met, she was all he thought about. It was no thanks to him the Navy had survived, since his mind certainly wasn't on his job.

In addition to etiquette, his father had taught Ian about birth control. But every lesson he'd ever learned had vanished the first time they'd made love. He wasn't usually irresponsible, but he'd been so crazy about Cecilia they'd both taken wild chances. He didn't care, because he loved her. If she did get pregnant, that would be all the excuse he needed to marry her. He *wanted* to marry her. With an attitude like that, it was bound to happen sooner or later—and for them it had been sooner.

It took him weeks to talk her into marrying him. That hadn't been easy on his ego. Her parents' failed relationship had left her with a real anxiety about marriage. The irony was that now *she* was the one who wanted out.

"I still remember our first kiss," she said in a soft voice.

"You do?" Ian was surprised she'd admit it.

"No man had ever kissed me the way you do…did."

"Do," he corrected, and then not giving a damn if anyone saw him, he leaned down and brushed his mouth over hers. That kiss was an experiment to see how receptive she was. When her mouth parted and her tongue met his, Ian could hardly keep from groaning aloud. Her lips were soft and slippery from the butter and she tasted like popcorn and salt. His heart went wild; he loved her so much.

He knew he should stop. They weren't teenagers without a place to go for privacy. Nor did Ian want anyone to find him necking with his wife in the back of a theater. But those thoughts had barely made it into his head when he found any number of compelling reasons to continue doing exactly what he was doing.

"Ian," she whispered, and slowly, reluctantly eased her mouth from his.

Ian kept his eyes closed and leaned his forehead against hers.

"Thank you for letting me use your car."

He wanted to tell her how much he loved her, but he was afraid she'd pull away and the moment would be ruined.

"I'll take good care of it for you," she promised.

"I'd rather you took good care of yourself," he whispered back.

The movie started then, and Cecilia settled back, her head resting on his shoulder. He slid one arm around her; she didn't object. Ian had no idea what the movie was about. He thought only of Cecilia, remembering the early days of their relationship and reveling in her nearness.

When the movie ended they walked slowly out of the theater, but Ian wasn't ready to leave her. "I want to come home with you," he said, standing next to her car, the driver's door open. Just so there'd be no misunderstanding about what he intended, he kissed her again, his mouth hard and hot.

Her eyes still closed, Cecilia broke it off and lowered her head. "I don't think that's a good idea."

"I do. Cecilia, we're married. It's been months since we made love."

"We're getting divorced."

"Fine, divorce me later, but love me now. I need you."

"Ian…"

She didn't say no, but she didn't quite say yes, either. Ian followed her home. When she arrived, he climbed quickly out of his car and opened the building door to let her in.

He waited in the hallway while Cecilia unlocked the apartment. She glanced over her shoulder.

It was all the invitation Ian needed. She met him just inside; he closed the door with his foot and reached for her. She came to him willingly, throwing her arms around his neck.

Ian lifted her from the floor and they kissed with such abandon that the world could have come to an end and they wouldn't have noticed. He removed her sweater and her bra, kissing her as he peeled away the layers of clothing. Her breasts seemed to throb in his hands.

"Don't make me wait," she pleaded.

Even in the dark, Ian had no trouble finding the bedroom. He held her by one hand and led her there.

He placed her on the bed, pressing against her, all the while kissing her slowly, dragging out each kiss until he thought he'd explode. The blood pounded in his ears as he stepped back and stripped off his own clothes. Cecilia shed her slacks.

It'd been so long, too long, and he was ready. He

prayed she was, too. His gaze sought out hers in the dim moonlight that filtered through the bedroom curtains. She smiled softly and lifted her arms to him. He felt overwhelming relief—and then he was on his knees over her.

She linked her arms around his neck and they kissed until they were breathless and he entered her. Slowly, so slowly, for fear of hurting her. When he paused, Cecilia whimpered, urging him to continue.

"Cecilia…" He groaned her name when he realized what he'd done. He had protection with him, and here they were risking the possibility of another pregnancy. "I didn't… I should—"

"No." Her arms tightened around him. "Don't stop. Not now. It's all right…this is my safe time."

God forgive him his weakness, but he did as she asked and poured his life into her.

Afterward Ian held her, kissing her repeatedly. Maybe now this insanity about divorce would be over. Maybe now they could go back to being married. But he was afraid to suggest it, afraid she'd reject him.

A few minutes later, he stood and retrieved his clothes. Cecilia sat up on the bed, clasping her knees with both arms, and watched him dress. He silently begged her to speak, invite him to stay the night.

She didn't.

This was crazy, idiotic! They'd just finished making love. She *had* to know how he felt about her. He hadn't tried to hide his feelings. He waited for her to say something, to stop him. A word, that was all it would take. One damn word. She wasn't willing to give him even that. So he left.

* * *

Grace was in a glorious mood. The entire world could now be viewed through rose-colored glasses, and all because she was going to become a grandmother. That news was just the boost her life and her marriage had needed. Dan's spirits, too, had revived, and they'd had a wonderful talk, reminiscing over the early years of their own marriage when their daughters were young. In the weeks since Kelly's phone call, Grace's love for her husband had been rekindled. The dark times they'd experienced recently had clouded her perspective on their years together. Maybe she didn't always get what she wanted from Dan, what she needed, but she did love him.

They'd been little more than teenagers when they got married. So young... It hadn't mattered that they'd lived below the poverty line, they were happy. Vietnam had shaken up their lives, but they'd survived and so had the marriage.

Wednesday night was her aerobics class, and Grace hurried in the front door, coming straight home from the library. To her surprise, the house on Rosewood Lane was dark and silent.

"Dan?" she called out. Almost always he was home before her.

Nothing.

The first thing her husband did when he walked in was turn on the television. He showered and changed clothes, but the TV was on, even if he wasn't watching.

He hadn't mentioned anything that morning about being late. She checked the calendar to be sure he didn't have a dentist's or doctor's appointment, but nothing was noted. Pulling hamburger out of the refrigerator, she hurriedly put together a casserole and placed it in the oven, then packed her exercise clothes and tennis shoes inside her gym bag.

The phone rang and she answered it immediately, expecting to hear Dan's voice. The caller was someone wanting to ask her questions for a survey; she got rid of him in short order. Answering the phone prompted her to check the machine, but there were no messages.

When the oven timer went off sixty minutes later, she took out the beef-and-rice casserole and set it on the stovetop to cool. Wednesday evenings were hectic for Grace. Dan didn't object to her attending the exercise class, but he didn't like waiting for her to return before he ate dinner. Consequently, Grace rushed home, got a meal on the table and then rushed out the door to meet Olivia for their seven o'clock class.

When it was obvious that Dan wasn't going to be there to join her, Grace ate alone. She picked at the casserole, which was one of his favorite recipes and not hers. Because she'd be leaving him, she always chose a dish she knew he'd enjoy. That was something she did, almost unconsciously, on Wednesdays.

As she sat at the table, the space across from her empty, Grace reviewed that morning's conversation for something she might have missed. The alarm had gone off at the usual time. Dan made the coffee and packed his lunch; Grace showered and dressed. They each had toast and homemade strawberry preserves while she wrote her list for the day and he read the *Bremerton Sun*. After thirty-five years together, they'd settled into the comfort of habit.

Grace couldn't recall Dan saying or doing anything out of the ordinary that morning. She'd kissed him on his way out the door, same as usual, mentioned what she'd be making for dinner and said she'd see him that evening. With his thermos and lunch bucket in hand, he'd headed for his truck and pulled out of the driveway. An hour later, after she'd finished wiping down the kitchen counter and running a load of laundry, Grace left for the library. Their morning routine had been the same as always. But where was Dan?

"You're making too much of this," Grace said aloud. It was just that the house seemed so empty. Everything felt slightly *wrong* without him there. He should've been sitting in front of the television, drinking his after-dinner coffee, watching the news.

Grace delayed leaving for her exercise class as long as she could. Before she went to the gym, she jotted a note and left it on the kitchen counter where Dan would see it when he came in the back door.

Driving into the lot at the YMCA a few minutes late, Grace noticed that Olivia was waiting for her. Her friend seemed positively lighthearted, and Grace wondered if her good mood could be attributed to the news about James or her dinner date with Jack Griffin.

"You're looking terrific," Grace commented, as they walked into the building.

Olivia laughed. "I *feel* terrific."

"How was your date?"

Olivia didn't answer right away. "Interesting."

"What does that mean?"

"It means I find Jack Griffin an interesting guy.

He's thoughtful, well-read, has strong opinions. He seems open and honest, and yet there's a hint of…mystery about him. It's probably nothing important, but you know how much I hate secrets and deceptions."

"What kind of mystery?"

"Well, for one thing, he's friends with Bob Beldon. Apparently they've known each other for ten years, but he never once mentioned how they met. It seemed odd, you know?"

Grace wasn't sure she did, but she let her friend continue talking because it distracted her from worrying about Dan. She was overreacting, she told herself again, but then she had a tendency to do that. Her imagination frequently got the best of her. The girls were never just late, they'd been in a horrible car crash and were lying in a ditch bleeding, calling out for her. That was just how her mind worked. It was probably all the murder mysteries she read.

"You're certainly quiet," Olivia remarked.

"Me?" Grace returned, acting surprised.

"Yeah, you. Is something wrong?"

"What could be wrong? I'm fine—great. Excited about Kelly's news."

"How's Dan?"

Olivia always did have a way of homing in on the problem. Grace glanced toward her and sighed.

"It *is* Dan, isn't it? Is he in another one of his moods?"

They entered the crowded locker room and Grace found a place on the bench. "No. Actually, his spirits have been good lately. I know we've had our ups and downs over the years, but this is a positive time for us both."

"Stan and I had our own roller-coaster ride."

This wasn't encouraging, seeing that her friend had been divorced for nearly fifteen years.

Olivia looked away. "You know what I mean."

Grace nodded. Olivia might be divorced but, regardless of anything she might say to the contrary, she remained linked to Stan by more than their children. He'd been the love of her life, and the death of their oldest son and the divorce that followed hadn't changed that. Stan would always be part of Olivia's life, even while he was married to another woman. Grace understood this. She doubted that Olivia fully recognized the strength of her bond to him.

"What's up with Dan?" Olivia pressed.

Grace stripped off her sweats and changed her shoes. "He isn't home from work yet." Then, before Olivia could chastise her for worrying, she added, "He probably had an appointment and forgot to tell me."

"He might have said something and it slipped your mind," Olivia suggested.

"Sure." Grace had already considered that scenario, but didn't really believe it. *Something was wrong*. Her heart told her and her head echoed that certainty, pounding with fear.

Probably because of her pent-up anxiety, Grace had the best workout of her life. By the time class finished, she was so weak she could barely walk back to the change room.

"Call me," Olivia said as they strolled toward the parking lot. The air was damp and cold, and their breath came out in little puffs of fog. The huge lights in the asphalt lot cast a bluish glow.

"I'm sure Dan's home by now," Grace murmured.

"I'm sure he is, too," Olivia said, but her words rang false.

Grace waited until Olivia was inside her car before she got into her own. As she turned down Rosewood Lane, her heart beat so loudly it sounded like a distant drumbeat in her ear. She felt almost as though she were sitting in a theater and the music preceding a tense moment in the story had begun, growing louder and louder around her.

Other than the porch light, the house was still dark. Dread suffused her whole being. She could hardly breathe.

Where the hell was Dan?

Then it occurred to her that he might be in bed. If he'd had to work overtime or been delayed in traffic, he'd probably arrived home exhausted. In that case, he'd have showered and gone straight to bed.

Only Dan's truck wasn't in its usual parking space. Going inside, Grace sat her gym bag in the laundry room, then moved into the darkened living room and slowly lowered herself into her husband's recliner. The cushion gave, broken down by years of use, and she sank into the comfortable old chair he loved so much. That was when she started to shake.

She waited fifteen minutes, then walked into the kitchen and reached for the phone. Without turning on the light, she dialed Olivia's number and let it ring until her friend answered.

"Dan isn't here."

Olivia didn't say anything for several tense moments. Then calmly, as though this was an everyday occurrence, she said, "I'll be right over."

Seven

Grace sat up all night, her fears out of control. Olivia had stayed up with her until after midnight, when she'd fallen asleep on the sofa out of sheer exhaustion. Grace let her friend sleep. There wasn't anything Olivia could say that would reassure her. Nothing either one of them could do, for that matter. None of this felt real.

At six-thirty, just as the first light of morning crept toward the horizon, Olivia woke. Bolting upright, she blinked rapidly and looked around.

"Have you heard anything?" she asked, rubbing her face with both hands.

Grace shook her head. She'd brewed a pot of coffee, more for something to do than any desire for caffeine.

"I think it's time I called Troy Davis," Olivia said in that no-nonsense way of hers. "It's been almost twenty-four hours, hasn't it?"

Grace nodded, and automatically poured them each a cup of coffee. She stood in the kitchen, sipping hers, while Olivia made the call to the local sheriff's office. She found it difficult to keep her mind clear and focused. The sleepless night hadn't helped. Her thoughts were fearful and obsessive—ideas of where Dan might be, what could have happened, what plausible reason he might have for not coming home.

"Troy isn't on duty until seven," Olivia explained when she'd finished.

"Should we go there ourselves?"

"No, I talked to Lowell Price and he said Troy would take a drive out here. He knows Dan and he'll want to handle this personally."

Grace felt a tremendous sense of relief. "Should I phone the girls?" After all those sleepless hours of worrying, she seemed incapable of making decisions.

Olivia appeared to weigh her answer. "Why don't you wait until after you've talked to Troy?"

"All right." She hated the idea of alarming her daughters, but they had a right to know their father had disappeared. Dear God, where *could* he be? Never in all the years they'd been married had Dan done anything like this. Something had to be very wrong.

"Have you given any more thought to where Dan might've gone?"

She had, but Grace found it hard to voice the words. "Lately…before Kelly announced she was pregnant, Dan's been…" She didn't know how to continue and struggled not to break into tears. "I think there might be another woman."

"Dan? No way! He's not the type." Olivia shook her head adamantly. "Not Dan," she repeated. "No way."

Grace found it hard to believe herself. But unlikely

though it seemed, the thought refused to leave her mind. "I realized a long time ago that we don't have a perfect marriage, but lately it's…it's as though something's changed in Dan. He's different." There, she'd said it, but putting into words exactly *what* was different about her husband proved far more difficult. She knew he was restless. He'd been moody for thirty years, ever since Vietnam, but lately the swings had been wider, more extreme. Whenever she tried to draw him out, get him to confide in her, Dan seemed to resent her effort. That had led Grace to wonder if there was someone else he was talking to, someone else he'd come to care about. The only time he'd been himself lately was when they'd heard Kelly's wonderful news. After their daughter's announcement, everything had been better—for a while. Now this.

"Dan just isn't the kind of man who would cheat on you," Olivia said in a confident voice.

"Do any of us really know our husbands?" Grace asked quietly. She didn't mean to be cruel, but her friend had learned that lesson the hard way. Apparently Stan had met his current wife while commuting on the ferry to his job in Seattle. Grace didn't think he'd been involved in an actual affair with Marge, but she'd offered a sympathetic ear after Jordan's death and had helped Stan deal with the guilt and anger that followed. His relationship with Marge had been one of emotional rather than sexual intensity. It was the only thing that could explain how quickly he'd remarried.

Olivia didn't answer right away. Carrying her mug, she paced the area in front of the sofa. "What makes you think Dan might be seeing someone else?"

Grace didn't have any specific details. "It's more of a gut feeling," she said with a helpless shrug.

"Think back over the last six months. Has he taken special care with his appearance, attended meetings at odd times of the day or night?"

Her mind was a blank. "Uh...not that I recall."

"Didn't you say he went hunting last fall?"

Grace nodded. He'd taken up the sport after a long absence, and while it wasn't something she could possibly like, she'd been grateful that he was showing interest in an activity other than watching TV. He'd left on a Friday afternoon in late October and returned on the Sunday evening. He'd spoken enthusiastically about his trek through the woods, more voluble than he'd been for quite a while.

"He went alone?" Olivia asked.

Dan hadn't mentioned anyone else, but at the time Grace hadn't thought of that as odd. He didn't have a lot of friends and often preferred his own company.

"Did he bring home any game?"

"No." But that made sense, too, since it'd been years since he'd gone hunting. Putting down her coffee, Grace frowned, remembering that weekend. "Are you suggesting he was with someone else?"

Olivia boldly met her look. "I wouldn't know, but deep down I think you do."

Perhaps she did. That free weekend had been wonderful for her. She'd spent a delightful two days with Maryellen and Kelly, shopping at an outlet mall in Oregon. It'd been their first "Mother-Daughter Getaway Weekend," an event they hoped to repeat annually.

"He seemed...happy," Grace murmured. He was so rarely in a good mood that it'd struck her as unusual. She couldn't believe that a man would go from another woman's bed and then home to his wife, without somehow betraying his guilt. She couldn't accept that her husband was capable of such a thing, and yet…

They heard a car outside and Olivia glanced out the living-room window. "Troy's here."

Grace had opened the front door and was standing on the porch as Sheriff Davis came up the walkway.

"Thanks for coming," Grace told him, grateful he'd decided to attend to this himself.

Troy removed his hat as he stepped into the house and nodded in Olivia's direction.

"I wasn't sure who else to call," Olivia explained.

"You did the right thing." Troy was a good-looking man who'd been two years ahead of them in school and the biggest heartthrob in Cedar Cove. He'd gone into the service after graduation, then joined the sheriff's department on his return. For the last thirty-eight years, he'd kept order in their community; ten years ago, he'd been elected sheriff. Folks liked and trusted Troy.

Grace invited him to make himself comfortable and he chose to sit in Dan's recliner. He carried a clipboard and had a pencil ready.

"I take it you'd like to file a missing person's report."

"Please," Grace said, nearly choking on the word.

"Tell me what you know," he said gently.

Grace told him everything she could think of. Although it broke her heart, she mentioned the hunting trip and Olivia's suspicions that there could be another woman in his life.

"Do *you* think there's someone else?"

Grace raised her hands in a gesture of defeat. "What is it people say? The wife is always the last to know." The more often she acknowledged the possibility, the more real it seemed to become. She told herself Dan wouldn't do that to her, to their daughters. She *had* to believe it. Yet she knew something wasn't right and hadn't been for a very long time.

"What happens next?" Grace asked once the report had been completed.

Troy glanced at Olivia and then back at her. "Actually, nothing."

"Nothing?" Grace was appalled.

"I've checked both hospitals in the area, but they don't have anyone admitted under Dan's name, nor do they have any unidentified patients."

"He hasn't been arrested, has he?"

"No," Troy confirmed. "Not by us and not by the State Patrol." In other words, no one knew anything about Dan or could guess where he might have gone. "As far as I can see, there isn't any evidence of foul play."

Grace nodded. She'd walked through the house a dozen times during the night, looking for even the tiniest clue that would tell her where Dan might be. She'd combed through his pockets, his dresser, everything.

"Then we have to assume Dan is missing of his own accord," Troy said calmly.

Confused, Grace looked at her friend. "What Troy is saying," Olivia told her, "is that it isn't a crime for an adult to run away."

"Husbands and wives abandon their families. Unfortunately it's a common occurrence."

"If that was the case," Grace snapped, "then Dan would've taken something with him, don't you think? All he had were the clothes on his back."

"I realize it might not make sense," Troy went on.

"Make sense?" Grace echoed. "This is ludicrous! My husband is missing and the police won't do anything to help me find him."

Troy held her gaze. "I'm sorry, Grace, but that's the law. If anyone sees him, I'll let you know."

"Thanks for nothing," she muttered, crossing her arms. She was furious, embarrassed and filled with a restless energy she didn't know how to dispel.

It was then that Grace heard the back door open and close. A moment later, as if he hadn't a care in the world, her husband walked into the living room.

"What's going on here?" he asked, obviously surprised to find Olivia and Troy in his home.

"Dan!" Grace's relief at seeing him was so great, she started to weep. "Oh, Dan. Dear God in heaven, where were you? I've been out of my mind with worry."

He ignored her. "Is there a problem here, Troy?" he asked stiffly.

"No." The sheriff stood, tore the report free from his clipboard and folded it in half. He handed it to Grace and, without a word of farewell, headed out the front door.

"I'd better get ready for court," Olivia said. She glared fiercely in Dan's direction and quickly left.

"You called Troy?" Dan said as soon as they were alone. He glowered at her as though she'd done something wrong.

"Where *were* you?" Grace cried again, unable to

hold back her anger or her tears. "Don't you realize what you put me through?"

"It's none of your damn business where I was."

"Like hell!" she shouted. "You're my husband."

Dan scowled darkly. "I refuse to allow this marriage to be a ball and chain around my neck."

Grace was so shocked, she couldn't restrain herself. "You go out and spend the entire night God-knows-where," she screamed, "and then casually come home as if nothing happened? You expect me to pretend everything's all right?" She couldn't do it. Wouldn't.

"Where I was and what I was doing are my own damn business." He marched into the bedroom. Grace followed him.

"You were with another woman, weren't you?" Her heart ached as she asked the question.

"Yeah, Gracie, I was with someone else."

"Who is she?"

Dan's responding laugh lacked humor.

"I have a right to know that much."

Dan refused to answer her question. Then he went to his drawer and took out a fresh change of underwear. "I haven't got time for this."

"*You* don't have time," she repeated. How dared he, after all the anguish he'd caused? For a moment she thought she was going to be physically ill.

He stomped into the bathroom. Grace went in the opposite direction and slammed the bedroom door so hard their daughters' graduation pictures flew off the wall. They crashed onto the hardwood floor of the hallway, shattering the glass.

Horrified by what she'd done, Grace stared at the

beautiful faces of her children and wanted to grind her teeth with frustration.

"Go to hell!" she yelled at her husband.

The bedroom door opened and Dan stood there. He wore a hard, unyielding look. "Been there, Gracie. What else would you call the last thirty-five years?"

Grace didn't show up for their next exercise class. Olivia knew that relations with Dan had been rocky since his disappearing act. Grace hadn't explained Dan's disappearance or where he'd been, and Olivia didn't pry. If there was another woman involved, then the matter was best settled between husband and wife. Still, Olivia couldn't help worrying.

In addition to that, she had other concerns. At the top of her list just now was Justine.

Her daughter had been avoiding her again, despite Olivia's efforts to build a bridge between them. She longed for them to be close, the way she was with her own mother. Perhaps it was too late for that; she hoped not and would willingly make any overtures. She vowed that under no circumstances would she bring up the subject of Warren Saget. Olivia's one wish was that she and Justine simply enjoy each other's company.

Olivia had invited Justine for lunch on Saturday, and Justine had accepted. Using one of her mother's favorite recipes, she prepared a main-dish chicken salad. Personally, Olivia would have preferred a restaurant meal, which would've been easier all around. Having lunch here, however, would allow for a more relaxed, casual atmosphere—and greater privacy. At a restaurant there was always the chance they'd run into someone they knew and get sidetracked.

Justine showed up right on time. She brought a small bouquet of yellow daffodils and gave Olivia a perfunctory kiss on the cheek as she walked into the house.

"How thoughtful," Olivia said, touched by the gesture. She found a vase for the flowers and set them in the middle of the kitchen table.

"It's been a while since we've gotten together for lunch," Justine commented, grabbing a breadstick from the table.

"Too long." Olivia removed the salad from the refrigerator, filled two plates, and carried them to the table. A kettle of water waited on the stove for tea later on.

Her beautiful daughter sat across from her, and Olivia had the sudden urge to speak from her heart. "I don't think I tell you often enough how much I love you."

Justine stared at her as if she didn't know how to react, then smiled. "This has to do with James, doesn't it?"

Nothing could be further from the truth. Still, she asked, "How do you mean?"

"I know it was a shock, his suddenly getting married like that, without any of the family even knowing or being there."

"This has nothing to do with your brother, and everything to do with us." Olivia found herself growing irritated with both Justine and herself. It shouldn't be so difficult to tell your child she was deeply loved.

"Oh, Mother, don't start."

"Start what?"

"You're worried about the fact that I'm seeing Warren and—"

"This has nothing to do with your boyfriend, either."

Her daughter laughed. "Boyfriend? You make me sound sixteen."

"Justine," Olivia said, trying to control her irritation. "As I told you, this isn't about your brother, your boyfriend, your job or anything else. I'm your mother, and I want us to be able to talk, to share, to laugh together, and I'm hoping you want that, too. I've felt...I don't know, that we're somewhat estranged these days. Distant. I don't know why it's happened, but I don't like it. I love you."

If Justine rolled her eyes, Olivia swore she'd...well, she didn't know what she'd do. Weep, maybe.

Justine didn't make a scornful face or flip remark; in fact she seemed to have difficulty taking in the words. She went still and after a moment, she met Olivia's gaze and whispered, "I love you, too, Mom."

Olivia swallowed the lump in her throat and picked up her fork. Perhaps there was hope of reaching her daughter, after all.

"What would you like to discuss?" Justine asked.

Olivia wasn't sure. She quickly reviewed a number of topics and remembered a notice in Wednesday's paper. Not wanting to mention the source for fear of diverting the conversation to her relationship with Jack Griffin, she spoke in an offhand manner. "It's your ten-year class reunion this year, isn't it?"

Justine set down her fork and sighed. "Yes, I know."

Ten years? It hardly seemed possible. "You'll be attending, of course."

To Olivia's surprise, her daughter hesitated. "Actually, I'm not sure."

"Why not?" But Olivia knew. Warren. It might embarrass Justine to show up with a man old enough to be her father. More likely, Warren would simply decline.

"I'd probably have to go alone. It's bad enough that I'm still single, but to come without a date—I don't know if my ego can stand it."

"You have several single friends who'll probably be there."

"I suppose," Justine said doubtfully.

This was exactly the sort of event that might open her daughter's eyes. Olivia hoped that if Justine saw her high-school friends, she'd recognize how completely wrong Warren was for her.

"There's a meeting later in the week," Justine said.

Olivia remembered that her daughter had been a senior class officer. Surely she'd be involved in planning the reunion. Since Justine was the local bank manager, the reunion committee would likely welcome her expertise with finances.

"Will you be helping?" Olivia pressed.

Justine sighed. "Probably," she said in a resigned voice. Then she brightened. "Do you remember Julie Wyatt and Annie Willoughby? I haven't seen either of them in years and they both live right here in Cedar Cove."

Olivia remembered both families well.

"Seth Gunderson still lives in town, too," Justine murmured.

Olivia remembered Seth because he'd been Jordan's best friend. He'd been fishing with his father in

Alaska at the time of her son's accident. Olivia had never forgotten the letter the thirteen-year-old boy had written her and Stan after he'd learned of Jordan's death. The few short lines, a simple expression of grief and condolence, had touched her heart.

"I always liked Seth," Olivia said thoughtfully. "Whatever became of him?"

Justine shrugged. "I'm not sure. I know he still fishes in Alaska every summer, which means he probably won't be home for the reunion."

That saddened her. If Olivia were to handpick a husband for her daughter, she'd choose a man like Seth.

"Oh, no, you don't, Mom." Justine good-naturedly waved her finger. "I can see the wheels turning in your head. You want to link me up with Seth, but I'm not interested."

"What's wrong with Seth?"

"Well, first of all, he hasn't got a brain in his head."

"Oh, Justine, that's not true!"

"All that ever interested him was sports."

"Ah, yes, he *was* good at sports." Seth had been the star football and basketball player through all four years of high school.

"He's a fisherman, for crying out loud!"

Olivia frowned; she hadn't raised her daughter to be a snob. "He's a hard worker, Justine, and there's nothing wrong with that."

"As opposed to Warren?"

"No!" Olivia refused to get drawn into that argument. "We're talking about Seth."

"Mother, he lives on his boat at the marina. I like Seth, don't get me wrong, but he's a big oaf. I haven't talked to him once since we graduated and I sincerely doubt we have anything more in common than we did in high school."

Olivia sighed inwardly. "Sweetheart, I didn't mean to suggest that Seth is the right man for you." Well, yes, she did, but she could hardly admit it. "Someday you'll find the one, and in fact you may have already." She had to grit her teeth to say it, but if Justine married Warren, Olivia would somehow manage to welcome him into the family.

Her daughter looked away. "When James first called to tell me he and Selina were married—and that she's pregnant—I was so relieved."

"Relieved?" That was a curious reaction.

"It took the pressure off me. I know you want grandchildren and I want you to have them." She straightened and met Olivia's gaze. "But unfortunately, you won't get them from me."

"Justine—"

"Listen to me, Mom, please, just this once. I have no intention of ever marrying or having children. I realize you're concerned about my relationship with Warren, but you don't need to be. He treats me well and I enjoy his company most of the time, but I'm not serious about him."

"You don't want to get married?"

She shook her head. "I know I'm a disappointment to you and I'm sorry, but please accept that I'm just not interested in being a wife or a mother."

Olivia let the words sink into her heart, then nodded. "I said it earlier and I meant it. I love you, Justine, not for what you do but for who you are."

Her daughter blinked back tears and lowered her

head in order to hide the emotion from Olivia, but it was too late. She saw.

"Thanks, Mom."

Then as if nothing noteworthy had transpired between them, they went back to eating their salads.

Every afternoon as Cecilia arrived for work, she looked across Cedar Cove to the Bremerton shipyard, where the *George Washington* was still berthed. It'd been more than a week since her dinner with Ian and she hadn't heard a word from him. Before he'd left her that night, he'd promised to get in touch prior to sailing. Apparently the aircraft carrier was still undergoing repairs.

Cecilia knew she had no right to feel disappointed that he hadn't called. He didn't have any reason to contact her, other than to leave her the keys to his car.

The dinner and movie had been wonderful; the lovemaking, too. Until he'd abruptly left, Cecilia had begun to feel that they'd made a breakthrough in their relationship. Now she wasn't sure what to think. And she was horrified that they'd done something as foolish as having unprotected sex. Granted, the likelihood of her being pregnant was very slight, but anyone might figure she'd learned her lesson the first time. Apparently not. When she was in his arms, she'd felt desired—and reassured. Safe. Then he'd dressed and run out as if he couldn't get away fast enough.

Now this silence. She didn't understand any of it.

Perhaps Ian was waiting for her to call him. She couldn't remember exactly what they'd said before he walked out the door. Nothing of importance. Noth-

ing she could even remember. All she could think at
the time was that she didn't want him to leave, but
couldn't ask him to stay, either.

The more she thought about phoning him, the
more appealing the idea became. By the end of her
shift on Monday night, she'd decided to call Ian first
thing after her classes on Tuesday.

All morning Cecilia found herself eyeing the time.
She had no idea what Ian's work schedule was. She
hoped he'd be available, but if not, she could always
leave him a message.

She knew he was living on base and had a cell
phone; she'd written the number in her address book
more than a year ago. She called from a pay phone
on the community college campus. The phone rang
four times and then she got his voice mail, inviting her
to leave a message.

"Ian," she said, worried now that she might be
doing the wrong thing. "It's Cecilia… I hadn't heard
from you and was wondering if you'd changed your
mind about the car…which is fine. I mean, I don't
need it or anything. My car's running great. I'll talk
to you later—that is, if you still want to talk to me."
The last part came out sounding defensive. He'd
wanted her badly enough earlier, but apparently sex
was all he'd been after. She quickly hung up the receiver and felt foolish, wishing now that she hadn't
given in to the impulse.

Wednesday afternoon when she showed up for
work, Cecilia was convinced that Ian wanted nothing
more to do with her. Just as the dinner hour was picking up and she was at her busiest, her father appeared.

"There's a call for you."

Her heart raced. "Me?" It had to be Ian. No one else would think to contact her here.

"You can take it at the bar," he told her, glancing around for their boss.

Cecilia quickly abandoned her duties and hurried in. Her hands were moist, her mouth dry with anticipation.

"This is Cecilia Randall," she said into the mouthpiece, eagerly anticipating Ian's voice.

Only it wasn't her husband on the other end of the line. Instead, Andrew Lackey answered.

"We met not long ago, remember?"

"Of course. Where's Ian?" He might have been transferred again. The Navy did that, often without rhyme or reason—at least in her opinion.

"Listen, I thought you should know. Ian's in the hospital."

She gasped. "What's wrong?"

"Nothing too serious. He took a tumble and wrenched his back. Apparently he hit his head, too, because he has a concussion. They're keeping him for observation."

"When did it happen?"

"Yesterday morning."

"Oh."

"There's nothing to worry about. I just thought you'd like to know."

"Yes, thank you."

As soon as they'd finished the conversation, Cecilia walked over to her father. "Ian's been hurt...I'm going to the hospital. Find someone to cover for me, would you?"

"Sure thing. You go, and I'll hold down the fort."

Grateful, she smiled at her father and impulsively hugged him. "Thanks, Dad." The tears sprang to her eyes.

"Hey, none of that. Now, give Ian my best and let me know if you need anything."

"I will," she said and hurriedly reached for her coat and purse.

The drive to the Navy Hospital in Bremerton seemed to take forever. Her car belched thick smoke as she turned off the freeway and headed for the extensive parking lot outside the hospital.

She quickly found out where she needed to go. Breathless, Cecilia charged into the elevator. Once she'd located his room, she paused in the hallway for a moment, just long enough to brush a hand through her hair and draw in a deep breath. Then she knocked at the door.

No one answered, so she opened it and stepped inside. At her first sight of her husband, Cecilia couldn't prevent an exclamation of shock. Andrew had led her to believe that Ian had suffered a minor fall, that the only reason he'd been hospitalized was as a precaution. One quick look told her his injuries were far worse than she'd expected.

Ian lifted his bandaged head and when he saw who it was, he groaned.

"What happened?" she asked, moving fully into the room.

"What are you doing here?" he demanded, and it was plain she was the last person he wanted to see.

"I-I... Andrew called me, and..."

He frowned, and winced; no wonder, she thought. One side of his face was swollen and badly bruised.

His left eye was completely shut and there was a bandage around his left arm.

"What's the other guy look like?" she asked, hoping a light approach would relax him.

He ignored the question.

"Ian…what's wrong?"

"I didn't ask you to come here," he returned gruffly.

"I know. I came because I wanted to make sure you were all right." She didn't mention that she'd risked her job to do so. Her father had said he'd cover for her, but in her rush, she hadn't spoken to her boss and had left without permission.

"As you can see, I'm just hunky-dory, so you can leave now."

His words stung. "That's rude."

"In case you hadn't figured it out, I'm not exactly in the mood for company."

"All right," she whispered and retreated a step.

"Go on," he urged. "Get out of here."

She blinked, unbearably hurt that Ian would speak to her this way. "If that's how you feel, then—"

"Go," he shouted, pointing at the door.

Turning on her heel, Cecilia ran out of the room. If he didn't want her concern or…or her love, that was fine with her.

"Cecilia!" he called after her, but she resolutely ignored him. She hurried to the elevator, pushing the button with more force than necessary. Maybe it was time to see her attorney, after all. She refused to stay married to a man who treated her like this.

Eight

The March rains had arrived, and the last thing Justine Lockhart wanted was to sit in a stuffy room with a bunch of classmates, planning an event she probably wouldn't even attend. But that was exactly what she'd have to do. As Justine had predicted, she'd been contacted by the reunion committee and asked if she'd be willing to help. In a moment of weakness, she'd agreed.

Unfortunately, Justine had made the mistake of mentioning the reunion to Warren. He'd refused to even consider going with her. After all the times she'd sat through dead boring meetings waiting for him or played hostess to a group of his business colleagues, she'd assumed he'd do this one small thing for her. She'd obviously assumed wrong.

He'd tried to smooth over their spat with a pretty sapphire necklace and an invitation to dinner. In the past, Justine had accepted his jewel-encrusted apologies, and they'd gone on as before. Justine was well acquainted with Warren's faults; she usually chose to ignore them. He could be entertaining and he tended to indulge her in return for her company. That might sound calculating but it was an arrangement that suited them both. Besides, for all his money, he had few friends. And neither of them was in this relationship for the long haul. Expectations were clear.

The planning meeting was held at the home of Lana Sullivan, who'd married Jay Rothchild. In the ten years since she'd graduated, Justine hadn't spoken to Lana once.

"Justine!" Lana greeted her enthusiastically, hugging her as though they were long-lost friends. "Come in! Seth's here and so is Mary."

Justine glanced into the living room and saw that Mary O'Donnell was several months pregnant. "Good to see you Mary," Justine said, smiling, then nodded at Seth.

The school's star athlete hadn't changed much—physically, at least. He was just as tall and muscular, although he'd filled out and had a more mature look. He remained strikingly blond. She didn't remember him being this handsome, but her high-school years were pretty much a blur.

"What are you doing these days?" Mary asked.

Justine shrugged. "I'm working at First National." She'd graduated from college with a degree in history; unfortunately, this hadn't translated into an employable skill.

"I hear you're the manager," Seth said.

"I am." It surprised her he knew that. He wasn't a customer.

Ill at ease, Justine claimed a chair across from Mary, tucked her hands under her thighs and made polite conversation with the small group, declining a cup of coffee. She wasn't sure when the strained atmosphere shifted into comfortable exchange, but it did. Soon she found herself laughing with these people who were little more than familiar strangers.

Once the schedule of events had been decided and committees formed, the meeting was over. Justine left at the same time as Seth.

"Have you eaten?" he asked, to her astonishment. He dangled his car keys as he waited for her reply.

Justine realized this was more than a mere inquiry; it was an invitation. "No, as a matter of fact, I haven't." Warren had suggested she phone when she was finished with her meeting—he'd said he might be able to take her out for a drink—but she was in no hurry to do so. "Would you like some company?" she asked.

"Sure."

As Justine had discovered early in the evening, Seth wasn't at all the way she remembered him. It hadn't taken her long to see that her view of him as an empty-headed jock was completely off-base. He had a sharp wit and the most wonderful, hearty laugh. She'd liked his ideas for the reunion, which revealed imagination combined with practicality.

They drove in separate cars to D.D.'s on the Cove, a fashionable seafood restaurant on the pier, close to the marina. The restaurant had opened that summer, and Justine had gone there for lunch but never dinner.

Since it was already past eight, they were seated right away. A prime table, too, by one of the windows overlooking the harbor, where they could see the lights from the Bremerton shipyard blinking across the cove. Justine glanced quickly at the menu and made her choice.

"It's hard to believe we graduated ten years ago, isn't it?" she said. "Nobody looks *that* different. Well, except for Mary…"

"I have mixed feelings about the reunion," Seth confessed.

"Why?" she asked with some puzzlement.

"If I go at all, I'll probably end up going alone. It kind of wrecks my image, you know?" He grinned, and Justine couldn't keep from smiling.

"You certainly had girls buzzing around you while we were in school," she told him.

"Except the one I really wanted." His deep-blue eyes held hers.

"Who are you kidding? You could've dated anyone."

"Not you," he said, still watching her.

"Me?" she said in shock. "You wanted to date *me?*"

This had to be a joke, and not a funny one. She was about to say so when it suddenly occurred to her that he might be serious.

"What do you mean?" she asked in a weak voice.

"I had the biggest crush on you."

"Not once did you ask me out," she reminded him.

"Would you have gone with me if I had?"

Justine didn't know.

"You saw me as a big dunce, and I don't blame you. Whenever I was around you, I got so flustered I couldn't speak. Anytime you were in the vicinity, I was in trouble. I couldn't say or do anything right. Then I'd feel like such an idiot I'd beat myself up about it for weeks afterward."

"I didn't have a clue," Justine said faintly, shaking her head.

"Thank God," he said with a chuckle. He returned his attention to the menu, as if he intended to say nothing more on this subject.

The waitress came with a basket of warm bread, promptly took their order and left. Justine reached for a slice of sourdough. Apparently Seth's "crush" had long since faded.

"I'll probably be attending the reunion alone, too," she murmured.

"You?" He made that sound entirely implausible. "I thought you and that Saget fellow are an item."

"We are…sort of." She wasn't sure how to explain her relationship with Warren and decided it was best not to try.

"You're dating other guys?"

Justine didn't think she wanted Seth to know she was available. His confession had a curious effect on her—it left her with the almost overwhelming urge to laugh. All through high school, she'd felt tall and awkward, on the very fringes of the popular crowd. She'd been too smart and serious for social success as defined in high school.

Seth tore off a piece of bread and smiled sadly. "It's all right. You don't need to answer that. I've made you uncomfortable, haven't I?"

"That's not it," she reassured him. "I don't know what to say. I never dreamed… You could've gone out with any girl you wanted!" She shook her head again. "I didn't date much in high school. It was a bad time for me."

"Because of Jordan?"

So few people mentioned her twin's name that it stunned her to hear it spoken. She waited for the shock to dissipate before answering. "Partly. We were close, you know, and well, nothing was the same after he died."

"For me, either."

Naturally Justine knew Seth and Jordan had been good friends, but she hadn't anticipated that her brother's death would've made such a lasting impression on him.

"I used to think if I'd been with him that day, he wouldn't have drowned."

Until Seth said the words, Justine had forgotten that this very thought had passed through her mind the day of the accident. She felt tears stinging her eyes and looked away, blinking furiously.

"Perhaps it would be best if we didn't discuss Jordan," she finally said, still staring out the window, although the lights of Bremerton were an indistinct haze. "The accident was a long time ago." It had been the turning point in her life. She'd lost not only her twin brother but her family, her security, her entire sense of self. Since the age of thirteen, she'd staggered through life looking for purpose—for something that would root her once again.

They were both quiet, as if caught in the memories of the past, then made a determined effort to move forward. By the time their meal arrived, they were chatting again, their conversation light and relaxed. They lingered over coffee, and he seemed as reluctant to leave as she was. When D.D.'s closed at ten, Seth offered to show her his boat, the *Silver Belle*. Justine agreed.

"It's not much."

Justine didn't expect that it would be; still, she was curious. They walked toward the marina. She hunched her shoulders against the cold drizzle that had begun while they sat in the restaurant. They stepped onto the floating concrete dock, which was slick with rain. The lights reflecting off the black water guided her as Seth skillfully led the way. He moved easily along the rocking walkway, and was several feet ahead of her before he realized that she lagged behind. When he noticed, he offered her his hand. She was amazed by the strength she felt in his fingers. His hands were those of a man who knew the value of physical work. This observation reminded her of what her mother had said. *He's a hard worker, Justine, and there's nothing wrong with that.*

During their dinner discussion, she'd learned that Seth not only lived at the marina, but helped manage it in the winter months. In the summers, he flew to Alaska and fished on one of the huge commercial vessels there. His father and grandfather had been fishermen before him. As Seth put it, fishing was in his blood.

He stepped onto the twenty-two-foot sailboat and helped Justine onboard. As soon as she was secure, he led her belowdecks. His quarters were cramped but tidy.

"Coffee?" he asked, as he reached for the kettle.

"No, I've had enough, thanks." She didn't want him to go to the trouble, especially since she didn't plan on staying long.

He stood with his hands tucked in his back pockets, looking indecisive. The tour of his home had taken all of about one minute.

"I'll escort you back to your car," he offered.

Justine was grateful; she didn't relish walking back along the floating dock on her own. Once again Seth took her hand, and neither spoke until they reached her vehicle. Before unlocking the door, she turned to him. "Thanks," she said lightly. "I enjoyed dinner and seeing your boat."

"I enjoyed spending the evening with you." He retreated a step. "Are you going to any more of the planning meetings?"

"I'm not sure yet, but I think so. What about you?"

"I will as long as I'm in town."

"Oh, right." Seth would be in Alaska fishing at the time of the reunion. Suddenly the thought of his not being there dejected her. When she'd first arrived at Lana's, she was so certain she had nothing in common with any of these people. She'd been delighted to discover that she did. With *one* of them, anyway...

"I'll miss you," she said.

"Do you mean that?" Seth stared down at her.

Justine nodded.

"I'm glad." Then, without giving her a chance to guess his intention, he drew her into his arms and slowly lowered his mouth to hers.

Very much aware of what she was doing, Justine closed her eyes and raised her face to meet his kiss. His lips settled warm and moist over hers. Wrapped in his embrace, she was astonished to realize that she *wanted* this. Wanted it badly...

There was excitement in his kiss, and gentleness. She hadn't expected a man of his size to be so...tender, but then Seth Gunderson had been full of surprises all evening.

* * *

The *George Washington* was gone and without a word from Ian. The fact that he'd left without notifying her was perfectly okay, Cecilia told herself bitterly. Their last meeting had been so horrible she didn't care if she ever saw her soon-to-be ex-husband again.

"You all right, kiddo?" her father asked Saturday morning when Cecilia dropped in at the restaurant to pick up her paycheck.

"Why shouldn't I be?" she snapped.

"No reason," he said, and held up his hands as though warding off trouble.

She hadn't meant to growl at him, but lately her father had developed this irritating habit of trying to be her friend, her confidante, and she rejected both roles.

"How's school?" he asked, obviously attempting to make conversation.

"Why the concern all of a sudden?" she wanted to know. When she'd first mentioned it, all the encouragement she'd gotten was some offhand comment about how *cool* that was.

"No reason," he said again. He turned away as if he regretted even asking.

Cecilia sighed, hardly understanding herself. "I'm sorry…I didn't mean that the way it sounded."

Bobby stared at her. "What's bothering you, kid? You've been in kind of a bad mood the last couple of weeks."

"That's not true."

He frowned, seemed about to protest, then shrugged. "Whatever."

"It's just that I've been working late, then getting up early for school." A feeble explanation, but the most she was willing to give. Lack of sleep explained a lot, but not everything.

"So you're still taking all those classes?" He seemed to think she would've lost interest by now.

"Yeah, I'm still in school." And loving the challenge, despite the drain on her time and energy.

"Ian around these days?" her father asked cautiously.

"Apparently not," she said, speaking in a nonchalant manner. "The *George Washington* left earlier this week." It wasn't as though she could ignore the fact. The media—both the local paper and the Seattle dailies, plus the TV news—had made a big issue of the repaired aircraft carrier departing for the second time within a month. Not only that, Cedar Cove had been full of talk about it.

"You speak to him lately?"

Cecilia noticed that Bobby stood several feet away from her. He seemed prepared to make a quick getaway if she snapped at him again.

"Ian and I are getting a divorce," she reminded him.

"I know," he was quick to tell her, "but I thought, you know, that you might be reconciling."

Cecilia had started to believe the very same thing. After the night they'd gone to dinner, and the lovemaking, she'd been hopeful. Excited. It was similar to the way she'd felt when they'd first begun seeing each other. Then, when he'd left her apartment that night, everything had changed, and she couldn't understand why.

"I wish you'd work it out," Bobby told her, "you and him."

Resentment swelled up inside Cecilia. "I wish you and Mom had tried harder, too, but wishing doesn't do me a damn bit of good, does it?" With that, she grabbed her paycheck and slammed out the door.

She was angry, without justification. Her father irritated her, her co-workers annoyed her—everyone did lately—and that wasn't like her. Bobby only wanted to be helpful and she'd immediately found fault with him. Not since her pregnancy had Cecilia been so out of sorts. She didn't have that excuse this time; her period had showed up right on schedule—thank God. Her bad mood was simply…a bad mood, she decided.

After depositing her paycheck, she went to the grocery store and picked up the few items she'd need to see her through the week. Although it was an extravagance she couldn't afford, she purchased a bouquet of spring flowers—for Allison. She hadn't visited her baby's grave in almost a month. Staying away was difficult for her. She'd had to make a real effort not to visit the cemetery every day. In the beginning she had.

She'd wanted to be more than a good mother; she'd wanted to give her daughter everything she herself had never had. Not material things, but attention and love and security. As it happened, she couldn't give Allison the most fundamental thing of all. Life itself. Her baby had been cheated from the first, and Cecilia, with all her good intentions, had failed. Rationally she knew she wasn't to blame, but emotionally… She couldn't get over the feeling that there must have been *something* she'd neglected to do. Something she should've done. The doctor had said that was a common reaction in such cases and had urged her to seek counselling. Cecilia hadn't been able to face it.

She didn't head for the cemetery until midafternoon. With tears in her eyes, she strolled along the pathway that led to the section of the cemetery with Allison's grave site. She stopped now and again to brush leaves or grass from a headstone, checking names and dates, wondering about each lost life.

When she arrived at Allison's grave, Cecilia noticed the bouquet of fresh flowers. Yellow daisies, which just happened to be Cecilia's favorite.

Ian. It could only be Ian.

He hadn't called to tell her he was being deployed, but he'd been to visit their daughter. Cecilia crouched down and placed her own bouquet next to the one her husband had left. She touched the daisies with one fingertip, wondering if this was a message to her.

No, she decided, steeling herself against any lingering emotion. Ian had made it plain that he didn't want her in his life. He'd wanted her body but not her. That message had come through loud and clear. He'd asked her to leave his hospital room in terms she couldn't possibly misunderstand. And he hadn't phoned to apologize. Fine, dammit! She didn't need his car, anyway.

The more Cecilia insisted she didn't care about Ian, the less she convinced herself. Not that she *wanted* to care. This depression and anger was all his fault. Once again she'd allowed him into her bed…and her heart. And now she was suffering the consequences.

It hurt that he'd left Bremerton without so much

as a word to her. Not *goodbye,* not *I'm sorry,* nothing. He'd been rude and unreasonable, and this wasn't the first time, either.

Back at her small apartment, Cecilia tried to do her English homework but her mind repeatedly wandered away from the English Romantic poets and down paths she'd prefer to avoid.

When the phone rang, she was jolted by the sudden noise. With an exaggerated sigh, she picked up the receiver.

"Hello," she said in a dull voice.

"Hi," came a cheerful woman's voice. "You don't know me, but I figured it was time I introduced myself. I'm Cathy Lackey."

"Who?"

"Cathy Lackey, Andrew's wife."

Ian's friend. "They're deployed, aren't they?"

"Three days ago. Ian didn't phone?"

"No." She tried to sound unconcerned, despite the pain it'd caused her.

"That coward! I'd like to give him a swift kick in the behind," Cathy muttered.

For the first time all day, Cecilia grinned. "You and me both."

"Listen, I realize we aren't even acquainted yet, but I'd like it if we could be friends. Andrew and Ian are such good buddies and...well, we were only stationed here a few weeks ago, and I haven't met very many people."

"I don't know a lot of people my age, either." Not unless she counted the women she worked with, and Cecilia had never truly fit in with the group at The Captain's Galley. Because she tended to be quiet and withdrawn, and her childhood had been so chaotic, she'd always had trouble making friends. "But sure," she added, "let's get together sometime."

Cathy would be able to tell her about Ian, too; that thought didn't escape her.

"Great!" Cathy seemed pleased. "Are you doing anything tonight?"

It was one of those rare Saturday nights that Cecilia didn't have to work. "What do you have in mind?"

"I was thinking we could rent a movie and make popcorn."

That was about all Cecilia could afford. "I'd like that. Do you want to come here or should I drive over to your place?"

"I'll join you, if that's all right?"

"Sure." Cecilia glanced around the apartment to be sure it was clean. She'd run the vacuum and straighten her books and papers; other than that, it was acceptable.

"Can you drive me back later?"

"No problem," Cecilia said. "Do you need a ride over here, too?"

"No, I've got Ian's car."

The words struck her like a lightning bolt. Before she could react, Cathy was asking, "Is six too early?"

"It's fine," she managed. "But—"

"I'll give you the keys and the insurance papers and everything then," Cathy continued.

"The...what?"

"For Ian's car. He was supposed to call you, but when I didn't hear from you, I figured he'd lost his nerve. Men!" Cathy giggled and Cecilia found herself frowning, hardly making sense of all this.

"You mean he said I should use his car?"

"He insisted on it," Cathy assured her.

Cecilia wanted to believe it, but wondered if she should. He'd sucker-punched her once already and she wasn't up to another round. "Was this before or after he went into the hospital?" she asked.

"After," Cathy said. "He gave me the keys himself and asked me to make sure you got the car."

"Oh," Cecilia said softly, and exhaled a long, slow breath. Despite her refusal to accept the use of his vehicle, he wanted her to drive it anyway. He *did* care. He did.

"I'll see you at six. And I'll get a video on the way—a comedy all right? What about *Notting Hill?* Have you seen it?"

"No, I never did," Cecilia said. "And I'd love to."

This latest recipe Charlotte had picked up—chocolate-chip pecan pie—was the best. She'd got it at the funeral for her next-door neighbor's elderly father. There'd been a good turnout, but that wasn't surprising since Herbert had lived in Cedar Cove for eighty-one years. The pie would make a perfect Easter dinner dessert. She'd bake her usual coconut cake, too. Her family would demand that, although she was certain Olivia and Justine didn't really understand how much work went into that darn cake.

Charlotte believed in doing things the old-fashioned way. She wouldn't use a cake mix if her life depended on it. Oh no, she baked from scratch, just like her mother had. And her grandmother. The coconut cake took three days and started with fresh coconut, but the result was worth all the effort. Tradition had a strong hold on her.

Thursday morning, as was her habit, she went to the Senior Center and visited with her knitting group. Her dearest friends sat around the large table, each working on her current project. Some knitted for their grandchildren, and others worked on projects for foster children or for charity. There was nothing more comforting than a sweater or blanket created with loving hands and a loving heart.

"Hello, Charlotte," Evelyn greeted her. She was almost finished with the afghan she was knitting for her daughter. The pattern was a lovely one and it had already been completed by several others in the group.

"Have you seen Jack Griffin lately?" Evelyn asked. Despite reassurances, she continued to have her suspicions regarding *The Chronicle's* editor. Evelyn was like that—especially after she'd learned how to log on to the Internet. She had doubts about practically everyone, and for the most part Charlotte chose to overlook her friend's lack of faith in others.

"Yesterday afternoon," Charlotte said conversationally. She'd been putting in a lot of extra hours on the Seniors' Page and was pleased with her efforts. Jack had liked her ideas and suggested she write a weekly column for the paper. At first Charlotte had balked. She wasn't much of a writer, and she hadn't thought she'd find enough news or ideas to fill a weekly column. But Jack had such confidence in her she'd decided to give it a try. Her first column had appeared on the Seniors' Page the week before and had included a recipe, some local history and a few recommendations, gleaned from Olivia's friend Grace, of new books available from the library.

"I tried your recipe," Helen told her, needles flying. She was working on a sweater for her fifteen-year-old granddaughter.

"The cheddar biscuits?" When it came to recipes, Charlotte was already three months ahead. Never lacking for new ones, she'd found it difficult to decide which to print first. "Oh, ladies, just wait until I tell you about the chocolate-chip pecan pie I tasted this week."

"Herbert Monk's funeral?" Bess asked.

"I heard about it," Helen said. "Word spreads when something really good is served at one of the wakes."

"All I ask is that someone make that broccoli lasagna for my wake," Evelyn tossed in. "Then everyone will know I've died and gone to heaven."

Charlotte chuckled.

"How's your friend Tom?" Helen put in.

Charlotte was beginning to feel guilty about Tom Harding. "I haven't seen him all week," she confessed. She'd been so busy working on the Seniors' Page, she hadn't gone to the convalescent center.

On her last visit, Tom had been rather subdued. She'd attempted to lighten his spirits, without success, although he sat and listened and occasionally responded. As always, Charlotte had chatted about all kinds of things. She told him she had his key in a safe place and he seemed reassured by that.

"I don't think he's doing well," Laura said.

Laura was a woman in the know. With seven children living in the community, she knew more about what was happening in Cedar Cove than the mayor.

"Really?" Charlotte hoped it wasn't serious. If so, she supposed Janet Lester would have called her.

"You might want to check on him yourself."

"I intend to do that this very afternoon," Charlotte said, a bit annoyed that Laura had been the one to tell her about her friend. Really, though, Charlotte had no one to blame but herself. It was just that she'd been so busy lately.

She stayed for an hour, visiting and knitting, then packed up her needles and headed for the convalescent center. Not bothering to stop at Janet's office, she went straight to Tom's room.

She'd learned from Janet that Tom had originally chosen Cedar Cove. He'd never indicated why. The storage unit remained a mystery. He hadn't explained that, and when she'd attempted to ask him about it, he'd pretended to fall asleep.

She'd brought her latest column to read aloud, plus a slice of the pecan pie she'd saved just for him. This would, she hoped, suffice as an apology for her lack of attention these last two weeks.

To her surprise, Charlotte found Tom's room empty. There'd been talk about getting him into physical therapy and she suspected that was where he'd been taken.

Anxious about Tom's condition, she hurried toward Janet's office. Charlotte knocked politely at the half-open door.

"Charlotte." Janet immediately stood, averting her gaze. "I should've phoned you earlier."

"You certainly should have." It was an embarrassment to find out from one of her friends that Tom wasn't doing well.

"I do apologize."

"Tell me what happened."

"We believe it was another stroke."

Charlotte gasped. Poor, poor Tom. Another stroke would certainly compound his health problems.

"How bad was it?"

"Bad?" Janet asked, sitting back down. "You don't know," she said slowly.

Charlotte shook her head, but she was beginning to get the feeling that this was worse than she'd imagined. Pulling out a chair, she sat down, too.

"Tom died late last night."

"Died?" It shouldn't come as a shock, considering his age and his poor health. Nevertheless, Charlotte felt she'd lost a good friend. "I…didn't realize. I didn't…" At this stage of her life, death was a common occurrence. She'd buried her husband years earlier, and every day, it seemed, there was an obituary for someone she knew. Still, the death of this man hit her hard.

"Are you all right?" Janet asked.

"Of course," Charlotte insisted, but she wasn't. Her hands trembled and she felt chilled.

"I know he appreciated your friendship."

Charlotte nodded, scrabbling inside her purse for a handkerchief to dab her eyes.

"Your visits meant the world to him."

"It's been two weeks—I should've been here."

"Charlotte, you couldn't possibly have known," Janet said gently.

Charlotte knew that was true, but she couldn't squelch the feeling that she'd let Tom Harding down. Before her work with the newspaper, she'd stopped by at least once a week. Tom had been the first person to hear her initial column. She'd read it to him herself and he'd smiled and approved of her efforts. Jack Griffin, on the other hand, had taken his sharp red pencil to her work and cut away at it until she'd barely recognized it as her own. Granted, she knew she wasn't an experienced writer, certainly not a professional, but it had wounded her pride. When she'd complained to Tom, he'd given her a sympathetic look, which was just what she'd needed.

That was the last time she'd seen him.

Janet reached for her phone and called down to the kitchen for tea. Five minutes later, one of the staff carried a tray into the office.

"He was a special man," Charlotte said, grateful for the hot, comforting tea. It helped ease the lump in her throat.

"Yes, he was," Janet agreed.

"What should I do now?" Charlotte asked.

Janet stared at her blankly.

"With the key? Remember he gave me the key to that storage unit?"

Janet frowned. "I guess the state will want it. You'd better return it as soon as you can."

Nine

Jack Griffin was strongly attracted to Olivia Lockhart, and that wasn't a good sign. Oh, hell, maybe it was. Still, pursuing this attraction meant losing emotional independence, and he wasn't sure he liked that. He couldn't help it, though—he found himself making excuses to talk to her. To learn more about her.

After the fiasco of their first date, he hadn't made a point of asking her out again. Mostly, he was afraid she'd turn him down flat and, frankly, he wouldn't blame her. He didn't want to give her any opportunity to reject him. Instead, he made excuses to be around her.

Jack Griffin spent many more hours at the courthouse than his job required. Plus, he made sure he was in the Safeway store every Saturday morning on the off-chance that he might run into her again. He had two or three times, and they'd ended up having coffee. Damn, but he liked her. Judge Lockhart was down-to-earth, smart and sexy. What got him, what *really* got him, was that she didn't seem to know it.

Friday afternoon, on his way home, Jack stopped at the dry cleaner. He rushed from the parking lot through the pulsing rain, cursing the foul weather under his breath. The skies had been a depressing lead-gray all week, with intermittent showers. The only bright spot on the horizon—so to speak—was a story he was writing about the Annual Seagull Calling Contest, being held that night.

He raced into the dry cleaner and nearly collided with Olivia. The shock of seeing her destroyed any chance of being clever. Her name was all he could manage. "Olivia."

Her smile was infectious. "Don't look so surprised. I do get my clothes cleaned regularly, you know." Her purse sat open on the counter.

"Me, too." Now that was brilliant. He nearly rolled his eyes. With other women he was a witty conversationalist, but Olivia unnerved him.

Duck-Hwan Hyo, who'd come from Korea in the 1960s, owned the dry cleaning shop. Jack had written an article about Duck-Hwan soon after he'd started as editor, impressed by the hardworking immigrant family. As soon as Duck-Hwan saw Jack, he rushed to give him the fastest possible service, in the process ignoring Olivia.

Jack felt he should explain.

"Don't worry," she assured him, "I'm in no hurry."

Friday night and in no hurry. Jack reached for his wallet and paid his bill, the whole time wondering if Olivia's response was her way of telling him she didn't have any plans for the evening. It almost seemed she was *hinting* that he should ask her out. Could that really be the case?

With the hanger for his dry cleaning hooked around his index finger, he waited for Olivia.

"You mean you're not going to the high-school theater?" Jack had figured that a good portion of the town would be turning up for the event.

"The Seagull Calling Contest is tonight?"

Before he could stop himself, he asked, "Would you like to go? With me?" He clarified his question so she wouldn't just assume he had an extra ticket he was willing to pass along.

"Sure," she said, agreeing instantly.

Jack was tempted to ask if she was sure, especially after their last date, then decided not to sabotage his good luck. "Great," he said. "That's terrific."

"I've waited a long time for you to ask me out again," Olivia said casually, walking toward the door. "What time should I be ready?"

She was joking, she had to be, but rather than leap up and click his heels in sheer jubilation, Jack merely checked his watch. "Is an hour too soon?"

"It's perfect."

Since he'd been lucky once, he was willing to try for twice. "How about dinner afterward?"

"The Taco Shack?"

He could see she was teasing him, but he let it pass. "If you want. Otherwise I suggest D.D.'s on the Cove or The Captain's Galley."

"Hey, I'm coming up in the world," she said with a laugh. "I'll let you decide."

What Olivia didn't know, because he didn't quite have the guts to tell her, was that dinner at local restaurants, including the more upscale places, was in exchange for advertising. The newspaper often traded advertising space for a restaurant credit; being able to take advantage of that was one of the perks that came with his job. The Taco Shack, for instance, owed the newspaper several hundred dollars and there were only so many tacos Jack could eat all by himself.

They parted outside the dry cleaner, and Jack hurried to his old Taurus, his step lighter than it'd been in months. Years.

Forty-five minutes later, he'd showered, changed clothes, cleaned out his car and was driving to Olivia's. She was ready, dressed in jeans and a hand-knit sweater and didn't bother with an umbrella. This was something he'd noticed living in the Pacific Northwest. Few people carried umbrellas. Anyone who did was automatically tagged as a tourist.

By the time they arrived at the high-school auditorium, the place was packed. Because he was with the newspaper, a pair of front-row seats had been saved for him.

No sooner had they settled down than Roy and Corrie McAfee walked over. Jack knew the couple from an article he'd written earlier in the year. Roy was a retired Seattle policeman who'd started his own detective agency; his background and experience made him a much sought-after private investigator. His wife ran the office and worked as his assistant. Roy and Jack had hit it off and gotten together a couple of times after that. Roy was an ardent hiker and Jack, who'd never been much of an outdoorsman, wanted to give it a try.

Roy reacted immediately to the fact that Olivia was with Jack.

"Hey, Judge, what are you doing with the likes of Griffin?" he teased her.

"Having a great time. Hello, Roy. Corrie."

Corrie took the empty seat beside Olivia, and Roy claimed the single one next to Jack. Before long, the two women were involved in a discussion of some sort, and Roy was talking to Jack about state politics. This wasn't exactly how Jack had pictured the evening, but on second thought it took the pressure off him to be a brilliant conversationalist.

Just as Mayor Benson walked onto the stage, Olivia leaned toward Jack and whispered, "Is it okay if Roy and Corrie join us for dinner?"

Jack hesitated. "Is it okay with you?"

"I don't mind if you don't."

Apparently she didn't, because she leaned close to her friend and he watched Corrie nod.

As he suspected, the evening's competition was entertaining. Jack learned that it had begun as a way to bring some laughter to a wet, gray spring. The contest had been going for a number of years. The rules were simple: Young and old did their utmost to sound like the cantankerous seagulls that populated Cedar Cove. Jack laughed, shouted, cheered and booed with the rest of the audience.

The winner, a fourteen-year-old boy, astonished everyone with his mimicry and won easily. Jack and Olivia walked close together as they filed out of the auditorium. He placed his hand protectively on her back—and wished he had the nerve to do more, to take her arm in his.

They met Roy and Corrie at The Captain's Galley a few minutes later. A sober-faced young woman who looked somewhat familiar led them to their table and gave them menus. Almost by rote, she wished them an enjoyable meal and departed.

"Who's that?" Jack asked.

Olivia's eyes widened; she was signaling that she couldn't discuss this. Not until later did it hit him. Their hostess was the woman who'd been in court the first day he'd seen Olivia. The woman she'd prevented from filing for divorce. He'd written about her—she was the Divorce Denied wife.

"How about a bottle of wine?" Roy suggested.

Everyone seemed to be in agreement. Jack studied his menu and let Roy do the ordering. When the waitress arrived with the wineglasses, he declined.

"Just one glass," Roy protested.

"No, thanks." He didn't drink and he didn't make excuses.

The restaurant had an excellent reputation, and Jack's meal certainly lived up to it. He ordered the fried oysters and Olivia had seafood fettuccine. After a congenial dinner, Roy and Corrie headed home while Jack and Olivia stayed for a second coffee.

The young hostess wandered past their table and Olivia glanced at Jack. "You recognize her now, don't you?"

He nodded, feeling a surge of sympathy for the woman, who seemed barely out of her teens. He'd sat in court and listened to a tragic yet all-too-common story. A story he knew well, about a marriage that couldn't weather a true crisis. A couple separated by grief. He didn't know what had happened since that day in court or whether they'd gone ahead with the proceedings. What he could see, just by looking at her, was that Cecilia Randall was very unhappy.

"Do you think she recognized you?" Jack asked.

Olivia shook her head. Jack didn't think she had, either.

"It makes me wonder," Olivia murmured.

Jack could tell she was upset. "You think you made the wrong decision?"

Olivia shrugged and stared down at her coffee. "The poor girl looks like she's got the weight of the world on her shoulders."

"Maybe she just had a bad night," he said.

"Maybe," Olivia echoed, but Jack could tell she didn't believe that and neither did he.

When Seth Gunderson left for Alaska in the first week of April, Justine was relieved. It was better this way. She thought about him far too often, treasured every minute they'd spent together. She didn't want to become involved with Seth. Didn't want to care about him, and most certainly didn't want to fall in love with him, but that was exactly what was happening—had already happened.

After their impromptu dinner date, she'd refused his next invitation. She knew trouble when she saw it, and was well aware of her own weakness. He wanted her and she, God help her, wanted him. But Justine was too smart to give in to those yearnings. She wasn't a woman ruled by emotions.

Seth, however, wasn't a man easily dismissed. He opened an account at First National Bank, and found an excuse to come in at least once a week. He didn't pressure her, didn't argue with her, didn't do anything out of the ordinary; he was just *there*. And one day she simply couldn't stand it anymore.

She followed him outside. "Why are you doing this?" she demanded, standing in the parking lot, the sun burning off a thick fog, threatening to break through at any moment. Justine felt like weeping, but she was too damned angry to let him know how much he'd disturbed her.

Seth didn't deny his intentions, but he met her anger with a gentleness that nearly broke her heart.

"If you want me to stop, I will," was all he said.

"Stop!" she cried, and marched back into the bank. A week later, after seven sleepless nights, she went in search of him. Not knowing exactly where to find him, she walked down to the marina.

He appeared almost immediately, meeting her out on the pier, wearing his heavy wool jacket, a knit cap on his head. She stood with her back against the railing, and Seth smiled and wordlessly pressed his warm hand to her cold cheek.

Justine resisted the urge to close her eyes and lean into his hand. "I'm here to tell you that Warren Saget is the perfect man for me," she said.

"No, he's not."

Justine wanted to stamp her foot the way a child does. She wasn't sure why she'd come—to assuage her longing to see him? To end this once and for all? But now that she was here, she knew it was a mistake.

"Warren is older, mature and wealthy, and you're none of those things."

"No, I'm not," he agreed.

She hated it that he so willingly accepted her arguments. It made everything ten times worse. "Warren's a respected businessman."

"And I'm a fisherman."

"Exactly," she cried, more angry with herself than with Seth.

"But it's me you want," he said simply.

Refusing to answer him, she'd vaulted from the dock and run back to work. She hadn't seen him since. The only reason she knew he'd left for Alaska was that she'd heard someone at the bank mention it earlier in the week.

Friday afternoon Warren phoned her at work. "How about dinner?" He sounded sure of himself, sure of her answer.

"Not tonight, Warren."

There was a short, uncomfortable silence. "Why not?"

"I'm not feeling well." Which was a slight exaggeration. She did have a headache, but nothing a couple of aspirin and a few minutes with her eyes closed wouldn't cure.

He didn't like it when Justine turned him down. Warren was a man accustomed to getting his own way. "You're still mad about that class reunion, aren't you?"

"Not particularly." As of this moment, Justine decided not to go. Seth might be there, and he made her weak in ways she didn't want to consider. One kiss had ruined her. One stupid kiss. Now, every time Warren attempted to touch her, she ran in the opposite direction. Seth Gunderson had a great deal to answer for.

"I have a killer headache," she told him, exaggerating in order to avoid another confrontation.

"Is there anything I can get you?" he asked, his voice soft, conciliatory.

"No. Have dinner without me and I'll talk to you soon."

"All right, sweetheart. You take care of yourself."

"I will." Justine intended on doing exactly that. After work, she headed straight to her apartment with a quart of her favorite gourmet ice cream and two rented videos.

When the doorbell rang and a deliveryman stood there with a huge arrangement of flowers, her first thought was that they were from Seth. Then she read Warren's name on the tag and started to cry for no discernible reason.

She dumped the flowers in the sink. Dressed in her oldest flannel pajamas, she sat cross-legged in front of her television, eating straight out of the ice cream carton.

Her doorbell ran again. Justine was in no mood for company. Stabbing her spoon into the ice cream, she shouted, "Go away! I'm busy."

Whoever was on the other side refused to take no for an answer. Angry now, she set the ice cream aside and got awkwardly to her feet. Drunk on her misery, she staggered to the front door and defiantly threw it open.

Seth Gunderson stood on the other side.

Justine took one startled look at him and gasped. "Justine?"

What an atrocious sight she must be. "This is your fault!" she raged. Then, throwing open the screen door, she grabbed him by the lapels with both hands and jerked him over the threshold. He stumbled into the apartment but she didn't give him time to speak before she hurled herself into his arms. Taken off guard, Seth lurched backward and nearly lost his balance before sliding his arms around her waist, locking her in his embrace.

Their kisses were full of passion and frenzy. Her lips were cold with ice cream; his were hot with longing. He was dressed for the outdoors; Justine was nude beneath the thin flannel pajamas. Her hands roved over his body; his hands pressed her close to his heart.

Struggling against him, Justine unfastened the big round buttons of his jacket and with clumsy movements peeled it from his arms. His shirt was next, but the buttons were more stubborn this time and she struggled, impatient and so damn hot she felt she was going to burst into flames if he didn't hurry and take her to bed. Her entire body pulsed with need. She wanted him as she'd never wanted another man in her life.

"Justine, no." Seth held her at arm's length, his chest heaving with the effort to break off their frantic kisses.

"No?" she cried in outrage. He'd created this wild fire that burned inside her, and he could damn well quench the flames.

"Not like this, when neither of us knows what we're doing."

"I know *exactly* what I'm doing," she challenged, her fists digging into her hips. "Are you rejecting me?" She noticed that her stance gave him a peek at her breasts and did nothing to shore up the gap in her pajama top.

Seth walked over to the sofa and sank wearily into

the cushions while Justine fought to hold on to her shredded dignity. She put on a brave front, but she already knew she'd done everything humanly possible to make a fool of herself.

"It would be the easiest thing in the world to haul you into that bedroom and spend the next two days making love to you," Seth told her in a low voice.

Her knees went weak, and she was almost—*almost*—reduced to begging.

"But I won't," he said, "because I love you. I've loved you from the time we were kids and I will not give either one of us an excuse to screw this up."

Her bravado was slipping fast. "Why are you here?"

"I couldn't stay away."

"You don't seem to be having that problem at the moment," she muttered.

Seth chuckled and said something under his breath that she didn't catch.

"What did you say?" she demanded, afraid he was secretly laughing at her.

He smiled faintly. "Trust me, you don't want to know."

She did, but she wouldn't press the issue.

He heaved in a deep sigh and held her look, his eyes a brilliant blue. "So you've missed me?"

"Yes, damn you."

He looked far too pleased by her confession. "I've missed you, too."

She glanced away rather than meet his gaze.

"Are you still seeing Warren Saget?"

Justine was grateful he couldn't see her eyes. "Sometimes."

Her response seemed to give him the incentive he sought. Seth stood up and scooped his jacket from the floor. "Let me know when you're not."

"What's that supposed to mean?" She refused to be Seth's exclusive property, just as she'd never belong to Warren. "I'll see him any time I please."

"I know."

The least he could do was argue with her instead of being so…so agreeable.

"I've told you before—Warren's not right for you," he said mildly.

"And you are?"

He nodded matter-of-factly. "Yes."

Justine had heard enough and apparently Seth felt he'd said everything she needed to hear. He walked over to the door and opened it. "Let me know when you've broken it off with Warren, all right?"

"You'll have a long wait," she tossed out, furious with him and unwilling to make the slightest concession, to give the slightest bit of hope. And yet, she couldn't have. It was over with Warren, and Justine knew it despite her words to the contrary.

"If you've learned anything about me at all, you should realize I'm a patient man." And with that, he left.

Although Justine was convinced Seth had stayed in town, she didn't hear from him the rest of the weekend. Then on Sunday night, he phoned.

"Where are you?" she asked, so grateful to hear his voice that she forgot to pretend she was angry.

"Alaska."

"You couldn't have called me while you were still in town?"

"No," he said, his voice husky and tired. "That would've been too easy."

"Do you always do things the hard way?"

"Good God, I hope not," he muttered.

"I suppose I should thank you," she whispered, keeping her eyes shut and cradling the phone against her ear as she dropped onto a kitchen chair. Seth had prevented her from making an even bigger mistake than just throwing herself at him.

"Don't," he said, his voice suddenly gruff. "I've kicked myself all the way back here. Next time I won't be so damned noble."

"Next time," Justine said softly, "I won't give you the chance."

Grace carried two heavy bags of groceries into the house and set them on the kitchen counter. It was Monday afternoon, after a relatively good weekend. She never knew what to expect from Dan anymore. Some days he was down and some days he was up. Recently, though, his moods seemed to be on a more even keel.

Kelly and her husband had been to the house for dinner on Sunday and it'd been a wonderful visit. The news of their daughter's pregnancy had brightened their lives. Grace longed for this baby; whatever was lacking in her marriage, she hoped to find in grandchildren.

The house was dark and still. She expected Dan home at any time. She'd taken off an hour early for a doctor's appointment that had lasted only a couple of minutes.

Grateful for this chance to organize her kitchen,

Grace started unloading the bags, then suddenly paused. Something wasn't right. She *felt* it. A sixth sense, a premonition, she wasn't sure which. Listening, she cocked her head to one side. Her first inclination had been to dismiss the feeling, but it refused to go away.

Drawing in a stabilizing breath, she walked into the bedroom, and stopped abruptly. The dresser drawers hung open; their contents dangled over the edge and spilled about the room. Her first thought was that an intruder had been in the house, but a quick inventory said otherwise. Strangely, nothing valuable appeared to be missing. Her jewelry was out in plain sight.

Moving into the living room, Grace threw herself into a chair and closed her eyes.

Dan wasn't coming home.

Again he'd taken nothing with him—only the clothes on his back. He'd abandoned everything else. His clothes, his personal possessions, his marriage and family.

She couldn't say how she knew, but she felt it with a certainty that was inexplicable.

She didn't contact Troy Davis or even Olivia; she wouldn't tell anyone until at least a few days had passed. Her husband had been furious with her the last time. He'd pulled this horrible stunt, worried her to the point of physical illness and then been outraged that she'd called the police. Dan had said she'd embarrassed him. Not once had he taken into account what he'd put *her* through. Two days of bitter, sullen silence had passed before they could speak to each other again. Now this.

Grace was right—Dan didn't come home after work, nor did he show up that night. Despite a determined effort, she didn't sleep. Her mind played tricks on her until, too exhausted to do anything else, she drifted off an hour before the alarm buzzed. She was tempted to call in sick, but decided against that. Staying home, pacing and worrying about where her husband might be or with whom, wasn't going to help.

Tuesday afternoon, she walked hopefully into the house and found it cold and silent. Dan wasn't back. The phone rang and she nearly tore it off the wall in her eagerness to answer.

"Mom, I just want to thank you and Dad for having Paul and me over for dinner."

"It was our pleasure," Grace said, doing her best to hide her fears.

"Daddy was in a good mood."

"Yes, he was." Grace closed her eyes in an effort to concentrate on the conversation.

"Mom," her daughter said cautiously, "is everything all right?"

"Of course…I think so," she corrected.

The line went silent, then, "What does *that* mean?"

Because she didn't know where else to turn, Grace told her daughter. "I haven't seen your father in nearly two days."

"You haven't seen Dad? But where is he?" Kelly asked, anxiety sharpening her voice.

"I…don't know."

"Shouldn't you call someone?"

"I phoned the police the first time and learned that—"

"This has happened before?" Kelly cried. "Why didn't you tell me?"

Her daughter was upset with her, and that was the last thing Grace wanted. Not with Kelly pregnant. A risky pregnancy at that.

"I'm on my way over," Kelly said adamantly.

"Kelly, no, there's nothing you can do."

"Does Maryellen know?"

Grace released a shuddering sigh. "I...I haven't told anyone."

"I'm coming over," her daughter insisted, and then slammed down the phone.

Twenty minutes later, both Maryellen and Kelly arrived. They stormed into the house like avenging angels.

"What happened?" Maryellen demanded. The two girls gathered around the very table where they'd sat as children.

Grace told them everything she could remember.

"Where would Daddy go?"

Grace forced herself to look away. Although she didn't want to admit the possibility, she had to let them know her thoughts. "I think there might be another woman."

Both of her daughters vehemently rejected that idea.

"No," Maryellen said first.

"Not Daddy," Kelly chimed in. "How can you even suggest such a thing?"

Dan had denied it, too. But he'd been so emotionally detached from her lately, so remote and moody. Another woman was the only plausible excuse that would explain his behavior.

"I don't believe that," Maryellen insisted.

"Then where is he?" she cried.

Neither of her daughters answered.

"Think," Kelly urged.

"What could Daddy have been looking for?" Maryellen asked. "You said it seemed like he was searching for something before he left."

"But he didn't take anything." Grace had carefully folded all his clothes and placed them back inside the drawers. Apparently he'd found whatever he'd been seeking with such impatience, although she couldn't find a single thing missing.

"He's coming back," Kelly said. "Otherwise he would've packed a suitcase."

"Of course he's coming back," Maryellen agreed, as though it was a foregone conclusion.

"I'm sure he will," Grace said. He had the first time, hadn't he? That gave her hope, although her heart told her something else.

They were all silent after that. There seemed nothing left to say. Grace reached for her daughters' hands and squeezed them, hoping to offer reassurance when she had damn little to give.

"What are we going to do next?" Maryellen, the no-nonsense one, was determined to take some kind of action. Grace didn't know how to advise her. Maryellen was the daughter of her heart. She didn't favor one girl over the other, but her oldest child was most like her. Maryellen had married young and unwisely, and, after one year, divorced. Now in her mid-thirties, she didn't seem likely to repeat the experience. Grace had wanted a different life for her, but Maryellen, who managed a local art gallery, seemed content, and that was all that mattered.

"We should inform the police," Kelly said.

Grace explained what she'd learned earlier. It wasn't against the law to disappear.

"We have to let the authorities know, anyway," Maryellen muttered.

"We can have posters printed up, too," Kelly suggested. She stood and started pacing.

"No." Grace adamantly opposed that idea. If Dan was coming back, and she suspected that eventually he would, he'd be furious if she allowed his face to be posted around town. "Your father wouldn't want that."

"Too bad. Then he shouldn't have left."

"I'd prefer to wait." Grace pleaded for time.

"How long?"

"One more day is all I'm willing to give him," Maryellen said, narrowing her eyes.

"If your father hasn't returned in another day or two, we should probably contact the authorities," Grace announced, knotting a tissue in her hand. "Other than that, I don't feel there's anything we can do. Your father has chosen to leave. He went of his own free will—"

"We don't know that," Kelly protested.

"It happened before," Grace reasoned. "He returned when he was ready."

"And he will again."

She nodded. "We'll just have to wait." Hard as it was, she couldn't see doing anything else.

"I don't know where Dad is, but I'm positive that he'd never leave you for another woman," Maryellen said softly.

Grace hugged her daughters and reluctantly let them go. She stood on the porch, both arms wrapped around her as they drove off to their respective homes. She was alone now, totally and completely alone.

Her daughters refused to believe that Dan had found another woman, but she'd suspected it for a very long time. She didn't want to believe it, either, but couldn't think of anything else to explain his disappearances.

Olivia knew the minute they met for their aerobics class that Wednesday. Grace didn't need to utter a word.

"Dan?"

Grace nodded as they walked toward the gym.

"When?"

"The last time I saw him was Monday morning."

"No word since?"

"None."

Olivia exhaled. "Are you all right?"

Grace bit her lower lip. "Do I have a choice?" Dan was determined to punish her for a list of sins she didn't even know she'd committed. The last laugh, however, would be hers. Grace had no intention of continuing this charade of a marriage.

Dan's latest disappearing act was the end. She was getting out. Dan might well return, and when he did, she'd have him served with divorce papers.

This was the end.

Ten

Cecilia had never been prouder of anything. The test paper had a huge A scrawled on the front and Mr. Cavanaugh, her algebra professor, had written *Well Done!* in bright red pen across one corner. She'd aced the test. After class Mr. Cavanaugh, who had to be in his late fifties, asked if she'd talked to a counselor about her next quarter's classes. She told him she hadn't and he suggested she take more math courses, since she showed aptitude in that area.

Cecilia had been giddy with joy ever since. The first person she thought to tell was her father, who spent most of his time at The Captain's Galley, on one side of the bar or the other. She'd see him soon enough, she decided. Cathy Lackey came to mind next, but it might sound as though she was bragging and Cecilia didn't want that. Feeling slightly deflated, she headed home, picking up her mail in the lobby.

She automatically tossed the envelopes down on the kitchen table and shrugged off her backpack. That was when she saw Ian's letter. Funny how a little thing like a letter could throw her for a loop. Cecilia stared at it a full thirty seconds before she reached for it and carefully tore it open.

April 12th
Dear Cecilia,
     Andrew got a letter from Cathy this week and she wrote that the two of you recently got together. I assume you have the car by now and hope you aren't too stubborn to drive it.

Ian Randall was a fine one to talk, Cecilia mused. Her husband was more stubborn than any man she'd ever met. But since she'd been driving his car for nearly a month, she couldn't very well complain.

     I realize you're probably upset with me over the way I acted when you came to see me at the hospital. I don't blame you. My only excuse is that I was in a lot of pain. I was mad as hell about being so stupid. It was my own carelessness that caused the accident. Andrew should never have told you; it wasn't necessary for you to know.

Cecilia disagreed. She was his wife and he'd been hurt. She was grateful Andrew had called her.

     We've had our differences the last few months, but after our "date," I had real hope we might look past all that. Then I had to go and blow everything. I'm genuinely sorry, Cecilia.

It damn well took him long enough to apologize! Nor did it escape her notice that he hadn't mentioned the lovemaking. If he was willing to ignore it, then so was she!

> I know you don't have a computer, but I'm including my e-mail address at the end of the letter in case you find a way of contacting me. Hearing from you would mean a great deal.
> Andrew said you and Cathy have become friends and started connecting with some of the other Navy wives. I'm glad. The Navy isn't so bad, you know. There are a lot of good people here.

Cecilia regretted rejecting those potential friends earlier.

> Tell me about school—if you write me back that is. I'll bet you're at the top of the class.
>   Love,
>   Ian
> Randall-Ian-M HT2 <iran-dall@bridge.navy.mil>
> P.S. About that night…is everything all right? You know what I mean.

He was asking if she'd gotten pregnant. He *should* be concerned. They'd been stupid and this wasn't the first time, but she swore it would be the last.

Cecilia read the letter through again. Her overwhelming reaction was pleasure. It wasn't a long letter, but she knew Ian had agonized over every word. The apology had been hard for him. Well, she deserved one. She was gratified that he'd asked about school; it was almost as though he *knew* she'd gotten the A on her final.

Cecilia left for work a few minutes early that afternoon and drove to the library. Fortunately, one of the computers was free. Cecilia slipped into the seat and logged on to the Internet. Her message was brief and to the point, because she didn't have a lot of time and because she wasn't entirely sure it would go through, anyway.

April 16th
Dear Ian,
        Your letter arrived this afternoon. Apology accepted. I miss you.

                                        Cecilia

P.S. Rest assured all is well.

Curiosity got the better of her the following day, and she returned to the library and was thrilled to find an e-mail waiting for her from Ian.

April 17th
Dearest Cecilia,
        I was really happy to hear from you. What did you mean, you miss me? Is it true? I don't care if it is or isn't, I'm taking it at face value. Andrew and Cathy e-mail each other nearly every day and she wrote about inviting you to the "girls' night out." I'm glad you're making friends.
        Life on an aircraft carrier is a whole lot dif-

ferent than a submarine. I didn't know if I was
going to like it, but it's all right, I guess.

Love,
Ian

P.S. Is all really well?

April 18th
Dear Ian,

My final grades are posted for the Algebra
and English classes and I got a 4.0 in both. I'm
so THRILLED! Mr. Cavanaugh suggested I
take an advanced Algebra class, and I am. I'm
still working weekends, filling in as a cocktail
waitress and am putting aside my tip money for
school.

I know you got the transfer to the *George
Washington* because of Allison, and because of
me. I appreciate what you did, but Ian, it was
too late. If you want to transfer back to the
submarine, then that's what you should do.

I have to hurry to work. Sorry, I wish this
could be longer. I will write you a real letter
soon, I promise. School starts up again in two
weeks.

Think of me.

Cecilia

April 19th
Dear Cecilia,

You asked me to think of you—that was a
joke, right? I think of you all the time. You're my
wife, no matter what the attorney tries to tell me.

Are we still getting the divorce? God, I hope not. I never wanted it. You know how I feel about that whole issue. Sorry, I didn't mean to harp at you about that. I'll live with whatever you decide.

You said something about me transferring from the *Atlantis,* and why I did it. This might come as a shock, but I didn't do it for you. Not entirely. I did it for me, too. When we were deployed that last time before Allison was born, you and I never suspected you'd have the baby while I was away. Neither of us had the slightest warning of what would happen. When I returned, our daughter had already been buried. You were hurting so badly, and I realize now that I wasn't much help to you, mainly because I was dealing with my own pain. I guess I really didn't know *how* to help. You hated the Navy, and I felt as though you hated me, too. It wasn't a good time for either of us. I never told you—perhaps if I had, we might not have gone down the path we did—but after my last tour on the *Atlantis,* I tried to get out of the Navy. My baby was dead and my marriage was falling apart and I was about as low as I've ever been in my life. I'm not blaming you, I swear it. My CO talked to me and arranged a transfer to the *George Washington.* The paperwork said it was for psychological reasons.

Congratulations on your classes! I'm proud of you. We'll celebrate when I'm back home. It's less than five months now. That seems like a lifetime, but the weeks will go fast. I love you and that's not going to change.

Ian

P.S. Don't freak out over me telling you how I feel. I haven't mentioned my feelings for you in a long time, because it didn't seem you wanted to hear. You still might not, but I'm hoping you do.

April 22nd
Dear Ian,

I had to wait until the library opened to e-mail you back—that's why the long delay. Cathy told me there are places I can go other than the library and after having to wait all weekend to contact you, I'm going to do it. I was so frustrated! Other than that, I had a good weekend.

I had my best tip night ever on Saturday. I know you don't like me working the bar. I don't much care for it myself, but it's the only way I have of getting ahead financially. The tips are decent and Bobby's around, so I don't have to put up with harrassment from customers. Believe it or not, he's keeping an eye on me. He even threatened to throw a guy out last week! Hardly seemed like my peace-loving father.

That's my little confession—I wanted to tell you about staying on at the bar after you explained about the transfer from the *Atlantis* to the *George Washington*. You're right. It would have helped if we'd communicated.

I know you love me, Ian. Through everything, I've always known how you felt, but sometimes loving someone just isn't enough. You asked about the divorce. I don't know how I feel about it anymore, but at the same time I don't know if I want to stay married, either. One thing I'm sure of—I don't ever want another child. This latest scare made that very clear to me. I can't believe we took such a risk again. The most profound lesson I came away with, after Allison, is that I was never meant to be a mother.

You deserve to be a father.

Considering that, you might not want to talk to me again. The choice is yours.

Always,
Cecilia

Charlotte Jefferson waited patiently until her daughter was finished with court for the day. Twenty minutes after the last case was heard, she knocked on her chambers door.

"Come in." Olivia sounded distracted, which meant she was probably reading briefs and preparing for her next session.

Charlotte turned the knob and peeked inside. Coming to her daughter with her own needs was not an easy thing to do. Olivia was a busy professional, and Charlotte tried very hard not to be a hindrance to her children.

"Mom." Frowning, Olivia stood up behind her desk. "What's wrong?"

Charlotte had hoped to disguise her tears. She'd been feeling depressed—that was the only word for it—ever since she'd heard about Tom Harding's death.

He'd been gone for more than a month now, and it hadn't gotten any better and she didn't feel she could delay this task any longer. Janet had already asked about the key; Charlotte knew she'd have to return it soon. But she'd already let Tom down once and she couldn't do it again.

Dabbing at her eyes, Charlotte came into the room. Olivia walked from her desk and placed her arm around Charlotte's shoulders. "Sit down, Mom," she advised gently.

Charlotte complied.

"What is it?"

Blowing her nose, Charlotte took a moment to compose herself. "I need your help." She sniffled, hating the tears that streaked her face, yet unable to keep them at bay. This emotion was difficult to explain, considering how many of her friends she'd buried.

"Does this have to do with Tom Harding?" Olivia asked, taking her own seat.

Charlotte nodded and wiped her eyes again.

"You miss him, don't you?"

"I do, but, Olivia, it's more than just missing him. I feel I was a sorry disappointment to Tom. We'd gotten to be such good friends. I know you probably don't think that's possible, with him not being able to speak...."

"I don't have a single doubt that you meant a great deal to one another."

"There was nothing romantic between us." Charlotte wanted that understood. The one and only love of her life was Clyde Jefferson, the dear man who'd been her husband.

"You were friends," Olivia said. "Good friends."

"I'm sure that's what Tom believed, but I fear I failed him. I got so involved with my work on the newspaper that I let myself get distracted." What distressed her most was thinking of Tom waiting to see her, waiting and waiting, and her being so caught up with her fifteen seconds of fame that she hadn't bothered to visit him at their usual time…or any other. She'd been too full of her own importance to spare him a couple of hours. And now it was too late.

"Mom, I'm sure Tom understood," Olivia said with such compassion, Charlotte had to resist the urge to openly weep.

"I hope he did." She wadded the linen handkerchief in her hand. "There wasn't even a burial service. I never had a chance to say goodbye…."

"You said you needed my help?" Olivia reminded her.

For a moment, Charlotte had almost forgotten. "Oh yes, the key."

"That's right," Olivia said, sitting straighter in her chair. "Tom gave you a key, didn't he?"

"It's to a storage unit. I want you to go there with me, if you would."

Olivia hesitated. She took her role as a duly elected judge far too seriously, in Charlotte's opinion. She could see that her daughter was weighing the possibility of any conflict of interest. "Is it nearby?"

"Yes, right here in Cedar Cove. Apparently he's had it for some time." This had surprised her, since he was transferred to the convalescent center from Seattle. The poor man must've had some connection with the area, some reason for choosing Cedar Cove.

"When would you like to go?"

"Can you do it now?"

Olivia closed the files on her desk. "That should work out fine. Do you want me to drive or should we meet there?"

Charlotte wanted Olivia to drive. As emotional as she was about Tom, she wanted the company. Besides, she was finding it difficult to turn and look behind her when using Reverse. Lately she'd been parking in spaces that didn't require backing up. Looking over her shoulder caused cramping in her neck. If she mentioned it to Olivia, however, her daughter might suggest it was time to stop driving and Charlotte couldn't give up her independence.

Olivia drove out on the highway, along the waterfront. The storage unit was off Butterfield Road on the way into Belfair, across from the drive-in theater.

"Do we need to check in?" Olivia asked, stopping in front of the office.

"I don't know," Charlotte said. It didn't look as though anyone was there. "I have the key and the receipt."

"Then we'll go directly to the unit." Olivia pulled forward until they located the number written on the receipt.

"This must be it." Charlotte climbed out of the car, taking her time. She didn't move as quickly as she once did, nor did she move as gracefully as she would have liked. It was especially difficult getting in and out of cars.

Olivia was waiting for her. The unit looked much bigger than Charlotte had anticipated. Olivia took the key from her and inserted it in the lock. The door swung upward. Inside the darkened space was one large trunk surrounded by assorted furniture. A sofa and chair, a saddle and what seemed to be a painting of some sort, covered by a blanket.

The painting interested Olivia and she lifted the blanket. Charlotte glanced at it; when she saw that it was a movie poster of a 1940s cowboy film, she quickly dismissed it.

Then, almost against her will, her gaze swung back to the poster. The man, on a rearing stallion with lightning flashing in the background, looked vaguely familiar. He should, she realized when she read the name. Tom Houston was "The Yodeling Cowboy," one of the most popular of the trick riders and cowboy film stars of the era. Many a schoolgirl afternoon had been spent in the theater, watching the wild horseman dash across the screen.

"Tom Houston." Olivia read the name aloud. "Have you ever heard of him?"

"Of course. You mean to say you haven't?"

"Sorry, Mom," Olivia said and released the blanket. It floated down over the poster.

That old movie poster must be worth something these days. It was a collector's item, no doubt.

"Shall we open the trunk?" Olivia asked.

"Just a minute." A thought struck Charlotte and she returned her attention to the poster. Throwing back the blanket, she took a second look. When she did, her knees started to shake.

"Mom!" Olivia was at her side instantly. "What is it?"

Sitting on the edge of the old trunk, Charlotte pointed with one hand at the poster while the other covered her mouth. "This *can't* be."

"What?"

"That's Tom Harding!"

"Who? The man in the poster?"

Was her daughter dense? "Tom Harding is…was Tom Houston."

"Really?"

Olivia clearly didn't appreciate the significance of her discovery. Charlotte took a deep breath. "Tom Houston was as popular as Roy Rogers and Dale Evans. He was as well-known as Gene Autry in his time. Oh my, I can't believe my own eyes."

"He could be a relative of your Tom," Olivia suggested.

"No, it's him… Oh my, he really was Tom Houston! You used to watch his television show when you were a little girl," Charlotte informed her. "Don't you remember? On Saturday mornings…Tom had his own television series for a couple of years in the nineteen-fifties, and then he faded from the scene."

"Tom Houston," Olivia repeated softly as though tugging at childhood memories. She shook her head and then it seemed to come to her all at once. "Tom Houston," she cried. "*That* Tom Houston?"

Charlotte saw that Olivia was truly excited now. A moment later, though, she frowned. "Oh, Mom, this has to be some kind of joke."

"No, that's Tom. Oh, he was decades older when I met him, but it's the same man, I'm convinced of that."

"Should we open the trunk?" Olivia asked obviously a little hesitant.

"Yes." Charlotte was adamant about that now. "I'm hoping we'll find some evidence of family."

"I thought you said Tom didn't have any family."

"That the state knows of," Charlotte corrected. "Which doesn't mean there isn't any." Everyone had family.

Olivia had a bit of trouble undoing the lock, but the struggle was worth it once they were able to pry open the trunk. Inside was a virtual treasure trove of memorabilia.

"Oh, my," Charlotte whispered, staring at the contents. The first thing she noticed was Tom Houston's signature white outfit. The good guys always wore white, and Tom was very definitely a good guy. His guns were there, too, along with a number of old television scripts that appeared to be originals. She also saw World War II medals, and remembered that he'd served in the military.

"This stuff must be worth a fortune," Olivia said in awe.

Filled with purpose, Charlotte straightened. "*This* is why he wanted me to have the key."

Olivia glanced at her as if she didn't know what to say. "He never gave you a hint about who he was, did he?"

"Not even one. He obviously didn't want me to know while he was alive." Charlotte was beginning to understand. Tom must have sensed that he could trust her. He must have realized she would do whatever was necessary to get these things—this *legacy*—to the people who were entitled to it. She might have let him down earlier, but by heaven, she wouldn't again.

"Mom." Olivia apparently recognized this look.

"He's entrusted me with his most precious items for a reason."

Olivia frowned. "And what's that?"

Charlotte frowned back. "I'm going to track down his people and—"

"*What* people? Even if he's got family, where are they? Why was he a ward of the state?"

"I don't know. But Janet told me Tom was transferred to Cedar Cove at his own request—it was his original choice. My guess is he's got family in the area."

"If that's the case, then why didn't Tom contact them himself?"

"I don't know," Charlotte said again.

"My point exactly."

Charlotte didn't see it that way. "He trusted me," she said stubbornly. "Tom wanted me to make sure all of this is properly distributed."

"Mother—"

"Furthermore," she continued, cutting Olivia off, "he knew he could count on me." That, as far as she was concerned, said it all.

From this point forward, Charlotte was a woman on a mission. She'd figured out how to make up to Tom for neglecting him the last few weeks of his life. As a woman of honor, she swore she'd do everything within her power to find Tom Houston's family. She wouldn't give up, nor would she rest until his legacy was passed to those who had the right to own it.

On her way home from the library, Grace collected the day's mail. That used to be Dan's task because he generally arrived at the house before she did.

It was three weeks to the day since his disappearance. Three hellish weeks, in which she'd been confronted by all the unanswered questions, by doubts and guilt and mounting frustration.

The little everyday things distressed her. Taking out the garbage, bringing in the mail, fixing the leaky faucet in the bathroom. All the things Dan used to do. Her fear and resentment intensified with each task.

At first Dan's employer refused to believe he'd simply walked away from his life. Grace could hardly believe it herself, but all the evidence pointed toward the likelihood of exactly that. Dan was gone. No one had come up with any reason for it, any hows or whys. Grace had questioned Bob Bilderback, Dan's boss at the tree service, at least five times, certain that he had *some* clue—even if he didn't immediately recognize its significance. Bob was as bewildered as Grace.

Walking into the house, Grace quickly dispensed with the mail. Two bills went into a pile to join the others on Dan's old desk. Money was tight. Bob had mailed her Dan's last check made out to her. Frankly she was surprised Dan hadn't collected that when he left, but then he had his credit cards.

Credit cards.

Grace hadn't even thought to look at the VISA bill until now. She raced into Maryellen's old bedroom, which had been turned into a den, and shuffled through the stack of unpaid bills on the desk until she reached the VISA statement still tucked inside the envelope.

Her hand shook as she tore it open and quickly scanned the list of charges. They all seemed to be in order with the exception of one. When she saw where the card had been used, her legs gave out. Bracing her back against the wall, she sank to the floor.

How long she sat there, staring at nothing, Grace

couldn't guess. She finally gathered the courage to call Olivia.

"Can you come over?" she asked. Her voice, which sounded scratchy, must have conveyed her urgency.

"I'm on my way."

Less than ten minutes later, her friend was at the front door. "What is it?"

"The son of a bitch," Grace cried, so furious she could barely contain herself. "Look at this!" She thrust the VISA statement at Olivia.

Olivia glanced at it and raised questioning eyes to Grace. "What?"

"Berghoff Jewelers in Bremerton. I didn't buy myself any jewelry."

"Dan?"

"Who else?" Grace raged.

"What would Dan buy there for 250?"

"A little trinket for his girlfriend, no doubt," she snapped.

"Well, let's find out."

Olivia was always sensible. It hadn't even occurred to Grace to contact the store. She hadn't cancelled the credit card, either, which was a mistake she planned to rectify first thing in the morning.

While Grace paced the living room, Olivia found the phone number and dialed. When she'd finished, she handed the receiver to Grace.

Anger shot through her. "Hello," she said, doing her best to sound calm and reasonable. "My name is Grace Sherman and I have my credit card statement here in front of me." She went on to explain the charge. "They're looking up the receipt now," Grace said, covering the mouthpiece with her hand.

In thirty-five years of marriage Dan hadn't once bought her a piece of jewelry. He considered it frivolous. She wore a plain gold band—the same ring he'd placed on her finger the day of their wedding. Over the years, the band had worn thin and should have been replaced, but never was. Her husband didn't wear a wedding band at all, not after he got out of the military. Working with heavy equipment made it dangerous for a man to wear any sort of ring.

The woman from Berghoff's returned with the requested information. "Mrs. Sherman," she said.

"Yes." Grace was instantly alert.

"The VISA charge is for a ring."

"I beg your pardon?" This was as strange as everything else about her husband's disappearance.

"A ring. I'm sorry, but it doesn't say what type."

Grace felt as if the wind had been knocked out of her. "That's all right. Thank you for your trouble." Quickly she replaced the receiver, then collapsed into a chair.

"What?" Olivia was at her side.

Grace stared down at the thin gold band on her left hand. She'd suspected for a long time that there was another woman; now she had proof. "He bought a ring."

"A ring?" Olivia said. "But why?"

"Isn't it obvious?" Grace cried. "That's why he left me his last paycheck," she added.

"It was supposed to pay for the ring?" Olivia asked.

"Apparently so." This was just like Dan and his twisted sense of honor. He thought nothing of walking out on her, without a word of explanation, turning her life into a living hell. Yet he made sure the last charge on their VISA account, one that had apparently paid for another woman's ring, had been covered.

"The other day," Grace whispered, struggling to hold on to her inner strength, "I came home from work and had the oddest sense that Dan had been in the house."

"You changed the locks, didn't you?"

"No." Maryellen and Kelly had talked her out of that. Both of them were convinced their father would return soon and explain everything. In the beginning Grace had thought so, too, but no longer. She didn't *want* him back. But if Dan ever did return, she wanted the distinct pleasure of telling him to his face that she was divorcing him.

"You think Dan was in the house?" Olivia asked.

"I'm almost positive…."

"Something was missing?"

If so, Grace couldn't detect what it was, although she'd torn through every room, searching. She shook her head.

"Then how did you know?" Olivia persisted.

"I could smell him."

"*Smell* him?"

"Working with trees all day, he often came home smelling like a freshly cut Christmas tree. The scent was there, I swear it, Olivia."

"I don't doubt you."

"I didn't tell the girls. They're upset enough as it is."

Olivia sat across from her. "Have you thought about talking to Roy McAfee? He has an excellent reputation."

"A private detective?" That sounded outrageously

expensive, and living on one income was already stretching her budget.

"It won't hurt to consult with him and find out what he'd charge to find Dan."

Grace nodded. Olivia was right.

The following day, Grace scheduled an afternoon appointment with the investigator. She'd met Roy a couple of times, and Corrie was a regular library patron.

Corrie was polite and friendly when Grace arrived, immediately putting her at ease. She led her into Roy's office and brought each of them a cup of coffee before gently closing the door.

"I understand Dan is missing," Roy said, getting directly to the point.

Grace could be equally blunt. Her patience with the situation was gone, especially since she'd learned about the ring. "How much would it cost to find him?"

"That depends on how long it takes."

Grace glanced down at her folded hands. "I don't think it'll be that difficult."

"Do you have any idea where he might be?" Roy asked.

"No. But I suspect he's with another woman."

Roy nodded. "Okay," he said, looking directly into her eyes. "How badly do you want to find him?"

"I don't. I mean, I don't want him back." Sadness settled over her. "I'd just like to see him long enough to slap the divorce papers in his hand."

Eleven

Cecilia had dreaded this day for weeks. May first.
Her wedding anniversary. A year ago, on this very
day, she'd stood with Ian before a Justice of the Peace
and they exchanged heartfelt vows. In a matter of
minutes, they'd joined their lives for what she'd believed would be forever.

The pregnancy was just beginning to show, and
Cecilia had felt it was silly to wear white. Instead
she'd chosen a lovely soft-pink dress and made a
matching veil herself.

Her mother had flown to Washington for the ceremony, brief though it was, and taken them both out
for dinner afterward. Bobby had slipped a fifty-dollar
bill in Cecilia's hand. Ian had insisted they have a honeymoon, and despite their lack of extra money, he'd
found a way. They'd spent two glorious days on the
Washington coast, the Long Beach peninsula. They'd
explored the beach and the small historic towns, like
Oysterville and Seaview. At night, they'd cuddled together in front of the fireplace in their rented cottage

and discussed the future. Everything had seemed so perfect then. It was on their honeymoon that they'd decided on names for their unborn child and talked about Ian's Navy career and Cecilia's role as a Navy wife. She hadn't understood everything that would require, but had been willing to follow her husband to the ends of the earth.

She'd followed him to the end of her sanity. Cecilia couldn't possibly guess that within a few months their child would be dead. She couldn't have known that all joy and purpose would disappear from her life.

A year later, May first was just another workday. Nothing special. Nothing out of the ordinary. As much as possible, she intended to ignore its significance, the same way she'd been ignoring Ian.

For a while, they'd been e-mailing back and forth—until she'd faced up to the reality of their situation. They remained legally bound, but they were no longer husband and wife, despite her lapse in judgment when they'd made love. Their separation had lasted longer than their marriage. What she'd said to him was true; he deserved to be a father. But as she'd told him in her last e-mail, he needed to accept the fact that she would never again risk that kind of heartache.

Ian's return e-mail had suggested she was overreacting. He'd said she would feel different eventually, that she'd want to have another child. He didn't understand. She didn't try to explain, because any response would've been an invitation for him to argue—and to continue their correspondence. So she'd stopped e-mailing him, stopped going to the library, stopped caring.

Unfortunately, that didn't mean she'd managed to

rid her thoughts of Ian. It'd been a mistake to write him, a mistake to get involved with him again, even through that series of short e-mails. No, her decision was made. As soon as she could afford it, she was going ahead with the divorce, which would be the best thing for both of them. In time Ian would see that, and in time, he'd find it in his heart to forgive her.

When she'd worked all of that out, she'd parked his car, refusing to drive it again.

Knowing what the future held for her and Ian, Cecilia couldn't allow the significance of May first to distract her. She headed for her advanced algebra class early that morning, driving her own car, determined to make the best of the day. This was the next level of algebra and far more challenging than her first course. It helped that Mr. Cavanaugh was teaching this one, too. She liked him a great deal.

Despite her efforts to concentrate during class, her mind drifted in various unsettling directions, finally landing on the very subjects she'd wanted to avoid. Ian, her dead baby and the hopelessness of ever getting an education one course at a time. When she finally graduated with any kind of useful degree, she'd be old enough to collect Social Security.

Feeling depressed, she waited to talk to Mr. Cavanaugh after class. Holding her books tightly against her, she walked to the front of the room.

"Yes, Cecilia," he said, giving her his attention.

"I...I thought you should know I've decided to drop out of class."

He didn't reveal any overt disappointment. "I'm sorry to hear that. Is there a particular reason?"

Several, but none she could mention. Hanging her

head, she shrugged. "I'm not sure where I'll use this knowledge. I'm a restaurant hostess, not some brainy type who'll have a career in math."

"Knowledge is never wasted. You're right, of course, you might never again have the opportunity to use the quadratic formula, but there's a certain satisfaction in being able to do so. Don't you agree?"

"I don't know."

"I see." He reached for his books and placed them inside his briefcase, then left the room.

Cecilia walked with him. Part of her had hoped he'd try to talk her out of quitting. "I did want to thank you."

"What about your other class? What was it again?"

"Business English," she supplied.

"Do you intend to drop out of that, too?"

She nodded, clutching her books tighter than ever. The school would refund a portion of the course fees if she pulled out before the end of this week.

"I'm sorry, Cecilia," he said again.

"I am, too," she whispered, even more miserable now.

"Give it to the end of the week, all right?"

"Okay," she agreed, but her mind was made up. She would use the money from the classes to pay for another appointment with Allan Harris. She'd ask him to try to get the prenuptial agreement overturned. He'd mentioned that they could appeal Judge Lockhart's decree, and with Ian out at sea, that was her only option.

After her classes, Cecilia drove her clunker back to the apartment, hoping to nap before work. Normally she started in on her homework, tackling it with enthusiasm, but not today. Not when there was a very real possibility she wouldn't be returning to Olympic College after Friday.

The light on the answering machine was blinking. Reluctantly Cecilia pushed the button.

"It's Cathy," came the cheerful voice of her friend. "A bunch of us are getting together tonight for dinner. Are you interested? It's a potluck at my place. I hope you'll come. Give me a call either way. I'd really love to have you here." Cathy had become a friend, a *good* friend, and they made a point of seeing each other every week. Sometimes with the other Navy wives, more often not. They'd scouted out garage sales, gone to an occasional movie, met for Sunday brunch.

But Cecilia couldn't go tonight, not when she was working the dinner shift at the restaurant. Cathy knew her hours and had invited her anyway, making a point of including her. Cecilia hated having to explain, since it should've been obvious that she couldn't get away.

Cathy answered immediately. "Cecilia," she cried, sounding really pleased to hear from her. "Say you'll come."

"I can't."

"But it won't be the same without you."

"I'm working and it's far too late to find a replacement." That was true enough.

Cathy heaved a sigh of disappointment. "Maybe we should all come down and see you. You know that old saying—if Mohammed won't come to the mountain…" She didn't finish the statement, but laughed as though she'd said something clever.

Cecilia didn't join in. "Maybe next time," she said in a dull voice.

Cathy hesitated. "Is everything all right? No, don't answer that. I can tell it isn't. What's wrong?"

Rather than tell Cathy the whole truth, she opted for the abridged version. "I'm dropping out of school."

"You can't! You love your classes."

"I need the money."

"I'll give you a loan."

Cecilia was shocked that a friend of such short acquaintance would make an offer like that. "You don't have any money, either."

"No, but I can get some…I think. Don't worry, if worse comes to worst, I'll take up a collection when I see the rest of the women tonight. We need to stick together, you know? If we can't give one another emotional support, who will? With our men at sea, all we have is each other."

Cecilia's spirits rose, but that was unavoidable with Cathy, whose optimism and generosity always made life seem more promising, somehow.

"I'll get back to you," Cecilia told her. Then, despite her mood, she sat down with the algebra book and began working on her assignment. When she looked up, it was past time to leave for work. She tore around the apartment, changing her clothes, and rushed out the door, arriving at The Captain's Galley just as her shift was starting.

As usual, Cecilia poked her head into the lounge to say hello to her father.

He raised his hand and called out "How's it goin'?" when he saw her.

"Fine." No use explaining her depression to him. He wouldn't know what to say if she did.

"Glad to hear it."

"Yeah, right," she muttered under her breath.

Cecilia hadn't been at work more than an hour when a deliveryman arrived with a huge bouquet of fresh flowers. Yellow daisies, her favorite, and big pink tulips and a variety of others. "I'm looking for Cecilia Randall," he said, reading the tag.

Taken aback, Cecilia said nothing for a moment.

"Is there a Ms. Randall here?" he asked, frowning.

"I'm Cecilia Randall," she told him.

The young man, probably a high-school student, thrust the vase filled with flowers into her arms and left. She didn't need to unwrap the cellophane and read the card to know they were from Ian. This was exactly the kind of low, underhanded thing he did just so she'd feel guilty. Well, dammit, that wasn't going to work. She refused to let it.

Setting the flowers down next to the cash register, she removed the plastic and dropped it into the nearby trash can. Then she reached for the card.

Happy First Anniversary. I love you. Ian

Her stomach cramped, and Cecilia feared she was about to be sick. Biting into her lower lip, she waited for the sensation to pass.

"Who are the flowers for?" her father asked curiously, walking into the restaurant.

She didn't answer right away. "Me, from Ian," she whispered.

"Really. Any special reason?"

She nodded. "It's…supposed to be our anniversary."

"Oh."

Tears slid down her cheeks. When her father noticed them, he patted her on the back and returned to the bar.

Justine sipped her wine and pretended to be listening intently to Warren as he babbled on. She'd lost track of what he was saying, but a response from her wasn't required. Any comment, other than praise or social small talk, wasn't welcome. Justine knew her role and it was that of a social accessory. This hadn't bothered her in the past and didn't really bother her now. She understood Warren, understood the terms of their arrangement.

"More wine?" Warren asked, lifting the bottle and replenishing her glass.

Dinner at this five-star Seattle restaurant was in celebration of some multimillion-dollar contract Warren had landed. Such celebrations happened every two or three months.

"Well," he said, gazing expectantly at her, "what do you think?"

"Think?" Warren didn't date her for her brains and wasn't really interested in her opinions. They never talked about *her* job; in fact, he avoided dealing with her bank.

He blinked hard. "Justine, weren't you listening?"

"I…I'm afraid it's the wine. I get kind of sleepy. I'm sorry, darling, what were you saying?" Announcing that another man had been on her mind was not likely to garner his sympathy.

Thoughts of Seth Gunderson consumed her day and night, but she'd have to be a complete moron to drop Warren for a man who lived on a sailboat. Seth infuriated her. He could have slept with her, would have if she'd had any say in the matter. Every time she thought about that night, Justine felt so angry and humiliated, she wanted to bash her head against the wall. Idiot! Idiot! Idiot!

In her weakness she'd encouraged him, and that had been a dreadful mistake. Seth believed she was leaving Warren for him. She couldn't. Warren needed her, and in her own way she needed him.

"I was talking about us," he repeated.

The conversation was about to become awkward. Justine could feel it.

"Oh, Warren, do you really think this is the time?" She pouted very prettily at him.

"Yes. Tonight's a celebration."

"I'm so proud of you."

He beamed her a smile and leaning across the table, clasped her fingers. Stroking his thumb over the back of her hand, he held her gaze. "You know how I feel about you."

She did indeed. Justine might be a lot of things, but she wasn't stupid.

"Move in with me."

"Oh, Warren." Two or three times a year he pressured her to make that decision. So far, she'd always managed to change the subject, cajole him out of his insistence on "taking the next step." Dating Warren was one thing; living with him was an entirely new scorecard. She'd never intended their relationship to go that far.

"Before you answer," he said, "take a look at this." He broke eye contact long enough to reach inside his pocket and bring out a jeweler's velvet case.

"Warren?"

So the pressure was about to intensify. It didn't matter. She wasn't willing to surrender her freedom, regardless of what he offered.

"Before I show you this, I want to explain." He took her hand once again, his eyes serious, then looked down at the table. "You never ask for more than I can give," he murmured.

By that he meant she accepted his inability to perform sexually. Actually, she didn't mind, even preferred the lack of a physical relationship. Justine kept his secret; she owed him that. She suspected very few people knew of Warren's problems. Apparently they were of a kind that a small blue pill wouldn't help.

"I like my freedom," she reminded him sweetly, not wanting to offend.

"You can have your freedom, baby."

"It wouldn't be the same."

"Sure it would," he argued. "In fact, you can have your own room if you insist."

He'd suggested that the last time he'd brought up the subject. She hadn't been interested then, and she wasn't now.

"It's because of your mother, isn't it?" Warren asked.

"That's not it." She knew it would be easy to lay the blame at her mother's feet. She was a judge, an important member of the community, but Justine was her own woman. What she did with her life shouldn't be any reflection on her mother's career.

"You're turning me down?" He wore the little-boy expression that might have been cute twenty years ago, but at his age left him looking merely pathetic.

"I'm sorry. You know I'd never do anything to hurt you."

"Good." He gave her a wide grin and flipped open the lid of the velvet case.

Justine gasped. It was the largest solitaire diamond she'd ever seen in her life, a good three or four carats. She brought her hand to her mouth, speechless.

"It's a beauty, isn't it?"

She could only nod.

"I want us to get married, Justine. This is your engagement ring."

"Married?" The room started to buzz and she felt a little dizzy.

"You're beautiful and a classy woman. When men see you with me, I feel like a million bucks. We make a good couple, baby."

She stared at him. His insensitivity was almost laughable. He was trying to persuade her to become his wife by telling her she enhanced his image. *That* was supposed to induce her to marry him?

"You told me once you don't want a family," he said.

"I don't."

"Well, that works for both of us, then."

Justine swallowed hard.

He glanced around him, then lowered his voice. "If you want to maintain separate bedrooms after we're married, that's fine with me."

"Oh, Warren."

"Think about it," he said. "Take the ring. Try it on."

She did as he asked, simply because she wanted to see what a four-carat diamond looked like on her finger. A man with romantic inclinations would have taken the opportunity to slip the ring on her finger himself. Seth would've—she was sure of it—but there was no way he could afford a diamond of this size…now or in any other lifetime.

The ring glided onto her finger as if it'd been designed for her. It was the most fabulous piece of jewelry she'd ever seen.

"Wear it for a while," Warren urged. "It's insured."

Justine gazed at the diamond, then reluctantly removed it from her finger. "I'm going to think very seriously about your proposal," she told him, and she meant it.

"Listen, if it's your parents that worry you, I'll talk to them."

"I make my own decisions, Warren." She shuddered at the thought of Warren confronting either of her parents. It wouldn't be a meeting of minds, that much she could guarantee.

"When will you have an answer?" he asked, ever the businessman. He wouldn't allow her to keep him dangling long.

"Next week," she told him. Even if she did reject his proposal, nothing about their relationship would change. Warren knew it and so did she.

Seth phoned Justine from Alaska the following night. She shouldn't have been surprised. He always seemed to know when she least wanted him to call.

"Hi," he said. His clear voice sounded as if he were across the street rather than a thousand miles north.

"Hello, Seth."

A short pause followed her greeting. "You don't seem happy to hear from me."

"I'm not."

"Any reason for that?"

She closed her eyes and sighed. She might as well tell him. The sooner Seth knew, the better—for both of them. "Warren asked me to marry him last night."

Another brief hesitation, then, "Have you accepted his proposal?"

"Not yet."

"Are you tempted?"

She wasn't, but letting Seth think otherwise was a sure way to get him out of the picture. "I don't know."

"When *will* you know?"

"Soon."

He didn't argue with her or try to persuade her to reject the other man. Nor did he say she'd be a fool if she agreed to marry Warren. Instead he asked, "Do you love him?" He kept his tone conversational, as though her answer was a matter of indifference to him.

"I haven't decided that yet, either." She was fond of Warren, but compared to the fire that surfaced whenever she was with Seth, *fond* was a bland emotion.

"Are you waiting for me to make your decision for you?" Seth asked.

"Don't be ridiculous."

"That's what it sounds like to me."

She sighed loudly. "I only mentioned it because I thought you should know."

He snickered, irritating her even more.

"What was that about?" she demanded.

"Did you tell your boyfriend how you practically dragged me into your bed?"

That was a low blow, and Justine had no intention of responding.

"Warren knows about you." She wasn't absolutely sure if that was true, but she had her suspicions. Most likely, her being seen with Seth was what had prompted the marriage proposal.

"I'll bet he does." Seth's anger had vanished as soon as it appeared. "Well," he said, apparently bored with the subject, "I guess you have an important decision to make."

"You're right, I do."

"Call me when you've made it."

Justine sensed that he was about to hang up, and perversely, she didn't want their conversation to end, not like this. And yet, she was helpless to do anything but agree. "I will," she whispered, miserable and furious at the same time.

"On second thought," he said, and she could practically hear his scorn, "don't bother. We both know what you're going to do." Having said that, he broke the connection. Justine was left holding the telephone receiver, which buzzed insistently in her ear.

The sun reflected off the bright green water of Puget Sound as the ferry pulled away from the Bremerton dock and moved smoothly through Rich Passage on the hour-long journey to Seattle. Standing at the railing, with the wind ruffling her dark hair, and breathing in the salty tang of the sea, Olivia turned to smile at Jack.

"It's just so beautiful this afternoon."

"Hey," he joked, "I ordered it just for today."

She rolled her eyes.

"This is no joke," he insisted, with a look so serious she was tempted to laugh outright. "I said, 'God, I've got this important date Sunday afternoon and I'd appreciate a little cooperation from you in the weather department.'"

"You said that, did you?"

"I did."

Olivia turned back to the railing, leaning her elbows on it, and waited impatiently for a glimpse of the Seattle skyline. Jack's son, Eric, was picking them up at the ferry terminal and the three of them would have dinner on the waterfront. This would be the first time Olivia had met Eric, and Jack seemed more nervous about it than she did.

"I've taken several vacations in the past few years," Olivia told him, "and traveled in a number of different countries, but I've never found any place more beautiful than Seattle when the sun is shining."

"It's lush and green, all right," Jack said, grumbling, "as it should be after three months of drizzle and rain."

"Is it time for you to sit under a happy light?" she asked, posing the question to him that she'd once asked her children. Whenever the day was especially gloomy and they'd argued and complained about being unable to play outside, Olivia had made them sit under a lamp and read. James had dubbed it the happy light because he'd figured out that until he smiled, she wouldn't let him leave the chair.

"Happy light?"

Olivia explained, and they joked for several minutes. When they fell silent, she noticed how tense he seemed. He left her at the rail and paced the length of the ferry, drank three cups of coffee to her one and fidgeted during the entire ride from the Kitsap Peninsula into Elliot Bay.

Olivia recognized Eric as Jack's son the instant she saw him. He was as tall as his father, with an athletic build, and other than his choice of clothing, they looked very much alike.

"Hello, Eric," Olivia said, extending her hand.

"This is Olivia Lockhart." Jack introduced her, sweeping his arm in her general direction.

Father and son didn't hug or exchange handshakes. Since Stan was quite demonstrative, it struck her as odd.

"How was the ferry ride?" Eric asked as they started walking along the waterfront.

"Great," Jack said enthusiastically, as though they'd just stepped off a cruise ship instead of a one-hour Puget Sound crossing.

"Are you hungry?" Eric asked next.

"Famished."

Olivia glanced at father and son, surprised by the awkwardness she continued to sense.

Eric told them he'd chosen a restaurant before their arrival and made reservations. "I hope you like crab," he said, leading the way.

"Love it," Olivia assured him.

Eric turned to his father. "I'm game," Jack muttered.

Apparently Eric wasn't acquainted with his father's tastes. That, too, seemed odd. The restaurant Eric had chosen specialized in freshly cooked crab, served on newspaper-lined tabletops. Each patron was supplied with a wooden mallet and a bib. By the time they finished cracking the steaming Dungeness crab and dipping the pieces in melted butter, they were talking with ease, bursts of conversation punctuated by laughter.

Everything about the meal was wonderful. When they'd washed up, Eric walked them back to the ferry. Once more he appeared rather formal, and the conversation, which had flowed so comfortably throughout the meal, suddenly seemed stilted. Jack's hands were buried inside his raincoat pockets.

"I had a good time," Eric announced. Was it Olivia's imagination or did he sound a little shocked by that revelation?

"I did, too," Jack said.

Eric didn't say anything for a moment. "Would you like to meet again sometime?"

"I'd like that very much," Jack said solemnly.

"Me, too."

Eric smiled charmingly at Olivia. "It was nice meeting you."

"You, too, Eric."

The cars started to leave the Bremerton ferry and it was time to walk onboard.

"I'll be in touch," Jack said, steering Olivia toward the terminal and the ticket booth for walk-on customers.

Eric raised his hand in farewell and eased away, taking small steps backward.

Jack purchased their tickets, and as they boarded the ferry, he said, "That went well, didn't it?"

"Very well."

She could feel his relief and found his reaction—his entire attitude toward his son—a bit puzzling. Still thinking about it, she followed him up the steps to the main deck. Jack hurried ahead of her toward the back railing and stood there, the wind in his face as he looked out over the Seattle waterfront.

"There he is," Jack called. He placed his finger between his lips and let out a piercing whistle.

Eric jerked around, saw them and waved once more.

"He's a well-adjusted young man," Olivia murmured.

"The credit for that goes to his mother."

"You weren't part of his life while he was young?" That would explain the awkwardness between them.

"I was around but…I wasn't much of a father."

Olivia understood what he was saying. Between law school and everything else that'd been crammed into the early years of her own children's lives, Olivia suffered her share of regrets. She'd longed to be a good mother, still did, but there were only so many hours in a day.

"I'm proud to be his father."

It was probably the best compliment a father could give his son, but unfortunately Eric hadn't been there to hear it.

"Do you see him often?" she asked, attempting to gauge the relationship.

"We try," was all Jack would admit. "However, we have a lot of issues—" he grimaced at the word "—that we need to work through."

She smiled at his distaste for what he called psychobabble. He'd told her more than once that he preferred plain speaking.

"But you and Eric are both making the effort," she said quietly.

Jack nodded. "Yes, we are." Then, as though

searching for a way to turn the subject from himself, he asked, "Any word from Justine?"

Olivia wanted to groan aloud. Her daughter was her main source of concern just now. Although Justine hadn't said anything to Olivia, word had filtered through town about her and Seth Gunderson. Olivia felt like cheering. Seth was exactly the kind of man she pictured for her headstrong daughter.

Then Seth had left for Alaska, and all of a sudden the gossip was about Warren Saget ordering a huge diamond ring from Berghoff Jewelers. Warren had purposely chosen a local jeweler, and the whys of it didn't escape Olivia. He wanted her to know. Coward that he was, Warren Saget didn't have the courage to confront Olivia face-to-face. He left the broadcasting of his intentions to the gossipmongers of Cedar Cove.

"You heard?" Olivia asked.

Jack gave a nonchalant shrug. "Did she say yes?"

"I have no idea." It hurt to admit that her only daughter hadn't even discussed a marriage proposal with her mother.

"If she says yes, what will you do?" Jack asked, watching her closely.

"Do?" As if Olivia had a choice. "What *can* I do? I'll grin and bear it, but I'll have a hell of a time calling Warren my son-in-law, especially since we're almost the same age."

"Is Seth Gunderson aware of the…proposal?"

That was the mystery of the hour. "I wish I knew."

"Are you worried?" Jack asked.

"Damn straight," she said grimly.

Jack threw his arm around her shoulder. "Everything's going to work out, just wait and see."

Olivia tried to think positive thoughts, but she wondered if Jack was referring to her situation, or his own.

Twelve

Charlotte believed with all her heart that Tom Harding had entrusted her with his most precious keepsakes for a reason. She was to find an heir or, failing that, make sure these things were properly displayed in a museum. It was a task she took seriously. Seriously enough to flirt with breaking the law.

For days she mulled over what to do. Because Tom had been a ward of the state, her biggest fear was that the saddle, guns, poster and television scripts would be confiscated and sold at auction in order to recoup the money spent on his care. According to Washington State law, Tom was only allowed two-thousand dollars' worth of property. At least, that was how Olivia had explained it.

"Can the state take all this away?" she'd asked her daughter the day of their discovery.

"Well…"

Charlotte knew what that "well" signified and, despite the risk, took action behind her daughter's back.

And the state's... If it meant she was about to be hauled off to the clinker, then so be it.

Since then, Olivia had been preoccupied with court issues, but Charlotte's innate honesty made it impossible not to tell her daughter what she'd done. She decided to pay a visit to the judge's chambers one Monday at noon. It wasn't likely that Olivia would have her own mother arrested.

Charlotte peeked inside and was instantly welcomed by the smell of old books and lemon oil. Looking up from her desk, Olivia frowned. "Hello, Mother."

"Do you have a minute?"

Deep in thought, Olivia took a moment to focus before answering.

"In case another time would be better, I want you to know I've been back to Tom's storage unit and have taken some of his things. I couldn't put it off any longer. Janet wanted that key."

"Mother," Olivia cried, covering her ears. Her daughter always did have a certain dramatic flair. "Don't *tell* me that."

"I have them in my safekeeping. We both know what'll happen once Social Service discovers Tom had anything of value." Charlotte simply couldn't allow that to happen.

Olivia stood, stared at her, then promptly sat down. She sighed. "Well...there's a case, weak though it is, for claiming that the items weren't of any real value until after his death."

That sounded like an argument an attorney would make, but still...an excellent justification, Charlotte thought with a satisfied nod. Anyway, it wasn't as though Charlotte had cleared out the storage unit.

She'd left the furniture, shabby and worn but still usable. She'd taken only what she felt Tom wanted her to save from obscurity. Only the things that should go to his family—if she could find anyone.

"Don't worry," Charlotte said. "I have everything under control." It worried her that Olivia had so little to say. Perhaps there were more legal ramifications than she understood, whole laws she didn't even know she'd broken.

"Your having control is what frightens me," Olivia said acerbically. Charlotte let that pass. "Have you tracked down any family members?"

"No…not yet, but I will. I—"

"Oh, Mother, this is a huge responsibility."

As though Charlotte needed reminding. "I feel it's my duty." Straightening, she decided she might as well confess everything. "I want you to know I've hired Roy McAfee to search out any heirs Tom might have."

"You did what?"

Olivia didn't have a problem with her hearing, so Charlotte left the question unanswered.

Olivia sighed again. "What did Roy tell you?"

Charlotte's fingers tightened around her purse, which was balanced on her knees. "I haven't actually spoken to him yet. When I phoned for the appointment, Corrie and I spoke. I explained why I need Roy's help. I'm seeing him this afternoon."

"Mother, *please* don't tell anyone else what you've done."

"Oh, not to worry. I won't mention how you went with me that first time, either."

Olivia groaned. "That would be appreciated."

"Do you want me to let you know what Roy finds out?" She had the impression Olivia would rather not be kept informed. The way her mind was all caught up with legalities, that was probably for the best. Charlotte often felt astonished by how frequently the courts abandoned common sense. "Never mind," Charlotte said, getting to her feet. "I'll fill you in later."

Olivia seemed decidedly relieved. "Okay, thanks."

The course of her action already determined, Charlotte walked out of the courthouse. Troy Davis nodded at her, and Charlotte quickly looked away, certain the chief of police would guess she was a felon on the run. Thankfully he didn't and merely strolled past. Really, it was a wonder that guilty people didn't give themselves away.

Later that same afternoon, Charlotte arrived at Roy McAfee's office a full thirty minutes before her scheduled appointment. She had her knitting with her and sat in his waiting room, her needles clicking at a furious pace. Illegal activities were one thing, but confessing them to a former policeman—well, that *really* tried her nerves.

Corrie was busy on the phone and apologized when she'd finished. "Roy won't be back for another twenty minutes."

"Oh, that's fine. I'm early," Charlotte returned. Olivia would protect her from the long arm of the law—or so she assumed—but she had no such guarantee with Roy. Well, so be it. Her resolve bolstered her spirits, although she didn't exactly savor the possibility of jail.

"Fiddlesticks," Charlotte muttered. It was a chance she had to take.

Corrie glanced up. "I beg your pardon?"

"Nothing," Charlotte said with a sigh. Roy arrived five minutes before her appointment time, and by then Charlotte had worked herself into a frenzy of worry. Corrie was aware of the reason for the visit, but Charlotte eluded her questions, preferring to speak to Roy alone.

Perhaps a minute later, Corrie announced that he was ready to see her. Stuffing her knitting needles and yarn back into her quilted bag, Charlotte stood up.

Roy sat behind a large oak desk littered with files. His computer was off to one side, and what files weren't on his desk were stacked around him on the floor. Charlotte had no idea a private investigator would have this much business, especially in a town the size of Cedar Cove.

"What can I do for you?" Roy asked in a crisp, professional tone.

Now that she was here, Charlotte wasn't sure where to start—probably *not* by confessing she'd recently committed a felony, if indeed that was what she'd done. "Did you ever watch Saturday cowboy shows as a boy?"

Roy grinned. "You bet." He held up his index finger and blew on it as though it were a smoking gun barrel.

"Do you remember Tom Houston?" she asked next.

"The Yodeling Cowboy?"

Charlotte brightened. "Yes. Well, you're going to be surprised to learn that until his death last month, Tom lived right here in Cedar Cove."

Roy leaned forward and his eyes widened. "You're joking."

"It's true," she said, beaming with pride that she knew this fact before anyone else. "We were good friends."

"You and Tom Houston?" Roy looked impressed.

"Well…" She released a deep sigh. "I didn't know he was Tom Houston at the time. He went by the name of Tom Harding." She explained the circumstances that had led up to their meeting and everything that had happened since his death. Including her raid on the storage unit.

"You have all the memorabilia at your home now?"

"I do." She'd avoided mentioning Olivia's name, but she could see that Roy had several questions. "I realize that what I did is flirting with civil disobedience," she began.

"Not quite."

Charlotte had trouble remembering all those fancy legal terms. "But…" Then she decided that if *he* wasn't worrying about the illegality of her activities, she wouldn't, either.

"What would you like me to do?" Roy asked.

Charlotte had thought that should be obvious. "I need to find out if Tom has any living heirs. Can you do that for me?"

Roy didn't hesitate. "I'm sure I can. Did you see anything in Tom's things that gave his Social Security number?"

"No, but I can get it." Janet Lester was sure to have it in the accumulated paperwork she had for Tom. She frowned, wondering exactly how to ask. As much as she liked and trusted the social worker, Charlotte hadn't told Janet any of this, including the fact that she'd taken things from the storage unit. No need dragging her friends to jail with her, if it came to that.

"Does anyone else know Tom's true identity?"

"Only Olivia."

Roy nodded approvingly. "Keep it that way until you hear from me."

It hadn't been easy staying quiet about all this, but Charlotte feared that once the story became public, long-lost relatives would be popping out of the woodwork, all eager to claim their inheritance.

"How long will it take?" Charlotte asked. Now that she'd officially hired Roy, she was ready for results.

"I can't promise you a definite time line," Roy told her. "If you'd like to make an appointment for two weeks from now, I'll give you a progress report."

"Can't you just look it up on the computer?" she asked, waving her hand in the direction of his monitor.

"I'll start there."

Charlotte had taken a basic computer class last summer. Using Olivia's old computer, she'd typed up her columns for Jack—because he'd insisted on it. But the best part about a computer was playing games such as solitaire, although the contraption made it impossible to cheat. What fun was that?

She planned to buy a new computer soon, with the money she'd earned from her contributions to the Seniors' Page. She had all kinds of ideas for future columns; once this was all settled, she might even write about meeting Tom....

"Two weeks, then?" Roy asked.

"I'll look forward to it," she told him.

As Charlotte walked out, she felt as though a great burden had been lifted from her shoulders.

Cathy laughed at Cecilia's caricature of a ditzy hairdresser. Cecilia was going to help her add do-it-your-

self highlights to her hair on this rainy Wednesday afternoon. Since that first video-and-popcorn evening
they'd found reasons to get together often. Neither one
could afford much, so they took turns having each
other over for various kinds of low-budget fun—like
movies or dinner. Gradually Cathy had drawn Cecilia
into a circle of other Navy wives. On the night of her
wedding anniversary, the whole group had shown up
at The Captain's Galley. Last weekend, Cecilia had
met Carol Greendale, another Navy wife who'd had
a baby girl the same month as Allison. She'd found it
hard—more than hard—to see Carol with her daughter. She'd made excuses to leave, but despite her vague
protests and paper-thin excuses, Cathy had patiently
convinced her to stay. In the end, Cecilia was glad she
had.

Cathy headed for the bathroom to wash her hair
while Cecilia read through the package directions.
"Did you bring a crochet hook?" she asked when
Cathy reappeared with a bathroom towel wrapped
around her head.

"No. Do we need one?"

Cecilia wasn't sure the small plastic hook included
in the kit would work as well. "Never mind, we'll
manage with this."

"Should I make a run over to K mart? I could pick
up another package to do your hair, too."

"Not this time, okay?" Cecilia shook her head.
"Look—I have to draw strands of hair through the
holes in this plastic cap…." She frowned as she studied the paraphernalia that had come with the kit.

"Have you heard from Ian lately?"

Cecilia shook her head. It'd been almost three

weeks since their anniversary, and she hadn't thanked him for the flowers, hadn't even acknowledged getting them. She hadn't contacted him in any way. Ian hadn't written her, either. Apparently her message had been received and understood.

"Andrew says they're putting into port soon."

"Australia?"

Cathy gave an exaggerated sigh and propped her chin on one knee. "I've always wanted to visit the South Pacific."

"Me, too."

"In his last letter, Andrew wrote about the night sky," Cathy said in a soft voice.

Cecilia stopped rereading the directions to listen. Ian loved the stars and was actually quite knowledgeable about the planets and constellations. She remembered the clear summer night he'd pointed out Cassiopeia and recounted the ancient Greek legend about its formation. Cecilia had been enthralled—and she'd learned something new about her husband.

"Andrew said there are a billion stars out at night," Cathy was saying. "At first he was disappointed because there seemed to be a thin cloud cover that obscured his view." She paused and laughed softly. "Then Ian told him the cloud cover he was complaining about was actually the Milky Way."

"Wow."

She nodded. "Andrew said he'd never seen anything like it."

Cecilia looked at her friend and was surprised to find tears in her eyes. "You miss him, don't you?"

Cathy bit her lip and nodded. "Cecilia," she whispered and reached for her hand, gripping it hard. "I'm pregnant again."

The *again* was what threw Cecilia. Andrew and Cathy didn't have children.

"I miscarried the first two pregnancies," Cathy explained in a voice that trembled with emotion. "I... don't know if I can go through that agony a third time."

Cecilia glanced toward her bedroom and the single photograph she had of Allison. It was a dreadful photo taken shortly after her daughter's birth. Allison had been so small, her skin so pallid. The hospital had stuck a tiny pink bow in her hair and someone had snapped the shot. It proved to be the only one she would ever have, and Cecilia treasured it.

Looking embarrassed, Cathy wiped her eyes and said, "I knew you'd understand."

"Oh, I do."

Impulsively they hugged. The damp towel slipped to the floor, and Cathy buried her face in Cecilia's shoulder.

"I figure it happened when the *George Washington* returned for repairs."

Cecilia was fortunate not to be in the same predicament herself. "You aren't going to tell Andrew?"

Cathy frowned. "He'll just worry. He's half a world away, and there isn't a thing he can do."

"You want children?"

Cathy nodded, but the admission seemed to cause her pain. "More than anything. Andrew, too. When I miscarried the first time, we were upset, but when I lost the second pregnancy, it devastated us both. I can't imagine what'll happen if I miscarry this time...."

"What do the doctors say?"

"That everything looks normal and healthy, but we were told the same thing before."

"Was there a medical reason for the miscarriages?"

"No. That's what makes it so frustrating. They couldn't find anything wrong."

"Oh, Cathy..." Cecilia didn't know what to say that would ease her friend's fears.

"No one can figure it out. Twice now, and I can't seem to stay pregnant for more than three months." She gnawed on her lower lip. "I'm about nine weeks along and I'm so scared." As if she were suddenly cold, Cathy folded her arms tightly. "I know this sounds crazy, but when I first found out, I actually considered terminating the pregnancy."

Cecilia said nothing. Cathy needed to confide in her, and this was not the time to be judgmental or to argue with her friend.

"I kept thinking I'd rather lose the baby early than build my hopes up. Now I realize how ludicrous that kind of thinking is." She drew in a deep breath. "No one else knows I'm pregnant, not even my parents. I didn't want to say anything until I'm in my fourth month...if I make it that far."

Cecilia could understand the fear and the doubt. It wasn't only her own hopes Cathy didn't want to dash. She was considering those of her husband and her family, as well. Cecilia knew what a difficult burden that was. And she knew that such a burden only grew heavier if you couldn't share it.

"I can't promise you that this pregnancy is going to be different from the first two," she said solemnly, holding Cathy's gaze. "No one knows what the future will bring. But I *can* promise that whatever happens, I'll be there for you."

"Oh, Cecilia, you don't know how much that means to me." Cathy wiped her cheeks with her fingers. "I'm so emotional when I'm pregnant."

Cecilia's laugh was poignant. "You and me both." The first few months she was pregnant with Allison, she'd wept at the flimsiest excuses. A sentimental television commercial could reduce her to a sniveling, tissue-packing blob. The bouts sometimes lasted for hours.

Cathy touched Cecilia's arm. "Are you afraid to have another baby, too?"

The mere thought resulted in stark terror. "I…won't. Ian knows how I feel." Cecilia stopped just short of confessing that this was one of the reasons she felt compelled to follow through with the divorce.

"Give it time," Cathy advised, and they hugged once more. "Good grief," she said, forcing a laugh. "My hair's dry already."

Grabbing the plastic hook, Cecilia held it up. "I'm ready to torture you."

"Just remember I get my turn later."

The afternoon passed in a whirl of giggles, chatter and popcorn, and by the time Cathy left, Cecilia was tired but exhilarated. The blond streaks were a success. But far more important, their friendship had become stronger and deeper because of what Cathy had shared. Cecilia understood why she'd confided in her. Cathy knew that, of all the women in their small group, Cecilia was the only one who could identify with the trauma and the recriminations that followed the loss of a child. It didn't matter that Cathy was only a few months pregnant when she miscarried. Her unborn children had laid claim to her heart.

As she readied for bed that evening, Cecilia stared at the one picture she had of Allison. The dried bouquet from her wedding had been fashioned into a heart-shaped frame.

"They're from your daddy," she whispered to her daughter.

Then, because she was weak and because her heart ached, Cecilia reached for a pad and pen.

May 16th
Dear Ian,

I wasn't going to write you again. I probably shouldn't now. Nothing has changed. Nothing will. Still, I find that you're on my mind and I hope we can at least be friendly toward each other.

I spent the day with Cathy Lackey. Don't tell Andrew, but his wife is partially blond now, thanks to me. While she was here, Cathy mentioned that the *George Washington* would be docking in Sydney Harbour this week. You always said you'd see the Southern Cross. Is it as incredible as you hoped? I imagine it is.

I was going to drop out of school. Really, I couldn't see the point of sticking it out. At the rate of two classes a quarter, it'll take me a hundred years to get a degree, but then I decided that it didn't matter if I ever got one. I like school, and as Mr. Cavanaugh said, knowledge is never wasted. I really like Mr. Cavanaugh. He's the kind of person I wish my father was, although I have to admit Bobby tries. He does. When the flowers arrived for our anniversary and I started to cry, he patted my back—and then walked away. Oh, well... But later he confessed that every year on the anniversary of his divorce, he gets drunk. I think that was supposed to comfort me. In some odd way, it did.

This isn't a very long letter and I'm not even sure I'll mail it. Basically, I wanted to thank you for the flowers and tell you Happy Anniversary, too.

All my best,
Cecilia

May 26th
My dearest Cecilia,

I've hardly ever been as excited as I was this morning at mail call. I'd given up on hearing from you. Andrew said my shout was heard three decks below. Thank you, thank you and thank you again for mailing that letter. You have no idea how badly I needed to hear from you.

I'm glad you got the flowers. *Happy Anniversary, Sweetheart.* It's been one hell of a first year, hasn't it? From here on out, it'll be better. You feel it, too, don't you?

I did see the Southern Cross, and it was even more exciting than I'd dreamed. That experience could only have been improved in one way—having you beside me when I found it.

I can't write much. I'm on duty in five minutes and I want to mail this as soon as I can. There's only one more thing I want to say. You mentioned that your father gets drunk on the anniversary of his divorce. He obviously has more than a few regrets. Don't make the same mistake he did, Cecilia. We need each other. *I love you.* There's nothing we can't work through. Not one damn thing. Remember that, all right?

Ian

"Anything?" Kelly asked hopefully as she slid into the booth at the Pancake Palace. The restaurant was a local favorite, where the food was good and the portions hearty. Sunday mornings, the lineup to get a table often stretched out the door.

Grace's daughter had phoned earlier in the week, and they'd agreed to meet Friday after work. With no reason to hurry home, Grace was free to have dinner out. Yet she felt an unaccountable urge to rush back to the house on Rosewood Lane. It was just habit, she decided. Thirty-five years of habit.

"No news," Grace answered.

"Mom, he can't have dropped off the face of the earth. Someone must know *something*."

If that was the case, no one had bothered to tell her. One thing Grace did know was that she could no longer afford Roy McAfee's services. He'd made some suggestions to help her track down her missing husband, but Grace had run into a solid row of dead ends. Discouraged and defeated, she'd given up trying. Even if she did manage to locate Dan, what could she possibly say? It wasn't as though she intended to beg him to come home.

The waitress brought them menus and Grace

chose a chef's salad and coffee, while Kelly ordered a chicken sandwich and a glass of milk.

"Why would Daddy do something like this?" Kelly asked—as she'd already asked dozens of times.

If Grace knew the answer to that, she could stop listening to the voices in her head. Besides her own emotions, she had those of her children to consider. Maryellen had reacted with outrage and anger. Kelly was more hurt. The younger of the two girls, she'd always been closest to her father. Even as a child, Kelly had followed Dan around; while she was a teenager, she and Grace had constantly been at odds. Yet even through the worst of her rebellion, Kelly had steered clear of any major confrontation with her father.

Grace waited until they'd finished their meals before she broached the subject she wanted to discuss. "Your father's been gone six weeks now."

"I know," Kelly said, sounding exasperated. "Mom, I'm so worried about him."

"I am, too." Although she was more worried about what she'd do once she found him. "I want you to know I've seen an attorney."

Kelly stared at her as if she didn't understand. "An attorney can help you find Dad?"

"No. I've decided to file for divorce."

Kelly reached for her water glass. She took a sip and Grace could see that her daughter was struggling to hold on to her composure. "Mom, don't! Please don't. Dad's coming back. I know he is—and when he does, we'll discover what this is all about. There's a logical reason he had to leave the way he did."

"I'm not doing this to punish your father. It's for legal reasons."

"Legal reasons," Kelly repeated, frowning.

She told her about the need to cancel all their credit cards and her responsibility for half of any debts he assumed. What she didn't mention was that Dan had used the VISA to purchase a ring for another woman. Every time she thought about her husband doing such a thing, knowing full well that she'd investigate the charge, she nearly broke down and wept.

"You still think Daddy's got a girlfriend, don't you?"

Grace heard the challenge in her daughter's voice. She wanted to protect her children, hide the truth from them, but the charade had become too much for her. Dan wasn't concerned about protecting *her*. He'd left her open to ridicule, speculation and embarrassment.

"You can't honestly think he'd do that," Kelly insisted.

"That's exactly what I think," Grace said without apology. "Everything leads me to believe he's involved with someone else."

Kelly shook her head so hard her earring flew across the table. "Not Dad."

"I don't want to believe it, either," Grace said quietly as Kelly retrieved the earring. "Do you think it gives me any pleasure to tell you I'm seeking a divorce? Your father and I have been married for thirty-five years. This isn't a decision I've made lightly."

"Wait," Kelly pleaded.

"For what?" Financial ruin? Dan could accumulate all kinds of expenses and as she'd explained, she'd be legally responsible for half the debt. A divorce would protect her from that.

"Wait until after the baby's born," Kelly whispered, her voice cracking.

"Oh, Kelly."

"Does Maryellen know you want to divorce Dad?"

"I talked to her last week." She'd delayed mentioning it to Kelly for exactly this reason. No matter what Dan was guilty of doing, Kelly would find an excuse for him.

"The baby doesn't have anything to do with the divorce," Grace said firmly. "Nothing at all."

Kelly's beautiful blue eyes clouded with tears. "Give him more time. It's only been six weeks."

Six hellish weeks. The six longest weeks of Grace's life. Her daughter apparently didn't understand what Dan's disappearance had done to her. It was difficult to hold up her head in public. Difficult to meet library patrons with a smile when it felt as though her life had been ripped in half. Grace saw the pitying looks in their eyes. She heard the whispers and knew they were talking about her.

"This baby deserves to be brought into a whole family," Kelly said stubbornly.

Grace wondered if it'd do any good to point out that *she* wasn't the one who'd splintered the family unit. Dan had walked out on her, not the other way around.

Then, as if she'd been waiting to deliver the final punch, Kelly reached for her purse and removed a shiny piece of rolled paper.

"What's that?" Grace asked.

"A picture of your grandchild."

Grace's heart started to pound faster. "You had your ultrasound?"

Kelly nodded. "Here's your grandbaby, Mother."

This technology hadn't been available when Grace was pregnant with the girls. She studied the circular array of lines and squinted, barely able to make out the baby's form.

"Oh, my goodness," Grace whispered, awed by the sight.

"That's Dad's grandbaby, too," Kelly said.

Grace's heart sank.

"Tell me you'll wait before you file for divorce."

"Kelly…"

"Please?"

Grace sighed. "All right, but just until after the baby's born. Deal?"

Kelly gave her a relieved smile. "Deal."

Thirteen

Olivia Lockhart left the Boeing 767 and stepped off the jetway. She was just returning from San Diego and a one-week visit with her son, his wife and their new baby. Isabella Dolores Lockhart was born in the wee hours of May eighteenth. The following morning, unable to stay away a moment longer, Olivia had boarded a plane for California. In seven short days, she'd fallen completely in love with her first grandchild.

Collecting her luggage, Olivia glanced around, wondering if Justine was late. Her daughter had volunteered to pick her up at Sea-Tac Airport and was normally punctual. Her suitcase in hand, unsure what to do, Olivia walked over to the bank of phones.

"Looking for a familiar face?" a man asked from behind her.

Olivia knew the sound of her ex-husband's voice as well as she knew her own. "Stan! What are you doing here?"

"What else? I came to collect you."

"But Justine—"

"I asked her to let me do the honors."

Olivia couldn't help feeling surprised. She rarely saw Stan and they didn't speak all that often. At fifty-six, he was still vital and handsome, and she smiled as he kissed her cheek, then relieved her of her bag. She'd vowed to love this man all her life—and despite the divorce, still did. It was a love that continued to this day because of everything they'd once meant to each other. Because of what they'd had—and what they'd lost.

"I thought this would give you an opportunity to tell me about the baby. How's James?"

After her visit, Olivia felt reassured. "I don't think we need to worry about James."

"You like his wife?"

"Very much," she told him. "I have pictures of the baby. Oh, Stan, she's adorable."

"Don't tell me you're turning into one of those silly grandmas with a purse full of pictures."

"In a heartbeat. I've waited a long time for this." Most of the friends they'd once shared were grandparents several times over by now.

Together they headed toward the short-term parking on Sea-Tac's lower level. Olivia told him about the baby as they went, barely paying attention as Stan paid for parking and led the way down the escalator. They walked along the row of parked cars until he suddenly stopped in front of a red convertible.

Olivia did a double take. Stan in a BMW? A convertible, no less. Leave it to her ex-husband to buy a convertible in a city that had three solid months of rain every year!

"When did you get this?" she asked, not even trying to disguise her amusement.

"Do you like it?"

"I absolutely love it! You'll put the top down, won't you?"

"If that's what you want."

He was smiling as he slid into the front seat. He started the engine and made a real production of lowering the top. When he'd finished, they were both laughing. "This reminds me of that beat-up old convertible you had in college," Olivia said between giggles. "Remember when the top got stuck halfway up?"

They talked comfortably throughout the drive. As they waited at a light, Olivia showed her ex the first photographs of their granddaughter.

"Born May 18th," Stan reminded her. "That's the day Mount Saint Helens blew, isn't it?"

As if either one of them was likely to forget. They'd driven to Portland for the weekend. Stan was attending some engineering conference and while he went to meetings, Olivia had taken the three children over to Lloyd Center. The shopping mall, with an ice-skating rink in the center, had fascinated eight-year-old Jordan. Olivia had tried to shop, but with three children constantly underfoot, it'd been an impossible task and she'd finally given up. After renting skates for herself and the kids, she'd spent a delightful day. Then early Sunday morning, when they were to drive home, Mount Saint Helens had the first of several volcanic eruptions. Plumes of hot gasses, ash and rock had shot sixty thousand feet into the sky. The falling ash had made the drive back to Cedar Cove nerve-wracking. For several hours, they'd been trapped on the Interstate with three whiny, frightened children in the back seat. Olivia had been no less terrified.

"You do remember May 18th, 1980, don't you?" Stan asked.

In response, Olivia shuddered elaborately. She'd never been happier to get home. The drive had been a nightmare, but time had a way of erasing the sharp edges of that memory. In later years, whenever the trip was mentioned, it was done with drama and lots of laughter.

"She's beautiful," Stan said, staring at the color photos while they waited for the light to change.

"James is happy, and Selina's perfect for him. She's just the kind of wife he needs." As the youngest, James had been badly spoiled—even more so after the death of his brother.

Stan had worried about their son. She knew that, but James was an adult now and made his own decisions. Often Olivia disagreed with what he chose, such as joining the military. Without a word to either one of them, he'd enlisted. Now he was married and a young father. This, too, had been accomplished without consulting either parent.

"I'm glad to hear that." Stan did sound relieved.

Olivia had liked her daughter-in-law instantly. They'd talked on the phone several times, but those brief conversations hadn't given her a clear picture of her son's wife. Selina belonged to a large extended and well-to-do family who'd welcomed Olivia with the same enthusiasm that they had James and the new baby. There were dinners and celebrations every night of her visit. James was genuinely happy. He and

Selina lived in a suite of rooms at his in-laws' home and amazingly, the arrangement seemed to be a success. Olivia was impressed by the amount of Spanish he'd learned since he'd met Selina. She'd quickly realized that Selina's family had been part of the attraction for her son. James had been only ten at the time of the divorce, and although both Olivia and Stan had tried hard to make the split as amicable as possible, their son had suffered. Every child did. Olivia saw the results of divorce every day in family court.

"How's Justine doing?" Stan abruptly changed the subject.

"Why? What did she say when you talked?"

"Not much."

He seemed worried about their daughter. "She still seeing that Saget guy?"

"He's asked her to marry him." By now, everyone in town knew about the diamond ring Warren had purchased. Justine, however, had yet to mention the proposal.

Stan cursed and swerved into another lane. "Is she going to do it?"

Olivia shrugged. "She doesn't confide in me when it comes to Warren Saget."

"Talk her out of it," he said urgently. "You're her mother—she'll listen to you a hell of a lot more than she will me. Marrying Saget would be a disaster."

"Yes, but convincing Justine of that isn't easy."

"She's stubborn, just like her mother."

Stan was joking and Olivia grinned, but his amusement didn't last long. "Marge's son is getting a divorce. She's pretty upset about it."

They rarely if ever talked about his wife.

"I think," he went on, "that one of the most difficult aspects of being a parent is watching your child make what you know is a mistake and not being able to do a damn thing about it."

"I'm sorry about Marge's son," Olivia murmured.

"It's really too bad," Stan told her. "He's got two small children and he's leaving them for some gal he met in his office."

Olivia wondered if her ex-husband saw the irony of the situation. Marge had divorced her husband and abandoned her children for Stan, and now history was repeating itself.

"I will talk to Justine," she said. "Unfortunately, we don't communicate well. But we've raised her to think for herself and make her own decisions, and we have to trust her to do so wisely."

"That's harder than it sounds."

Olivia didn't need him to tell her that.

By the time they hit the Seattle freeway, the sun had come out from behind the clouds. The wind and the traffic noise made conversation difficult. The hour's drive through Tacoma and over the Narrows Bridge passed quickly, especially when Stan plugged in a sixties rock-and-roll CD—music they'd danced to in their college days. Olivia was soon lost in happy memories.

She felt almost disappointed when he pulled onto Lighthouse Road.

"Oh." She reacted with surprise when she noticed Jack's clunker parked outside her house behind Justine's car.

"Someone you know?"

"Jack Griffin. He's the editor of *The Chronicle*."

Stan darted a glance in her direction. "Isn't he the one you had a date with the night I phoned? Is he a...boyfriend?"

"Oh, hardly. Jack's a *friend*."

"That's what Justine said when I first asked her about Saget," he muttered. "The next thing I know, he's pressuring her to get engaged."

"I don't think you need to worry about me marrying Jack," she assured him.

He parked at the curb and cut the engine and then said the oddest thing. "Good."

Good? He didn't want her to remarry? What a strange reaction, considering that he'd been married to Marge for fourteen years. Before she could ask him about it, her front door opened and Justine stepped onto the porch—with Jack right behind her.

He smiled and raised his hand in greeting, but his gaze slowly shifted away from her. Stan and Jack locked eyes.

"Welcome home," Justine called, oblivious to the tension between the two men. She ran down the porch steps to greet her.

Olivia hugged her daughter, and with her arm wrapped around Justine's waist, walked toward her home. She was much too old to get excited about the attention of two men, she told herself. But then—was she really?

"It's great to be back," she said, leaving Stan and Jack to follow if they chose.

"I'm dying to hear all about the baby. You didn't mind Dad picking you up, did you?"

"Not in the least." If anything, Olivia had enjoyed it too much.

* * *

Charlotte Jefferson could hardly wait for her daughter to return from California. She had so much to tell her. Although she knew Olivia would be exhausted from the trip, Charlotte couldn't delay talking to her another minute.

The last thing she expected when she arrived at Olivia's was a houseful of company. Anyone might've thought she was having a garage sale.

Naturally she recognized Justine's SUV, and the Taurus looked like the one Jack Griffin drove, but the red BMW had her baffled.

Olivia answered the doorbell and relaxed noticeably when she saw her. "Mother." After a quick hug, Olivia brought her into the house. A pizza delivery box lay open on the table and a bottle of red wine was there, too.

"Anything left for me?" she joked.

"Get your grandmother a wineglass," Olivia instructed Justine.

"Stan!" Charlotte was delighted to see her ex-son-in-law. She'd always been fond of him. The divorce had been as hard on her as it'd been on her daughter and the children. "Don't tell me that red convertible belongs to you?"

"It does." He set his wineglass next to the pizza box. "I hate to eat and run, but I've got to get back to Seattle."

"Already?" Charlotte would have dearly loved a chat.

"Another time," he promised. He bent down and kissed Charlotte's cheek, then hugged Justine, who was busy pouring a glass of wine. The two men exchanged brief handshakes and Olivia escorted him to the door. Charlotte soon realized that Stan had picked up Olivia from the airport. She realized something else, too. The two men had not taken a liking to each other. Now, *that* was interesting.

"I should be leaving, too," Justine announced. She gave Charlotte a half-full goblet and a kiss, then promptly disappeared.

That left Jack, who showed no sign of departing in the near future. Well, Charlotte needed to talk to her daughter, so she intended on waiting him out. "Tell me all about the baby," she said, settling in for a long visit. "Did James and Selina like the blanket I knit?" Then sighing, she added, "I do hope you brought back pictures."

"I sure did. Oh, Mother, she's so beautiful."

"See you Wednesday?" Jack asked, sounding a little dispirited.

Olivia hesitated a moment, then nodded. Apparently she'd just agreed to a date, which cheered Charlotte immensely. She didn't want Olivia to be alone the rest of her life, and she liked Jack Griffin.

"I should be heading out, too," Jack said reluctantly—as though he wanted Olivia to ask him to stay.

She didn't. One look from Jack told Charlotte he wanted to be alone with Olivia, but she wasn't budging.

Soon enough he'd departed. *Privacy at last.* Charlotte released a deep sigh. Olivia sat down next to her with a glass of wine, feet propped up on the coffee table. "It's been quite a week."

"For me, too," Charlotte said excitedly.

"You heard from Roy?"

Charlotte grinned widely. "Yes, and guess what? Tom has a grandson living right outside Purdy." The town was only a few miles down Highway 16 from Cedar Cove. Charlotte was thrilled with the news. In her heart of hearts, she'd known Tom had chosen to spend his last days in Cedar Cove for a reason.

"His name's Cliff Harding. Ever heard of him?"

"Can't say I have." Olivia rubbed her eyes, and Charlotte could tell that her daughter was tired.

"He raises quarter horses." Roy had told her that, along with the other information he'd unearthed. Cliff was a Boeing engineer who'd opted for an early retirement. He'd moved to the Kitsap Peninsula five years earlier.

"I suspected Tom had family in the area." Charlotte felt downright proud of that.

"Yes, you did."

"I didn't want to be intrusive, so I wrote Cliff to ask him to get in touch." The letter had gone out the very day she'd heard the news, but to her disappointment, she hadn't heard back from him.

"That's great, Mom."

"I thought so, too." She finished her wine, and then, because it was obvious that her daughter wasn't in the mood for more company, Charlotte decided it was time to leave.

After a quick peek at the pictures, she gathered her things. Olivia made a token protest, then escorted her to the door.

"I'm glad you had a good trip. And I'm thrilled about James."

"Thanks, Mom." Olivia hugged her. "Did you feel this elation when you first became a grandmother?"

It hadn't been so long ago that Charlotte had forgotten. "Twins, no less. That was one of the happiest days of my life."

"And mine," Olivia told her, but a sadness came over her, a sadness Charlotte felt, too, as they remembered Jordan and the happy, carefree boy he'd been.

On her drive home, she thought about Cliff Harding. He would certainly have received her letter but for some reason had either put off answering, or—worse—decided not to answer at all.

Perhaps she should have called, instead.

Yes, that was what she should've done, all right.

Unable to resist, as soon as she walked into the house, Charlotte located his number, which Roy had given her.

The phone rang four times before the receiver was abruptly lifted.

"Harding," said a gruff male voice.

"Jefferson," she returned in the same clipped tones. "Charlotte Jefferson."

Silence.

"I'm phoning to see if you got my letter," she explained. She knew he most likely had but that seemed the easiest way to introduce her subject.

"I got it."

Charlotte paused, wishing she'd thought this through more carefully. "Perhaps right now is a bad time?"

"It's as good a time as any. Basically, I'm not interested in anything to do with my grandfather."

Charlotte frowned in disapproval. "I'm sure you're going to reconsider when you see what I have."

"Listen, Mrs. Jefferson, I realize you mean well, but—"

"Were you aware that your grandfather recently died right here in Cedar Cove?"

"Your letter said as much."

"Mr. Harding, I have risked a great deal to find you."

"I'm not ungrateful, but—"

"I could do jail time for what I've done and at seventy-two, I don't intend to spend the rest of my life rooming with someone named Big Bertha."

He howled with laughter. How dared this young man be amused when she was dead serious?

"What exactly did you do to risk facing Big Bertha?"

Charlotte told him, sparing none of the details. "I have everything under my bed."

"That's probably the first place the police will look, don't you think?"

Charlotte suspected he was still mocking her—a little bit, anyway—but she gave him a straightforward reply. "I did think of that, but my knees are too tired to be traipsing up and down the basement stairs."

"My suggestion is that you give it all back to the state. Let the authorities sell it and recoup whatever expense they put out on my grandfather's behalf."

"You can't mean that!" Charlotte was outraged. "My dear boy, this was your *grandfather*."

"He was as much a grandfather to me as he was a father to my dad. In other words, not at all. Dad saw him a grand total of three times in his entire life. I never had the pleasure nor would I have cared to."

"All the more reason to learn what you can about him now," Charlotte argued.

"Frankly, I don't care. So what if he was a movie

and TV cowboy from the forties and fifties. The 'Yodeling Cowboy,'" he added scornfully. "Well, my dear Mrs. Jefferson, I don't give a damn."

"It's his blood that runs through your veins."

"I'd rather it didn't. Like I said, he wasn't any kind of a father or grandfather, and I sincerely doubt he cared about me in the slightest."

"I beg to differ." Normally Charlotte wasn't this argumentative. But she refused to let this…this arrogant whelp turn his back on his heritage. "You have a great deal in common with your grandfather, young man."

Cliff snickered softly. "I doubt that. And I'm not so young."

"Don't you raise quarter horses?" This was part of the information Roy had given her. "Where do you think that interest in horses came from?" she asked grandly.

He didn't answer her question. "I'm sorry to disappoint you."

"Mr. Harding, please. Considering the risk I've taken, the least you can do is look at what I've rescued. There just might be something here you'd want."

"You mean like a Yodeling Cowboy lunch bucket? No, thank you."

"I mean like his saddle and his six-shooter."

"You have a saddle?"

"Yes, I do." Charlotte suspected that was probably the one thing that might interest Tom's grandson.

"I understand it's a federal crime to steal a gun."

Charlotte bristled. "Are you trying to frighten me?"

He chuckled in response. "All right, listen," he said as if making a big concession. "I'm willing to look over all this junk."

"It most certainly is not junk." She could think of several museums that would leap at the opportunity to display some of the items she had under her bed.

"That's a matter of opinion."

"Will you come into Cedar Cove or do you want me to find you?"

"I avoid inviting known burglars into my home."

Charlotte was not amused. "Then you'll just have to drive to Cedar Cove."

"All right, Mrs. Jefferson. I can see you're not a woman who takes no for an answer."

"In this instance, you're right."

Grace enjoyed her job as head librarian. Per capita, there were more library cards issued in Cedar Cove than in any other city or town in the entire state. She took real pride in that.

The Cedar Cove Library, with the mural painted on the outside of the old brick building, was one of the most attractive structures in town. For the one-hundred-and-fiftieth anniversary of the township, the Chamber of Commerce had commissioned several murals to be painted on civic buildings around town. The waterfront library had been among those chosen; the artists had created an 1800s scene of a waterfront park with people in period dress enjoying a summer's afternoon—children and dogs cavorting, families picnicking and, of course, people reading.

The downtown community was a lot like a family, Grace often thought. The business owners looked out for one another and encouraged the Cedar Cove population to shop locally. These days, when large conglomerates were moving into small towns and destroying independent businesses, Cedar Cove's downtown thrived. This was thanks in part to the library, the marina and the brand-new city hall, which was the most prominent building in Cedar Cove, rising from the steep hill above the waterfront like a protective angel standing guard over the town. The bells chimed on the hour; some people loved them and others cursed the constant interruption.

With Dan missing for almost two months now, Grace was more grateful than ever for her job. Aside from financial reasons, she valued the fact that it helped distract her, helped keep her mind from the constant wondering and worrying about her missing husband. At least it did for eight hours a day.

"Hello, Mrs. Sherman." Jazmine Jones, a five-year-old with a precocious wit and two missing front teeth, stepped up to the front desk and placed both hands on the counter.

"I'll bet you're here for storytime," Grace said.

Jazmine nodded. "Are you reading today or is Mrs. Bailey?"

"Mrs. Bailey."

"That's all right, but..." Then, as if she didn't want to hurt Loretta Bailey's feelings, little Jazmine glanced over her shoulder and whispered, "You're a better reader."

"Thank you," Grace whispered back conspiratorially.

Tuesday afternoons were often slow, and while Loretta entertained the children, Grace handled the front desk. She was busy doing some paperwork concerning interlibrary loans when the glass door slammed open and Maryellen rushed in.

At the unexpected noise, Grace glanced up from the desk and discovered her daughter flushed and breathless.

"What's wrong?" The first thing that came to Grace's mind was Kelly and the baby.

Breathing hard, Maryellen staggered toward the desk. She placed her hand over her chest as though her heart needed to be held firmly in place.

"Dad," she managed, barely able to speak.

"What?" Grace had already come out from behind the counter.

"He's here."

"Here?" This was unbelievable. "Where?"

"The marina."

Grace was halfway out the door, with Maryellen stumbling behind her.

"You saw him?"

Maryellen shook her head. "John Malcom did."

Even as she raced out the library parking lot toward the waterfront, Grace was trying to remember who John Malcom was. Then she remembered. John and Dan had worked together years ago. John was another logger whose career had been wiped out in the controversy involving the spotted owl. Entire forests had been closed to cutting in an effort to save the endangered species, destroying the livelihood of certain communities in the shadow of the Olympic rainforest.

"Where is he?" Grace cried.

"Down by the foot ferry."

"Did he get on the ferry?" Panting, she could hardly get the question out.

"No," Maryellen shouted, gaining on Grace. As

luck would have it, Grace had worn high heels that morning and they made running nearly impossible. Maryellen had on flats and was much faster, but Grace wasn't any slouch. She took that aerobics class precisely to experience the benefits. Her adrenaline surging, she pounded down the sidewalk, putting everything she had into reaching Dan before he disappeared again. Suddenly she stumbled, then tripped over a water hose. She went down hard on the sidewalk, scraping her knees. Grace didn't give herself the luxury of checking her injuries.

"Mom!"

"I'm all right. Go! Go!" Ignoring the pain, she picked herself up, paused only long enough to remove her shoes and then started running again, limping as she went. By the time she reached the foot ferry, Grace felt as though her legs were about to collapse.

John was there, pacing back and forth. He came toward them as soon as he heard Maryellen's shout. "He's gone."

"Gone?" Maryellen cried. "You said you'd stop him."

"I tried." John's sober gaze refused to meet Grace's. "I'm sorry, really sorry. He was here, and I kept an eye on him like you asked me to. About five minutes ago, a pickup drove to the curb and he climbed in and there was no way I could stop him."

Grace fell onto a park bench, her knees throbbing and her legs trembling.

"Start at the beginning," she pleaded, barely able to talk. The frustration and anger were almost more than she could stand. Dan was *that* close, taunting her, daring her to find him, mortifying her in front of the entire town.

"You're *sure* it was my dad?" Maryellen asked.

John nodded. "I'm positive. I worked with him for years. I know what Dan Sherman looks like, all right."

"How'd you get involved in this?" Grace asked her daughter.

"I just happened to take a late lunch today. I closed the gallery and decided to walk down to Java and Juice for a latte," Maryellen said.

"I heard about Dan turning up missing and all," John went on. "There's been a lot of talk down at the Pelican's Nest about what might've happened to him."

The local watering hole was one of the most popular drinking spots in town. "Have you been drinking, John?"

"No, Grace! I swear it was Dan."

"He didn't know what to do," Maryellen interjected, "and he was halfway to the library to get you."

"I thought you'd want to know," John said, looking miserable. He shoved his hands in his coverall pockets and stared at the pavement.

"That was when he saw me," Maryellen explained.

"Your daughter said she'd get you and sent me back to keep an eye on Dan."

"Mom, your knee!"

Blood trickled down Grace's leg; the nylons were already soaked.

"Are you all right?" John asked.

"I'm fine. Tell me about the pickup." Grace wanted as much information about Dan as she could get. She'd take care of her knees later.

John hung his head. "I should've gotten the license plate number, but it happened so fast I didn't think to look."

"Did you see who the driver was?" Maryellen asked.

"Sorry, no."

Maryellen sat down next to Grace, both hands over her face, and hunched forward.

Grace placed a comforting arm on Maryellen's back. Caught up in her own misery, she'd failed to see how upset her oldest daughter was by Dan's disappearance. Kelly had been much more forthcoming about her emotions, and Grace had assumed Maryellen was taking the situation in stride. As far as anyone could...

"I can't tell you how sorry I am about all this," John Malcom said again.

"You didn't see who was driving?" Grace asked one final time.

John shook his head. "It wasn't anyone I recognized. Not from around here, leastways."

"Male or female?"

John hesitated and looked away. "Female."

Grace bit her lower lip to keep it from trembling. John wasn't telling her anything she didn't already know.

Fourteen

Cecilia would forever be grateful that she hadn't given in to the impulse to drop out of her community college classes. The day of her wedding anniversary, she'd been feeling depressed and regretful. She thought now that her desire to quit was a way of punishing herself—by taking away the very thing in life that brought her joy. She couldn't understand why she'd wanted to do such a thing. Thankfully, Mr. Cavanaugh had been kind enough to reason with her. He hadn't tried to pressure her or talk her out of it, but he'd been sensible and matter-of-fact.

She loved her classes, especially advanced algebra. On a Sunday afternoon when she was free to go anywhere and do anything she wanted, Cecilia chose to work on problems in her textbook. Problems that hadn't even been assigned. That said a lot. Recently one of the other students had flippantly called Cecilia the teacher's pet. She didn't believe it since Mr. Cavanaugh wasn't the sort of teacher who played favorites. But afterward Cecilia had smiled all day.

Never in her life had she experienced anything like this sense of approval and success.

She enjoyed telling Ian how well she was doing. They were back to e-mailing and writing. Yesterday, she'd received a postcard from Australia. He hadn't chosen one with a picture of the famous opera house, the outback or even the Barrier Reef. No koalas or kangaroos, either. Instead, Ian had mailed her a photograph of the night sky. It showed the Milky Way and what looked like millions upon millions of stars. His message on the back was full of praise for her high marks and the promise of a celebration once he got home.

Cathy was still keeping the news of her pregnancy from Andrew. It was all Cecilia could do not to tell Ian. Every day that Cathy remained pregnant was a triumph. She'd miscarried the first pregnancy at eight weeks, and the second at twelve. Already this pregnancy had lasted longer than the first two, but Cathy couldn't trust that all was well—not yet, anyway. Cecilia was the only person she'd told. Not even her mother knew, and Cecilia regarded the news as sacred information.

At a little after one, she decided it was time for lunch. With the radio on in the background, she was opening a can of soup, when a news bulletin interrupted the Top 40 song that was playing.

"This is a KVI news bulletin. There's been an explosion aboard the *George Washington,* the Bremerton-based aircraft carrier. Details are just coming into our newsroom now. At this early hour we have no idea as to the cause of the explosion. The possibility exists that this is the work of a terrorist group. There has been loss of life, but how many casualties and the extent of damage to the aircraft carrier is unknown at this point. We'll keep you updated."

Cecilia gasped and dropped the soup can. The contents spilled out over the counter, dripping onto the floor. Unrolling some paper towels, she started wiping it up when the phone rang.

"Hello," she nearly shouted as she grabbed the receiver.

"Did you hear?" It was Cathy.

"Just now. What do you know?"

"Nothing…just about the explosion. I called the ombudsman, but she'd just heard it herself. The Navy has set up a meeting area on base for husbands, wives and family members to wait for news. We'll get information there more quickly than we will at home."

"I'm on my way." Cecilia didn't waste time worrying about the appropriateness of being on base. Although she hadn't lived with Ian in many months, she was still his wife.

"That's one of the reasons I phoned," Cathy said, her voice faltering. "Could you swing by for me?"

"I'll be there as fast as I can." Then it hit her. "Cathy, is everything all right?"

Cathy released a sob. "I think so…I don't know."

"Cath? You'd better tell me."

Cecilia heard her friend struggle not to cry. "I…I've started spotting."

"When?"

"This morning."

"How bad is it?" It might be more important to drive Cathy to the hospital first.

"Not bad—much lighter than the first two miscarriages." Cathy made it sound like a foregone conclusion that she would lose this baby, too.

"I'll be there in ten minutes."

"Oh, Cecilia, I don't know what I'd do without you." The tears were back in her voice.

Dumping everything in the sink, Cecilia didn't change clothes or bother with her hair or makeup. She refused to think of what might be happening to her husband half a world away. If there was one thing she'd learned this past year, it was that she couldn't take anything for granted. She could only hope for the best.

Cathy was sitting on the front porch steps outside her rental house, waiting for her. As soon as Cecilia approached, Cathy stood. She looked shaken and deathly pale.

"Did you hear anything else?" Cecilia asked.

"No. You?"

Cecilia had turned on the all-news radio station on the drive over. "Just what was on the local news."

"A number of…deaths have been reported."

Cecilia couldn't bear to think about that. "I'm taking you to the hospital."

"No, I have to find out what I can about Andrew first," Cathy said. "If we go to the hospital, it'll take hours and they might keep me. I need to know if Andrew's all right. Then I'll go, I promise."

"Are you still bleeding?"

Cathy shook her head. "No, thank God."

Cecilia headed toward the Bremerton Navy base and joined the cars streaming toward the checkpoint at the entrance. It seemed that every spouse, parent and sibling of each enlisted man and woman sought information. A large hangar was set aside for the purpose; hundreds of chairs had been brought in, along with drinks and snacks.

Women, older men and children gathered together in small groups. Cecilia was astonished by the speed with which rumors started to circulate. By three that afternoon, word arrived of five confirmed deaths. Then Cecilia heard ten had died and with every hour the number grew. The truth remained unknown, lost amid all the speculation.

An officer announced that the explosion had been due to human error and was not a terrorist attack as first suspected. Terrorists were prominent in everyone's fears, Cecilia suspected, especially after what had happened to the *USS Cole*. Australia was a friendly port, but one could never be sure.

Next, they learned that the explosion had occurred in the munitions area, which sent gasps of horror rippling through the room. Three known dead, the officer said, but in such a volatile spot on the ship, that left a lot of uncertainty regarding the number of injuries.

By nightfall they were told that everything was under control. The fires were out; the aircraft carrier was secure. At last came the moment they'd all been waiting for. The base commander moved to the front of the room to read a list of those who'd been injured. "Lieutenant Wayne Van Buskirk. Ensign Jeremiah Smith. Chief Petty Officer Alfred Hussey. First Class Gunner's Mate Gerald Frederickson. Third Class Gunner's Mate Charles Washington. Seaman Janet Lewis…" Cathy and Cecilia clung to one another. Each name echoed through the room like a bombshell, followed by a gasp or a cry of alarm. And then Ian's name was called out. Cecilia heard her own shout of panic; her legs went slack and she slumped into a chair.

"Ian." She wasn't prepared, wasn't ready to deal with this. Cathy gripped her hand and Cecilia squeezed so hard, her fingers lost feeling.

"I'll wait for you here," Cathy told her.

Until that instant, Cecilia didn't realize any other instructions had been given. Cathy hugged her and explained that she was to proceed to the front of the room and speak to the Information Officer.

Weaving her way through the crowd of Navy family and friends, Cecilia seemed to be walking in slow motion. She heard the sounds of conversation and weeping and occasional nervous laughter as though from a great distance.

"I'm Cecilia Randall," she told the officer. She gave him Ian's name and rank, and showed her military identification card.

He directed her to another officer. By then, Cecilia was nearly at the point of passing out. This all seemed so unreal. It *couldn't* be happening. Not to Ian. Not to her. She'd already lost her daughter. Surely life wouldn't be so cruel as to claim her husband, too. Clenching her hands at her sides, Cecilia held her breath and waited.

"Mrs. Randall?"

"Yes." Instantly alert, Cecilia stepped forward. "I'm the wife of Ian Randall."

The officer smiled reassuringly. "Your husband has sustained cuts and bruises."

"Is—Is he hospitalized?"

"No." He tore off a sheet and handed it to her. "The reason we ask to speak to all the relatives of those injured is to inform you that you can talk to your loved one."

"Talk?" She didn't understand.

"We have a bank of phones in the other room. If you'll go over there, your name will be called shortly. Give the officer this sheet."

She was going to be able to talk directly with Ian. Cecilia resisted the urge to sob with joy and relief. Waiting in the inner room with several other wives, she realized how fortunate she was that her husband had only minor injuries.

It wasn't long before her name was called. She reached for the telephone and cried out, "Ian?"

"It's all right, sweetheart. I'm fine. I really am." He briefly relayed what had happened and said it looked like he had a couple of cracked ribs. "I'm tough, you know that."

"Yeah, right," she joked through her tears.

"How did you hear about the accident?" he asked.

"I had the radio on while I was studying—"

"Algebra, I'll bet," he interrupted.

She smiled. "Yeah. Guess what?" she added. "Mr. Cavanaugh suggested I take an accounting course next quarter. I'd never thought about doing any bookkeeping."

"Does that interest you?"

"I'm not sure yet." But the more she thought about it, the better she liked the idea.

"I've only got a couple of minutes," Ian said. Obviously someone had told him to hurry it up.

"I know." She'd been warned about the time limitations. "I'm glad you weren't badly hurt." An understatement if ever there was one.

"I am, too. I'm missing you something fierce. Don't stop writing me, okay?"

"I won't," she promised. She looked forward to hearing from him, too. It felt almost as though they were dating again, only this time their dates came in the form of e-mails and postcards. Their communication was comfortable and yet intimate and helped remind her of all the reasons she'd fallen in love with him.

A minute or so later, it was time to end the conversation, long before Cecilia was ready.

"I love you," her husband told her.

"I love you, too."

Her words were followed by a short silence. Then, "Say it again, Cecilia. I need to hear it."

"I love you, Ian Randall."

Cecilia was feeling warm and safe when she returned to the main room, where Cathy waited for her. Her friend watched her anxiously. "He's got two cracked ribs and is in a lot of pain, but he's okay." Even though Ian had done a good job of disguising his discomfort, she knew he was hurting.

"You ready to head to the hospital?" Cecilia asked.

Cathy nodded. She wore a look of serenity. "We can go," she said, "but I have a strong feeling that everything's just fine. Somehow, I had this sense, when I found out Andrew wasn't one of the injured, that I had nothing to fear."

Cecilia sincerely hoped her friend was right.

Grace wasn't sure why she looked inside the drawer on Dan's nightstand. She sat up in bed reading and for no obvious reason she found herself staring at it.

Moving slowly, she set aside the latest John Lescroart hardcover and stretched across the bed. Dan's nightstand was exactly as he'd left it. A crossword puzzle book lay open, the spine bent. The glass jar where he tossed his loose change was untouched.

She frowned, pulling open the drawer. Inside were a deck of cards, some receipts and a paperback novel he hadn't finished. Then she saw it. There in the corner. His wedding band.

He hadn't worn it in years. After he started working in the forests, he'd removed it and worn it only on special occasions. The last time he'd put it on, the ring had been tight; it had barely fit. She picked it up and held it with two fingers. She gazed at the ring as though this inanimate object could reveal her husband's secrets.

Why had he come back to Cedar Cove? Why risk being seen? Then again, perhaps that was what he wanted. To taunt her, to humiliate her. So he'd come here with another woman.

Grace gritted her teeth and studied the wedding band, comparing it to her own, which was thin and worn. After all these years his ring still looked brand-new, as if when he accepted it, he'd had no intention of honoring his vows.

Anger boiled up inside her. Suddenly, she rolled onto her back and with every bit of strength she possessed, hurled the ring across the room. It hit the wall and tumbled across the carpet. Her labored breathing continued for several moments as the rage held her in its grip. Finally she managed to calm down.

Reaching for the novel, she repositioned herself against the pillows, but quickly realized she wouldn't be able to concentrate on her book. The fierce anger returned. She struggled to regain her composure, but it was like trying to avert a windstorm by holding out her arms.

Not knowing what to do, she slid off the bed and stood barefoot in the middle of the bedroom. Her hands were so tightly clenched her nails bit into the soft flesh of her palms.

"How dare you show up in Cedar Cove with her," she hissed.

Her daughters refused to believe Dan had another woman, but Grace knew. She'd known for months. There was someone else and, she thought now, that someone else had been in his life for a very long time.

Kelly had insisted there'd be some evidence, but Grace had all the evidence she needed. It'd started years ago. The emotional distance and the wild mood swings had been going on for so long, she couldn't remember when they'd begun. Evidence, she realized, of someone dealing with guilt and remorse.

By God, she'd prove it. Not to her daughters but herself. Dan *had* left some evidence; he must have. It was right here in this room—where else could it be? After years of reading mysteries, she should've thought of this sooner. The evidence she sought was probably something ordinary, something right in front of her eyes. Something tangible… Proof that Dan was living with another woman.

She banged open the sliding closet door and jerked a shirt free of its hanger. The force of her rage left the wire hanger swinging like a pendulum. She checked the pocket, tossed the shirt aside and reached for another one.

Nothing.

He'd been too smart for her, or so he thought, destroying all the evidence. But Grace wouldn't be foiled, not this time.

The second shirt joined the first one on the carpet. Soon the floor was heaped with Dan's clothes. Her shoulders heaving, she grabbed as many as her arms could carry and hauled them through the house, dumping everything at the front door. Staring at the heap, she unlocked the dead bolt and threw open the door with a fury that made it crash against the opposite wall. Then, standing on the top step, she flung her husband's clothes into the night. Trip after trip, she repeated the action, until his half of the closet had been stripped bare and every bit of clothing Dan owned was sprawled across the porch and the sidewalk.

Then, nearly tripping over her cotton nightgown, she kicked a dress shirt on the top step, and sent it soaring into the darkness. A pair of work pants went next as she got caught up in a frenzy of kicking, hurling his clothes one piece at a time.

Sobbing now, she sank onto the porch step and covered her face with both hands.

"Dan!" she screamed. "Where are you? WHERE ARE YOU?"

Only silence answered. Her rage hadn't brought him back, nor had her love. All that was left were her tears. The emotion poured out of her until she was spent and weak.

Wiping the tears from her face, she staggered back

into the house, not bothering to lock the door. If someone wanted to break in and kill her, she'd welcome death. It was better than this nightmare that had become her life, better than having to walk into an empty house every night and acknowledge that the man she'd loved no longer wanted to be with her.

What was it Dan had told her? His idea of hell was spending the last thirty-five years living with her. Right to her face he'd said such a thing, not caring how that made her feel. Not caring that his words were as brutal as any weapon.

"I hate you…" she whispered as she crawled back into the bed. "Oh, God, I hate you." Curling into a fetal position, she began sobbing again, until there were no tears anymore.

Grace woke at first light. She didn't move, but remained in the same curled-up position, her knees tucked against her stomach. The memory of the night before flooded her mind. She'd been like a wild woman, purging her life of Daniel Sherman.

A sound came from the front room. Dan? It'd be just like him to appear now, she thought wryly. Just like that bastard to show up and behave as if there was nothing out of the ordinary.

"Mom? Are you all right?"

"Mom?"

Maryellen and Kelly. Dear God, not her daughters. Grace didn't want them to find her like this.

Maryellen stepped into the bedroom, and sobbing openly, Grace covered her eyes.

"Mom…" Maryellen leaned forward, and wrapping her arms around her, pressed her cheek against Grace's hair. "It's all right. Don't cry, Mom, please don't cry."

Grace's eyes burned, and even after sleeping for what must have been several hours, she felt as though she hadn't rested a single moment.

"What happened?" Kelly begged. "Tell us what happened."

Grace didn't know how to explain that the clothes strewn across the front yard had been the result of a temper tantrum. "Why are you here?" she asked instead.

"Mrs. Vessey phoned," Maryellen explained. "She woke up and saw all Dad's clothes outside and was worried about you."

"Oh."

"Did you hear from Dad?" Kelly pressed, and it killed Grace to hear the eagerness in her child's voice. With all her heart, Kelly believed that Dan loved them all. Soon, any time now, he'd return with a perfectly logical explanation of where he'd been and why.

"Do you know where Dad is?" Maryellen asked gently.

"No."

"Daddy...where...are...you?" Kelly raged. She started to sob.

Grace didn't have any answers for her daughter. All she could say for sure, as she caught a glimpse of gold on the other side of the room, was that when Dan had left, he hadn't bothered to take his wedding band with him.

Justine couldn't concentrate on banking. Already she'd made two mistakes and it was only eleven o'- clock. This was not the way she wanted to start her work week. The problem had to do with her class reunion. The planning committee had gotten together Friday night for an informal dinner and discussion. Everything had been set in motion weeks earlier and the reunion was less than a month away.

Justine had never intended to get this involved. She blamed Lana Rothchild for being so eager to enlist her help. And she blamed her mother for encouraging her. Before she could back out, Lana had her collecting the money and paying the bills. At the last meeting, Justine discovered she was also expected to be part of the decorating committee. Now it would be impossible not to attend.

It wasn't only the reunion that was getting her down. Seth was on her mind constantly, although she hadn't heard from him since the night Warren proposed. Not one word. For a man who claimed to be so crazy about her, he did damn little to show it.

She'd thought… She'd hoped… The hell of it was, Justine didn't know *what* she thought anymore. Not about Seth and certainly not about Warren.

She and Warren weren't getting along, either. It'd serve Seth right if she did accept Warren's proposal. Even as that idea went through her mind, she knew it was the worst thing she could possibly do.

"Looks like you've got company," Christy Palmer whispered as she walked past Justine's desk.

Seth. It had to be Seth. Her head shot up with a smile she couldn't restrain.

Only it wasn't Seth who strolled into the bank, but Warren. He carried a huge bouquet of fresh flowers in a glass vase. Every eye in the room turned to him as he headed directly for her office.

If Justine could have slid out of her chair and hidden beneath her desk, she would have. She'd promised an answer to his proposal, and the deadline had come and gone, and still she didn't know what to do.

"Hello, baby." Warren greeted her loudly enough to ensure that everyone in the bank heard him.

"Hi, Warren," she returned without emotion.

"I came to invite you to lunch."

"Sorry," she said, fighting the urge to be flippant, "but I have a noon meeting." That was true enough, but she didn't mention it was a meeting with one of the tellers and would take all of five minutes. If that.

Warren sighed. "I'm still waiting, you know."

"For what?" She closed the file she was working on.

"You still haven't given me your decision."

"I told you," Justine said impatiently, lowering her voice, "that if you pressure me, the answer is no."

"Hell, I figure we might as well get married, seeing that all we've done lately is argue. Is that what you want? What's happened, baby? We used to be close and now all of a sudden, it's like I'm not good enough for you."

"That's not it." How could she explain something she didn't fully understand herself?

"It's that high-school reunion of yours, isn't it?"

Justine didn't know how many times she'd had to tell him otherwise.

"If that's not it, then it has to be that old boyfriend you met up with."

Seth wasn't an old boyfriend. "I never went out with him."

"But you wanted to."

"No." Not when she was in high school, at any rate. The problem was a more recent one.

"We need to talk," Warren said urgently.

"Warren," she began, doing her best not to show her frustration, "I can't just take off in the middle of the day because you want to chitchat."

"You could if you married me—you wouldn't have to work."

Justine narrowed her eyes. "Don't say another word."

"All right, all right." He held up one hand, smiling. "Come on, this'll only take a moment." He set the flowers on the corner of her desk and pleaded with his eyes.

It wasn't like Warren to be humble. She realized this must be important, at least to him. Normally he went out of his way to act arrogant.

"Fine," she said, motioning for him to sit down.

"I'd rather do it someplace more private," he whispered, glancing over his shoulder.

Justine darted a look at her watch. "Listen, I have an appointment in ten minutes. I can leave after that. Would you like to meet outside? We could talk there."

"All right."

Justine thought he seemed relieved.

Sure enough, Warren was waiting for her when she left the bank. He was leaning against his car and straightened when she stepped outside. Hurrying around to the passenger side of the car, he held the door and Justine climbed inside. He didn't need to tell her that the engagement ring was stored in the glove box.

"I only have a few minutes," she reminded him when he slid into the seat beside her. "I've got meetings all afternoon." A slight exaggeration, but in a good cause.

"You sure you can't get away for lunch?"

She answered him with a hard look.

He shrugged. "Just asking."

"What's all this about?"

Warren gazed out the side window. "I wanted to talk to you about us getting married."

"Warren!"

"I think I know the reason you can't make up your mind."

Great. If he had any insight into that, she'd gladly listen.

"You've got the hots for Seth Gunderson."

For one moment she was too breathless to respond. Breathless with embarassment—and chagrin. "I most certainly do not! That you'd even say such a thing—"

"Now, don't get mad. The least you can do is hear me out before you get all riled up." He clenched the steering wheel with both hands—the only outward evidence of tension.

"Fine," she said curtly. This was what got her about Warren. As insensitive and blind as he could sometimes be, every now and then he had the uncanny ability to know her better than she did herself.

"You don't have to hide the way you feel about Seth."

She crossed her arms irritably. "Is that right?"

"I can give you the things a woman wants. Jewels, gifts, status."

Justine rolled her eyes. "That's what a woman wants? You sure, Warren?"

In response, he leaned across her and opened the glove compartment, withdrawing the ring box. He flipped open the lid and she nearly gasped, seeing all four gorgeous carats of the diamond in the full light of day. It sparkled like nothing she'd ever seen.

"You tell me," Warren said. "You're a woman meant to wear a ring like this."

Justine didn't argue with him. He was right; this was an incredible diamond and any woman would feel beautiful with it on her finger.

"Well?" he pressed.

She gave a long, drawn-out sigh, conceding. "You've made your point."

"That's what I thought."

"Is there anything else?" she asked. "I need to get back to work."

"You want the ring, and I want you to have it, but you're still hesitating and I think I know why."

Justine said nothing.

"I can give you all the things you deserve in life, but we're both aware that there's one thing I can't give you."

"Warren…"

"Hear me out. You want Seth Gunderson. You're young and healthy, and hell, I'm not blind." He held her look, then pointedly slid his gaze past her. "But I can be."

Justine frowned. "I don't understand."

Warren slid his arm along the back of her seat. "Baby, you want sex. What woman doesn't? So go ahead, with my blessing. Screw his brains out if that'll make you happy, and then come home to me."

The crudeness of his words made her gasp. "You're sanctioning an affair?"

"If not Seth, then someone else. You pick."

"That's not the kind of marriage I want!"

He spoke as though he hadn't heard her. "The only thing I ask is that you tell me who it is."

Justine couldn't believe they were having this conversation or that Warren would suggest something so…so reprehensible. "I'm not like that, Warren."

He grinned with the amusement of a man who'd seen it all. "You never know, Justine. You just never know."

Fifteen

As a single man, Jack Griffin didn't make a habit of turning down dinner invitations, especially ones that came from Bob and Peggy Beldon. Peggy was an extraordinary cook, and meals at their bed-and-breakfast were the stuff of culinary legend.

Jack had been friends with Bob for more than ten years; Bob and Peggy had owned Thyme and Tide for seven. It was on Lighthouse Road, a mile or so from Olivia's house. The two-story white structure with the black wrought-iron fence had been called the Mansion before Bob and Peggy bought it. A Navy Commander was said to have built it in the early 1900s. It had turrets, one at either end of the house, and the larger of the two had a widow's walk.

The B and B had been successful from the outset, due in no small part to the Beldons' skill as hosts—and of course, to Peggy's cooking.

Jack arrived with a bouquet of flowers and a healthy appetite.

"Welcome," Peggy said as she opened the door and

kissed him on the cheek. "We don't see nearly enough of you. Our guests aren't scheduled to arrive until late, so we're free to relax for a few hours." Her eyes crinkled in a smile. "I always enjoy the opportunity to feed someone who appreciates my cooking as much as you do."

"Invite me to dinner any time you like," he said enthusiastically.

"Did I hear the doorbell?" Bob walked in and the two men exchanged handshakes.

"I'll take care of these flowers," Peggy said and left the room.

Jack followed his friend onto the patio behind the house. Its location granted a full view of the cove, with the Bremerton ferry in the distance.

"I've already got the cribbage board set up and ready to go," Bob told him. "How about a glass of iced tea?"

"Sounds great."

While Bob hurried into the kitchen for the tea, Jack inspected Peggy's herb garden. It was lovely to behold, a delight for all the senses. Even Jack, who liked to say that he had "a green thumb—green with mold," derived real pleasure from Peggy's garden. Many of the fresh herbs were used in her prized recipes, and he wondered what she'd serve tonight.

Bob returned with two glasses of iced tea. "This retirement is for the birds," he muttered. "It looks like the house is going to need painting this summer, and Peggy thinks I should be able to do it myself."

"She's joking, right?"

"I hope so." Bob sank down on one of the lounge chairs. "Can you believe it's the middle of June already?" He sat upright with a startled look.

"What's wrong?"

Bob glanced away and seemed embarrassed, as though he'd said something he shouldn't have. "Nothing," he said, shaking off the question. "Just another one of life's regrets. Let's not discuss it."

Jack frowned, but if there was anything he understood it was regrets.

"So—you've been here almost a year," Bob said casually, reaching for his tea.

Jack nodded. A year. Well, it would be in October. Busy as he was with the newspaper, the months had flown by. It seemed only a few weeks ago that he'd sat in Olivia's courtroom that first time…. He was shocked to realize that six months had passed.

"What do you think of Cedar Cove now?"

"Hey," Jack said with a grin. "It's my kind of town." Bob and Peggy had been raised in Cedar Cove. They'd graduated from high school together, and then Bob had been drafted and gone off to fight in Vietnam. He'd come home haunted by demons— memories and experiences he could scarcely speak of, even now. Those demons had led him to look for oblivion in the bottom of a bottle. Jack had faced his own demons from Nam and they, too, had led him to the deceptive gratifications of alcohol. He'd met Bob in a rehab center, and they'd struck up a friendship that had grown over the years. Although he had ten years' sobriety now, the consequences of those hard-drinking years still lingered. Only now had Eric begun to trust him.

"I thought we'd eat out on the patio tonight," Peggy announced, joining the two men.

That suited Jack just fine. After a week of intermittent rainfall, the evening was clear and warm. A soft breeze came off the water, and with it the faint scent of the sea.

"So," Peggy said, taking the wicker chair next to Bob. "How's the paper doing?"

"It's thriving." Jack was proud of that. He'd made a lot of changes in the last eight months, added a second edition each week and followed his instincts. One of his most popular innovations had come from Charlotte Jefferson. Her Seniors' Page had become a huge hit with the community. Olivia's mother was a natural. Her chatty column every Wednesday was full of tidbits about local happenings. If Mrs. Samuel's grandson was visiting, Charlotte reported the news. If the Robertsons' dog had puppies, she wrote about them, guaranteeing the litter good homes. She passed on recipes and some great old-fashioned household hints. Who would've guessed vinegar had so many uses? She wrote about the past, discussing local history, especially events that took place around World War II. And she threw in bits and pieces of her own wisdom.

"What about you?" Peggy asked. "Are you thriving, too?"

"Me?"

"Are you happy?"

"I'm sane and sober, and that's about as good as it gets for me."

"What about Olivia?" Bob asked.

His buddy would ask the one question he didn't want to answer. Jack shrugged.

"What kind of answer is that?" Peggy scolded. "A few weeks ago, you had lots to say about the judge."

"She's in love with her ex-husband," he said bleakly. He'd seen it the day Olivia returned home from her trip to California. Since then he'd only heard from her once, when she called to break their date for the following Wednesday. There'd been no contact between them after that. He sighed, remembering how she'd come back from the airport with her ex, the top down on a fancy red convertible, music blaring. They'd had eyes only for each other. Anyone looking at them would think they were lovers. Jack wasn't a man who walked away from a challenge, but he was smart enough to avoid a losing proposition—like falling for a woman still involved with her ex.

"I thought Stan remarried," Bob said, turning to Peggy.

"He did."

"That doesn't change the way Olivia feels about him," Jack insisted.

"Did you ask her about it?"

Jack shook his head. More than willing to move on to another subject, he said, "What do you hear from the kids?" Bob and Peggy had two children; Hollie, their oldest, lived in Seattle and their youngest, Marc, was in Kansas.

"They're both fine," Peggy told him. "What do you hear from Eric?"

His son didn't make any effort to keep in touch with Jack, which he supposed was fair. For a good portion of Eric's life, Jack had been absent, if not in body, then in spirit.

"Not much," Jack confessed.

"When was the last time you talked to him?"

Jack had to think about that. After their dinner with

Olivia, he'd phoned to invite Eric to Cedar Cove, but his son had refused, offering a convenient excuse. He had a date. This wasn't the first time Eric had mentioned the girl he was seeing. Shirley or Shelly—her name was something along those lines. It seemed Eric might be serious about this one, and Jack had made the mistake of saying so. He'd suggested it was time Eric thought about marrying and settling down. His son had nearly snapped his head off.

There was a reason for Eric's reactions. He couldn't father children, due to the massive doses of drugs he'd been given as a child, and had never gotten around to telling Shirley…or Shelly, who apparently wanted a family. The conversation had ended on that sour note, and Jack hadn't called him since.

He would soon enough, but he needed to give Eric time to forgive him for his careless remark. He longed to forge a path to his son, not destroy the fragile groundwork that had painstakingly been laid.

"Dinner will be ready in half an hour," Peggy said, leaving the two of them. She returned a moment later, carrying out a large salad.

"Let me help," Jack said.

"Nonsense." Peggy waved aside his offer. "You two play cribbage. Bob's been looking forward to it all day."

Jack was more than willing to comply. Bob had the cribbage board set up on the table, and Jack sat down opposite him, his back to the sea. He didn't want to be distracted. Bob was a good player, quick and decisive, and Jack needed all his wits about him.

"Is Peggy all right?" Jack asked after Bob had dealt the first hand.

Bob put aside the deck and reached for the seven cards. "What makes you ask?"

Jack wasn't sure. Peggy was as warm and welcoming as ever, but he sensed that something was troubling her.

Although he appeared to be studying his cards, Bob had the look of a man deep in thought.

"That bad?" Jack teased.

Bob frowned in confusion.

"The cards," Jack explained.

"No, no." His smile seemed forced.

Jack set his cards aside. "Everything's all right with you and Peg, isn't it?" he asked, his voice worried.

"After thirty-two years, it should be, don't you think?"

"You never know." He desperately wanted evidence of one solid marriage, just to prove it was still possible in these days of easy divorce. One marriage that could survive a crisis… He thought of his ex-wife—and he thought of Olivia. He'd never wanted a woman with the intensity he wanted her. He—

"Jack?" Bob's voice broke his concentration.

He glanced up.

"Are you going to stare at your cards all night or are you going to discard?"

"Discard."

"Something on your mind?" Bob asked.

"Like what?" Jack said.

Bob grinned, obviously a man capable of reading all the signs. "Like Olivia."

Jack gave an exaggerated shrug. "That readable, am I?"

Bob chuckled. "No more readable than Peg and me."

"Nothing wrong, is there?" He didn't mean to belabor the point, but the thought of problems between Bob and Peggy depressed him. They were the one couple he knew who'd found happiness and clung to it through all the years, both good and bad.

"We're fine. What about you?"

"I'm okay, just a bit disappointed."

"Olivia?"

Jack nodded, and nothing more was said.

They finished the first game, and by then Peggy had dinner dished up and ready to serve. Good food and good friends. It was the best meal he'd had in weeks, but Jack decided that the company was even more satisfying than the food.

The accident aboard the *George Washington* made headlines on the national news for several days. Cecilia was in daily contact with Ian. Some days she couldn't get to a computer, so she wrote out her thoughts. These letters would take a week or longer to reach him, but Ian said he enjoyed hearing from her in any form.

With finals in only two classes, Cecilia had one day in which she didn't have to be in school. Since she wasn't scheduled to work until late afternoon, she decided to celebrate and made plans to spend the morning with Cathy.

After examining her at the Navy Hospital, the attending physician had told Cathy that the pregnancy was safe but suggested she quit her job as a cashier at the local grocery. Being on her feet for an eight-hour shift wasn't good for her or the baby. Not wanting to take any chances, Cathy had immediately handed in her notice.

When Cecilia arrived at her friend's duplex, she discovered that Carol Greendale had stopped by, too. Cecilia almost changed her mind and turned around. Almost. Carol's little girl was just a day or two older than Allison would have been. Cecilia dreaded seeing the baby and was drawn to her in equal parts.

"Hello, Carol," she said in a friendly voice, pretending she was at ease with the other woman. Little Amanda was toddling happily around the apartment, examining everything in sight, reaching for books, trying to grab knickknacks, pulling at the curtains.

"Come here, Amanda," Carol urged, holding out her arms for her daughter. The child immediately lurched toward her mother, shrieking with pleasure.

"I'm glad you're here," Cathy said, gripping Cecilia's hand tightly as if to let her know she understood.

"We were just talking about the *George Washington,*" Carol explained, bouncing the child on her lap.

"Carol came by with the latest news," Cathy said.

"I just heard they're heading back," Carol squealed.

"The *George Washington*'s coming back to the shipyard in Bremerton?" Cecilia wanted to make sure there was no misunderstanding. Where the aircraft carrier would go for repairs had been undecided.

"Yes!" No one could doubt Cathy's excitement.

"When will they get here?" Sheer joy raised Cecilia's voice.

"It shouldn't be long."

Cecilia felt hopeful about her marriage, especially after the last few weeks. Ian had communicated with her practically every day. In the beginning, most of what they'd exchanged had been ordinary, everyday information. Facts more than feelings. But as the weeks went on, they'd both felt ready to venture into more dangerous territory—their daughter and her death.

In the process, Cecilia realized that she'd heaped too much of the blame on Ian's shoulders. She hadn't meant to, but trapped in grief and pain, she'd lashed out at him. It wasn't fair, she'd known that even at the time, but she hadn't been able to prevent those reactions. Dealing with his own shock, Ian hadn't been much help to Cecilia. Almost a year had passed now, giving each of them a new perspective on the role they'd played in nearly destroying their marriage.

"Let me get the baby a cracker," Cathy said, moving into the kitchen.

"That's not necessary," Carol told her.

"Oh, I want to."

Cathy looked pointedly in Cecilia's direction. "Come and give me a hand," she murmured.

Cecilia jumped up with alacrity.

Carol seemed confused and a little affronted. Cecilia felt bad about that, but Cathy obviously had something important to tell her.

"Andrew knows about the baby," Cathy whispered the minute they entered the kitchen.

"How?"

"I told him. I had to. He wanted to know why I quit my job. I tried to edge around the truth, but we made a promise never to lie to each other and so I...I explained that I'm pregnant."

"And?"

Cathy stared down at the floor. "He's afraid, just like I am, and kind of hurt that I hadn't told him sooner."

"Under all of that I'm sure he's thrilled."

Cathy nodded. "I know he is. We both want this baby so much."

Cathy seemed about to dissolve into tears and might have if little Amanda hadn't let out a frustrated cry. Cathy hurriedly found a soda cracker and brought it into the living room.

Carol was busy picking up toys. "It's time I went home," she murmured.

"You just got here," Cathy protested.

"I know…it's just that…" She glanced at Cecilia, as if to say that now Cathy's other friend had arrived, she was obviously less welcome.

Ever sensitive, Cathy shook her head. "I hope you'll forgive me for being so rude, but I needed to tell Cecilia something. I didn't mean to exclude you."

"I understand," Carol said. She reached for Amanda, who eluded her mother's arms and waddled toward Cecilia. The baby stumbled and Cecilia instinctively thrust out her arms. Drooling as she smiled, Amanda gazed up at Cecilia, her eyes wide with interest. Cecilia froze, unable to stop looking at the baby girl who in other circumstances might have been her own.

Little Amanda returned her look, then smiled and raised her arms, wanting Cecilia to pick her up.

The decision was automatic. Cecilia leaned over and lifted the child. Then Amanda, as though she understood the significance of the moment, wrapped both chubby arms around Cecilia's neck. Cecilia knew she was being fanciful, but she felt that this child, this year-old baby, recognized all the love stored in her heart for Allison. The daughter she'd never hold again, or sing to, or kiss good-night.

Cathy and Carol paused for breathless seconds, watching Cecilia's reaction to Amanda.

Tenderly Cecilia brushed the wispy hair from the child's forehead, kissed her there, then set her back on the floor, where Amanda teetered, recovered herself and walked unsteadily to her mother's side.

"Carol, I'm going to tell you, too," Cathy said. "I…you know I recently quit working. Well, there's a reason for that. I'm pregnant."

Carol's eyes lit up. "That's great!" Her smile faded when she realized that neither Cathy nor Cecilia seemed completely delighted. "What's wrong?" she asked, glancing from one to the other. "Aren't you happy?"

Cathy was quick to assure Carol she *was* pleased. "It's just that I miscarried the first two pregnancies, and I'm scared to death."

"I would be, too." Carol handed Amanda the soda cracker; the little girl was content to sit on the floor, gnawing it. "I'm so sorry, Cathy. I can't even imagine…" She turned to Cecilia. "Weren't you in the hospital about the same time as me?" Carol asked.

Cecilia nodded. "My little girl was named Allison."

"I remember. I always wanted to tell you how bad I felt, but you…well, you didn't seem to want to talk to anyone."

"I regret that now," she said. "I could've used a friend."

"I could use one myself," Carol said.

The military might have its heroes, but the wives were the backbone of the Navy, Cecilia reflected. These women—and she was now one of them—supported their husbands, their country and each other.

"I don't know how this pregnancy will go," Cathy told them, "but I do know that Andrew and I will be able to deal with it, no matter what happens."

No matter what happens, Cecilia mused. If her friend could be this brave, then she could, too.

Hurry home, Ian, she prayed. *Please be safe and hurry home.*

Sixteen

If not for Olivia, Grace would've dropped out of the Wednesday-evening aerobics class ages ago. But since Dan's disappearance, she'd found that working out was a great stress-reliever. Never had she sweated so much or breathed so hard. Every movement was done with enthusiasm and energy. Before, she'd always been the one who lagged behind; now she led the class.

"Keeping up with you is going to kill me," Olivia complained as she followed Grace into the shower room. "What's gotten into you lately?"

As if Olivia didn't know. "You have to ask?"

"Well, yes, I understand you're upset about Dan."

"That's not the half of it."

Olivia wiped her face with a hand towel. "Have you had dinner yet?"

Grace shook her head. With only herself to cook for, it was easier to toss a frozen entrée into the microwave. Wednesdays she generally skipped dinner altogether. By the time she got home from aerobics, she was too tired to eat.

"Not yet."

"Want to meet at the Pancake Palace?" Olivia suggested.

Grace wasn't hungry, but it beat walking into an empty house. "Sure."

She took her time showering and changing into her street clothes. She hadn't done more than chat with her friend in several weeks, and she was looking forward to a real conversation. Sure, they saw each other, but there was rarely an opportunity to say more than a few words in passing.

Olivia had already secured the booth when Grace arrived. She slid in across from her and reached for the menu tucked, as always, behind the napkin canister.

"Wasn't this our booth back in high school?" Olivia asked.

Grace had to think about that. Was it? "I don't remember, but it might be."

"Remember how Kenny Thomas broke up with me right here in the Pancake Palace?" Olivia reminded her.

"The rat fink."

Their eyes met and they smiled, chasing memories. But Grace's amusement faded as she recalled how often she'd met Dan here during their high-school days. How different her life might have been if he'd broken up with her, or she'd had the courage to return his high-school ring. Even then, while she was still a teenager, Grace had sensed that they didn't bring out the best in each other. Deep down, Dan had known it, too. Then, just before graduation, Grace had discovered she was pregnant. Dan had wanted to marry her and she'd managed to convince herself it was the right thing to do.

"Kelly and I met here for dinner not long ago," Grace told her, breaking off her thoughts before she fell into the abyss of self-pity. It was the night Kelly had persuaded her not to file for divorce. She'd promised to wait until after the baby was born, but she'd regretted that decision ever since.

"I envy your relationship with your daughters," Olivia admitted.

"Aren't you and Justine getting along?"

Olivia gave a slight shrug. "We don't argue, if that's what you mean, but we don't talk openly. I heard through the grapevine that Warren's asked her to marry him, but she hasn't even mentioned his proposal to me."

"Maybe she knows what you'll say."

Olivia's eyes turned thoughtful. "I've vowed not to be negative, but it isn't easy."

One thing Dan's disappearance had done was bring Grace closer to her daughters. They talked at least once a day, mostly to encourage and support each other. After the latest episode, they'd decided they could no longer bear not knowing where Dan was. The girls were willing to help with the expense of the private investigator; they felt as desperate for answers as Grace did.

"I hired Roy McAfee again last week." Grace had talked to him soon after Dan's disappearance, and decided after his initial investigation that she couldn't afford his services anymore. As the weeks crept by, she'd come to understand that neither she nor the girls could afford *not* to hire him. They had to know what had happened to her husband, and there seemed to be no other way. "The frustration is driving me insane."

"Do the girls approve?"

Grace nodded. "They're the ones who talked me into it. They want answers as badly as I do. Badly enough to help foot the bill." Hiring a private detective was expensive, but as Maryellen had said—only half joking—the medical bills for a nervous breakdown would be far higher.

Something inside Grace had snapped the night she cleared out Dan's closet. She should probably have checked herself into a psychiatric ward. She'd reached her limit, and her daughters had immediately recognized it even if she hadn't.

"What did Roy say?"

"I gave him what information I could, and he promised to get back to me."

"Did you tell him about your suspicions?"

Grace sighed and picked up her fork, squinting at the water spots. "He didn't agree or disagree with me. But I have faith that if there's another woman, he'll find out who it is."

"And," Olivia said, leaning forward, "what proof were you able to give him?"

"Not a damn thing." Grace had searched through everything Dan owned and come away all the more confused. How careful he'd been, how clever. Not a shred of evidence remained—at least, nothing tangible she could hand over to Roy.

"But gut instinct tells you there's someone else?"

She nodded slowly. "As I think back, I see more and more clues."

"Such as?"

"You know Dan. He didn't care much about appearances, but recently I started remembering little things about the first time he went missing."

"Like what?"

"That morning was the same as always, but I realized later that he'd combed his hair and shaved. Dan usually shaved at night. He altered his routine that day."

"He was meeting her?"

"That's my guess."

"What about this time?"

Grace had reviewed their last morning together a hundred times or more. "I can't remember exactly, but I think so." What she did recall was the faint scent of his aftershave as he collected his lunch bucket from the counter and headed out the door.

"I remember a year ago I asked him if he felt guilty about something because he was acting kind of… furtive." That incident had played back in her mind, too. Dan had shot her a stricken look as though she'd caught him red-handed. Naturally he'd denied everything, and because she'd *wanted* to believe him, she had.

"Have you heard anything from Roy yet?"

Grace wadded up the paper napkin in her fist. "He phoned this afternoon."

"And?" Olivia's eyes widened with anticipation.

"Nothing. He said that if Dan does have another job, he's not using his social security number."

"What about the woman? Did Roy give you any ideas on who it might be?"

"No. He's asked around, put out feelers in Seattle

and beyond, but he hasn't come up with a single lead. Whoever it is, I suspect they've been meeting for years. She probably got tired of Dan's inability to make a decision and told him it was either her or me." Although Grace spoke without emotion, plenty of it churned inside her. It had become more and more apparent that Dan had been under pressure. He wasn't by nature a cruel man, although at times he was capable of saying and doing cruel things. Whoever this woman was, Dan must have loved her very much.

"It's like he disappeared off the face of the earth."

"I know." Grace stared down at the table. "All I want is an answer," she whispered. "I know it might be hard to believe, especially after everything he's put us through, but I want Dan to be happy." She'd never been able to fill the emptiness inside him. It'd been worse after Vietnam. Then Kelly had been born, and it was as though this second daughter had renewed his purpose. For a few years they'd been happy. Dan had encouraged Grace to get a college education, and was an invaluable asset with the girls. They'd been a team, a family. Now he was gone.

"What if you don't get those answers?" Olivia asked gently.

Grace had considered that, too. It was a very real possibility. Dan didn't seem willing to tell her why he'd left—not to her face, at any rate. Perhaps that was the reason he'd decided to make a brief appearance in Cedar Cove. He'd wanted to be seen. Perhaps he was telling her he'd gotten on with his life and now she should do the same.

"If I don't get any answers, I'll deal with it just as I have everything else."

Olivia shook her head admiringly. "You're a brave woman, Grace Sherman."

Grace didn't view herself that way but accepted the compliment. "Hey, when are we going to get some service around here?"

Olivia placed two fingers in her mouth and gave a low piercing whistle. She'd always been proud of her ability to do that—and it had certainly impressed her sons.

"Hold on!" the sixty-year old waitress shouted from the other side of the restaurant. "I've only got two hands."

"Same ol' Pancake Palace," Grace laughed. Some things never changed, and for that she was grateful.

The last week of June, Olivia suddenly realized she hadn't heard from Jack Griffin in more than a month. Not since she'd returned from California. It wasn't until she started planning her mother's birthday celebration that she noticed it'd been so long. Between her work in family court, the problems with Justine, James's new family, her mother's obsession with Tom Houston and Grace's troubles, Olivia had been caught up in everyone else's life. She'd nearly forgotten she had one of her own.

Home from court early on a Monday afternoon, Olivia was in a rare domestic mood and prepared a batch of her favorite breakfast muffins, a family staple.

Since Jack hadn't seen fit to phone her, she decided to call him. It wasn't her habit to contact men, but this time she had a perfectly good excuse—an invitation. She didn't have a home number, so she called him at the office.

"Jack Griffin," he snapped, answering as soon as the receptionist had rung through.

"Hello, Jack."

"Oh—Olivia."

He sounded as if she'd knocked him off-balance. "I guess you weren't expecting me," she said.

"You could say that." His voice softened.

It was probably best to get to the point right away. "Have you got plans for the fourth of July?"

"Depends," he said cautiously. "What do you have in mind?" He didn't wait for her to answer before he offered his own suggestion. "There's an article I've been meaning to write about a nudist colony out by Home. Are you interested in tagging along?"

Her laugh was answer enough.

"That's what I thought." He muttered in a resigned voice, and Olivia laughed again.

"Actually, it's my mother's birthday on July fourth," she said, "and I was planning a small surprise party."

"How small?"

"You, me and Mom." Justine had been invited, too. She would likely make an appearance without Warren, but Olivia doubted her daughter would stay long.

"Can I get back to you?"

"By all means." They ended the conversation soon after that, and Olivia hung up with a sense of disappointment. Perhaps she'd offended Jack, although she couldn't imagine when or how. She'd had to cancel their last date, because of a Bar Association meeting, but he'd sounded almost relieved and she hadn't heard from him since.

Five minutes later, the doorbell chimed. When Olivia answered, she was astonished to see Jack Griffin leaning against her doorframe, doing his damnedest to look like Cary Grant in *His Girl Friday*.

"Jack? What are you doing here?"

"I thought it over," he said, grinning sheepishly. "I'd love to come to your party."

"Great."

"Are you going to invite me in?"

"Oh, of course." She moved aside and he stepped into the house, following her into the kitchen, where she'd brewed a fresh pot of coffee. The muffins were just out of the oven.

"This is a family recipe," she told him as she set a warm muffin on a plate. "Mom frequently reminds me how good bran is for the older person." She rolled her eyes on the word *older*.

"Bran apple muffins? Your mother included the recipe in one of her first columns."

"The very ones." Olivia reached for a muffin herself and joined him at the table.

"I'm glad you called," Jack told her. "It's been a while since we talked."

"You could've phoned me, you know."

He hesitated. "I, uh, wasn't sure that was such a good idea."

"Why not?" she asked, her tone forthright.

He hesitated again, weighing his words. "I know you've been divorced a long time, but it seemed to me—and I could be wrong—that you and your ex are—"

"Friends?"

Jack's gaze held hers. "More than friends," he said. "Are you still in love with him, Olivia?"

It was a question she didn't need to consider long.

"Stan and I had three children together. We'll always be linked through them."

"That wasn't what I asked you."

"I know." She wished she could explain what she felt for her ex-husband, but her feelings were complex and something of a mystery even to her. She took a deep breath. "You're right, we're divorced. I do love him, but it isn't the same kind of love we had as husband and wife."

Jack looked away as if he didn't understand the answer. Or perhaps he *did* understand, but didn't like what he'd heard. Olivia felt her words were woefully inadequate. The bond between her and Stan was more than the children they'd brought into the world, more than the child they'd buried. It was everything they'd shared. There were things they knew about each other that no one else could possibly know.

Legally they were separate. Stan had a new wife and a new family, but a court decree hadn't completely divided their hearts.

"I don't really get it," Jack said, his face darkening. "Basically I'm wondering, seeing how you feel about your ex, if there's room in your life for someone else." He straightened and threw back his shoulders. "Actually, I should be a little more specific. Is there room for *me?*"

"That shouldn't be such a difficult question to answer," Jack muttered, when she didn't speak right away.

"It isn't," she tried to assure him. "I'd very much like there to be."

He stared at her. "Really?"

Olivia laughed. She found Jack Griffin smart and

funny and in some ways almost childlike in his enthusiasm, his sense of adventure. She loved the spontaneity she saw in him.

"I like you, Jack."

He beamed at her. "I like you, too. A lot. It's probably not good strategy to admit it at this early stage, but what the hell do I know about strategy anyway?" Having said that, he leaned forward and kissed her.

Olivia was sure his original intention had been a friendly peck, a short kiss to seal this new understanding. However the moment their lips met, moist and warm with freshly brewed coffee, the kiss became…real. Passionate. Jack wove his fingers into her hair and he rose to his feet to lean closer. Olivia reached for him.

The intensity of the kiss heightened as his mouth expertly molded against hers. It'd been years since a man had touched her like this. She'd ignored that sensual part of her, let it grow dormant, and now Jack had brought it back to life.

A discordant sound drifted toward her, and Jack abruptly broke off the kiss. "Someone's coming," he whispered.

"Mom!"

Olivia jerked back and nearly fell off her chair. "Justine."

"Oh, hi." Justine stood framed in the kitchen doorway. She looked sharply from Olivia to Jack. "I'm not interrupting anything, am I?"

"No!" Olivia shouted. "I mean…" She glanced at Jack and—damn it all—blushed.

To her surprise, her daughter laughed. "Honestly, Mom, it's no big deal. If you two want to continue whatever you were doing, go ahead, with my blessing. I'll come back at a more convenient time."

"Ah…"

"I think I should leave," Jack said. He kissed Olivia's cheek. "See you on the fourth. Do you want me to bring anything?"

Her mind a blank, Olivia shook her head. For the life of her she couldn't remember what they were doing on the fourth. Oh, yes, her mother's birthday.

Jack sidled past Justine, and whistling a catchy tune, let himself out of the house.

"Mother," her daughter said, arms folded. "I'm shocked." Her delight was unmistakable.

"Don't act so amused. I'm not as old as you think."

"*I* know that," Justine assured her, "but I wasn't sure *you* were aware of it."

Olivia stood on feet that felt a little unsteady. Jack's kiss had shaken her more than she cared to admit. She walked over to the coffeepot and refilled her cup, then automatically poured one for her daughter. What had prompted this visit, Olivia couldn't even guess.

"So how long have you and Jack been involved?"

"We're not."

"He was at the house when you returned from California, remember?" Justine reminded her.

"Yes, I know." She hated the way these questions flustered her. Nothing had been settled between her and Jack. Not really. Okay, so they'd agreed to start seeing each other, but it was too early to know how significant their relationship would become.

"I asked Jack then, and he claimed you were only friends. Foolish me, I believed him."

Justine certainly seemed to be enjoying this.

"We *are* friends."

"Oh, yes," her daughter teased.

"Justine!"

"Friends and then some."

Olivia shook her head. "All right, if you must know…this is a recent development."

"How recent?"

Olivia peered at her watch. "Twenty minutes."

"Mother!"

"It's true." And Olivia felt good about it. Optimistic. No way of knowing what would happen, of course, especially as they hadn't yet defined their relationship. But she couldn't help wondering where the kissing would've led if they hadn't been interrupted.

"Enough about me," Olivia said abruptly. "To what do I owe this unexpected visit?"

"Well," Justine said, sinking down in the chair recently vacated by Jack, "I came to see what you had planned for Grandma's birthday."

That was only an excuse; Justine could easily have asked over the phone. "I thought we'd have a small picnic."

"Waterfront Park?"

"I hadn't decided where, but that sounds like a good idea." Her mother's home was within walking distance of the waterfront area, and there'd be a lot of festivities there on the fourth. "Can you come?"

"I should be able to drop by for an hour or so."

Not looking at Justine, she reached for her muffin. "Will Warren be with you?"

"Probably not, but we're still seeing each other."

Olivia was afraid of that. More than anything she wanted to ask her daughter what the future held for her and Warren, but she dared not say anything that would upset the delicate balance of her relationship with Justine.

"The truth is, Warren and I haven't been getting along lately."

In one way, Olivia was glad to hear that, although she chastised herself for such an ungenerous reaction; in another way, she was distressed by Justine's evident unhappiness. If Warren was what she really wanted... "Any reason?" she asked carefully.

"Oh, I don't know." Justine exhaled sharply. "We're different people."

Different generations, too, but Olivia didn't mention that. "You might want to remember what attracted you when you first started seeing each other."

"I've been thinking about that a lot lately." Her hands cradled the coffee mug. "I was drawn to him right away—he was so polished and successful. I'd dated other men and they were always pressuring me, wanting more from the relationship." She hesitated. "That's probably an oversimplification." Lifting her mug, she stared at the coffee and then lowered it to the table without taking a drink. "Actually, I was the one to blame for past dating failures. I don't want a long-term committment or a family." She stared at Olivia. "I've told you that before. I know it upset you, and I'm sorry, but it's the truth."

"Warren's already been married," Olivia said, wanting to keep Justine talking, hoping that as her thoughts emerged, she'd gain insight into her daughter's emotions.

"Actually, he's been married three times."

Olivia had only known about two of his former marriages, but wisely refrained from comment.

"His children are raised."

From what she'd heard, Warren Saget had a daughter four years younger than Justine.

"In other words, he wouldn't be interested in starting a second family."

"Yeah, you could say that."

Olivia merely nodded.

"Warren represents safety and security to me," Justine said in a low, serious voice. "It's comfortable being with him. It seemed that everything I objected to in other relationships isn't a problem for him. He's always been good to me and I didn't need to worry about…you know."

Olivia wasn't sure she did, but again she held her tongue. "You're looking sad." Reaching over, she stroked the side of her daughter's face.

"I am sad," Justine repeated as though this was a revelation. "That's exactly what I am."

Olivia searched for something comforting to say, some wisdom she could pass on to her daughter. Unfortunately her mind was a blank. Every day she sat in court and issued judgments that would alter the way families lived their lives. But when it came to her own child, Olivia was at a loss.

"Have you decided to break it off?"

It was the wrong thing to ask. Justine instantly bristled. "That's what you'd like, isn't it?"

"No," Olivia responded, sorry now that she'd said a word. "Whatever happens between you and Warren is your business. It's obvious that you care for him."

"I do. Sometimes he irritates me, and then sometimes he's so kind and thoughtful…. I know what you think, Mom, what everyone thinks, but Warren's got his insecurities, just like most people. And in his own way, he loves me."

"I'm sure that's true."

Justine stood and deposited her coffee cup in the sink, as though preparing to leave. "Thanks, Mom, I feel better."

Well, that was good, but Olivia felt confused. She had no idea what the visit had been about; she only knew she didn't want it to end. "Isn't your class reunion coming up shortly?"

"Next month," Justine mumbled, reaching for her car keys. "I doubt Seth will be there in case you're wondering."

"I'm not," Olivia lied. "But...why not?" she asked, surprised that her daughter had voluntarily brought up the other man's name. Generally Justine went out of her way to avoid the subject of Seth Gunderson.

"He's in Alaska, and this is his busiest time of year. He won't be able to take four or five days off and fly home for a class reunion."

"Perhaps not," Olivia agreed mildly.

Then out of the blue, Justine looked her square in the eye and blurted out, "Falling in love with Seth would be a terrible risk."

"Why is that?"

"Oh, Mom, think about it. I have nothing in common with him. He's just the type of man I want to avoid. He's a fisherman—that's a dead-end career if there ever was one. Besides, he lives on a *boat*. I have more tablecloths than he has dishes. We just don't...mix."

"But you're attracted to him?"

"He makes me crazy." She clamped her mouth shut and folded her arms tightly across her chest.

"Loving him *is* a risk," Olivia repeated her daughter's words back to her.

Justine groaned. "I *know* that, Mother."

"Oh, Justine," she whispered, hugging her daughter. "Think about it. Everything of value in life involves risk."

Her daughter pressed her forehead against Olivia's shoulder. "Oh, Mom, I wish I knew what to do."

"Follow your heart."

"I can't," she whispered brokenly.

"Why not?"

"I'm afraid it'll lead me straight to Seth."

Olivia patted her back gently, but found it impossible not to smile.

June 25th
Dearest Cecilia,

I know it's probably a shock to get a letter from me. I've gotten into the habit of sending e-mails because they're convenient and easy, and so much faster. Today, however, e-mail just seems too impersonal. It doesn't feel right to sit down at a computer. Not today, June 25th.

You didn't say anything, but I'm sure Allison Marie has been on your mind. If she'd lived, we'd be celebrating her first birthday. And this year, just like last year, her daddy's out at sea.

I don't know if there are words enough to tell you how much I regret not being with you when Allison was born. I would've done *any-*

thing, given everything I possess or ever will, to have the opportunity to hold my little girl just once. There's an ache inside me that will never go away, knowing that not only could I not be with you, but I was denied the one opportunity I had to see my daughter.

Your getting pregnant when you did last year wasn't a real surprise. A part of me was looking for it to happen, I think. I was crazy about you from the moment we met, and despite the separation, that hasn't changed. Allison Marie was a gift from God. I don't know why she had to die or what purpose her life served, but I do know I have no regrets about us marrying. Not a single one. Together we created a beautiful baby and together we loved our child. We still love her. The key word here is *together,* Cecilia. And that's the way I want us to stay.

After the accident on the *George Washington,* you told me you love me. Oh, honey, you don't know how good it was to hear you say it. My ribs hurt like hell, otherwise I would've been shouting loud enough for you to hear me all the way in Cedar Cove.

Let's not do anything foolish—like get that divorce. When the *George Washington* pulls into Bremerton shipyard, I hope you'll be there with all the other wives, waiting for their husbands. I don't want this to be the end of our marriage, but the beginning of our lives together. I think Allison would approve of her mommy and daddy celebrating her birthday, don't you? After all, she brought us together, didn't she? It's time we put away the pain and celebrated her life, short as it was. Because of Allison, you're my wife and I'm your husband and that's how we should remain.

I love you so much.

Ian

Seventeen

Charlotte was fast losing patience with Cliff Harding. He'd assured her he'd come to town to look over the things she'd taken from Tom's storage unit, but that was more than a month ago. Cliff continued to delay the meeting. Although his excuses sounded plausible, Charlotte could see that this simply wasn't a high priority for him.

That distressed her, but she wasn't sure what to do about it.

"I'd drive out and see him myself," her friend Laura told her on the Monday following her birthday.

Charlotte was with her knitting friends at the Senior Center. A few weeks ago she'd casually mentioned talking to Tom's grandson, but hadn't told them everything involved. She wasn't about to admit, even to her nearest and dearest friends, that she'd committed a felony.

"I would, too," Evelyn added. "From what you said, it isn't that far."

"It'll mean driving on the highway." Any road with more than two lanes terrified Charlotte. Cars whizzed past, and no matter what lane she was in, she seemed to annoy the other drivers, especially if she followed the posted speed. What did these people think the speed limit was, anyway? A suggestion? Everyone seemed to be in such an all-fired hurry these days. She'd drive over to see him if she had to, but she wouldn't like it and she'd make darn sure Cliff Harding heard about it.

"I don't know what it is with young people today," Helen muttered, jerking on her yarn with unnecessary force. "They don't respect their elders the way *we* were taught to."

"I couldn't agree with you more." This came from Bess, who nodded emphatically.

"You were his grandfather's friend. One would think he'd welcome the opportunity to thank you."

"It didn't escape my notice," Helen said, leaning toward Bess, "that he didn't visit his grandfather, either."

"I'm going to phone him again," Charlotte said, decision made. "And I'll let him know when he can expect me." She'd put it off for nearly five weeks already. Cliff Harding always had an excuse. There had been that business trip, and last week there was a brief message on her answering machine—one of his horses was about to foal and he couldn't leave. Charlotte could only imagine what his excuse would be *this* week. And the next. No, Laura was right, it was time to take matters into her own hands.

When Charlotte returned home, she tucked away her knitting, made a fuss over Harry, and then, filled with determination, headed toward her phone.

Tom's grandson answered, sounding far more congenial than he ever had before.

"This is Charlotte Jefferson," she announced.

"Yes, Mrs. Jefferson, I've been meaning to get in touch with you."

Charlotte just bet he had. Probably with another of his lame excuses. "I'm sorry to trouble you again, but seeing that you've been unable to keep your appointment with me—"

"That was what I planned to discuss with you. Would this afternoon be convenient?"

The indignation that had been bolstered by her friends' well-meaning advice was suddenly unnecessary. "This afternoon would be fine," she muttered, feeling deflated and, truth to tell, a little disappointed. She'd been ready to blast him; she'd even worked out some very effective remarks about family duty on the drive home. Now she wouldn't be able to use them.

"I imagine it's a bit disconcerting to be sleeping with a gun under your bed."

Charlotte heard the teasing in his voice and decided to ignore it. "Actually, I moved the gun to my underwear drawer." She didn't mention that she'd wrapped it in an old girdle.

"Your underwear drawer?" he repeated.

Again, she'd amused him, but this time she couldn't fathom why. That was a clever hiding place in her opinion. No one breaking into the house, if they got past her overprotective cat, would think to search for anything of significance in a drawer of cotton panties. Anything that was the least bit important in Charlotte's house invariably ended up there. Her savings passbook was tucked inside her support panty hose. No thief was going to catch her off guard.

"What time will you be here?" she wanted to know.

"Is around four okay?"

"That would be perfect." Charlotte gave him directions to her home and they ended the conversation. Then, because she wanted to be hospitable, she baked cookies. The recipe had been given to her three years ago at a seniors' potluck and it always went over well. Men, especially, seemed to like these cookies, which were thick with chocolate chips, coconut and pecans.

She'd just finished scraping the last of the batch from the cookie sheet when the doorbell rang. Charlotte hurried toward the front door, picking up Harry to keep him from escaping. Her cat purred in her ear as she turned open the three locks. The last one had been installed only recently. Charlotte wasn't going to make a thief's job easy for him, no sir. She couldn't afford one of those fancy security systems, but she had her own safeguards.

The man who stood on the other side of the threshold was a good six feet tall with a small paunch. He wore a cowboy hat and boots, blue jeans with a brown jacket and a string tie.

"Mrs. Jefferson?"

"Yes. You must be Cliff Harding." She unlocked the screen door and held it open for him. "Come in, please."

He stepped into her modest home and sniffed appreciatively. "You been baking cookies?"

"I just wanted to be neighborly," she said, inviting him to take a seat on her sofa. She was ready. The silver service was set up, the pot filled with fresh coffee. The service was used only on rare occasions, but she wanted to make a good impression on Tom's grand-son. The cookies were still warm from the oven.

Charlotte noticed that she didn't need to urge Cliff to help himself. She sat down across from him.

"How much do you know about your grandfather?" she asked, pouring for them both.

Cliff leaned forward and accepted the delicate china cup. "Only what my father told me." This was said with a scowl. "And frankly, it wasn't compli-mentary. Tom Harding was a scoundrel and a wom-anizer."

"That I wouldn't know. I only knew him during the last few months of his life."

"Were you aware that he abandoned his family in order to pursue his film career? My grandmother and father lived on charity and died in poverty while Tom Houston, The Yodeling Cowboy, lived the high life. If I have no interest in his effects, I'm sure you can understand why."

Charlotte found it difficult to think badly of Tom. This wasn't the man she knew. "By the time I met Tom, he'd suffered a stroke and had lost his ability to speak."

"You said he requested to be transferred to Cedar Cove?"

"That's my understanding." Charlotte reached for a cookie. She should avoid the unneeded calories, but these were simply too good to ignore.

"Do you think I was the reason?"

"I'm positive." Charlotte didn't doubt it for a mo-ment. "What you said about your grandfather may very well be true. I can't possibly know, nor is it im-portant that I do. But I *can* tell you about the man who became my friend. He wanted to meet you, I'm convinced of that, but I think he was afraid."

"Of me?"

She nodded. "He moved to Cedar Cove because it was the closest facility to where you lived. It makes sense, doesn't it?"

"I suppose." He didn't seem convinced.

"I understood Tom. Don't ask me how or why, but the two of us bonded. Some days it was almost as if we *could* talk. I understood what he wanted to say and he appeared to understand me."

"My father said he always did have a way with the ladies."

Charlotte stiffened, then decided Cliff was probably right. She wouldn't take offense, although that was her first instinct. "Your grandfather never had the chance to tell you he loved you."

"Loved me?" Cliff flared. "He never even met me."

"You're right, of course, but you were his only living relative. He'd obviously kept track of you. Otherwise, how would he have known where you were living or that you raised horses?"

"Are you *sure* he knew that?"

"I believe he did. The same way I'm confident he wanted you to have the things I took out of his storage unit. He wasn't able to be part of your life. Perhaps he felt he didn't have the right to intrude on you. But it's his blood that runs through your veins. He was proud of you—I know it. Proud to be your grandfather. This is all he had to give you."

Cliff Harding set down his coffee and stood. Staring out the window, he turned his back to Charlotte. "I came this afternoon to thank you for your efforts on my grandfather's behalf and to tell you I wanted nothing to do with the man."

"And now?"

"You're a very persuasive woman, Mrs. Jefferson."

"Does that mean you'll take his things home with you?" She hoped he would. And more importantly, she wanted him to examine each piece and discover the man Tom Harding had been. She feared Cliff would pack everything away without learning about his heritage.

"I'll take them."

"And you'll carefully study what your grandfather left you?"

He nodded.

"I believe you've made a wise decision." Sighing deeply, Charlotte knew she'd put in a good day's work. Somehow, she'd accomplished what Tom had wanted her to do. And on a more personal note, she'd be glad to remove the gun from her girdle.

Justine bought a slinky blue dress for her ten-year class reunion, but she didn't know who she was hoping to impress. Her one consolation, as she headed out the door for the festivities, was that Seth Gunderson wouldn't be attending. She should know. As the treasurer for the reunion, Justine had compiled a list of who'd signed up and who'd paid. Seth had done neither.

She felt humiliated arriving without a date, but why should this night be different from any other high-school function? Justine had been an outsider all through those years. She was the class brain, the valedictorian and the girl voted most likely to succeed.

With several scholarships offered, she'd dutifully chosen a prestigious East Coast school and followed the course set out for her, but she was never truly happy.

She hated life on campus, hated being away from Cedar Cove. After her graduation, she'd taken a job at First National. In the years since, she'd been promoted steadily. Now she was the youngest branch manager in Cedar Cove history, and one of the bank's youngest senior employees. Justine loved the challenge of her job and enjoyed playing an active role in financing the growth of her community. But she considered her personal life a dismal failure.

Warren would have attended the reunion with her if she'd pressed him. She hadn't, afraid her former classmates would assume he was her father or, even worse, an old teacher they couldn't quite place.

The high-school gymnasium looked great, if she did say so herself. The decoration committee, of which she was a part, had worked hard and done a fabulous job. Fresh flowers were everywhere, on the tables and in huge rented vases along the walls.

The band was already playing, and almost involuntarily Justine tapped her foot to the music as she waited in line to collect her badge and sign in. Everyone around her was talking; she was surrounded by squeals of recognition and "do you remember when's." Just as she had in high school, she remained the outsider, listening in, smiling and pretending she felt at ease when she didn't.

Attending this reunion was a bad idea. Her instincts had told her that months earlier, and she should've heeded them.

"Justine!" Lana Rothchild hurried around the sign-in table and hugged her as though it'd been years since they'd seen each other. Actually they'd worked on the decorations together that very morning. "I *love* your dress."

"Thanks." The metallic-blue dress had short sleeves and a deep V in front. Knee-length, it clung to her trim figure. She'd bought the dress on impulse and had decided not to think too hard about it.

"Do you need any help?" Justine asked, looking for a way to appear busy and needed and part of the group.

"Everything's under control. You just enjoy yourself."

Justine wondered if that was possible.

"I can't thank you enough for all the help you gave us," Lana said as she handed Justine a badge.

With no further excuse to linger, she walked into the main part of the gymnasium. A few couples were dancing, a clump of women had gathered on one side, a group of men on the other—not all that different from the high-school dances she'd attended. Thinking a glass of wine would relax her, she found the bar and ordered a zinfandel, then stood by herself on the outskirts of the dance floor. It had been the same ten years earlier.

"Hello, Justine."

Seth Gunderson stood directly in front of her, deeply tanned, his hair so blond it was almost white. His eyes had never looked bluer.

"What are you doing here?"

He grinned. "I graduated the same year as you, remember?"

"I mean…" She found it difficult to think. "Aren't

you...I thought...well, of course we graduated the same—"

"I flew home for the reunion," he said, answering the question she couldn't seem to get past her teeth.

"I realize that...what about..." Rather than continue making an idiot of herself, she simply stopped talking.

"You're surprised to see me. Actually, I surprised myself by deciding to fly down at the last minute."

Surprised was an understatement, as far as Justine was concerned.

"Would you like to dance?" he asked.

She couldn't stop staring at him. No man on earth had a right to look this good. Refusing him would have required more effort than she could possibly muster. Oh, yes, she wanted to dance with him. Wanted to slide into his arms, be held by him...

Rather than attempt to respond verbally—at the rate she was going she hadn't a clue what might actually come out of her mouth—she nodded and put her wineglass on a nearby table.

Seth led her onto the dance floor and turned her into his embrace. Naturally—fittingly—the band was playing a slow dance and she lifted her arms as he held her loosely. Justine was amazed at how well-suited they were physically. At five-ten and in heels, she was taller than most of the men, but Seth still had several inches on her. She rested her head against his shoulder and breathed in his clean, outdoor scent.

This was the first time she'd ever danced with him.

"You came alone?" he whispered.

"Yes."

The music was mesmerizing and it was all she

could do not to close her eyes and give herself completely over to it. That couldn't happen, especially with Seth. She couldn't allow herself to be trapped in the magic of the moment. She refused to let her guard down, certain that as soon as she did, Seth would ask her about Warren, or the engagement.

"I did, too," he said after a minute. "Came here alone, I mean."

He wrapped his hand around hers and brought it to his chest. Justine felt the solid, steady beat of his heart. It seemed to travel through her hand and the pulse in her wrist, directly to her own heart. His eyes held her, and with their steps in unison, this was the most sensual, seductive moment of her life.

When the love song ended, Seth released her. She moved away from him and clapped politely.

"Do you have a table yet?" Seth asked.

"Lana asked me to sit with her and Jay."

"Well, Jay invited me to sit with him and Lana," Seth told her, eyes twinkling.

So the Rothchilds were involved in a little matchmaking. Just now, it was very easy to forgive them.

"The buffet isn't until nine."

"I know," she said, wondering if he was inviting her to dance again. If so, he didn't need to ask. When the music started, they moved toward each other as though magnetically drawn.

Other than the few times they stopped to talk to friends, Justine and Seth danced every dance. Soon the buffet table was ready and a line of revelers straggled around the gym floor. Seth bought them each a glass of wine and sat next to her at the table for eight.

It wasn't long before Justine fell into conversation

with the others. Soon pictures of her classmates' children were passed around and she found herself looking at the cherubic faces and listening to stories full of love and pride. Justine carried a small photograph of her newborn niece and showed it to Seth.

"James is married? When did this happen?"

"Earlier in the year. Isn't Isabella beautiful?" Justine had made a firm decision not to be a mother, but as she studied the photographs she was handed, she felt an intense and unexpected longing. It would eventually pass; she recognized that, even as she struggled to deal with a slew of unwelcome emotions.

"Excuse me," she said, getting to her feet. Instead of heading for the ladies' room, Justine walked outside, out the front door, letting the cool air revive her. She leaned against the flagpole and closed her eyes, breathing in the night air and with it the return of her rational self. She wasn't like those people back inside the school. She never had been. She was separate, different. Not above them, just not one of them. She'd known it in high school and felt it even more profoundly ten years out.

"Justine?" Seth joined her. "Is something wrong?"

"No." She was quick to assure him that everything was fine, but he wasn't fooled.

"What is it?"

She shook her head. She couldn't explain to Seth, of all people, that she'd come outside in order to clear her head and put her life back in perspective.

"You look like you're about to cry," Seth commented.

"That's ridiculous." She turned away, but Seth caught her hand and drew her gently into his arms.

She could have resisted at any time—but didn't. She knew he intended to kiss her even before his lips claimed hers. This wasn't their first kiss, but Justine had conveniently forgotten what this man was capable of doing to her resolve.

The effect of his kisses was like putting a match to lighter fluid, each one hotter and more explosive. "This isn't a good idea," Justine cried, tearing her mouth from his, her breathing labored.

"It's a terrible idea," Seth agreed, but it was clear he was teasing her as he brought his mouth to hers. He held her head between his hands, but Justine wasn't struggling. She submitted fully to the kiss, starved for his touch.

"We have to stop," she whimpered.

"The reunion…" he murmured.

"Yes…yes, we should get back." Justine broke away and hid her face against his collarbone as her shoulders heaved.

Seth held still, arms around her waist, until his ragged breathing slowed.

"This *really* isn't a good idea," Justine finally said, and broke free from Seth entirely.

"Why isn't it?"

"You aren't going to like the answer," she told him.

"What?" he asked. "I suppose you're going to say you've decided to accept Warren's proposal, after all?"

She attempted a smile, one that would show him she was confident in her decision. "Actually, I have."

"You're going to marry Warren Saget?" The question sounded incredulous.

She lowered her eyes and nodded.

Seth didn't say anything for several seconds, then exhaled slowly. "If that's your choice, I'm obliged to honor it. I only want the best for you, and if that's Warren as your husband...I won't try to change your mind."

He spun on his heel and returned to the reunion alone.

Dan had been missing for over three months now, and as the weeks drifted by, Grace had become almost accustomed to living alone. She'd adopted a routine of sorts, which helped her forget that the man she'd been married to all those years had abandoned her and their two daughters. She couldn't understand why he hadn't stayed long enough to see their first grandchild. Kelly had convinced herself that her father would be back before the baby was born, but Grace held out no such hope.

Roy McAfee continued to give her biweekly updates on his progress, but so far he had nothing of significance to report. There'd been no more sightings of Dan in town after that one time. Grace suspected there wouldn't be. Her husband had come to deliver a message and Grace had received it loud and clear. He hadn't been to the house again, either.

Thursday evening after she'd closed the library for the night, Grace walked toward her car, which she'd left near Waterfront Park. Concert on the Cove—a summertime music series sponsored by the downtown merchants—was on tonight. This was exactly the kind of social gathering Dan hated; in all the years the performances had been offered, Grace hadn't attended a single one.

Families came with their children, senior citizens brought their own chairs, teenagers hung out in groups. Most people brought a take-out dinner. The blend of young and old drew the community together.

As she reached her car, Grace heard sixties rock-and-roll and sang along with an old Diana Ross hit. All at once it dawned on her that there was nothing to keep her away. There hadn't really been a good reason in the past, and there wasn't now.

Dan would never have told her she couldn't attend, but she hadn't wanted to go alone. She was alone now, with no reason to hurry home. She could stay or leave as she wished; it was entirely up to her. How odd that this insight should give her such a profound sense of freedom. It felt as if shackles had been unlocked and the weight she'd carried had fallen from her shoulders. She was free—free to attend the concert. Free to enjoy life without catering to Dan's likes and dislikes. Free to do what *she* wanted.

Walking over to the park, Grace stopped long enough to pick up an order of chicken teriyaki from the Japanese restaurant across the street.

Most of the seating had already been taken. Grace stood and watched, delighting in the fact that so many people were enjoying the concert. A trio of women cavorted on the bandstand. Dressed in miniskirts, pageboy haircuts and pink feather boas, The Blondells performed the old Supremes hits from the '60s, and Grace found herself smiling at their energy and high-spirited fun.

"Grace!" Charlotte Jefferson raised her arm in order to attract Grace's attention. Her best friend's mother sat on the outer edge of a semi-circle of lawn chairs, with a blanket spread in front of her.

Grace made her way over to Charlotte, maneuvering slowly through the crowd.

"Sit here with me," Charlotte invited. "I have something I want to discuss with you later, all right?"

"Sure." Grateful for the invitation, Grace sat down on the blanket and leaned against one leg of Charlotte's chair. Her back would start to ache soon, but she would enjoy this as long as she could.

"This is such good music," Charlotte announced when the intermission was announced.

"It's fabulous," Grace agreed.

"You know, I was just thinking of you the other day," Charlotte said. "I have something for you."

"Me?"

"I talked it over with Olivia, and she thinks it's a good idea. Exactly what you needed, she said."

Grace was intrigued.

"A friend of mine, a good friend, has a wonderful companion, and well, she's moving to a retirement complex and needs to find a home for Buttercup."

"Buttercup?"

"Harry's been such a loyal friend, and seeing that you're alone, I thought…" Charlotte looked uncertain. "I did plan to ask you first, but as I recall you've had dogs in the past."

Dan had loved his dogs, and throughout their marriage they'd had a number of family pets. Two years ago, their small cocker mix had died peacefully in his sleep and Dan had decided they wouldn't have any more animals.

"What kind of dog is Buttercup?" she asked.

"A golden retriever."

"I'd love a dog," Grace said decisively. "I really would."

Charlotte rubbed her hands together. "I'm so pleased. Olga's been terribly worried about finding a good home for her dog. I *knew* you were the right person."

"I'd be happy to take Buttercup over to visit Olga now and then, if that would put her mind at ease."

"Oh, Grace, what a thoughtful gesture. Olga would be so appreciative."

That weekend, the golden retriever became part of Grace's life. She wasn't sure how well the dog would adapt to a new environment, but the moment Grace brought her into the house, it was as if Buttercup recognized it as her home and prepared to settle in.

"Well, Buttercup," she said, releasing her from the leash. "What do you think?"

With her tail wagging, the golden retriever examined each room, paused in the middle of the living room and then jumped into the old recliner that had been Dan's chair. Dark eyes watching Grace, she rested her chin on her paws.

Grace couldn't help it; she burst out laughing. Of all the places for Buttercup to claim as her own, she'd chosen Dan's chair. Somehow she'd instinctively known that space was available.

"We're going to be good friends, aren't we, Buttercup?" Grace murmured to the dog.

This, too, Buttercup appeared to understand.

Grace poured herself a cup of coffee, reached for

a crossword puzzle book and settled down in the chair next to that of her newfound friend and companion.

Life continued without Dan. He'd apparently found someone else and—Grace smiled over at Buttercup—so had she.

Eighteen

Olivia felt good. Better than good. She felt confident, successful, at the height of her powers. She'd put in a fabulous day in court, and, since summer was now apparently in full bloom, she intended to enjoy what remained of her afternoon.

This was perfect weather for sitting at a café along the waterfront and enjoying a bottle of wine and some delectable Hood Canal shrimp. She could think of no one she'd enjoy doing that with more than Jack Griffin.

He'd proved to be delightful company. In the three weeks since the Fourth of July picnic, they'd attended a political rally, on which Jack had written an article. Then she'd tagged along while he interviewed the lady who crocheted beautiful tablecloths for the Saturday Farmers' Market. That article had appeared in Wednesday's edition of *The Cedar Cove Chronicle*. Last Friday night, Jack had taken her to dinner at Willcox House, a B-and-B in Seabeck that Bob and Peggy Beldon had recommended. The house boasted a room

Clark Gable had once stayed in, and the food was incredible. Once again, Jack was writing an article. It was high time they went out just for pleasure, she decided, instead of combining it with business.

Leaning back in her office chair, she reached for the phone and punched out his number. "Hi," she said when he picked up.

"Hi, yourself. To what do I owe this pleasure?" He sounded genuinely pleased to hear from her.

"I'm about to make you an offer you can't refuse."

"Sounds interesting."

"I promise you it will be." Olivia loved the banter between them.

Jack chuckled. "I can hardly wait. What do you have in mind?"

"Close your eyes," she whispered seductively. "Think of sitting out on the Cove."

"Am I with anyone?" he interrupted.

"Naturally. You're with me."

"What are you wearing?"

"Jack!"

"Well, it's important."

She sighed in mock annoyance. The teasing was all part of the Jack she enjoyed most. "Okay. I've got on a sleeveless top and walking shorts, a big sun hat and dark glasses."

"I like you in dark glasses. They make you look mysterious."

She laughed; there wasn't a thing mysterious about her—certainly not her growing attraction to him.

"Next, consider the background music."

"Dire Straits? Guns n' Roses? Red Hot Chili Peppers?"

"No," she said with a beleaguered sigh. "I was thinking more along the lines of Neil Diamond, Barry Manilow, Henry Mancini."

"*Barry Manilow?* Please, not Barry Manilow."

"I happen to like Barry Manilow," she chided.

Now it was his turn to sigh. "I don't know if there's hope for this relationship."

"All right, we'll compromise on the music."

"If you like Manilow, there's nothing I can do."

"Okay, Eric Clapton," she suggested.

"Bob Dylan's better. Agreed?"

"All right. May I continue?"

"Go ahead," he urged, as if she'd been the one holding up the proceedings.

"We're together on the Cove watching the sun set, music is playing softly in the background and we're sipping glasses of wine." She hesitated, certain he was about to launch into a discussion regarding the wine. "Do we need to argue about the wine, too?"

"No," he assured her, "you choose."

"All right. A nice fruity Gewürztraminer."

"Hmm. Isn't that a little sweet? Are you sure you wouldn't be interested in something—"

"I thought we weren't going to argue about the wine. You can drink what you want and I'll drink what I want."

"Fine with me." He was certainly amicable all of a sudden.

"A waiter appears with a menu," she went on.

"If the menu's got tassels, I can't afford to eat there."

"No tassels."

"Good." Jack said immediately. "Now, did the waiter bring the bread basket yet? I'm getting hungry."

"Don't rush him, we're still enjoying our wine."

"While you're drinking the wine, I want the warm bread and butter."

"You're making this difficult, Jack."

"Okay, okay, continue, but I should tell you I worked through lunch today, so if you're going to start listing the specials of the day, I'll have to make a run to the candy machine."

Olivia heard drawers opening and closing. "What are you doing?"

"What do you think? I'm looking for something to eat." A grumbling sound followed his explanation. "The best I could come up with was a roll of Tums."

"Poor baby. I guess that means you don't want to hear about the seafood fettuccini, dripping with spicy shrimp, seared scallops and bits of lobster, stirred together in a creamy Alfredo sauce."

"You are a cruel woman, Olivia Lockhart."

Olivia laughed delightedly. "You just wait until I show you how cruel I can be."

Jack sucked in his breath. "I love it when you talk dirty."

Olivia growled.

"When, where and how long will it take me to get there?"

"Tonight at seven."

He hesitated. "I…can't."

"Six?"

"That won't work, either."

"All right, eight, but that's really kind of late for me."

"What about tomorrow night?" Jack asked.

"Can't. I've got a judicial committee meeting. Why can't you go to dinner tonight?"

"I just can't."

He was certainly being cryptic about it. "Jack, have you got another date?" she asked, half laughing as though it was a joke. Neither of them had made any promises. He was free to date someone else, just as she was. But she hadn't.

He paused before answering. "Not exactly," he said.

"Not exactly," she echoed. What the hell did that mean? "Are you doing something illegal?" she asked.

"No."

"Just secretive," she muttered under her breath.

Again the pause. "If you want to put it that way."

Olivia hated secrets. "I see," she said, not bothering to hide her disappointment.

"Olivia, I'm sorry. I'd love to have dinner with you, but you'll have to choose some other night."

Olivia was a woman whose life was open to scrutiny; she disliked the way he chose to keep parts of his life hidden. If he had some dark secret, she'd rather know now.

"Come on, honey, it's not that big a deal, is it?"

Honey. Now she was his honey.

"Another evening, all right?"

"No," she said softly but with conviction. "It isn't all right."

"Let me make sure I'm getting this," Jack said after a long pulsing silence. "You're angry because I can't go to dinner with you at the drop of a hat."

"No, Jack, that's not it at all." She straightened in her chair. "Listen, I'm sorry. It seems I've been reading more into our relationship than warranted–"

"Olivia…"

"No, please, I understand."

"You don't."

"I do," she countered. He wanted everything on *his* terms, which meant that any relationship could only be a surface one. He had his secrets, and she was just supposed to overlook that.

"Olivia…"

"I'm sorry you can't make it for dinner," she said, interrupting him a second time. "We'll do it another night." *Maybe ten years from now.*

"Don't hang up that phone!" Jack shouted.

She was too stunned to react.

"I know what you're going to do. The next time I call and suggest we get together, you'll have a reason you can't. The time after that, it'll be the same, until I've got the message. Dammit, Olivia, I won't let that happen."

"Then I'll be up front with it. Jack, I don't think it's a good idea to continue seeing each other."

"Why? Because I can't go to dinner with you tonight?"

"No," she said swiftly. "Because I was married to a man who chose to keep secrets from me. I'm not willing to get involved with anyone who can't be open and honest."

Silence.

"I'm right, aren't I?" she pressed. "You're a man with secrets."

It took him forever to answer. "If it gives you any pleasure, then I'll say it. You're right—I have my secrets."

He replaced the receiver, and Olivia listened to the

buzz droning in her ear. Jack should've known her better than that. She derived no pleasure from being right.

The instant Grace pulled into the driveway, Buttercup bounded out the doggie door at the back of the house and raced to her side.

"Hello, girl," Grace said as she stepped out of the car. She leaned down and scratched the dog's ears, then the two of them walked to the mailbox to collect the day's offerings.

Along with a couple of magazines and a few odd bills, Grace got the *Bremerton Sun*.

"Are you ready for your dinner?" she asked Buttercup, unlocking the door that led to the kitchen.

The golden retriever dutifully walked to her water bowl and lapped up a drink, then waited patiently while Grace opened the closet door and brought out the large bag of dog food. She filled the dog's dish, then settled down to glance at the mail.

Nothing important.

She set the magazines on the table and as she did so, noticed that the message light was flashing.

"Grace, it's Roy McAfee. Give me a call when you get home."

Dan.

Roy must have learned something about Dan. Her hand trembled as she looked up Roy's number and immediately returned the call.

Corrie, Roy's wife and assistant, connected her right away.

"Roy, this is Grace Sherman. Have you located Dan?"

"No, but I got the report from the Assets Check and thought you might be interested in what I found out."

After running into nothing but dead ends, Roy had suggested they request a computer check for assets, but Grace had balked at forking over the extra two hundred-dollar fee required for the search. Learning that Dan held title to a piece of land wasn't going to help her locate him. In a community property state, any bank records would be open to her without cost.

"So—anything interesting?"

"Yup. The report listed a license application Dan made last June."

"A year ago."

"That's right. You didn't tell me you two owned a travel trailer."

"We don't."

"According to state records, Daniel Clayton Sherman residing at 204 Rosewood Lane, Cedar Cove, Washington, applied for a license for a travel trailer."

"When?" Grace asked. "*Exactly* when?"

"June sixteenth of last year."

The date was meaningless, and Grace felt numb. "I…I don't know about any travel trailer."

"I called the private party who sold it to him and discovered he paid cash. It's a twenty-four footer. The other person wasn't likely to forget, since Dan arrived with the money in fresh one-hundred-dollar bills."

"How much?"

"According to the seller, thirteen-thousand dollars."

"Cash?" They didn't *have* thirteen-thousand dollars in cash. Any extra money had been invested. Nearly everything they'd managed to save over the years was in stocks and bonds.

"The man made quite a point of telling me it was all one-hundred-dollar bills. Actually, he was quite shaken when he was handed that much cash."

"Where would Dan get that kind of money?"

"I can't answer that," Roy told her.

Neither could she. "Dan couldn't have taken out an equity loan without my knowing, could he?"

"He didn't," Roy said. "Not according to the bank records I have."

And surely she would've received some sort of statement for any other kind of loan.

"This doesn't make sense." But then, very little of what Dan had done in the last year was logical.

"So you don't know anything about this travel trailer?"

"Not a thing. Do you think Dan's traveling around the country?" she asked, searching desperately for answers.

"I really don't know. Haven't come across any evidence of that—no credit card charges, for instance. None in his name, anyway."

"Then what's he using for money?"

"If he had thirteen-thousand dollars in cash you knew nothing about, there's no way of knowing how much money he had squirreled away."

"Where could he have kept this money?"

"Do you have a safety-deposit box?" Roy answered her question with his own.

"Yes…no. I don't know anymore." They did have a box at some point, but she hadn't seen the renewal application in years.

"Tell me this," Roy said. "Who brought in the mail every day?"

"Dan."

"That's what I thought. Another possibility is that Dan has a post office box you know nothing about."

All the secrets Dan had kept from her. Grace didn't know how she could have lived with him for more than thirty years and not known the man who was her husband.

"The report didn't show a safety-deposit box?" she asked.

"No, but if Dan has one strictly in his name, the bank isn't legally obligated to report it. Some banks will as a matter of course, and others only if a court order is issued."

"Will we need a court order?"

"We'll face that when we come to it."

"All right."

As if she understood that her new mistress was feeling anxious, Buttercup walked over to the phone and stood next to Grace. She leaned down and stroked the dog's head, which calmed both of them.

She spoke with Roy for a few more minutes. When she hung up, Grace experienced a new sensation. Considering the range of emotions she'd already become familiar with, she wouldn't have thought that was possible. Since Dan's disappearance, she'd felt disbelief, shock, grief and outrage. Lately she'd discovered a certain peace that came with resignation and acceptance. Roy's latest news didn't infuriate her. Instead, she was left feeling *stupid*.

Sitting at the table, she leafed through the latest issue of *Sunset Magazine*. Something must be wrong with her, she mused. Her life was falling apart and she was reading a chicken enchilada recipe.

The phone rang and for an instant Grace hesitated, uncertain she wanted to talk to anyone. But it was bound to be one of her daughters, and if she ignored the call they'd both worry.

"Hi, Mom."

Grace was right. "Hello, sweetheart. How are you feeling?"

"Pregnant," Kelly complained. "Six weeks to go."

The time had passed quickly for Grace, but she doubted her daughter would feel that way.

"Any news on Dad?"

Grace was always astonished by the way her daughters seemed to sense any new developments regarding Dan.

"Mom?" Kelly pressed.

"Can you get your sister on three-way calling?" Kelly had the option on her phone, whereas Grace didn't.

"You learned something?"

"Get Maryellen on the line and I'll tell you both at the same time."

"Okay." Grace was accustomed to the procedure. She was put on hold while Kelly dialed her sister's phone number, and then once Maryellen was connected, Grace would be able to speak to both her daughters at once. She closed her eyes, her mind spinning as she waited.

In the beginning, Grace had wanted to protect her children from what Dan had done. Her reaction had been instinctive, but it'd also been wrong. Maryellen and Kelly were entitled to know. Furthermore, they might be able to provide an answer. For all Grace knew, Dan might have said something to one of the girls that would give her—or Roy McAfee—some kind of clue.

"We're both here," Kelly said anxiously.

"Are you all right, Mom?" Maryellen asked.

"No." It was time for honesty. "Roy discovered that your father purchased a twenty-four-foot travel trailer last year."

"Dad bought a trailer?" The question came from Kelly.

"Where did he keep it?"

That was a question Grace hadn't thought to ask. "I don't know, but I'm discovering that I knew very little about your father."

"There's more, isn't there?" Again it was Kelly who asked. Kelly who was so close to her father and so confident he'd return before her baby was born.

"Yes," she said reluctantly. "He paid cash for the trailer."

"How much?" Maryellen asked.

"Thirteen thousand," Grace said. "In fresh one-hundred-dollar bills."

Kelly gasped.

Maryellen said nothing.

"I don't have a clue where he got that much money," Grace told her daughters. It was as much a mystery as his disappearance.

"Mom, do you think the other woman might have bought the trailer for him?" Maryellen asked softly.

"Then why not register it in her name?"

"Maybe she wanted you to find out about it," Maryellen suggested.

"Stop it!" Kelly shouted. "There *is* no other woman. Dad wouldn't do that."

"Grow up," Maryellen said sharply. "When are you going to quit looking at Dad like he's some kind of saint? He didn't just leave Mom, you know. He walked out on you and me, too."

"Don't say that," Kelly cried, breaking into huge sobs. "I don't believe it. I'll never believe it."

"Girls, please…" Grace felt close to tears herself.

"Do you still think Dad's going to magically reappear before your baby's born?" Maryellen asked. "Get a grip! He doesn't care about either one of us."

"Maryellen, stop." Grace refused to allow her older daughter to continue. This was hard enough without the two of them turning against each other.

An awkward moment passed, then Maryellen whispered, "I'm sorry, Kelly. I was upset and I took it out on you."

"I'm sorry, too," Kelly said. "For you and Mom. One day we're all going to discover the truth about Dad. I don't know why he's doing this or where he is, but there's a perfectly logical explanation for his disappearance."

Her daughter had said this many times before, and Grace let her say it again. Neither she nor Maryellen challenged what they both saw as a fantasy. They understood that Kelly needed to believe it.

Justine had been downright miserable since the reunion. She'd announced to Seth that she intended to marry Warren, but she hadn't gotten around to mentioning it to Warren himself.

Friday night, Warren planned to take her to dinner

at D.D.'s on the Cove, and she thought she'd tell him then, as long as he understood she wanted a long engagement. Eventually they'd ease their way into marriage.

"You look fabulous," Warren said, kissing her cheek when he picked her up after work. The bank was open until six on Friday nights and after a ten-hour day, Justine was tired. Warren might think she looked good, but that wasn't how she felt.

Because they were close to D.D.'s, Justine suggested they walk over to the waterfront restaurant.

"Let's drive."

It seemed ridiculous to drive to a restaurant less than two blocks from the bank, but Justine didn't want to start the evening with an argument.

Warren held open the car door for her and she discovered a small wrapped package on the passenger seat. "What's this?" she asked.

"Open it and see."

"Not another gift. Warren, please, this isn't necessary."

"Says who?" he joked. "It's the only way I can prove to you that I'll be a generous husband."

"Warren."

"All right, all right, no pressure." Chuckling, he hurried around to the driver's side.

Justine waited until he was seated before she opened the jeweler's box. Inside was an oblong-shaped black pearl in a gold oyster clasp; it was suspended from a fine gold chain. The pearl was exquisite.

"A friend of mine picked that up for me in the South Pacific," he told her.

"It's lovely."

"You deserve to wear diamonds and pearls."

"Oh, Warren."

"Come on," he said, grinning. "Let's get to the restaurant. I could use a drink."

Justine enjoyed a glass of wine now and then, but she wasn't a heavy drinker. Warren often overindulged and when he did, she drove them both home and spent the night in his spare room. She knew what people thought and was content to let their assumption stand. Warren appreciated her discretion. Evenings of this kind happened often enough that she kept a spare set of clothes at his house.

The parking lot at D.D.'s was already almost full, and they were fortunate to find a space. Instead of requesting a table for dinner, Warren led her into the cocktail lounge, where they sat at a circular booth overlooking the water.

Warren had two double scotches in quick succession. He'd just ordered his third when Seth Gunderson walked casually into the lounge.

Justine's shocked gaze clashed with his. She'd had no idea he was still in town. The last place she'd expected to run into him was here.

Seth looked slowly from Justine to Warren, a disgusted expression on his face.

Since it would be rude to ignore Seth completely, she attempted a smile. He acknowledged her briefly by inclining his head in her direction, then made for the bar. He took a seat with his back to her.

"What's wrong?" Warren asked.

"Nothing," she assured him, staring out over the waterfront and the marina.

"Who's he?" Warren asked, glancing at Seth and then, as if he'd figured it out, he reached for his drink and tossed it down in one swallow. "Damn," he said, shaking his head.

"Don't worry about it, Warren. I'm with you, not Seth." Agreeing to marry Warren right then and there would reassure him, but she couldn't make herself do it.

"You want him, though. Don't you?"

"Of course not." How easily the lie came to her lips.

"Who do you think you're kidding?" Warren said scornfully. "It's written all over both of you."

"That's not true." She repulsed Seth. Everything he did told her as much. He sat at the bar with his back to her, letting her know that he couldn't bear the sight of her.

"You can't take your eyes off him," Warren commented and oddly, he sounded amused.

"Don't be ridiculous."

"I'm going to clear the air here and now."

"No! Warren, no." She tried to grab his arm as he slid out of the booth, but he was too fast for her.

Horrified, Justine watched as Warren walked over to the bar. She could only speculate about what he said, but he appeared to be inviting Seth to join them. Seth declined, and obviously Warren persisted, encouraging him. Justine wanted to crawl under the table when Seth finally gave in, picked up his beer and followed Warren back to their booth.

"Sit down," Warren said jovially.

Seth hesitated. The option was to sit next to Warren or to slide into the booth beside her. He chose to sit by her, so she was trapped between the two men.

She noticed that Seth was as far removed from her as he could possibly be and still remain in the booth. Warren moved closer to her and wrapped one arm around her shoulders.

"I understand you two know each other from high school."

Seth didn't seem too interested in answering.

"We were friends even before that," she murmured.

"Did you enjoy the reunion?" Warren asked, directing his question to Seth.

"Parts of it." His gaze burned into Justine's. "I understand congratulations are in order. Justine told me she's agreed to be your wife."

Warren's arm tightened around her shoulders, as if to tell her how pleased he was. Then—pretending he knew—he said expansively, "That's right. As you can imagine, I'm a happy man." He threw Justine a bold smile.

"A lucky one," Seth added without emotion.

"But not a selfish one," Warren said, not quite under his breath.

Justine pressed her hand against his arm, fearing what he seemed about to say.

"What do you mean?"

"Warren, I think it's time we had dinner," Justine said, eager to end this conversation.

"Not quite yet."

"Warren, *please*."

"In a minute," he said a little more firmly. "I can see what's happening between you two," Warren went on.

"Not a damn thing, I can assure you," Seth informed him stiffly.

"Maybe. I'm not here to judge. I know how Justine feels about you, Gunderson. She's got the hots for you."

"Don't do this," she pleaded.

Seth frowned, his face darkening.

"You aren't any better at hiding your feelings than she is," Warren continued. "Well, more power to you."

"Justine's already agreed to marry you," Seth reminded him.

"True, but we both know she's more woman than an old guy like me can handle."

"Oh, God." Never in all her life had Justine been so humiliated, so embarrassed. She tried to leave the booth, but with Warren on one side and Seth on the other, she couldn't escape.

Seth leapt out of the booth as if it'd suddenly caught fire. "I've heard enough of this conversation to know I'm unwilling to listen to any more."

"Don't be hasty," Warren said with a congenial laugh. "I'm just trying to show you both how open-minded I am. If you want Justine, you can have her with my blessing."

Seth's earlier look of contempt didn't compare to the one he cast Justine now. Contempt…and pity.

"I'm afraid you're mistaken," he said, slamming down his beer. "I have no interest in Justine." Then he walked out of the lounge, not sparing her so much as a backward glance.

Nineteen

Cecilia felt the joy, anticipation and excitement as Navy wives and families crowded the pier, awaiting their husbands and fathers. She had truly become one of those wives. She stood with Cathy, who was obviously pregnant now. They held on to each other, fearful of being separated in the large group. In some ways, Cathy was like the sister she'd never had. She hoped that the bond they'd built in the past months would continue for a lifetime. Her friend had taught her so much about courage and hope. Lessons Cecilia had carried with her ever since the accident on the *George Washington*.

"I think I see Andrew," Cathy shouted.

Andrew Lackey stepped off the gangplank and peered expectantly around. Cathy shrieked and ran toward him, arms flung wide. Andrew caught her around the waist and half lifted her from the ground. As they kissed, Cathy threw her arms around her husband's neck.

Feeling a bit awkward watching them, Cecilia

looked away, hoping to catch sight of Ian. Her heart sank; he wasn't anywhere to be seen. Glancing back at her friend, Cecilia felt tears in her eyes as Andrew flattened his hand against Cathy's belly. Standing where she was, Cecilia could feel his relief and his sheer happiness that this pregnancy was secure. The most dangerous months had passed, and although there were no guarantees, a miscarriage was far less likely now. The doctors were pleased with the way the pregnancy was progressing.

Then all at once Cecilia saw Ian. He paused at the top of the gangplank and scanned the crowd, searching for her.

"Ian!" she shouted and her arms shot into the air to attract his attention. "Here! I'm here." She took off running toward her husband, ducking and weaving through the crowd, and literally flew into his embrace.

Cecilia had thought she was ready for this moment, but nothing could have prepared her for the wild burst of happiness. When Ian returned shortly after Allison's burial, she hadn't come to the base to meet him. At the time, she couldn't. She just couldn't. But everything had changed, and now Ian was home and they were beginning a new life together.

"Oh, honey." Her husband's hands were in her hair and they kissed frantically, straining against each other, eager to give and receive, holding back nothing.

"Welcome home." As long as her arms were around his neck, she didn't care if her feet dangled inches off the ground. "How are your ribs?" she asked, afraid all this hugging might hurt him.

"They burn like hell, but I'd rather put up with the pain than not hold you." He kissed her again. The passion between them was back, the way it had been at the start.

Tears welled in Cecilia's eyes. She hadn't expected to cry, but it felt so...so *good* to be with Ian. The months he'd been at sea had been a time of healing for them both.

"I love you so much," she whispered over and over.

"I love you, too."

Ian had proved it in more ways than she could count. She was grateful for his patience and his refusal to give up on her or their marriage. If it hadn't been for his repeated attempts to resolve their differences, she was sure they would've been divorced by now. Neither Ian nor the judge had made divorce an easy option and Cecilia was truly thankful.

"I've made a decision," she told him as they walked toward the car, their arms locked around each other. Now that he was home, any separation, even that of a few inches, seemed too much.

"I hope it involves living with you again," he murmured.

"Yes, it does." Actually Ian was in for a surprise. With Cathy's help, she'd moved her husband's things back into their small apartment. Some of his stuff was still on base, but everything he'd left with the Lackeys had been brought to their home.

"I want my wife with me." He stared into her eyes.

"I want another baby, Ian." There, she'd said it. The words came straight from her heart.

His steps faltered and he stopped abruptly. "I thought...you said..."

She knew he was confused and could hardly blame him. "You can thank Cathy and Andrew for my decision." If her friend could face a third pregnancy with hope and a positive attitude, then Cecilia, too, could learn to let go of her pain and look toward the future.

"You're sure? Because I've made up my mind to leave it entirely up to you. Don't misunderstand me, I want a family, but it's more important to me that *you* feel you can go through with another pregnancy."

Cecilia leaned her head against his shoulder as they resumed walking. "I've given this a lot of thought in the last few months. I'd like to continue with my schooling."

"You should, Cecilia. You're very intelligent, and you show real ability with numbers."

"But I want a family, too. Our family. I'd like to wait a couple of years, though."

"Whatever you decide."

"I wish you'd been this agreeable a few months ago," she teased, then changed her mind. He'd been stubborn, all right, but she'd been no less so.

"Someday soon I want to go back and visit that judge."

"Why?"

"She had the courage to tell us to stay together. She didn't say it in so many words, but that was her message. I want to thank her."

"I do, too," Ian said. And he gently kissed the top of her head.

The telephone woke Grace out of a sound sleep. Heart pounding, she jerked upright and automatically groped for the receiver.

"Yes?"

"It's time," her son-in-law said.

"Kelly's in labor?" Grace was already out of bed, holding the telephone to her ear, turning on lights, looking for clothes. The digital clock-radio told her it was three-fifty.

"The contractions are five minutes apart, and we're on our way to the hospital."

"I'll meet you there. Do you want me to call Maryellen?"

"Thanks. She's the next name on the list."

After throwing on a pair of sweats, phoning Maryellen and making herself a cup of instant coffee, Grace was ready to head out the door in less than fifteen minutes.

"Buttercup!" She called her dog, needing to let her out in the backyard before she left.

The golden retriever ambled slowly out of the bedroom, obviously not pleased to have her sleep interrupted. "I'll be back before you know it," she promised, and then because she was just so excited, she announced loudly, "I'm about to become a grandma!"

Maryellen was at the hospital's birthing center by the time Grace arrived. They met in the waiting area. Paul's mother, Margaret, was there with her camera and cross-stitch project.

"I've been through this before," she explained, settling down in a chair and taking out skeins of embroidery thread in various colors.

"I can't believe I'm doing this," Maryellen muttered, cradling a cup of convenience-store coffee in her hands. "I haven't been up this early since drill team in high school." That comment was followed by a huge yawn.

"Where're Paul and Kelly?"

"Back there." Maryellen waved absently toward a set of double doors.

Grace was approaching the nurses' station to ask for news when Paul appeared. "Kelly's getting checked now to see how far she's dilated. She's doing great."

"How about you?" Grace asked.

Paul nodded excitedly. "I'm ready for this."

"He *thinks* he is," Paul's mother teased.

"Your life is going to change forever," Grace told him.

"Believe me, I know that. Kelly and I very much want this baby."

Before he left, Grace hugged her son-in-law, grateful to Paul. He'd been a wonderful help in the months since Dan's disappearance. Grace knew he'd given Kelly unwavering comfort and support, as well as commonsense advice; she herself had leaned on him many times when something around the house needed fixing. Not once had he complained. She'd gradually become stronger, braver, more determined to get on with her life, but she didn't think Kelly felt that kind of resolve yet—or resignation.

"How do you think Kelly's going to deal with Dad not being here?" Maryellen asked, as if reading Grace's thoughts.

Grace couldn't answer that. Kelly had clung to the hope that her father would reappear as soon as her baby was born, absolutely refusing to accept that he'd abandon her at this crucial time.

"He isn't coming," Maryellen whispered, leaning forward. "Dad's not going to walk through that door and there isn't going to be a joyous reunion, is there?"

"Probably not," Grace agreed. "Kelly will deal with it in her own way. Right now, though, she has enough to think about."

"You're telling me," Maryellen muttered.

Grace leaned back in the hard plastic chair and closed her eyes, fighting off the urge to sleep. A part of her wanted to be with Kelly, but she also recognized that this special time was reserved for Paul and she didn't want to intrude. Maryellen, long-divorced, had shown no interest in motherhood, nor had she revealed any desire to marry again. Grace sometimes wondered if Maryellen had put her emotional life on hold while concentrating on her professional life. Grace's only concern was that Maryellen have no regrets about the choices she was making.

At seven-thirty, Kelly was ready to deliver. Paul brought them that update and then dashed out of the waiting room at lightning speed. Maryellen, Grace and Margaret gathered in the hallway outside the delivery room. Not long afterward, their tension was broken by the cry of an infant.

Paul appeared a few minutes later. "It's a boy," came his jubilant shout. "A boy!"

Grace didn't know Margaret Kelso very well, but all of a sudden Maryellen and Grace were hugging Paul's mother as if she were their closest friend. Tears of joy crept down Grace's cheeks.

"Mother," Maryellen chided. "Just look at you."

"I have a right," she laughed, wiping the tears from her face. "I'm a grandmother!"

At nine that morning, while Kelly slept, Grace sat in the rocking chair with this precious new life cradled lovingly in her arms. "Welcome, little Tyler Daniel Kelso," she whispered, rocking gently. The commotion had died down. Margaret had taken her pictures and returned home to her husband. Maryellen had gone into the art gallery, refusing to allow a little thing like becoming an aunt—and getting hardly any sleep—to keep her away. Grace, however, was in no hurry to leave.

"Mom," Kelly whispered from her bed. Grace glanced up to find her daughter watching her. "He's so perfect, isn't he?"

"Precious child." Grace kissed Tyler's forehead.

"You don't mind that we named him after Dad, do you?"

Grace assured her she didn't. "I don't know where your father is," she told her, "and there are no guarantees I ever will, but I'm sure of one thing. He loves you and he'd be very proud to know that little Tyler is his namesake."

"Do you really think so?"

"I believe that with all my heart."

"Thank you, Mom," her daughter whispered, then closed her eyes.

Grace continued to rock her grandson, holding this much-loved child close to her heart. Dan was gone. His leaving had torn a gaping hole in her life. She'd lived with her husband's disappearance all these months, struggling to find answers, knowing that might never happen. But just now, holding this grandchild, she felt as though none of that mattered.

In confronting her doubts and fears, Grace had learned something vital. Everything she needed for happiness lay deep within herself. Her grandson, this perfect little boy, gave her the inspiration and courage to go on. She wished her husband well, wherever he was, and whoever he was with. Then, eyes closed, Grace released Dan, mentally and emotionally. She was ready to let go even without the answers.

It wasn't easy, but Justine couldn't leave things as they were between her and Seth. She hadn't seen him since that horrible night when Warren had confronted him at D.D.'s on the Cove. Never in all her life had she been so humiliated. She supposed she should be grateful because that night had opened her eyes to what she'd become.

Seth was back in town, although Justine didn't know for how long. Realizing she'd lose her courage if she thought about this too much, Justine went over to the marina.

Seth was busy working on his boat, stripping paint. He seemed oblivious to her. Her footsteps were heavy with shame and dread as she walked down the dock toward him. She stood in front of his slot. Not sure what to do with her hands, she tucked them in the hip pockets of her jeans.

"Hello, Seth."

He stopped his work and slowly turned to face her. His mouth was set and tight. "Hello, Justine."

He didn't seem receptive to her presence. But then, he didn't have any reason to be. "I imagine you're wondering what I'm doing here," she mumbled.

"Not particularly."

She ignored his lack of welcome. "I wanted to apologize for the other night."

"No problem, it's forgotten." He returned to his task, as if everything had already been said. He certainly wasn't eager to talk with her, which made this even more difficult than it already was.

"Do I...disgust you?" she asked.

He paused, glancing in her direction. "What I think of you or Warren shouldn't concern you."

"It does because...because, dammit, Seth—oh, never mind." She bolted and got maybe half a dozen steps down the dock when she stopped abruptly. She had the horrible feeling that if she walked away from Seth now, she'd regret it for the rest of her life.

When she turned back, she was surprised to find he'd leapt onto the dock and was only a step or two behind her.

"You care what I think?" he demanded, his brow furrowed.

Her voice deserted her; she simply nodded.

"Fine, then hear me out." Everything about him told her he was angry. His stance was confrontational, his fists clenched, his eyes narrow and hard. "You're a fool if you marry Warren Saget, and I don't suffer fools gladly."

"I know."

"You're still going to marry him?"

"No," she cried. "I broke it off with him that night."

Seth's head reared up. "You're not seeing Warren anymore?"

"No." She didn't mention any of the things Warren had said and done to win her back, but there weren't enough gifts in the world to accomplish that.

"I doubt he took the news sitting down."

"He's had trouble believing me, but he'll accept my decision in time." He wouldn't have any choice.

"So what's next?" Seth asked.

The answer was completely up to him, but Justine couldn't tell him that, so she shrugged. A heartfelt shrug, conveying uncertainty…and hope.

"What did that mean?"

"What?" she asked innocently.

"That shrug."

"I don't know," she said desperately. "I guess I'm just letting you know I'm here."

He frowned. "Here?"

"You told me once that I should come to you when I broke it off with Warren—and well, I'm here."

"I said that?"

"Close enough."

"If you think I'm just going to—"

"Yes," she interrupted.

"Then I've got news for—" He stopped. "What did you say?"

She squared her shoulders. "When? Just now? I said *yes*."

"What was the question?"

"Well," she said, exhaling slowly, "I didn't quite give you time to ask, but what I said was *yes*. Meaning I'll marry you."

Her answer appeared to confuse him further. He stared at her for the longest moment and, still unsure of his reaction, Justine said nothing. He started toward her, then halted, then walked directly past her. He'd gone four or five feet before he turned back. "Are you coming or not?" he asked impatiently.

"Where are we going?"

"To get a marriage license."

"Now?"

He smiled then, the most wonderful smile she'd ever seen. "I don't believe in long engagements."

Justine threw back her head and laughed. "As it happens, neither do I."

The front door of 16 Lighthouse Road was open. Olivia sat out on the porch with her needlepoint in her lap, the portable phone at her side. The wicker rocking chair had been her mother's and she loved spending summer evenings right here, enjoying the view and watching the sun set over the Olympics.

The phone rang, disturbing her solitude, and Olivia answered without giving it a chance to ring again.

"Mom, it's me—Justine," her daughter said. "Okay, listen. I have some news and I don't want you to be angry with me."

"Why would I do that?"

"Well, because—"

Olivia heard someone arguing with her in the background. "Justine?"

"Mom," her daughter cut in, "I'm married."

The needlepoint project fell off Olivia's lap as she bolted upright. "Married?" So Warren had finally worn her down. "Congratulations," she said, doing her best to sound enthusiastic. She'd always said that if her daughter chose to marry Warren Saget, she'd smile and welcome him to the family.

"Here, talk to Seth."

"*Seth?*"

"Oh, did I forget to mention that I married Seth Gunderson?"

For a moment, Olivia was too shocked to respond.

"Mrs. Lockhart, it's Seth. I know you're probably upset—"

"On the contrary, I couldn't be more pleased. Where are you?"

"Reno."

"Why Reno, for heaven's sake?"

"I'll let Justine explain."

Her daughter got back on the phone. "Are you upset with us, Mom?"

"I'm surprised…but delighted."

"Seth doesn't believe in long engagements."

"Nor in a long courtship, it appears."

"No…what happened is this— We decided to get married and it just made sense that we get the license at the courthouse and have you or even Pastor Flemming marry us, but that would've taken three days."

"That's Washington State law," Olivia reminded her.

"I know. It's just that we didn't have three days."

This was getting more interesting by the minute. "And why not?"

"Seth has to be back in Alaska by Sunday night and he won't be available for almost five weeks, and it was either now or wait."

"And you didn't want to do that?"

"I couldn't, Mom! I just couldn't. He didn't want to wait, either. I know this is probably the most impulsive thing I've ever done, but I know marrying Seth is the *right* thing. I'm sure of it. Oh, Mom, I love him so much and *please* don't be upset with us. We can have a second ceremony with you and Grandma and Dad later on, can't we?"

"Of course. Oh, Justine, I'm so happy for you and Seth."

"You like him, don't you?"

"You know I think the world of Seth."

"Me, too. I have to go now. We're phoning Seth's father next. And then Dad. After that, we've only got about twenty hours before we have to drive back. I'm happy, Mom, happier than I've been in my entire life." She paused. "Oh, would you call Grandma for me?"

Olivia swallowed the lump that had formed in her throat. "I'm happy for you, too," she said again. "And of course I'll call your grandmother."

They ended the conversation, and Olivia walked inside in a daze. She went into the bedroom and sat on the edge of her bed. She needed a few minutes to absorb what she'd just learned. Her daughter was married. To Seth Gunderson. Oh, this was wonderful, wonderful news!

Her first instinct was to phone Stan, but she decided against it. Justine would tell her father, and he'd call once he'd heard. So, both of their children had chosen to marry without either parent there. She wondered if that meant anything.

She phoned Charlotte, who wasn't home; she left a message, saying simply, "Call me when you get in."

Then she returned to her needlepoint project. Feet propped up on the porch railing, she continued her stitching, grinning every now and then. Who would've believed Justine would do something so spontaneous?

When a battered blue Taurus parked in front of the house, she strained to see if it was who she thought. It was.

Jack climbed out of his vehicle and stood on the sidewalk, watching her nervously. Did he expect her to walk inside and bolt the door? Or to offer him an invitation? She did neither.

He walked to the bottom of the steps. "Hello, Olivia."

"Beautiful afternoon, isn't it?" She was cordial, but not excessively so.

"Very."

"What can I do for you?" She didn't think this was a social call.

"Do you mind if I sit down?"

"Go ahead."

Since there was only the one chair, which she occupied, he climbed the stairs and sat on the top step. "Are you still angry with me about that dinner date?"

Men! He seemed incapable of understanding a concept like mutual trust and respect. "No." A one-word reply should satisfy him, without leading into a dead-end conversation.

"But you're still unwilling to go out with me?"

"I don't know," she answered honestly. She hated to admit how much she missed his company. Maybe she'd been expecting too much, but she couldn't tolerate the fact that he'd created secrets between them.

"That's what I thought." He looked out over the Cove, its sparkling, distant water tinged by the pink of a slowly setting sun.

"I moved to Cedar Cove to start a new life," Jack

told her. "But the past has a way of catching up with people, doesn't it?"

Olivia nodded; she saw the evidence of that every day.

"Bob's advice is that I simply tell you—that I should have months ago. But I was afraid if you knew, you wouldn't want anything more to do with me."

"More secrets, Jack?"

"No, just the reason I couldn't go to dinner with you."

"It isn't necessary, Jack." He'd made his decision and so had she, although she had to confess to being curious.

"I think it is," he countered. "If you and I are to continue, at any rate, and I want that very much."

"I have this thing about secrets. I detest them." She realized that a lot of her feelings were tied to her long-dead marriage. Stan had been unfaithful before the divorce, if not physically then emotionally. After the crisis of Jordan's death, it'd been another woman who'd helped Stan deal with the loss. Another woman he'd confided in.

"I'm a recovering alcoholic, Olivia."

"But…" She paused, certain she'd recently seen him with a drink in his hand. No, she thought. That was at Willcox House, and he'd had sparkling water while she'd had wine. He'd said it was because he had to drive….

"The reason I couldn't go to dinner with you was because I had an AA meeting to attend. I have ten years of sobriety. It's been ten long years but not a day goes by that I don't think about booze. I'm one beer away from destroying everything."

It took a lot of courage to tell the truth. Olivia rose from her rocking chair and sat on the porch step beside Jack and reached for his hand.

He wrapped his fingers around hers. "I've stood before a lot of judges in my time, but I've never dated one," he said. "The truth is, I wasn't sure how you'd feel about seeing me once you knew."

"Actually, it explains a great deal."

"How so?" he asked.

"Well…I figured there had to be a logical explanation for why you don't like Barry Manilow."

Jack chuckled. "Are you saying only a drunk wouldn't appreciate him?"

Olivia threw back her head and laughed.

"My mind was pickled for twenty years, but thankfully I've managed to keep my sense of humor."

"Good thing. You're going to need it living here in Cedar Cove."

Jack raised her hand to his lips. "Friends?"

"The very best kind."

"Lovers?"

"Don't press your luck."

He sighed. "I'm free tonight for that dinner, if you're so inclined."

"As it happens, I do have a reason to celebrate. I'll tell you about it later."

"What's wrong with now?"

"I don't want to disturb the sunset. Oh, Jack, isn't it beautiful?"

"It is," he whispered, slipping his arm around her, bringing her close to his side.

As the sun set over Cedar Cove, Olivia rested her head on Jack's shoulder. This had been a good summer. Both her children were married now, and James was a father. Justine sounded genuinely happy. Her mother's health continued to be good. Her dearest friend had suffered a blow, but Grace had accepted what she couldn't change; she was refashioning her life, and Olivia was proud of her.

And Olivia herself… Olivia was with Jack, and their relationship was secure. She didn't know what the future held for them, but she couldn't help feeling it was positive.

The sun sank below the Olympic Mountains. Its deep-pink glow fell across the water and spilled onto 16 Lighthouse Road. It crept through the town of Cedar Cove and gently touched the house at 204 Rosewood Lane. Grace Sherman looked out her window and smiled.

Welcome to
Blossom Street

Make time for friends. Make time for

DEBBIE MACOMBER

Take a trip to
Cedar Cove

Make time for friends. Make time for

DEBBIE MACOMBER

Spend Christmas with
DEBBIE MACOMBER

Make time for friends. Make time for
DEBBIE MACOMBER

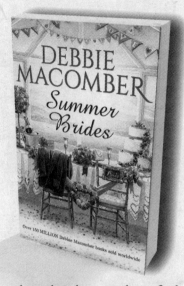

Finding love was never easy...

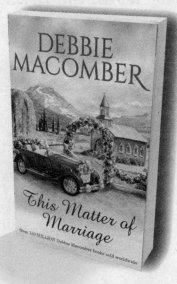

The alarm on Hallie McCarthy's biological clock
is buzzing. She's hitting the big three-0 and
there's no prospect of marriage, no man in sight.
But Hallie's got a plan. She's giving herself a
year to meet her very own Mr Right...

Except all her dates are disasters. Too bad she can't
just fall for her good-looking neighbour, Steve
Marris—who's definitely *not* her type.

From convenience to true love—there'll be plenty of confetti this summer!

Savannah Charles believes in the value—and the values—of marriage. She's a wedding planner who finds herself saying yes when divorce attorney Nash Davenport unexpectedly proposes. Even though it's strictly a business proposal, Nash isn't convinced that love and marriage necessarily go together. Yet he's never expected to marry Savannah, the most passionate woman he's ever tried not to love…

Make time for friends.
Make time for Debbie Macomber.

Loved this book?